YOUNG MR KEE

Seen at a fashionabl ancisco,
Jimmy Keefe nother
of those come
of age nia,
like ot e,
persona rriages
neverthel oo much, and
who so t along the way.
But Mr K just another' young man.
Haunted by h es and failures, desperately trying to find a meaning and purpose in his life, he is fiercely and unforgettably an individual. "Let's call it the Blazing Fifties," cried his best friend's wife Claire, "Our candle does more than burn at both ends – we toss the whole thing into the fire! . . . We're a generation that feels the world owes us a living, just because we're attractive!" Young Mr Keefe wondered, was it true that they were people with everything to offer, yet who actually offered nothing? At the back of his mind there was always his family in New England – they could supply him with a ready-made security – as well as a social position that he could never bring himself to accept. Since his separation from his wife he had spent more and more time with Blazer and Claire Gates, themselves New Englanders exiled in the wilds of California. At first they played as if they were in college together. But the pace became faster and the parties wilder; Claire was ready for new excitements, and Jimmy could feel her undeniable attractiveness.

CW01637456

Also by Stephen Birmingham from Futura

THE AUERBACH WILL
HEART TROUBLES
THOSE HARPER WOMEN
BARBARA GREER
THE LEBARON SECRET

Non-fiction
'OUR CROWD'
'THE REST OF US'
THE GRANDEES
REAL LACE
DUCHESS

STEPHEN BIRMINGHAM

Young Mr Keefe

Futura

TO NAN
with love

A Futura Book

Copyright © Stephen Birmingham, 1958

First published in Great Britain in 1958 by
William Collins, Sons & Co., Ltd

This edition published in 1987 by Futura Publications,
a Division of Macdonald & Co (Publishers) Ltd,
London & Sydney

All rights reserved
No part of this publication may be reproduced, stored in a retrieval system, or transmitted, in any form or by any means without the prior permission in writing of the publisher, nor be otherwise circulated in any form of binding or cover other than that in which it is published and without a similar condition including this condition being imposed on the subsequent purchaser.

All characters in this publication are fictitious and any resemblance to real persons, living or dead, is purely coincidental.

ISBN 0 7088 2828 0

Printed and bound in Great Britain by
Cox & Wyman Ltd, Reading

Futura Publications
A Division of
Macdonald & Co (Publishers) Ltd
Greater London House
Hampstead Road
London NW1 7QX
A BPCC plc Company

PART ONE

I

THE apartment was ready. Now there was nothing to do but wait for them, and they were always late. He knew they would be late to-night. Their habitual lateness was by no means innocent. It was as though, secretly, they hoped that being late would make their presence all the more exciting when they came. They were like that. They enjoyed planning the effect they would have on other people.

He looked at his watch. It said six thirty-five. He decided to check it, and went to the telephone and dialled. Presently, a voice said, "At the tone, the time will be six thirty-seven, Pacific Daylight Time." Cradling the telephone between his shoulder and his ear, he adjusted his watch. Then he replaced the receiver. They were over half an hour late already.

Jimmy Keefe was tall. He was twenty-four, with a long, rather thin face and black hair. He was slender, but looked as though he had once been heavier. He had been drinking coffee, cup after cup, ever since coming home from work that afternoon, while he cleaned the apartment. As a result, his hands felt a little tense and jumpy. He began to fidget with little things—arranging the silver ash-trays on the coffee table, the stack of freshly purchased magazines. He had bought *Vogue*, *Harper's Bazaar*, *Mademoiselle*. He had bought these magazines for a reason. He plumped up the pillows on the sofa. He moved back and forth across the room, and made periodic stops, looking around with indecision at the appearance of everything. He lighted a cigarette with one of the silver table lighters and took several deep puffs. He rested his cigarette on the edge of an ash-tray, and then, because it was freshly polished, removed the cigarette quickly, took it into the kitchen, and rested it on the edge of the sink. In a blue dish, on the counter, he had placed the broken pearls.

The kitchen faced Capitol Avenue. The street was quiet now. From the open window, he could hear the pounding sound of the springboards at the public plunge in the park three blocks away and the gentle splashing sound of the lawn sprinklers next door. Then he heard the sound of the newsboy's bicycle tyres as they spattered through the puddles that the sprinklers made along the sidewalk. It had been a hot June day; it was still hot, but the trees—sycamores, live oaks, and magnolias—along Capitol Avenue created a long, shaded tunnel with their branches. The street was broad and flat and cool. The slanting California sunlight was almost completely excluded.

At number 3360, across the street, Jimmy watched the newsboy's bicycle stop with a squeal of brakes. The afternoon paper was tossed on the front steps of the big grey-shingled house. A woman, in shorts and halter, appeared from around the side of the house, and picked up the paper. She was carrying a round fat pitcher decorated with red cherries and green leaves, in which ice cubes and chunks of lemon swirled. Iced tea, probably, Jimmy thought. She glanced at the headlines, put the paper under her arm, and disappeared around the house. In California, Jimmy thought, all life exists in the back yard. The newsboy parked his bicycle in front of the apartment house and walked up the walk to the front door with a stack of papers under his arm. He disappeared within, and Jimmy could hear him, downstairs, stuffing papers into the seven letter boxes.

The apartment house consisted of two floors, built around a central courtyard, Spanish style. The first-floor apartments opened on to the courtyard. The second floor opened on to a balcony that ran around above the courtyard and that was approachable by a flight of rough-hewn redwood steps. Although Jimmy's apartment was smaller than most of the others, it rented for more because it was on a corner. It was called a " studio " apartment—with a large all-purpose living-room, a kitchen, and a bath. The sofa opened into a double bed at night. The furniture, which came with the apartment, was California modern—blond wood, formica, glass. The arm-chairs in the living-room were upholstered in a rough, tweedy, brick-coloured fabric that was shot through with gold threads. The walls were painted slate grey, and the two huge picture windows in the living-room were draped with a heavy rust-coloured fabric imprinted with green tropical leaves. Jimmy considered going downstairs to get his paper, then decided against it.

There was a Thermos of martinis in the refrigerator—a large Thermos, freshly made. He took this out and poured himself a drink in a jelly glass. Then, with his drink in one hand and his cigarette in the other, he went back into the living-room, picked up a magazine and tried to read it. He found little that interested him in *Mademoiselle*; he put it down again. He got up and turned on the radio. " Welcome to the Burgemeister Ballroom," a woman's voice said. " Brought to you through the courtesy of Burgemeister Beer . . ." He turned it off again and looked at his watch. He found himself suddenly wishing that they wouldn't come, or that he had arranged to meet them somewhere else. He wished he had told them the truth, that he would rather be left alone. Then he wondered if perhaps they had come while he was out buying the gin for the martinis. What if they had come, rung the bell, waited, and finally decided to go on without him? Then he thought no, they would have left a note. Or broken in. Or scrawled a message in lipstick on his window. He thought it was quite possible that they weren't coming at all, that something else had come up, or that they had forgotten entirely. He realized that the parties and plans lately had all had a quality of indefiniteness, of indecision. Whichever way the wind happened to blow, whichever way the day happened to dawn decided which thing would be done that day. And it didn't matter if you decided not to do it after all—if you invited people to your house for the evening and decided to go to a movie instead. Everyone understood. No one expected you to be where you said you would be, at the time you said you would be there.

This plan, for example, had been made coming down in an elevator of the Mark Hopkins Hotel in San Francisco, a week ago. They had all had cocktails, and someone had invited them all somewhere, but they were not going to go. They were going, instead, to a new place in the International Settlement, where a girl did a strip tease to the hula, and Claire Gates had suddenly turned to him and said, " I have it—the *idea*! "

" What is it? " he had asked.

" Next week-end—let's go camping. Let's pack knapsacks, take sleeping-bags, citronella, and go up to the mountains.

Around Tahoe or Squaw Valley, and find a little lake. There are lots of little lakes up there. We'll swim in the nude and sleep under the stars, and do all sorts of things." She turned to her huband. "What do you think, Blazer? Won't that be fun?"

Blazer had agreed. "We'll drive up to Sacramento Friday night," Claire had said. "We'll pick you up at your apartment and go out to dinner. Blazer and I will stay at a motel somewhere, and then we can all get an early start Saturday morning. When we get to the mountains, we may never come down!"

"I have a sleeping-bag," Jimmy had said.

"So do we," Claire said. "Blazer and I will bring the food."

"Will Helen be back then?" Blazer had asked. "Will we finally meet the mysterious Helen?"

"I don't know," Jimmy had said vaguely. "I doubt it. But we three can go anyway."

"Honestly, that wife of yours!" Claire had said. "We've been seeing you for weeks and we've never once laid eyes on her. When I meet her, I'm certainly going to scold her for leaving you alone and uncared for so long. Where is she now?"

"Still at her mother's."

"Oh."

Remembering all this now, he wondered why he had let himself be carried along into their plan, when it had involved such an elaborate scheme of pretence, pretending that Helen was still here. Buying the magazines, cleaning and polishing, arranging flowers in a vase, trying to make the apartment look the way it had before. While all the time, in his dresser drawer, there was a growing file of letters, from her lawyer and his lawyer . . .

He suddenly felt tired. He stood up and went into the kitchen and filled his glass once more, carefully. He drank a little, and the warmth of the liquor relieved him somewhat. He sat down at the kitchen table and picked up the telephone. Perhaps telephoning would cheer him up. Some of the numbers he called were numbers that he was fairly sure wouldn't answer, but, after two martinis like that, it was pleasant to have someone to talk to, even if that someone was only Long Distance. In the end, he didn't reach anybody. It was Friday night, and three hours later in the East. His friends were at dances or parties, or at the club for dinner, or in Europe for the summer. He talked, indirectly, with several maids, mothers, butlers, in many cities—heard the clipped, cultured voices of Park Avenue women, the slow drawls of negro servants. There was some difficulty with a Tampa number—a boy from his class at college—and the operator would call him back. He put the phone down and poured himself another drink from the Thermos. If Claire and Blazer didn't come soon, he thought, they would find him drunk. He decided to give them another half-hour. If they didn't come by seven-thirty, he would go out to a drugstore for a sandwich and then to a movie. They could go to hell. He lighted another cigarette with the enamelled kitchen lighter. *Be careful*, Helen used to say, *that lighter throws out sparks*.

A great, heavy loneliness dizzied him then, just for a moment. He looked into his glass and wondered if the loneliness would end at the bottom of it. He tried talking to Helen. " My God," he said softly to the empty room. " My God, you didn't have to do this. We could have tried again. It didn't have to end in a mess like this." He tried to hide himself in thought of other things. He took another walk around the apartment. His knapsack and sleeping-bag were rolled in a corner of the living-room, ready to go. Oh, hell, he thought, hell, we'll have fun. We'll have fun, if they ever come. He would have one more drink.

It was nearly two hours later when they finally came. He had fallen asleep on the sofa, his head resting on his forearms, his glass beside him on the floor. They came and interrupted a dream he was having in which Helen figured only slightly, as the audience, more or less, to something he was doing. He tried, half asleep, to continue the dream, to see what was happening. It was dark, and there were Chinese lanterns blowing wildly around a white house, his mother's house in Connecticut. The lanterns were set up for a wedding. He was playing with a calendar, tearing the pages from it, one by one, and as he tore off each page the wind took it, whipped it away. April, March, February. Then he realized that he was going through the calendar backward, back six months to his own wedding day. Helen laughed. He turned the calendar over and began again. Claire and Blazer pounded on the window. Through veils of sleep, he heard them try the front door. It was locked, and so they walked back along the balcony to the window, raised the screen, and climbed in.

"He's asleep," Claire said.

"No, he's not," Blazer said, "he's just faking. Wake up! Wake up, Keefe-o! We're here!"

Jimmy rolled over and looked at them. Blazer wore a faded pair of suntans and a baggy Shetland sweater. Claire had pulled her blonde hair back and tied it in an orange scarf. She was wearing a white blouse and Bermuda shorts.

"Well," Jimmy said, "where the hell have you been?"

"Are we late?" Claire asked innocently. "We drove like the wind." They both flopped down on the couch beside him and stretched their legs in front of them. "We drove like the wind, didn't we, Blazer?"

"I went out a while ago. I came back and thought maybe you'd come and gone without me."

"Poor little boy!" Claire said in mock baby talk. "Poor little lonely, neglected boy! Thought he'd been left out of the party—so he had a little party of his own." She picked up the glass and sniffed it.

"What took you so long?"

"Well, first of all, we had trouble getting over the Golden Gate," Claire said. "They're tearing up the highway for miles and miles, and then we ran into an accident on Route 40——"

"Hey, wait a minute," Jimmy said. "What highway are they tearing up?"

"Don't try to pin me down!" Claire said. "Of course it's a fib, but why make me admit it?" She looked around the room. "So this is the apartment," she said. "It's very nice—bigger than ours, don't you think? And your furniture is in sensational taste. I love that lowboy with stirrups for handles."

Jimmy laughed. "I bought it for a song in a very, very old motel in Salinas. The driftwood lamp came across the continent on a prairie schooner."

"There *was* an accident," Blazer put in. "That part is true -three people killed. It was awful."

"Nobody knows how to drive in California."

"And then we stopped somewhere to eat," Claire said.

" Oh, that's nice," Jimmy said. " I've been waiting to have dinner with you. It's now nine o'clock, and you've already eaten."

" Well, you wouldn't have wanted to eat where we ate. The carhops were all dressed to look like jockeys with little short skirts. Their buttocks were absolutely flapping in the breeze. We decided there must have been a house rule banning girdles."

" And requiring chewing gum."

" We had two lovely, leathery hamburgers."

" Mine had a hair in it——"

" And mine had a few bristles from a suède brush——"

" And the waitress went off duty while we were waiting for our check."

" And of course," Claire said sadly, " Blazer's been horrible to me all the way up. We've been parked in front of your building for the last hour—squabbling."

" Oh, so that's it."

" He's been just awful," she said. " He had me in tears."

" She's a psychotic crier," Blazer said. " She's a compulsive weeper. A manic depressive."

" Blazer says I'm a manic depressive. Well," she said, turning to him, " did it ever occur to you to be just a little bit *nice*——"

" Just because I pointed out that she was driving like a madwoman," Blazer said.

" But would he offer to drive instead? Oh, no—he was too tired! All he could do was criticize, and——"

" She always starts talking about me in the third person," Blazer said. " As though I weren't here."

" Isn't he horrible? "

" Isn't he *horrible*! " Blazer mimicked.

" If my mother ever heard how he talks to me! "

" Now, speaking of your mother——"

" Listen to him talk about my mother! "

" You haven't even given me a chance! "

Jimmy stood up. " Drinks, quick," he said. " Drinks for both of you! "

Their quarrels weren't real quarrels. It was a familiar pattern to Jimmy. He had heard them, bickering like that, in hotels, bars, restaurants—anywhere—and the purpose of it all was really only to entertain the people they were with, or, possibly, to amuse each other. They pretended that this was the consistency of their marriage, and yet, Jimmy noticed that when the quarrelling grew dull, or the accusations grew flat, they seemed to sense it together, and stopped. Jimmy now rose and patted Claire on the shoulder affectionately. "I think Blazer's a complete bastard," he said. "I'm totally on your side—because you said you admired my furniture. Now, I want to show you the largest jug of martinis in the world. You'll have to drink them because they're all I have." He went into the kitchen and brought out the Thermos and three cocktail glasses.

"What in the world is that?" Claire said.

"A gallon Thermos. For our trip."

"But it will be so heavy!"

"Let's lighten it right now." Jimmy filled the glasses. "I must admit I tapped it while I was waiting for you."

Blazer lifted his glass. "Here's to the trip," he said.

Claire sat back deep in the sofa cushions and sighed. "I'm so *tired*," she said. "I feel as though I'd spent the whole day on the Pennsylvania Railroad—on a flatcar—with thousands of little tramps. I feel so dirty. I feel as though I should put some Mum on. Do you have any?"

"In the bathroom, yes."

"Well, never mind. You'll have to bear me as I am. I hate bugs."

"Bugs?"

"Yes. California bugs. Our windshield is smeared with them. I don't remember Connecticut having so many bugs in summer."

"It's the valley," Jimmy said. "They breed in the tules—in the marshes, out in the delta."

"Ah——"

"And it's hot," Blazer said. "Christ, it's hot. It's much hotter here than in San Francisco." He pulled off his sweater.

"Valley again."

"How do you stand it?" Claire asked. "Why don't you come to San Francisco with us?"

Jimmy shrugged. "I've got a job here. Remember?"

"Oh, yes. A job. How dull. Why don't you quit work and just play? Live on the Keefe millions."

"What Keefe millions?"

" Don't tease me," Claire said. " I know all about the Keefe millions."

Jimmy looked at her. " I don't think that's very funny," he said.

" Sorry. Why are you ashamed? After all, we're all from the same, shall we say, background? The flowering of New England and all that."

Jimmy laughed dryly. " I notice Blazer works," he said.

" Oh, I know, I know." Claire let her blonde hair in the orange scarf fall back lazily across the back of the sofa. She looked up at the ceiling. She was in her bored Katherine Hepburn mood, sucking in her cheeks and blowing a long thin stream of smoke from her lips. " I'm so glad you came to California, Jimmy," she said. " We were wretched here among all these primitives, until you came. It's a shame we didn't get together until a month ago."

" When are we going to meet that wife of yours? " Blazer asked suddenly.

" Well," Jimmy said quickly, " her mother's sick—as I told you—and——"

" I hope we'll like her," Claire said. " Even if she is a Californian."

Jimmy extracted a cigarette from a pack and lighted it with the enamelled lighter. *Be careful*, he remembered, *that lighter throws out sparks.*

There was a pause, and then Jimmy said, " You've seen this picture of her, haven't you? I took it in Nassau." He handed them a photograph in a small leather frame.

Claire took it and studied it. " I think you're making her up," she said. " You don't really have a wife. This is just a picture of a pretty girl."

Jimmy laughed. " She is pretty, isn't she? " He accepted it as Claire handed it back and looked at it. There she was, in a loose yellow sweater, her camera slung over the handlebars of her bicycle, her short light-brown hair blowing in the wind. She looked distant, fragmentary. She was looking away from him, towards something. What had it been? A sailboat on the horizon, a cloud? The expression on her face was not exactly a smile. It was tense, preoccupied. She eluded him now, as she had eluded him then. " That was on our honeymoon," he said.

" Yes, I've heard about your honeymoon," Claire said. " You went everywhere under the sun for months and months."

" Six weeks," he said. " That was all."

" Is it all right if Claire and I sleep here to-night? " Blazer asked, pouring himself another drink from the Thermos. " It's a little late to find a hotel room."

Jimmy hesitated. " Well, the accommodations will be a little on the Youth Hostel side," he said. " The sofa opens out into a double bed—you and Claire can have that. I can take my sleeping-bag into the kitchen and sleep on the floor."

" You can put our two sleeping-bags underneath you for a mattress," Claire said.

" You don't need to sleep in the kitchen," Blazer said. " Just spread out here on the rug. We don't mind."

" Doesn't give you much privacy, old man.'

" Privacy, schmivacy."

" If you get chilly, you can crawl right in with us," Claire said. " I've always wondered what it would be like to sleep with two men."

" Don't worry—I don't mind the floor."

" Do you talk in your sleep? " Claire asked. " If you talk in your sleep or snore or do anything uncouth like that, you *will* have to sleep in the kitchen. Blazer does both. With two of you doing it, I couldn't bear it."

" It all seems rather modern and casual, doesn't it? " Jimmy said.

The telephone rang. " Oh, God," he said. " Do you know what that is? It's Jeep Tanner. I called him in Florida this afternoon. Do we want to talk to Jeep Tanner? "

" Jeep *Tanner*! " Claire said. " Do you mean that dreadful football player with the Buick? Let it ring."

" All right."

" Jeep Tanner would break the spell."

" Why in the world were you calling Jeep Tanner? " Blazer asked.

" This afternoon—I didn't have anything else to do. It was beginning to look as though you two weren't coming. I wanted to hear a friendly voice."

" You *are* in a bad way," Claire said. " Fill my glass with that golden elixir! " She extended her glass to him. He filled it and she put it down carefully on the coffee table. The phone stopped ringing. Claire stretched her arms high over her head and yawned. " Blazer says I'm ugly and fat. Am I? I think I'm rather gorgeous, what do you think? "

" I think you're splendid," Jimmy said.

In a way, she was, though she was not gorgeous. Her legs were a little too heavy, and her nose was too small. But she had, Jimmy thought, a wonderfully elfin face, and her blonde hair, long and twisted into that strange bright scarf, fell across her back and made her look like a polished urchin, or a little girl who had been left alone for the first time with her mother's cosmetic tray. She used too much make-up, but somehow got away with it. Her lips were rouged a dark creamy red, and her pale blue eyes were accented with dark mascara and eye shadow. Claire wanted to look worldly. She dreaded looking " Smithish," as she put it. But under her movie-star patina, her face was round and smooth and snub as a cherub's.

" I'm glad that one person agrees with me," she said.

" Tell me what you brought for food," Jimmy said, before he realized that now he, not Jeep Tanner, was breaking a spell.

Claire let her arms droop. " Everything," she said sadly. " I brought everything except eggs. I decided eggs would break. I brought bread and butter and jam and corned beef hash and tomato soup. I brought chicken gumbo soup. That's Blazer's favourite kind. I brought everything. You'll see. I even brought my silver knives and forks. Much nicer for a picnic, don't you think? "

" Our packs weigh fifty pounds apiece," Blazer said. " You'll have to carry all three sleeping-bags to make up for it."

" Why don't you let me carry Claire's pack? " Jimmy said.

" He'd never let me live it down," Claire said. " He doesn't think girls are worth anything if they can't do everything a man can."

" Do her good," Blazer said. " Carrying that pack may help her whack off a few pounds."

" Hear him? " she said. " He talks to me that way all the time. Do you know what he did the other day? I called him from work the other night to tell him what was in the refrigerator——"

"Did you say from work?" Jimmy asked.

"Oh, yes! Didn't I tell you? As of three days ago, I'm a working wife. It's terribly exciting. True to Smith tradition, I'm doing case work. I had to do something. I couldn't spend my entire day admiring the view from Russian Hill! But Blazer called me—or rather I called Blazer—and I said there were some tomatoes and some tuna and so forth. And then, all of a sudden, I heard this *peculiar*, this unidentifiable—this sound—from the other end of the wire. Well!"

"Well—what was it?" Jimmy asked.

"Well, it was—well, I can't bring myself to say it. It was too terrible a thing."

Jimmy laughed. "I'm only slightly confused," he said.

"Not an uncommon occurrence when Claire tells a story," Blazer said. "Not only does the story have no point, in the first place—but when she gets to it, she won't tell you what the point is."

"Isn't he dreadful? Isn't he awful?"

Jimmy laughed again. "He certainly is."

They laughed and joked aimlessly, pointlessly, through another cocktail. Claire had learned to do the hula. They had finally gone to the place in the International Settlement. The strip tease had been a disappointment. But the hula! Claire performed it for them: "Lovely hula hands, hands that seem to say, 'I love you,' lovely hula hands——" They applauded her. Claire said suddenly, "Jimmy, are we really clever and amusing? Or are we only silly?"

"Both," he said. "Clever and silly. It's a pretty combination."

She sat down. "I have a terror of being silly," she said. "Blazer says I sometimes am. Don't let us be silly people, Jimmy. Really—the only thing I want to be is young!"

"You are young."

"Jimmy—old sobersides Jimmy. Even when you laugh and smile, I think you're being very serious, thoughtful, deep inside. You're the audience to everything; you have that quality. Even when someone says something very silly—as I did, just now, when I said I wanted to be young—you turn to me and nod, very seriously, and say, 'You are young.' You're a funny boy."

They decided that it was time for bed. Claire went to the linen closet and took out sheets and pillow-cases. "I hate to say it, Jimmy," she said, "but you're a terrible housekeeper. Look at this linen closet. Everything's stirred in the middle."

"Well, as soon as Helen gets back——"

The three of them, pulling together, separated the sofa bed into its component parts. Jimmy stretched two sleeping-bags on the floor and tested them for softness. "Better than the Statler," he said. "I don't usually wear pyjamas, but since you're company, I'll put some on."

He went into the bathroom, changed into his pyjamas, and when he came out, Blazer was already in bed and Claire was sitting on the edge in neat white boyish pyjamas that looked starched, and stood out all around her. She had pinned her hair on top of her head, and she looked roughly twelve. She stood up and opened the window. They stood there, Jimmy and Claire, in their bare feet, surveying themselves and the disorder they had made of the room, and laughed. They were still laughing when Claire got into bed and Jimmy crawled into the sleeping-bag on the floor. And when they had turned out the lights, and the room was dark, and Claire and Blazer pretended to fight for the covers, they were still laughing softly.

"If we had a picture of this——" they said.

"If Mother could see us now——"

"If Helen should walk in now——"

"If there were a fire and we all had to jump out the window into a net——"

"If the police should come——"

They lived in their laughter, Jimmy thought. They had found a world in which everything, even tragedy, had its humorous side. The Korean War was over. They laughed, because they had missed it; they had been too young. An earthquake in Tehachapi had sent timbers of houses shuddering to the ground. They laughed, because who would want to live in Tehachapi? Claire told of a flood that had threatened Mars Hill, her mother's house in Connecticut; Mrs. Denison had been without water and electricity for two days. They had had to carry water from the swimming-pool. Wasn't that funny? Claire had sold some Wrigley stock from her grandfather's estate to buy their new car. Why Wrigley? Because it had the funniest name . . .

Laughing with them, Jimmy tried to live in their laughter too, tried to move into its warm and wonderful comfort. " What if I should crawl in? " he said. " What if I made advances on you, Claire? What would Blazer do? What would you do, Blaze? "

" Blazer would say, ' Make a little less noise, please,' and go back to sleep. Ah, the pleasures of married life! Where have they sped, on what wings——"

" I can tell you," Blazer said.

" Think of to-morrow. Think of *Sunday* morning on the mountain—when the dawn, in russet mantle clad——"

" Make a little less noise, please," Blazer said.

" Ah, we're deep," Claire said. " Aren't we deep? About as deep as three frying-pans." They laughed again.

Jimmy thought: If Helen should walk in now. For several minutes, he thought of what she would say, of what he would say to her. He pictured the little scene, the elaborate explanations, the pyjama-clad introductions. It was a funny thought. But of course she would not walk in now. Or ever. Never no more, he thought, but he clung to that moment.

They sang, " I'm tying the leaves so they won't fall down . . ." But they had forgotten most of the words. Then the room was quiet. A full moon appeared and cast the shadow of the eucalyptus tree in the courtyard across the floor.

Sleep was tricky for him. It had been so lately, and it was getting no better. He had brief, vivid dreams that were unpleasant only for their vividness and realness. He woke and tried to sleep again, but it was difficult. He knew it would be difficult; he had tried it before. It was as though, shoeless, in pyjamas, you were asked to climb a tree or a mountain, and every false step meant disaster. Indeed, he thought, he was on a mountain now, with nothing to do but look downward, or even upward to where nothing at all lay. Helen was asking too much of him to expect him to survive on these slopes. There were several things he wanted to ask her. " Where are you? " was the first of them. He had written her letters; she had not answered.

The second—what was the second thing? He couldn't think of the second thing; he was going to sleep again.

He dreamt of Claire and Blazer, and they suddenly were all on their trip, the mountains flattening out in front of their heavy strides. Their hearts were beating audibly in the high air; he could hear three heartbeats. He looked at Blazer and Blazer was a little boy. The little boy he had grown up with at home, in Connecticut, that he had roomed with at prep school and college, with whom he had fought over girls and patched things up later. It was Blazer Gates before he had married Claire Denison, before all of them, by sheer coincidence, had ended up three thousand miles from home. Blazer was smiling at him, saying Jimmy could count on him.

Then suddenly the dream switched, became frantic, fast. Claire was saying something about soap, that they had forgotten it. " How then shall we be cleansed? " she asked. Then they were sitting at the camp-fire. Then the camp-fire disintegrated. Claire threw her mink coat from her shoulders and sighed. She removed her diamonds. " These rocks made me *sweat* so! " she said. She was in a car, arguing her way out of a ticket. " I've been to the most boring cocktail party, officer, and I suddenly decided I had to get home as fast as possible. That's why I was speeding. You understand." Then, for no reason, she was behind a desk, interviewing a charity case. " My wife has left me," the man explained. " I don't have enough dough to feed the kids. They're starving. My mother-in-law insists that I support her. My wife's lover insists that I support him. My wife's lover's mother insists that I support her. My problem is that I can't support anybody, but everybody expects me to. What should I do? "

" Well," Claire was saying, " don't you think you're letting this situation get the better of you just a teeny bit? Who sent you to our charitable agency, you dear old soul? I was at a cocktail party the other night and heard a story very similar to yours—all lies, of course—but still it convinces me that your problem is not a unique one." She was standing up, extending to him an arm that was a-glitter with precious and semi-precious stones. " Don't be afraid," she said, " just because I'm rich and you're not. No. No! Don't touch my hands, that's against the rules. Go out and find yourself a highly paid position, move to a respectable neighbourhood, and you'll be all right." She buzzed her secretary. " No more charity cases to-day," she said. " My hang-over is killing me."

He woke with a mild start. In half sleep, he was filled with a resentment of Claire, for what she was doing to Blazer. My God, she's ruining him, he thought wildly. Ruining Blazer, his friend, who was nicknamed for a jaunty jacket that he used to wear with scuffed-up white buck shoes, dirty chino pants, and open-collared shirts. Then, further awake, he realized that it was a dream, and that the room was getting cold. He crawled out of his sleeping-bag, tiptoed across the room, and closed the window quietly. He avoided looking at them, then did. The moonlight through the eucalyptus branches moved across their faces. Claire lay with one arm extended whitely on the pillow. Her hair had tumbled down. Her white pyjamas were tangled about her neck, and she was twisted fanta[illegible]lly in the bed-clothes. Blazer lay beside her, breathing s[illegible] They looked very happy. The dream, like all his drea[illegible]tely, had no relation to the fact. They were happy. Miserably, he wondered where he had turned wrong, where he had lost touch, how he had missed the thing they seemed to share so perfectly.

He looked at Claire again. It would not be hard to love her, not hard at all. He went back and lay down again, trying to untangle his thoughts. Claire stirred. " Hmmm? " she said. " You awake? I'm getting cold."

" I just closed the window," he whispered.

" Blazer," she said, poking him with her feet, " I'm getting cold."

Blazer turned sleepily. " Go to hell," he grumbled.

" The perfect marriage! " Claire said.

They were silent. Presently, Claire got out of bed and went into the bathroom. Jimmy politely pretended to be asleep through the sounds of the plumbing. When she came back, she stood in the centre of the room shivering, hugging her pyjamas around her. " Now I really am cold," she said unhappily. " Wake up, everybody! I'm cold. Let's all do something about me being cold."

Jimmy sat up. " Here," he said, " take one of these sleeping-bags." He pulled one out from underneath him and handed it to her.

" Thank you." Standing there, she stepped into it and zipped herself in. Then all she could do was hop. She began hopping as though she were in a potato-sack race. She hopped to the bed and fell flat across it. " I'm in the bag," she said, and giggled.

And then, after a minute, she said, " Oh, this is marvellous. It's like being between two slices of warm toast, or two pancakes. Blazer," she said, " look at me."

" Shut up, please," he said.

" Are you still awake, Jimmy? " she asked.

" Yes."

She talked in a husky whisper. " There is *one* nice thing about being married," she said. " When you sleep with someone then, you don't have to worry about touching them. I mean, when you sleep with another girl, you've always got it on your mind not to roll over against them, or touch them. For fear they'll think you're peculiar or something. I imagine it must be the same with two boys in the same bed, not wanting to touch each other . . ."

" A profound observation," Blazer said. " Go to sleep."

" Though I saw two little Air Force cadets one night on a plane," she said, " and they had literally fallen asleep in each other's laps. They looked awfully cute and sweet, sleeping there like that. Babes in the wood. I kept wanting to take them both in my arms . . . the madonna in me . . ."

Jimmy laughed softly.

" Blazer and I—what a silly pair we are! But we have fun. We started this ' Shut up, please,' and ' Quit it, please,' routine —but it's just a routine we go through. We tell each other to shut up, please, or to quit it, please, at least seventy-five times a night . . ."

" Shut up, please," Blazer said. " And this time I mean it."

But after a moment, Claire went on. " The funniest thing is in the morning, before we get up. We have these funny arguments. Someone says, ' Shut the window, please,' and the other says, ' I shut it yesterday.' ' Yes, but I set the alarm . . .' ' Yes, but I made the bed yesterday, and that's supposed to be your job . . .' ' Yes, but I shut the window two days in a row last week, so it's your turn.' And we go on like that. We sometimes get quite mad about it. Isn't that awful? "

Jimmy laughed again.

" Am I keeping you awake? Do you ever have trouble sleeping? "

" Sometimes," Jimmy said.

" I'm sorry." She paused. " You're the strangest person, Jimmy," she said. " You really are. I never quite believe you're happy. But it's all right—you do your best not to let on, if you're not."

" Thanks," he said.

" You love Helen terribly, don't you? " she asked suddenly.

" Yes."

" But that doesn't make you happy, does it? "

He didn't answer her.

" Does it? Does it? "

2

In the morning, when Jimmy woke, they were having one of their arguments. He listened to them.

"What do you mean, so *many* martinis?"

"I mean about eight martinis. That's what you had."

"*Eight!* It was more like three!"

"You were loaded."

"Well, I may have had a couple of cocktails, but I wasn't loaded."

"How do you know you weren't loaded? No one ever knows when they're loaded."

"Well, I wasn't. And you're being mean."

"Mean?"

"Yes. All the way up in the car yesterday."

"In the car?"

"Yes, in the car. In the car was when you were being so mean to me."

"I merely said you were driving like hell, and you were."

Claire's voice was small. "I wasn't."

"Yes, you were."

"No, I wasn't."

"You've reached sort of an impasse there," Jimmy said.

"Well, I wasn't," Claire said. "I didn't smash into anybody, did I? I got us up here in one piece, didn't I?"

"She's got a point there," Jimmy interjected.

The two of them paused for a moment, then continued.

"You're getting to be a compulsive alcoholic as well as a compulsive weeper," Blazer said.

"Is an alcoholic having three cocktails? Which is what I had?"

"She's right," Jimmy said.

" Well, if you only had three, you certainly let them get you stinko."

" I certainly wasn't stinko! "

" You said you couldn't find your watch, and you had it on all the time."

" She did have it on, that's a point," Jimmy said.

Claire began to laugh softly. " Wouldn't it be awful, darling," she said, " if whenever we were having an argument, a little voice kept chiming in from somewhere—making comments and taking sides? "

There was some discussion about their dressing, deciding what to wear. What did the best-dressed young people wear to climb a mountain? Blazer was pulling his belt from the loops of his khaki trousers, and strapping a knife case to it. " I think we've thought of everything," he said. " Except—oh, Christ, we need an axe! "

" We don't need an axe. Why do we need an axe? " Claire asked.

" To cut pine boughs with," Blazer said.

" Pine boughs? "

" For our beds. We have to make our beds with pine boughs."

" But we have the sleeping-bags."

" We'll need pine boughs underneath them."

" Suddenly," Claire said, " this trip sounds very exhausting. Do you mean to say we'll have to *work* when we get up there? "

" We can stop somewhere along the road and buy an axe," Jimmy suggested.

" I've brought a revolver," Blazer said.

" Do you think we'll need a revolver? "

" You never can tell."

" In case we meet the Abominable Snowman," Claire said. She went into the kitchen. " Jimmy? " she called. " Have you got any eggs? Milk? Bread? Things for breakfast? "

He hesitated. " I'm not sure," he said. " Helen and I aren't big milk drinkers."

Claire opened the refrigerator door. " Well," she said, " you don't have a very well-stocked larder. There's practically nothing here but some mouldy lettuce and a can of apple juice."

" I usually eat breakfast out," Jimmy said.

" And much as I hate to say it, dear," Claire said, " this refrigerator needs a bath. It needs to be defrosted. It smells of something."

Jimmy forced a laugh. "Helen and I hardly ever use it," he said. "It's really just for decoration."

Claire opened the closed cupboard doors. "We'll have to have spaghetti," she said finally.

"For breakfast?"

"I think it might be good for breakfast."

While the spaghetti was heating, Claire asked, "Is this Helen's silver pattern, Jimmy?"

"No," he said, "it's some I bought——"

"Where's hers? Doesn't she have any silver?"

"It's all packed away somewhere."

"Goodness," she said, "I don't see how you two survive at all."

"We eat out quite a bit."

"How long have you been married?"

He was beginning to be annoyed with her. "You ought to know," he said sharply, "you were invited to the wedding. In January."

"Don't get huffy," she said. "Blazer and I couldn't come to the wedding. We were back East."

"Well, what do you mean, asking me how long we've been married?"

"I was just—I was just wondering. Where's the silver water pitcher we sent you?"

"Packed away. Everything's packed away."

Claire set the kitchen table with plates, knives, forks, and paper napkins folded to look like little hats. "Does it look like a party?" she asked gaily.

She filled three water goblets from the sink. "What's this?" she asked suddenly.

"What?"

She picked up the blue plate on the counter. "A pearl neckface," she said. "Did Helen break her pearls?"

"Yes," Jimmy said.

"What a shame."

They sat down. "When we get up there, the first thing we have to do is find a camp site," Blazer said. "Then we have to build a fire."

" Do you have your *Boy Scout Handbook?* " Claire asked between mouthfuls. " I hope you know how to do all these things. Jimmy and I have never been on a camping trip, have we, Jimmy? " She turned to him.

She was chattering too brightly, too enthusiastically, Jimmy thought. It was as though she had sensed something, and was now trying to erase the things she had said about Helen. The silver pattern, the wedding, the pearls. The pearls had been his fault. He wished he had not left them there. He felt the deep, swelling loneliness rising in him. He put down his fork.

" I camped out once when I was little," he said. " In Colorado. It wasn't much fun. It rained, and we had to soak the wood with fly spray to make it burn."

He excused himself and went into the bathroom. He felt a little sick. He rested the palms of his hands on the edge of the sink and looked into the mirror. Oh, God, he thought, why don't I tell them the truth?

Claire called to him. " Don't you want anything more to eat? "

" No, thanks."

When he came out, they were ready to go. Claire had washed the dishes. The knapsacks and sleeping-bags were rolled and stacked by the door.

" I've left some intimate apparel in your closet," Claire said. " I hate to think what Helen would say if she came back unexpectedly and found it."

" I've got to water my avocado," Jimmy said.

" What? "

" I'm trying to grow an avocado."

" Now, really——"

" I am. What's funny about that? " He went into the kitchen. On a corner of the window-sill, behind a fold of the curtain where it would get plenty of sun, was the brown avocado pit, suspended above a glass of water with projecting toothpicks. Carefully, he lifted the stone from the glass. Already, a white root, perhaps an inch long, was sprouting from the base of it. He ran fresh water into the glass and replaced the stone. Claire had followed him to the kitchen door, and stood there, watching him. " The miraculous leaf of life," she said.

" What? "

" The miraculous leaf of life. Before I was married, when I lived alone, I bought a miraculous leaf of life. It grows on air. It's just a leaf, but it begins to sprout new leaves all around. Horticulture. It's a sign of bachelorhood, I guess."

" This is the remains of a salad," Jimmy smiled.

" The miraculous leaf of life cost twenty-five cents. But " –she shrugged—" it died."

" Let's go! " Blazer called.

Carrying their packs—they were awkward and heavy—they staggered down the flight of steps to the courtyard, and through the arch on to the sidewalk. The street was still cool; the heat would come by midafternoon, but by then they would be in the mountains. A trace of wind rustled the leaves of the live oaks. At the corner, they waited for the light to change. Then they crossed the street to where Blazer had parked his crimson Jaguar.

When they had arranged everything in the trunk, Claire went across the street again to the drugstore. After a few minutes, she came out with a box of Saltines, a quart of cold root beer, and three pairs of sun-glasses. " I thought these might come in handy," she said, distributing the glasses. " And this is stuff to munch on in the car."

" Great," Blazer said. And he gave the command. " Ten-shun! Don glasses! " They donned the glasses and started off. When they stopped, a little later, at a hardware store for the axe, Jimmy disappeared for a moment and made a couple of purchases. He bought a plastic toothbrush holder and a long-handled bath brush with bright red bristles. " We can nail this on a tree for our toothbrushes," he said, " and I don't know what this is for. I bought it because it matches Blazer's car."

" Just think! " Claire said. " A lonely hunter—years from now—may come wandering through the mountains and come to a place where he's sure no white man has ever been before him. And then, lo and behold, he'll spot our toothbrush holder nailed to a tree."

" When our civilization is dust, this plastic will remain," Blazer said solemnly.

" A thousand centuries from now "—Claire intoned—" or maybe next week—when the world is blown to atoms, some cruising man from Mars may find this bit of floating plastic coasting by his spaceship—radioactive, of course.

"Oh, let's flame!" Claire said suddenly. "Let's be flaming youth! Our parents had so much fun at it. Let's make this the Roaring Fifties!

"Only let's call it something else. I know—let's call it the Blazing Fifties. After Blazer! That sounds wonderful, don't you think? The Blazing Fifties! Our candle does more than burn at both ends—we toss the whole thing into the fire! The Blazing Fifties—after Blazer and his car!" She began to laugh. She laughed so hard that she turned to Jimmy and put her hands on his shoulders, clung to him, and buried her head against his arm, laughing.

Driving across the warm Sacramento Valley on Route 40, heading east, they passed from the lush and irrigated farmlands outside the city into the parched tall grass of the foothills. The names of the towns began to have a Western, gold-rush ring—Red Dog . . . Last Chance . . . They passed the root beer bottle back and forth between them, and munched Saltines. Jimmy had never seen Claire quite like this before.

"Look at these lousy California drivers," Blazer was saying. "Nobody in this state knows how to drive. Have you noticed that?"

"I've noticed something," Claire said. "Which is, the way all of a sudden it's next year. Have you noticed the way it does that? I can't believe that Blazer and I have been married nearly a year—that a year ago we were all secure, back in New England."

"I don't really like California," Jimmy said. "I've tried to like it—because of my job and all—but I can't get too whipped up about it. Look at this valley—flat, flat . . ."

"But we're getting into the mountains."

"I prefer the Berkshires."

"Ah!" They all thought fondly of the Berkshires.

"Blazer and I spent our honeymoon at Stowe, did we tell you? It was Blazer's idea, of course. December—we spent nearly every day ski-ing. I used to sit around the lodge worrying, thinking I'd be a widow at the tender age of twenty-two. You and Helen must come ski-ing with us next winter."

"I'd love to."

"Does Helen ski?"

"A little."

" Good."

" Helen and I——" he began.

" What? "

" Well, we're not very athletic," he said lamely.

They stopped, after a while, at a little tearoom on the road and had ice-cream and pie, and were badly served. Claire began talking in a Bronx accent, pretending that she was their pick-up. Their waitress eyed the three of them with disapproval. When they walked back to the car, they pretended to be drunk, and Claire stole a large thermometer that was hanging on a tree that said GOLDEN STATE ICE-CREAM on it. " So we can tell how cold it gets up there," she said.

Blazer made her return the thermometer, but they started off again in fabulous spirits, anyway. Soon they were really in the Sierras, and the red car climbed and twisted between the low peaks, into the higher ones, up and up, and the trees became shorter, spikier, and, when they stopped for gas, they asked the attendant, " How far up are we? "

" Five thousand feet," he told them.

Jimmy offered to drive for a while, and Claire, who had been sitting on the outside, slid across the seat so that she could sit between them. " Helen doesn't think much of my driving," Jimmy said. " I hope you won't mind it."

After a few minutes of his driving, Claire said, " I don't see why Helen should object to it. I think you drive beautifully."

" Yes," Blazer said. " Maybe even better than me."

" Helen probably drives like a Westerner," Claire said. " She just doesn't understand the way an Easterner drives. Californians don't appreciate cautiousness. Why in the world did you have to marry a California girl? "

They watched the signs now, carefully. The changes in elevation were marked. Soon it was six thousand, then nearly seven thousand feet above the level of the sea. They were beyond the timber line, and ledges and shelves of rock jutted out sharply all around them. In the distance, the tallest mountains were capped with clouds and fringed, below, with patches of summer snow. They reached Donner Summit, and stopped and got out of the car for a moment. Their ears were ringing with the altitude, and the cold wind whipped around them. Donner Lake glittered a thousand feet below them, and, far beyond, the deep blue shadow of Lake Tahoe hung below the sky.

" If I leaned over, I could spit into it," Claire shouted against the wind. " But I won't. It's too beautiful! "

In the car again, in that rarefied air, a strange thing happened. For as they talked, they suddenly found that each of them knew all the dirty words that the others knew—all the graphic, beautiful four-letter words of the Anglo-Saxon. They began using them freely and without inhibition. They became incredibly vulgar, and if anyone was shocked, no one would have dared to show it then. They laughed and told stories, and sang, over and over again, a very dirty song called " I Don't Want to Go to War." The fences were down, and the effect they created upon each other was drunken and supreme. In the middle of all this entered Squaw Valley.

" I've been thinking," Claire said, as they drove up the drive towards the low, handsome redwood and glass lodge, " why don't we see if the ski lift is running? If it is, we can go up the mountain on that, climb over the ridge, and go down the other side."

" It seems like a lazy way to climb a mountain," Blazer said.

" Yes, but so much easier! "

" All right."

They parked the car, got out, and walked around behind the lodge, and saw, ahead of them, that the lift was working. Although there was no snow here, the lodge was making money towing sight-seers up and down the mountainside. " When we come back down to-morrow," Claire said, " let's stop at the pool for a swim. After all, we don't want this week-end to be *too Field & Stream*, do we? " They went back to the car, took out their knapsacks and the roll of sleeping-bags, and strapped them on.

When they reached the foot of the lift, and the double chairs were swinging by them, starting their ascent, there was some indecision as to how the three of them would split up for their trip. Blazer settled it by hopping into one of the chairs as it went by and waving good-bye to Claire and Jimmy as he started up. Jimmy and Claire stood side by side and were scooped into the next chair together. It tugged them into the air; their feet brushed through the tree-tops.

Blazer, ahead of them, was now out of earshot. " Isn't this wonderful? " Claire said excitedly. And she added confidentially, " I'm glad you could come with us, Jimmy, I really am."

" I'm always afraid three is a crowd," he said.

" It's not. It's not a crowd with you. I don't know why, but it just never is."

" Well, I'm glad I came, too."

" My, aren't we polite! " After a moment, she said, " You've lost weight, haven't you? "

" I've been on a diet."

" Enforced? "

" Self-enforced, yes, if that's what you mean." He removed a cigarette from his pocket, and, with a little trouble, lighted it and handed it to Claire. Then he lighted another for himself. The smoke, in the high air, tasted strange and sharp in his throat.

" How strange," Claire said. " Most people—most men, anyway—seem to put on weight after they're married. Have you noticed that? Blazer's put on nearly ten pounds already."

" That's why I went on a diet."

There was a pause, and Claire said, " I'm not sure I like it. I think I liked you better when you were chubbier."

" What do you mean? "

" I don't know. It just seems to me that when you were at college, you were always so cheerful and light-hearted and gay. And now—oh, you know how you were in college."

" How was I in college? "

" You know. You were—you could have had any girl you wanted for the asking, for one thing. Even at Smith I heard tales of the great Jimmy Keefe. You were a legend! "

" Jimmy Keefe—the all-American party boy."

" Not that. Not just that. You were always graceful."

" *Graceful ?* "

" Yes. Graceful about being rich. Not like some people——"

" You have an obsession about this business of being rich, don't you? " he said.

" No, I don't. But I understand it. I'm rich, too, remember. Or I will be some day. It's just that I never could be graceful. I was always more blatant. But you're different now——"

" I'm blatant, you mean? "

" No, just not as happy. You're quieter. I think you drink more, don't you? I mean, last night. I think you'd really had quite a bit to drink before we came."

He gave her a sardonic smile. " Now it's out," he said. " My ugly secret."

" Oh, I don't mean to scold. Probably we all drink too much. It's an easy thing to do. But I just don't think anyone should ever drink alone."

" Next time I feel like drinking alone," he said, " I'll call you up. Will you come over and join me? "

Claire laughed brightly. " I'll go like the wind from San Francisco to Sacramento—just to join you in a drinking bout, darling," she said. " Of course, it will take me a couple of hours, but you'll wait."

" With open arms and open bottle . . ."

" You're not taking me seriously at all! "

" Hey! " he said. " You're Claire Denison—Mrs. Stuart Gates. Blazer Gates's wife. Nobody's supposed to take you seriously."

She frowned. " Yes, they are," she said. " When I talk like this, they are."

" I'm sorry."

" Blazer used to say, when we were all still in college and I'd come up from Smith for all those fantastic house parties and week-ends, that all he wanted to do was stay drunk all the time! I couldn't understand that in him. It worried me. I think I see now why it was—why he felt that way. Lord, but he used to drink a lot."

" Why do you think it was? "

" I think it was just loneliness. People like Blazer—like you, too—are gregarious. You're meant to have other people around, nice people who love you——" She paused again, and then she said, " Besides, I think now that you're thinner, you have sort of sad lines around your eyes."

" Really? "

" Really. Sort of worry lines. Around your mouth, too."

" My job keeps me pretty busy. I may be behind in my sleep."

" That's not all," she said.

" What do you mean? "

"Oh, Jimmy. Poor, silly Jimmy. You know what I mean."

He was silent for a moment or two He pulled on the end of his cigarette and then crushed it on the sole of his shoe and let the dry tobacco and ash fall to the rock below. He looked ahead; they were nearly half-way up. The line of towers which suspended the cable stretched precariously higher. Finally he said, "You mean because Helen has left me? Is that what you mean?"

"Yes."

"How did you know? How the hell did you know?" Suddenly he was angry with her. "Look," he said, "have you been laughing at me the whole time? Is that it?"

"Oh, no!" she said. "That isn't it at all. I don't care why it is. I don't want to know anything! But I just don't want you to go on feeling you have to lie to me."

"Thanks," he said sharply. "Thanks for that consideration."

"Please don't be sarcastic." She put her hand gently on his knee. "Jimmy," she said, "I love you. Did I ever tell you that? You're like—well, you're like a brother! I know it sounds trite, but——"

"How did you know?" he said quietly.

"I'm a woman. I'm really more than Claire Denison, queen of the Senior Prom! I know what a woman does and what a woman doesn't. I hadn't been in that apartment ten minutes before I knew. There was nothing—not a thing of a woman's in that whole place. Bobby pins. When I was in the bathroom, I looked for bobby pins. That's one thing a woman always has around. I couldn't fine one. And of course there were none of her things in the closet—nothing in the kitchen. And those pearls! Really, Jimmy, what an obvious plant! Those were dime-store pearls, dear. A woman wouldn't save them in a dish to have them restrung if they broke. I knew that was probably the only thing she left behind, probably in a waste-basket——"

"You must have had a good laugh," he said. "It's pretty funny, isn't it?"

"No! I felt more like—like crying! Why did you feel you had to pretend?"

"Look," he said, "I just didn't see any point in trying to inflict my problems on the two of you. I didn't want you to feel you had to be sorry for me, or polite or anything. I wanted everything to be natural. I didn't want you commiserating——"

" I wouldn't have—if you hadn't wanted me to. I told you, I don't want to know anything about it. I'm sorry if you're upset, but that's all."

" You've told Blazer, I suppose."

" No. I thought if you didn't want him to know, there was no point in my telling him——"

" Well," he said, " thanks for that." He turned to her. " I'm sorry I got mad just now," he said. " You're pretty fantastic, you really are."

" Nonsense. I like you, that's all."

" I'll have to tell him, I suppose," he said. " Christ, Claire, I don't know whether you understand how hard it is for me to tell people about it. The whole thing seems to call for explanations and post-mortems. I guess it's because this is the first thing in my life that hasn't gone hunky-dory. My first failure."

" Why should you feel that way? " Claire said. " Couples separate all the time."

" I just feel as though I've made such a flop of things. Do you know what hell I've been through? "

" I can imagine."

" Oh, it's all very pretty. Shall I tell you about some of the fights we had? About the time she tried to kill herself? "

" Please," she said. " I'm just sorry—terribly sorry that it happened."

" My God, it's been——"

" Jimmy," she said, " you love her, don't you? You're just feeling a little sorry for yourself, aren't you? "

He sighed. " Yes, I suppose I am."

" I don't mind. Everybody does that. I just hope you're not fooling yourself—that you don't think these things to yourself all the time."

" I do, part of the time."

" What about the other part? "

" I just want her back, I suppose."

" Of course. Oh, it's too bad. But we are different."

" Who is different? "

" You and Blazer and I—different from Helen. We must be. After all, we're New Englanders. She's from California. California people are different from Connecticut people. They really are. We were raised differently—secure, conservative . . ."

" Baloney."

" No, I mean it. I know your family, and you know mine and Blazer's. We'll never surprise each other. We'll always do expectable things. We're all living on our granddaddy's money. We're sheltered, protected. If we're a boy, we go to Kent, Choate, or Hotchkiss. If we're a girl, we go to Farmington, Westover, or Ethel Walker. Then we go to New York to the Junior Get-Togethers, and the débutante parties, and we get on invitation lists, and dance to Lester Lanin's orchestra. Then we go to some nice all-male or all-female college and join a fraternity and go to more parties, to Bermuda for Easter week, to a ranch in Wyoming in the summer. We meet each other over and over again, in the lobby of the Biltmore before Thanksgiving, at Joe King's, at the parties and weddings—the same old faces! We gather together in little knots wherever we are and talk about the same things. And sooner or later we marry each other—like Blazer and me."

" Yes . . ."

" You were the maverick. You whirled off and married a Westerner. ' Tut-tut,' everybody said. ' It'll never last,' they said. ' Who *is* she? ' they asked."

" Do you mean I shouldn't have married a California girl? "

" No, no. I'm just saying that perhaps that difference between the two of you somehow accounted for it. Does that make any sense? "

" Claire," he said, " you know you're rather amazing. You can be so damned *motherly* sometimes! "

" Oh, God! " she said. " I didn't mean to be! "

" I don't mean it unkindly——"

" I know. You like me because I'm home. I'm familiar. I'm part of your upbringing and background. We talk the same language. I can say ' Biltmore ' to you and conjure up a picture of what the Biltmore is to us. You like Blazer and me because we're a relic of the East. We're New York, New Haven, and Hartford wherever we go."

" A fragment of a foreign shore that is for ever Fairfield . . ."

" But it is too bad. It's a shame that things have to happen to us while we're so young."

Jimmy looked at her and thought he saw tears in her eyes. With one hand, she pushed a lock of yellow hair back across her forehead. "I thought you were the great advocate of breaking away from the pattern," he said.

"Oh, I am. But sometimes it seems impossible. I try to avoid the Smith look—that well-*groomed* look! I used to wear my hair in bangs and wear black stockings. I smoked with a long green holder and read Kant. But all the other Smith girls were wearing bangs and black stockings and reading Kant. I wore baggy tweed suits and found all the other Smith girls wearing baggy tweed suits. I can't escape it. I'm sure that if I shaved my head and wore my dresses backward, all the other girls from Smith would be doing the same!"

"Look at the other Yalies," Jimmy said. "They're getting married, wearing hats to work, renting little apartments in Larchmont, taking junior memberships in the country club—they're not getting fouled up with divorces after six months of marriage. I'm a freak."

"Oh—is it going to be a divorce?"

"Sure. I suppose so. What else? We have Eastern lawyers, Western lawyers, complaints, cross-complaints . . ."

"Oh, lord, lord!" Claire said. "Why *can't* people——"

"Damn it," he said, "this is what I didn't want to have happen. I didn't want you feeling sorry for me."

"All right." She reached out spontaneously and took his hand. "Enough. We've said enough, I've said enough. Look," she said, "look at that mountain! Can you believe we're going to climb it? It's the biggest mountain in the world. I can't, I simply can't—not with this knapsack. You'll have to leave me behind on the way."

He looked at the mountain, and it was indeed an impresive sight. Pinnacles, peaks, crests, and crevices. It had shot itself into the sky one volcanic morning long ago, and, in an attempt to be higher than all other mountains, it had made one noble thrust. It had clutched at the sky, groped, and missed. And it had cracked and broken on the final slopes, and its rocks had shaken away and rolled into the valley. Now it was tired and through, satisfied to be a pile of jagged stone. The air made Jimmy breathless. "It is beautiful," he said.

Through the wind, ahead of them, Blazer was shouting something to them. They couldn't hear him.

They hallooed back to him, and suddenly they were both at a high pitch of excitement. " I can't wait," Claire said.

" Be careful getting off the lift."

Claire looked at him. " We've been holding hands! " she said. " Like children. Like kids on their first Ferris-wheel ride! " They both laughed. Then Claire was suddenly serious again.

" There's just one thing," she said.

" What? "

" Some day—you must tell me how the pearls broke."

He thought of the awful, the terrible noise that the pearls made as they fell, one by one, from the string, slipping, and sounding like tiny bells as they struck the tile of the bathroom floor. And how they rolled, this way and that, about the floor for moments afterward.

" I broke them," he said.

" I thought so. You see—we do the expectable thing."

He looked at her steadily, wondering whether she wanted his defence, the explanation, or whether, perhaps, she knew it already. Finally he said, " You know too much. You know entirely too damn' much."

Then they both laughed again, turned, and pulled their pack straps tighter. They were ready to get off.

Suddenly Claire cried, " Blazer! Wait for us! " Blazer, who had jumped from the lift ahead of them, was already half-way across the ridge.

3

THEY started across the ridge together, Claire ahead, Jimmy close behind: they had agreed that the slower of the two should set the pace. The surface ahead of them, across which they had to climb, was composed of loose, drifting shale, pieces of the flatness and size of dinner plates. There was no vegetation; there were no twigs or branches to grasp on to. They decided that the safest course was parallel to the slope, moving gradually upward to the sharp spine of the ridge. Blazer was more familiar with mountains, or perhaps had more bravado. He climbed faster, and straight up. At times, he would disappear in front of them. " What's his damn' hurry? " Jimmy said.

" He wants to be first. Everything's a race with Blazer."

Rocks slipped under their feet and clattered downward. They both thought *avalanche* simultaneously. There was not much breath now for conversation. They proceeded slowly, step by step. The falling rocks suggested a game; Jimmy began pretending that Helen was there. Fancifully, he began plotting an elaborate revenge. " See the view from here," he said, motioning her closer to the precipice. His legs felt tight and the back of his neck ached. Ahead of him, he could hear Claire's painful breathing. He wondered: Why in God's name are we doing this?

He tried to move faster. There was a declivity, a cavern. Here, he thought, would be a good place to do it. Then he thought of the long loneliness afterward. In his mind, she died; once again, he buried her, brought flowers to her grave.

They climbed in silence, and suddenly Blazer, far ahead of them, stopped and opened his lungs in a magnificent yodel.

Claire called, " Can we stop a minute? " But he had not heard her, and had turned away, so Jimmy and Claire climbed on.

" Hate him, hate him, hate him! " Claire whispered. " Why does he have to drive us so? "

Jimmy tried again to figure out what had gone wrong between him and Helen. Was it only the sex thing? Or was there something else, something that was his own fault? He had agreed to stay in California, which had pleased Helen. He had taken the job with the public relations firm; they had found the apartment. Once more, the gloom settled, dispersed for a moment the way a clock striking would make it do, then settled for good. For one thing was sure: the trouble, the beginning, was before the apartment. By the time they moved into the apartment, hurting each other had already become a force, a sickness. They hurt each other with looks, with silences, with words. Everything that happened in California—the quarrels, Helen's father's death—had been preceded by other things, farther back. On their trip to the Caribbean, or even before.

Remembering the apartment on Capitol Avenue as it had been with Helen there, Jimmy found himself wondering: Does the living-room have one window, or two windows side by side? Are the walls pale green or pale grey? Recapturing the apartment in his mind was like trying to move back into a dream after waking. It was different from his home in Somerville, which could be remembered, lovingly, inch by inch. The apartment was colourless, shapeless. Only small, unimportant details stuck out. Like the gilt birds on the window-sill, poised for flight—a wedding present, gone with Helen. And the low glass bowl by the sofa in which she sometimes floated red camellia blossoms. Another wedding present, also gone. He remembered the Venetian blinds behind the curtains, slanted to keep out the heat of the afternoon, and, sometimes, the curtains pulled tightly across the blinds to achieve a cool, restful twilight in midday. He remembered watching a piece of purple fluff from her skirt floating and settling on the glass top of the coffee table. He remembered ash-trays, clean and cool, sweating slightly from the heat outside. He remembered Helen at night, coming to bed, waiting anxiously a few feet away, waiting for him to say something or do something, or repeat a question.

" Do you love me? " he asked her.

" Yes," she said softly.

Then, quite suddenly, her shoulders shook with sobs and she

threw herself across the covers and cried silently into the pillow.

He had met Helen at a party in New York. He had graduated from college the week before, and had been staying in Manhattan while he looked—in rather desultory fashion, perhaps—for a job. It was a hot June night, and the party, at an apartment in the East Sixties, was a cocktail party that had gone on too long by the time Jimmy arrived. His friend Charlie Somerby had taken him by the arm and said, " Hey, I want you to meet a new girl—she's from the Golden West." They threaded their way through the noise and people to the other side of the smoky living-room. " This is Helen Warren," Charlie had said. Helen was small and dark. Her slim arms were deeply tanned and her figure was compact and boyish. There was something in her appearance—whether it was her small, finely boned features, her colour, or her extremely white, extremely even teeth—that immediately made her stand out, emphatically, against the others in the room. Jimmy had been attracted by the breathless way she talked—she began talking almost at once—and the quick, nervous way she smoked. She had a bright, sudden laugh, tossing her short brown hair back, and she laughed at nearly everything he said. People crushed around them. There was a shriek as a pack of matches went off in a girl's hand, and, in the ensuing scramble to put out the flames where the girl had dropped the matchbook, someone spilled a drink on Helen's dress. He mopped at it with his handkerchief. " Let's get out of here," he said. No one noticed when they left the party. They went down into the street. " How did you get mixed up in that? " he asked her.

" In what? Oh—that party, you mean? "

" Yes."

" Cousins of cousins of my mother's," she said. " They heard I was in New York and called me. My first New York cocktail party."

" What did you think of it? "

" Well——"

They stood on the sidewalk. " Where would you like to go? " he asked her.

" You decide," she said. " I'm just a tourist and this is my last night here."

" Then where do you go? "

" Back home. Back to California."

They started walking slowly west, towards Fifth Avenue. " And then what? " Jimmy asked. " What will you do? "

" I don't know," she said. " I may go back to school in the fall. I don't know. I was at Cal—but I dropped out. Or I may get a job. I just don't know. What street is this? "

" Fifth Avenue," he said.

" Oh, yes—Central Park. Isn't it beautiful? "

" Do you like New York? "

" Oh, yes," she said. " It's—well, it's almost a little overpowering. Like that cocktail party. Is that typical? Are all New York cocktail parties like that? "

" I'm afraid a lot of them are."

" Oh, but I do love New York."

" You mean——? " he began, looking at her.

" Yes! " she smiled. Then, in chorus, they said, " It's a nice place to visit, but I'd hate to live here." And they both laughed.

They were walking south now, on the park side of Fifth, towards the Plaza, and suddenly Jimmy said, " You know—I've got a real tourist's idea. Let's get a hansom cab down here and drive through the park. Or have you done that already? "

" Never! " she laughed. " But I'd love to."

A few minutes later they were in the cab, trotting slowly through dark tunnels under trees. " Isn't it strange," Helen said, " to be moving so *slowly*! In a city that I'd always thoughts of in terms of people running about, hurrying everywhere! It's so slow! " Her face, in the shadows, was warm and animated, her lips parted. Impulsively, he kissed her. " We can get out and take a taxi," he said. " We don't need to go slowly."

" No, no," she whispered, holding his hand.

" You know," he said, " it's funny, but you're terribly different. I mean, back at that cocktail party—you didn't belong there at all! I took one look at you and saw you didn't belong there. I don't mean that unkindly either. But did you take a look at any of the other girls there—the New York girls? Those Finch types—pale, kind of haggard-looking, and "—he mimicked them, talking with the broadest possible *a*—" ' My deah, so terribly, terribly weary and bored with it all—you can't imagine how bored. And how *initiated*! ' "

She laughed softly.

" But you're different," he said. " You don't belong with them. You belong out on a hill somewhere, or on the deck of a yawl, or——" He broke off. " Do you really have to go back to-morrow? "

" Yes, I'm afraid I do."

" I wish you wouldn't."

" I wish so, too," she said.

Later, when the driver returned them to the Plaza, Jimmy said, " Where would you like to go now? You name it. Statue of Liberty . . . Staten Island Ferry . . . Grant's Tomb . . .? "

Helen laughed. " I'm afraid I've seen all those things already." And she added, " It's nearly midnight."

" Look," he said suddenly, " I have an apartment on Sixty-eighth Street—it's not mine, but the people are away and have let me use it. Would you like to go back there? "

" Well——" she said.

" I mean," he said hastily, " I could fix us some coffee—something to eat. And it's near the river—there's a good view."

" All right," she said.

They had gone, and he had mixed her a drink, and had put a record on the phonograph—Marlene Dietrich singing her sad songs. In the kitchen, he fixed a plate of crackers and cheese and returned with this to the living-room. They ate in silence. " I can't get over it," Jimmy said once again. " How different you are from the other girls I've known. Not just *healthier*—but —I can't put my finger on it."

She said nothing. " Do you like "—he said, his chest feeling tight—" do you like Marlene Dietrich? "

" Yes."

And suddenly they had been in each other's arms. She had kissed him fiercely, almost angrily. Then she had pulled her face away and put her head back, letting her short brown hair fall loose. " Oh, hallelujah! " she had cried. " Oh, hallelujah! Hallelujah! " They reached, together, for the light; the phonograph played on.

Later, in the dark, she had whispered, " *Jimmy?* "

" Yes? "

" Darling—am I—am I your first girl? "

He hesitated, wondering whether to give her the answer he had read somewhere young men his age were supposed to give, or whether, with Helen, to tell the truth. And then, because he suspected that she knew the truth anyway, he told the truth. " Yes."

It had happened so fast—the sudden burning, almost unquenchable love. For Jimmy, it was an emotion unlike anything else he had ever experienced. And somehow her departure—she had flown back to California the next day as she had said she must—only served to heighten it. Nearly every night after that he telephoned her. Once, a few weeks later, his father had driven down from Connecticut to have lunch with him. Jimmy had got nowhere with the job hunting; he hadn't tried. In his talks with Helen it had been decided somehow that he would go to California, marry her, and find a job there. He tried to explain this to his father as they sat over drinks at the Yale Club. " But you don't seem to know too much about her, Jim," James Keefe, Sen., had said. " You don't know her people, for one thing. You've only just met the girl. Oh, I know—at twenty-three you're ready to win the world. But be a little common-sensical, Jimmy. Don't feel you've got to marry the first pretty face you see! " His father had grinned at him.

After that, his father wrote him a long letter in laborious longhand—an indication of how important his father considered the letter to be—about maturity and responsibilities, urging Jimmy finally to come to work for the Keefe Company, where, as always, a slot waited for him.

Nevertheless, one rainy day in December he went to the savings bank and withdrew money that had been placed there for him by his parents, grandparents, aunts and uncles on every birthday and Christmas of his life; money that represented income from a trust set up by his father, and money that his mother had sent him from time to time to " tide him over " in New York—the total came to a little over nine thousand dollars—and deposited this in his checking account.

That night, without telling anyone, he took a plane to San Francisco. Helen met him at the airport, and in a rented car, they had driven to Reno. There they had been married in a wayside wedding chapel that offered the services of a justice of the peace, an organist, and, on the premises, a motel. The next day there had been a series of telephone calls—anxious, tearful, and admonishing—to and from the two families, back and forth across the continent. Both families urged their children to come home immediately. But Jimmy and Helen went on to Yosemite, and did not return to Helen's home in Rio Linda until a week later.

In the meantime, it had been agreed between the Keefes and the Warrens, negotiating over Long Distance, to treat the elopement as though it had never occurred. A formal wedding, with invitations and announcements in the New York and San Francisco newspapers, was scheduled for early in January. The Keefes prepared to fly to San Francisco, with as many relatives as they could muster on such short notice, and to ensconce themselves in a series of suites at the St. Francis Hotel. It was Jimmy's first brush with the power and influence of his family. In his attempt to have his marriage with Helen kept secret, spontaneous, and private, he found himself defeated. When they returned from their single secret week in Yosemite, he discovered that his marriage was going to involve many more people than himself and Helen. He spent the weeks between the two weddings receiving and dispatching lengthy legal documents—wills, trusts, community property agreements. Jimmy's father expressed annoyance with Walker Warren, Helen's father. "This gentleman," he wrote, "fails to comprehend the tax advantage to be gained for you if the actual, proper wedding were allowed to fall within the current calendar year, instead of in January. Now, for your greatest tax saving, you must use the Nevada wedding date on your return when you file in April."

And Helen? He tried to remember Helen's face, her reactions, through all of this. But of course, he thought, even by then, it had begun.

Jimmy climbed on close behind Claire. The straps of his knapsack burned into his shoulders. "Oh!" Claire gasped. "Let's stop!" They stopped and he looked down. For a moment, he imagined that he could see the world below turning. A blue sliver of Lake Tahoe had appeared between the mountains—the same sliver they had seen from the summit in the car. Beyond the lake lay the wastes of northern Nevada. He wondered wildly if that odd little wayside chapel was somewhere in that expanse. Directly below, the white roof of Squaw Valley Lodge looked like a pale linen handkerchief that had been tossed down. Next to it, the swimming-pool was a vivid blue rectangle that caught the sun. " Looking down makes me dizzy," he said.

Dizzily, though, he continued to look down. With the nerve, with the right persuasion, he thought, he would go down himself. He would tumble his troubled frame down, and the rocks would spring up to catch him, to cradle him . . .

As though she sensed his thoughts, Claire said amicably, " Death wish? "

" Uh-huh," he said. " Will you jump with me? "

" Yes."

" All right, then."

" All right."

She laughed at him, and reached for his hand. In the effort, suddenly she slipped and fell face forward across the rocks. She screamed and clutched at a stone. It came loose and she slipped farther. He went to his hands and knees, tried to reach her, and lost his own footing. Then they were both motionless. A clatter of stones loosened, fell, and echoed below them. " Don't move," he said. " For Christ's sake, don't move! "

" I can't! " she sobbed.

" If I move, I'll slip on top of you, and we'll both go down. Don't move until I think of something."

" Oh, God! " said Claire.

He tried to steady himself, and when he thought he had, he tried to reach down to her again. Blazer was far ahead, out of sight.

With his fingers, he groped for her hand. " Don't touch me! " she screamed sharply. " Don't touch me! "

" Let me try to get your pack off."

" Don't touch me! " And suddenly she said, " I'll get out of this myself, without your help. You only want to make me grateful! "

Stung, he drew back his hand. " All right," he said. Slowly, he inched himself forward, placed his knee against a rock, and stood up. He stood, looking down at her, watching her as she crawled painfully up. Tears streamed down her face. She had cut her chin, and the tears mingled with blood. He watched as she slid upward across the shale until her toe found a firm place. Then she stood up.

" I'm sorry," Jimmy said quietly.

Her face was still white. She laughed shakily. " Blazer would never forgive me," she said, " if I couldn't make it up this little mountain by myself." She reached in her pocket and removed a handkerchief. She dabbed at her chin. " Just a scratch," she said.

They went on in silence, and after a while, the worst of it was over, and they reached a high level stretch where Blazer was sitting cross-legged, waiting for them. The westward side of the mountain sloped off gently. They started down, and suddenly there was a low clump of trees, and, in a hollow, a spring that bubbled out of nowhere into a pool. They walked to the edge of the pool, turning the rocks over carefully with their toes.

" This is a large arrowhead," Blazer said, kicking over a stone.

" A particularly large arrowhead," Jimmy said.

" Probably a deadly weapon."

" A blunt instrument, anyway," Claire said.

" And look at this curious fossilized dingbat," Blazer said. " Centuries ago, it lived and walked among us."

" Well, not *us*," Claire said.

" And here is a relic of the Pleistocene Age . . ."

Tadpoles darted from the edges of the pool where they stepped.

" How do they *get* here? " Claire asked. " Such nice big fat ones, too! "

" They're disgusting," Blazer said.

" Yes," Claire said, " but don't forget they turn into butterflies."

" No, they turn into swans," said Blazer.

" No," Jimmy said, " they turn into frogs that turn into princes. I read it somewhere."

There was another short rise to climb before the whole panorama of the western slope came into view. The lake, and Nevada, had passed behind the ridge. They were looking across a greener, softer expanse into California. There was a small lake below them, rimmed with small firs. " Look," Blazer said, " that's where we'll camp! "

" We can swim with no clothes on," Claire said. " We can skinny-dip! "

" Let's go." Blazer looked at her. " How'd you cut your chin? " he asked.

" A branch snapped in my face," Claire said casually.

Going down from there was mostly running and leaping from stone to stone, and half falling, slipping, and sliding. At times, they lost sight of the lake, and then again they would see it, correct their course, and head for it again. Although it was past noon, the sun was still on the morning side of the mountain, and they were in the mountain's dark brown shadow. Soon they were among sequoias and pines and thick patches of sweet fern, stepping and climbing over fallen trees that resembled giant graves. They came unexpectedly to a clearing in the trees where the grass was thick and tall and green and spattered with buttercups. Claire flopped on her stomach in the grass. " I've wanted to do this all day," she said.

" All of a sudden, it's hot," Jimmy said. He unbuttoned his shirt and let his shirt-tails hang loose.

" But, oh, God, what a lovely day! " Claire said. " Does anybody feel like gambolling? Let's gambol on the greensward."

For a while, they gambolled. They played hide-and-seek for a minute or two, but there were no good places to hide. They played run, sheep, run. They chased each other until Claire said, " Oh, dear, I'm getting a headache. Let's stop now." They took off their shoes and sat in the grass and dug their bare toes into the moist earth. They sang songs and tried to remember good rhymes. " On the top of the mountain," Claire said, " I remembered Edna St. Vincent Millay—' The world stands out on either side, no wider than the heart is wide.' Isn't that the loveliest thought? She was nineteen when she wrote that." Claire produced some sandwiches from her knapsack. Later, Claire said, " Let's climb trees," and they did. When Claire reached the outermost branch of her tree, she hung on, swaying fantastically, and called, " I'm never coming down! No, no, never-nonnie-nay! "

Then, since it was getting late, they picked up their packs again, and went on through the last remaining stretch of woods. Presently they reached the lake.

" This makes it worth all the trouble," Claire said. " It's not real—it's a Maxfield Parrish painting."

And it was. Even though it had formed itself in a hollow of

the mountains, there was a long strip of sand along its shore, and another section where the shore was cragged with rocks and boulders that stretched like huge stepping-stones into the water.

They took off their packs and sat down, looking at it. Fish plopped quietly out of the water for flies, and, except for this noise, it was remarkably silent. The slanting sunlight came through the trees and struck every ripple. The branches of the spruces and hemlocks swayed, and a few birds called. Nothing else. Blazer started working on the camp-fire.

" Collect small sticks," he said.

They did this, and when they returned with them and heaped them on the fire, it burned well, throwing a deep, pungent, piny smoke into the air. Jimmy took the axe and began cutting pine boughs for their beds. " Don't take too many branches off a single tree," Claire said. " We mustn't spoil the beauty of it here."

" How shall we arrange the beds? " Blazer asked. " It would be easier to make one big bed than three little ones."

They considered this for a moment. " Well," Claire said, " I think it would be better to make a big one for you and me, and a smaller one for Jimmy."

" All right."

Claire started unpacking the knapsacks. " What's this? " she said, holding up the large Thermos bottle. " This isn't ours."

" I told you last night," Jimmy said. " That's my contribution to the larder."

Claire opened it and sniffed the contents. " You were serious! " she said. " You *did* bring martinis! I thought you were only joking. How degenerate! Imagine bringing martinis on a camping trip! "

" Why, I think they might go well," Jimmy said.

" Well, I'll have one," Claire said, lifting the bottle to her lips. " Just to show you I'm a good sport." She passed the Thermos to Blazer. " Cocktail hour, darling," she said.

" I've never felt less like a martini," Blazer said. " But what the hell."

Later, Claire said, " It's only six o'clock, but it's beginning to get dark." She lay on her back on the bed of pine needles with her drink, in a paper cup, resting on her stomach. " I guess if you live between two mountains, you only have about a seven-hour day. We'd better do something about eating."

She stood up and began opening cans. Blazer and Jimmy stretched the sleeping-bags across the pine beds. " Now, one thing about selling," Blazer was saying, " is that you've got to be so God-damned nice to so many God-damned bastards, all day long. You know, whether you like them or not. That was what used to gripe me when I first took this job. You know why I really took it? Because of the travel. There's a hell of a lot of travelling connected with it. Not just up and down the state of California—but, hell, I may go to Honolulu in a month or two. And I may go to Manila. Well, everything has its compensations, I guess. I used to think I'd like to be a lawyer. But a lawyer stays pretty much in the same place."

Claire returned with a dipperful of water from the lake. " Are you talking about *business?* " she said. " How can you—out here in the wilderness? " She put the pan of water on the fire. " I hope this water is pure," she said. " It has a funny smell. It might be safer to cook with martinis." She filled her paper cup from the Thermos.

" Of course it's pure," Blazer said.

" It tastes like pine needles."

" That's a good taste."

" The martinis are beginning to taste like pine needles," Jimmy said.

When it was dark, they sat in a circle around the fire and ate corned beef hash. When they finished, they tossed their paper plates into the fire and watched them burn. The moon was coming up, filtering through the trees, shining on the lake. " Let the still moon sleep on the lake," Jimmy said. " Does anyone know who said that? "

" I do," Claire said. " William Blake."

" Yes."

" Let's find a tree and lean against it," Claire said. " I'm deliciously, marvellously drunk." She looked up at the sky. " I three see moons," she said, and laughed. " Let's tell ghost stories." They found a tree and sat around it, but it was soon uncomfortable. They went back to the edge of the fire and sat on the ground, back to back, and leaned against each other.

" No ghost stories? Then I'll begin the story of my life," Claire said.

The fish jumped still, and there were a few night birds here and there, but all sounds were either very close or far away. " I like college week-ends," Claire began. " And I like week-ends like this, deliriously. I like doing nothing at all. I like boys who wear dirty old scuffed-up white buck shoes in college towns, and polo coats. I used to like fraternity parties hopelessly, but now I'm jaded. They bore me. I like people—nice, silly people, who do silly things in silly places. You have to know all this before you understand the story of my life," she said parenthetically. Her voice trailed off. " But I realize," she said sadly, " that I am one of the silliest people who does the silliest things in some of the most ridiculous places, like the Biltmore."

" Well, you're also one of the nicest," Jimmy said.

" Ah—do you think so? "

" Sentimental," Blazer said. " You and Claire are just alike. You think everybody should be nice and warm and wonderful and funny and amusing. And when you find out they're not, you can't take it. You act all hurt and bewildered."

" I have my serious side," Claire said. " Do you know something that worries me? Look at us! We're not people who have fought the wars. When the First World War was fought, we weren't even born. When the Second World War was fought, we were children. When the Korean War was fought, we were going to football week-ends at Yale and both of you were marching around campus in the R.O.T.C. It's all kind of an illusion with us, isn't it? Anzio Beachhead, Heartbreak Ridge . . . they're just quaint romantic names. They have no real, personal meaning to us. We weren't there—we weren't even *aware*! We've contributed nothing. We're a generation that feels the world owes us a living, just because we're attractive."

" Now, that *is* a serious thought! " Blazer said.

" Of course. We've never been tested. If we were given a challenge, how do we know we'd stand up! The biggest challenge we've ever had is—well, it's climbing a mountain."

" But don't worry," Blazer said, " we'll have wars to fight before we're through."

" I think we hope so, don't we? We really hope so, so that we'll have a chance to prove ourselves."

They were silent, thinking about this.

" And then," Claire said, " of course we're idlers. We work, but only because we feel we should. It's expected of us. We like to think of ourselves as staunch New Englanders, with lots of Puritan spirit. But we're just living on money that our grandfathers and great-grandfathers made. Blazer and I—we don't live on Blazer's salary. The little dividend cheques come in every three months . . . we're just spending money somebody else had to work to make. We won't make any fortunes of our own. Our children, or our grandchildren, will have to start all over again. There won't be any left for them."

" Claire feels guilty because her old man's got millions," Blazer said.

" I do. Why should I feel proud? I didn't do anything to make them."

" Well, neither did he. All he did was vote the Republican ticket."

" Still, we're living on the fruits of somebody else's work, someone we don't even understand. Jimmy, am I making any sense? "

" I know what Claire means," he said.

" In California, the fortunes are being made now. Here. To-day."

" But who wants California? " Blazer asked.

" I know . . ."

" California is damp and dreary."

" But this place is nice," Jimmy said.

" Yes, because we're here," Blazer said.

" Oh, do you think this place is nice only because we're here? " Claire asked.

" Yes."

Claire said, " That may be true. I detest towns with Spanish names."

" And missions . . ."

" And abalone . . ."

" And avocados."

" Jimmy's growing one in a glass of water."

" My pet peeve is Mexican food . . . enchiladas! "

" I hope I've seen my last artichoke."

Claire said sleepily, " I'm dreadfully homesick. Mother and Daddy are probably at the Cape now . . ."

" I'm glad we're not with them, though," Blazer said.

" Well, so am I, in a way."

Jimmy said, " We're all New Englanders, transplanted. Our roots don't seem to take to California soil." He yawned and stretched his feet closer to the fire.

The three New Englanders, transplanted, were rooted there against the night's green bank, no one daring to speak now, to say a word, or move. Caressing the fat, cold dew drops with their toes in the deep pine needles, smelling of soap and Seaforth and Chanel Number Five, they were indeed a tragic sight. They were on a merry-go-round in the blackness beyond the limits of their fire, and it was anyone's guess which star they might be thrown off on. Nursing their desperate, self-pitying dream, they sat, all shoulders touching, back to back. (Jimmy thought: *Perhaps we are not really troubled; perhaps we only long to be. Is it that simple?*) A star fell. That was Claire's star. And then another one for Blazer, and then three rapid ones close together, any one of which Jimmy could have had for the asking. These lovers, these hybrid flowers struggling in an unfriendly land, drew close together and tried to remember shows they had seen, night-club banquettes they had sat upon, what the signs said twinkling on the Jersey shore from the West Side Highway, what the mother swan said when she found her ugly duckling missing, and where Moses was when the lights went out. . . .

" If ever a day should end, it should end now," Jimmy said. And the night was still, pierced only with the glow of the fire, and their cigarettes.

4

ALONE in his sleeping-bag, Jimmy thought about what Claire had said. Was it true that they were people who had everything to offer, yet who actually offered nothing? In some ways it was true, disturbingly true. He tried to think about it, but realized that he could only think about his own particular problem—his loneliness, confusion, not being able to sleep without having gaudy, nightmarish dreams. My world is as small as this sleeping-bag, he thought. He thought of himself. James Lyndon Keefe, Jun. He thought of his mother and father. For no reason, he suddenly remembered the night, a year ago, when he tried to tell his mother about Helen. She had been dressed and leaving for a party, her crimson silk coat rustling about her, her fine white hair piled high upon her head. The Chrysler was waiting, parked in the lighted driveway. " I've met this girl——" he began. But she was already late. " Can it wait? " she said. " Can you tell me about it later? It sounds terribly exciting, darling, but I must rush. " " Can you wait just a second, Mother? " he had asked. " Dear, I *can't*." She offered her cheek to be kissed. It smelled of powder and perfume, and the high collar of her silk coat tickled his neck. " We won't be late," she said. " I'll stop by your room when I get home." He kissed her; that night, he heard her come in and snapped on the light, waiting to hear her footsteps come down the hall. But she had forgotten. He turned off the light and angrily swore that he would never try to tell her anything again. And yet, he thought now, it would be unfair to blame his parents for everything. He rolled over on his back and looked up; the mountains all around reached out in silence. He wondered if another drink would help him sleep. He crawled out of his sleeping-bag and felt his way across the ground to where the Thermos lay.

In May, after Helen had left, he had flown back to New York to tell his parents about the separation and the divorce. What had he expected from them? His mother was sympathetic, warm. But it was just one of those things, she said. She had thought Helen a terribly *possessive* girl, didn't Jimmy think? Possessive—it was certainly the last adjective he would have thought to apply to Helen; it was just an adjective his mother had found floating in her head, and felt it was an appropriate one to use. Of course, his mother said, she had hardly known Helen. She had hardly been given the chance, she said reproachfully. The whole business had been so terribly rash and hasty. Didn't Jimmy agree, she asked, that so often those rash, hasty marriages ended this way? The thing to do now was simply to forget about her. Forgetting Helen would be as easy as rolling off a log—wait and see. Just to prove it, just to get his mind off her, to-morrow they would all drive to the beach with a picnic lunch, and there would be plenty of salad and French bread, and the spiced chilis that he liked so much. And they would take—let's see—they would ask the Mortons if they were free, and Jessica. Jessica was home from Foxcroft for the weekend, and was looking lovely. Jessica would get his mind off Helen. Now, there was a nice girl. Had Jimmy ever considered *doing* anything about Jessica? Why, she asked him, did he insist on going back to California to that silly advertising job? (It's not advertising, Mother, he had reminded her, it's public relations.) If he really wanted to forget Helen, he would stay right here. If he didn't want to work for Daddy, he could go down to New York again and let Daddy help him find a job with some nice company. He could live at the Yale Club, where Buzzie Washburn was living. Let Helen get her divorce or whatever. There was no point in his sticking around Sacramento while she got it.

The next day, his father had called him to come down to the office. Sitting with his father, when he arrived, were two other people—Miss Maitland, his father's secretary, and Turner Ames, his father's lawyer. James Lyndon Keefe, Sen., was cheerful and to the point. He took his son's hand and shook it, and motioned him to one of the heavy leather chairs. Miss Maitland smiled effusively, remarked how well Jimmy looked; Turner Ames ruffled through papers in a brief-case which he held on his lap. "I think we might as well turn this little meeting over to Turner," his father said. "Turner has worked out all the details."

Turner Ames cleared his throat. "Your father tells me," he began, "that you've—ah—had a bit of bad luck, and that the—ah—younger Mrs. Keefe is initiating a divorce action. Well," he said, and smiled, "these things can be unpleasant, Jim, but I'd like to tell you here and now they could be a lot worse. Fortunately"—he turned and smiled at Jimmy's father—"your father is a foresighted man. A very foresighted man."

"Tut, tut, Turner," his father said, "all that was your doing, not mine."

"Well," Mr. Ames went on, "whether you realized it or not, we worked out a very satisfactory arrangement prior to the marriage. For example, you both signed a community property agreement. This is very important under California law. It will be impossible for her to claim any of your present property as jointly owned. Bank accounts were maintained separately . . ."

"I don't think Helen has any idea of doing anything like that," Jimmy said.

"Well, we never can tell," Mr. Ames said. "Now, there is also the matter of alimony. Since the marriage was of such short duration, it seems incredible to us that alimony will be asked. However, since we may assume that Mrs. Keefe, Jun., has been apprised of some of the Keefe family—ah—holdings, she may get the idea that she can hold us up for a fancy figure——"

"Look," Jimmy said, "Helen's not like that. She's not a gold digger. She's——"

Mr. Ames held up his hand. "Ah," he said, "we musn't go into this with our eyes closed. You'd be surprised at some of the things a woman will do when she smells money." He smiled at Miss Maitland, and Miss Maitland smiled back. "However," he said, "we are prepared to make a reasonable offer—not large, but reasonable under the circumstances. It will, of course, be discontinued in the event of her remarriage. I would say it was likely that she will remarry, wouldn't you?"

Jimmy sat back in the leather chair. He felt his stomach tighten, and wondered if he was going to be sick.

"Tell him about the other business, Turner," his father said.

"Ah, yes," said Mr. Ames. "This is definitely on the pleasant side of the ledger, Jim. You have, from your grandfather's estate, some shares of Keefe Company stock. That amounts to —let's see"—he shuffled through his papers—"three hundred and fifty-one shares. Where that odd share came from, I can't imagine. Ha ha," he said. "Well, your father has worked out a very astute plan for you——"

"Nonsense, Turner, you worked it out," his father said.

"In the interests of reducing some of his holdings, and reducing the size of his estate, your father is making available considerable amounts of this stock for purchase. Certain amounts are being offered to officers and executives of the company. I am flattered to say that your father has offered a portion of this stock to me. He will also arrange for you to purchase, on a regular, continuing, annual basis, additional stock from him. This purchase will be facilitated for you by means of an annual cash gift from your father. Unfortunately, Uncle Sam won't let gifts of this sort be over a certain amount. But let me add that, through an accounting gimmick that we've worked out, your father will be able to sell his stock at a loss. This works to both your advantages. Now, I have here a cheque to your order signed by your father which, if you will endorse and make payable to the Keefe Company . . ."

He had gone on, explaining about estates and trusts and taxes. He read a list of properties ("Lots 347, 348, and 350, Crescent Avenue . . . Lot 14B, Hall Street . . . Lot 69, Hall Street, known as the Loew's Theatre Building . . .") which were being set aside in a separate trust, the income from which would be utilized to defray . . .

Jimmy had stopped listening. Turner Ames passed papers to Miss Maitland, who glanced at them, passed them to Jimmy's father for inspection, who passed them to Jimmy for his signature, who returned them to Mr. Ames. The documents circled around the room for nearly an hour. Then, when they were finished, they all stood up. Mr. Ames clapped a hand on Jimmy's shoulder. "Well, my boy," he said, "you may never be rich, but you'll never be in the poorhouse, either. Ha ha." He laughed, to imply that the path to the poorhouse would indeed be long and roadblocked by generations of corporate wizardry. "Going to stay in Somerville awhile?" he asked.

"No, I'm afraid this is just a two-week vacation," Jimmy said. "I've got a job in California to get back to."

His father frowned. "Do you really mean that?" he asked.

"Of course," Jimmy said. "I've just started this job. I can't run off and quit just like that."

"Want to make good on your own, eh?" Mr. Ames asked.

"That's right."

"Well, that's fine, fine," Mr. Ames said. "But we'll get him back, won't we, J. L.?" He winked. "He'll have his fill of those movie stars before long."

Remembering all this, alone in the mountain night, he shivered and took another drink from the Thermos. How little they understood, and how hopeless it was to try to make them understand. Yes, he thought, perhaps Claire was right. None of them had been tested. But this was a test that he was giving himself. Maybe it wasn't war, but it required bravery of a sort. He had failed in his marriage, but he must not allow himself to fail in his job. He must not take the easy way out, which was home, to Somerville, to the Keefe Company, to the calculated heartiness of Turner Ames, and Miss Maitland's simper.

His mother had hoped that Jessica would make him stay. That day at the beach, Jessica had talked about the sailboat races on the lake that summer which he shouldn't miss. She talked, gaily, about how long her tan would last, the party she was going to give, the people she was going to invite. She talked of the familiarity of Massachusetts, Connecticut, Rhode Island and Vermont. Jessica had learned an interesting trick at Foxcroft. Taking the matches from her pack, she placed them side by side along the sea wall. Then she showed him how she could make five out of three, ten out of two, three pairs of four by only moving one, six out of twelve. Her lacquered fingertips moved deftly, carefully through the magic, and the order she desired resulted. "I didn't say they couldn't be *Roman* numerals!" she laughed, as, halfheartedly, he accused her of cheating. That night, once again, he had told his mother, "I am going back to California. I'm sorry, but I am." She shook her head and said that never in this world would she be able to fathom the reason why.

He had kept his promise. He had actually cut his vacation

short and flown back ahead of time, telling his parents that he had remembered an important piece of work that he had overlooked. Back at his desk, he had tried to keep himself exceptionally busy. One of the firm's clients was the California Tomato Growers' Association. He looked at a picture of a pretty girl holding a bushel basketful of tomatoes in her arms. She was wearing a farmerette's hat. "How many tomatoes can you count in this picture?" he led off the caption, and he wrote a few more words about the special lushness of California-grown tomatoes, tomatoes from the land of eternal sunshine. The picture, caption and all, was then mailed out to a long list of newspapers. A few weeks later, Burrell's clipping service would respond with the tally. "You're doing great, Jim," Bob Maguire, his boss, had said. "There's a great future for you here, boy." Jimmy was almost absurdly pleased with the compliment, but, with Helen gone, there was no one to tell it to. He was seeing Claire and Blazer that week-end in San Francisco. But they were a special case; if he told them, they would think he was trying to be funny.

He poured himself another drink. Probably he was drinking too much, he thought. But there was so little else to do, in the evenings, when he was alone. Bob Maguire was very kind. He and Margie, his wife, invited Jimmy to dinner every few weeks. In their split-level, ranch-type house in Fair Oaks, a newly developed suburb that was burgeoning east of the city—a suburb that was still a treeless, lawnless stretch of redwood and plate-glass houses—they tried to make him feel at home. They knew that he and Helen had separated. Margie Maguire fixed asparagus with Hollandaise sauce, and fresh fat lamb chops, and the inevitable California garden salad. She had given him the avocado stone and told him how to make it grow, on toothpicks in a glass of water. She had a profusion of avocados growing in her picture window. For dessert, for a touch of gaiety, she served vanilla ice-cream topped with green *crème de menthe*. He had made the mistake of mentioning this dessert to Claire one time. She had made a face. "Why doesn't she serve it on top of mashed potatoes?" she asked.

After dinner, Bob Maguire liked to bring cold beers—quick-chilled in the freezer—into the living-room. They would lower the lights and watch television. The Maguires were fond of

I Love Lucy, and, thanks to the fifty-foot antenna which was almost a requisite in the valley, the reception was good. Jimmy realized that he was really leading three lives. One was the quiet, polite, weekday evening life of the Maguires, thanking Margie kindly for the nice dinner, bringing her, occasionally, the box of Mary See's chocolates that she liked. The second was the week-end life, shared with Claire and Blazer in their apartment on Russian Hill in San Francisco, seeing, from time to time, old friends from the East who were always passing through, on their way to or from Hawaii or Southern California, and who were always ready for a party. The third was his lonely private life, like now.

He had told the Maguires about Claire and Blazer, his friends in San Francisco, his friends from home. Margie Maguire had asked him to bring them by. She might be able to introduce them to some new people, to some of their Sacramento friends. But Jimmy had been wise enough to see how hopeless this would be—how dull Claire and Blazer would have considered the Maguires to be, how strange and Bohemian Claire and Blazer would have seemed to the Maguires. He could imagine the things Claire would have to say about the Maguires. About their little house, their tiny fruit trees, their backyard barbecue, their picture window.

Yes, he was moving in three worlds, really. No two of them were compatible. And, in a way, all three seemed empty. . . .

The liquor swirled inside and warmed him. The night was cold and ominous; it was easy to imagine himself the only living, pulsing being in it. Yes, he was drinking too much. For too much of a reason. That was the frightening thing. Perhaps his mother had been right. Perhaps he should have let his father help him. Perhaps he should have gone to New York, found a job with a brokerage house, gone to work carrying an umbrella. And yet he was sure that he was doing the right thing. It was a challenge—this was—the sort of challenge Claire had meant, the challenge none of them seemed to have, but all of them needed. He wanted to meet it, and he would meet it, he told himself. If only he didn't get lost along the way. Perhaps he could explain to Claire. He thought of her face, white and tear-stained, on the mountainside when she had slipped. "I'll make this without your help!" she had said.

And for a moment, in her eyes, he had glimpsed a kind of bone-hard courage. This is what I must have, he thought.

All right, he thought. The drink in his hand glowed palely in the moonlight. With a quick, angry gesture, he threw it on the ground. He stood up and walked back to his sleeping-bag. The ground was cold and frosty under his bare feet. He felt good—as though he had argued something out with himself, and settled something for all time. If Helen should appear now, he would have the right answers for her. As he crawled back into the sleeping-bag, he realized that he had not really been thinking about Helen at all. Just as well, he thought. I won't think about her any more to-night. I will turn my mind off now.

5

THERE was a noise in the night quite close to his shoulder and he sat up abruptly. " *Jimmy?* "

" Who is it? "

" It's me—Claire."

" What's the matter? " he whispered. She was obscured in the shadows and he could barely see her.

" Let's go for a walk."

" Where's Blazer? "

" Asleep."

He crawled out of his sleeping-bag and stood up beside her. " God, you scared me to death," he said. " What's the matter? "

She laughed mockingly. " I couldn't sleep. Let's go for a walk. Just down by the water. I feel like talking."

" All right." He shivered. " Christ, it's cold."

She laughed softly again. " Well, put on your jacket, silly! I have mine on. You don't need to impress me with your broad bare chest."

He was wearing only a pair of suntan pants. He knelt and felt around on the ground for his windbreaker, found it, and put it on. He pulled wool socks over his bare feet and put on his sneakers.

" I was having the funniest dream," Claire said.

" What was it? "

" Oh, I don't remember all of it. It was all mixed up. I was married to you . . . you were Blazer, only you were yourself. Very confusing."

" I'll say." They walked carefully and slowly towards the water.

They found a wide, flat stone at the edge of the lake. " Let's sit down here," she said. They sat down. " I haven't finished telling you the story of my life."

" This is a great time to tell it," Jimmy said. " In the middle of the night . . ."

She went on, as though she hadn't heard him. " I have this great frustration," she said. " When I got out of college—remember—I went to New York for a while. I wanted to go to Europe, but Daddy wouldn't let me go alone. New York was the next best thing. I lived on West Twelfth Street, in the Village, and went to art school in the evenings. You can imagine what everybody in Mars Hill thought of that! You know Mars Hill . . ."

Jimmy knew Mars Hill. Claire's grandfather had built it on a high bank of the Naugatuck River, in Connecticut, about twenty miles from Jimmy's home in Somerville. Originally, Mars Hill had been planned as a summer place, and though it contained over fifty rooms, it had been built without central heating. Claire's family occupied the house now; they had modernized parts of it, closed parts of it off, torn parts of it down. Still, from the road below, Mars Hill was an astonishing sight—built in a variety of styles, part medieval, part Renaissance, part Tudor. It had gargoyles, crenellated roof-tops, and a complex of towers and chimneys that rose above the surrounding trees. Jimmy remembered Claire's coming-out party there. The house had been opened up. Brightly coloured balloons had been floated in the lighted pool that cast kaleidoscopic shadows into the trees above the outdoor dance floor.

" I wanted to be an artist," Claire said. " Nobody in Mars Hill could understand it. They thought I was sowing wild oats, or whatever it is girls are supposed to do at that age. They smiled and said, ' She'll be back.' Of course they were right. I got a job. I sketched housewares for Macy's, in the advertising department. Housewares—I should say electrical appliances. Steam irons . . . stoves . . . refrigerators. One of the other artists had a lamp to draw. It was a hideous lamp—but how I wanted to sketch it! But they wouldn't let me! ' You're doing beautifully on appliances,' they said. There I sat in front of my little easel. Then one morning the art director called me in and said that all my sketches looked as though they were sitting in piles of coal. The appliances were white! I had to put them on dark backgrounds! But they didn't understand. They put someone else on appliances. I wanted to try fashion.

The last thing I drew was a dress shield. How ironic! That was the closest I ever came to fashion."

"Not exactly an exciting career," Jimmy said.

"So I quit. Then I wrote some sort of silly heartbroken, mixed-up letter to my mother about all my unfulfilled desires. Well, you can imagine what happened. Mother and Daddy drove down to New York and needless to say they were *appalled*. Imagine, Junius Denison's daughter living in absolute squalor—the cute little apartment I had told them about—it was unheard of. It shook their very foundations! Of course, I was whisked home. They thought I was repudiating them, or whatever it is that children nowadays are supposed to do to their parents. I wasn't repudiating them. I just thought they were dull!"

"I can picture your dad's face."

"Yes. And so I went home with them—back to Mars Hill, to the warm womb of love. I took tennis lessons instead of art lessons, and started seeing Blazer again. We had sort of broken off. But Mother and Daddy always liked Blazer, so I married him."

"Claire, why are you telling me all this?" In the darkness, he tried to make out her face.

"I don't know . . . I guess it's because I think you understand. My one big dream. Blazer doesn't understand. Jimmy," she said suddenly, "do you want Blazer and me to be happy?"

"Why do you ask me that?"

"I don't know that, either. Sometimes I wonder if I love him as much as I should."

"Don't say that."

"It's true. I'm so sorry I was unkind to you this morning—when you wanted to help me. It was just crazy—I felt that Blazer would have wanted me to get out of that jam myself. I wanted you to help me, really. A woman doesn't always want to be self-sufficient. Still, that's what Blazer wants me to be."

"I understand."

"Do you? Sometimes I worry about Blazer and me. Blazer is so fond of Daddy, for instance. When Daddy phones me from home, Blazer gets on the phone . . . they talk for hours. Blazer tells him all about how many hundreds of dozens of sheets he's sold . . . how he approached a prospect, how he followed a lead. All about business. Daddy loves that, of course. He says Blazer has his feet on the ground now—even though he used to be a little wild. He says Blazer is a solid citizen. Remember *Death of a Salesman?* Is Blazer turning out like that? I have a terror that Daddy's right—that Blazer is turning into a solid citizen. A stuffed shirt—like Daddy!"

"He takes his job seriously, that's all," Jimmy said. "I take my job seriously, too."

"Too seriously! You should hear Blazer when he gets going on the soft-goods business. He can be such a bore. I want him to be funny and gay. I have to supply all that myself now. Blazer and Daddy have hit it off so well, I'm afraid one of these days Daddy is going to offer Blazer a job . . . and I'm afraid Blazer will take it! I'll be right back with everything I've always tried to run away from. Am I shocking you, talking like this?"

"No, not really . . ."

"When Blazer's company transferred him out here, to San Francisco, I thought everything was going to be different. We'd be away from that warm womb of love at home—build one of our own, perhaps. But we haven't."

"Of course you have."

"No, no. Look at that moon!" she exclaimed. "It should have a bird flying across it now, shouldn't it? Except for that one detail, don't you think it's awfully well done?"

He laughed. "Yes," he said, "it certainly is."

"Let's get into it," she whispered, and stood up. "Over here."

They walked, a few feet apart, along the strip of beach, into the moonlight. Claire began scuffing her toes carelessly into the sand, and Jimmy tried matching his footprints to hers so that their tracks would be one. "There's no tide up here," he said, "to wash our footprints away."

Claire started taking bigger steps. Away from the trees, their shadows stood out clearly on the sand beside them. "Do you know why I'm named Claire?" she asked him. "It's for '*Clair de Lune*.' Years ago, when Mother was a girl, Debussy played '*Claire de Lune*' for her on the piano. Mother says he wrote the song for her . . . but I don't know. Let's sprawl here." She took a little nose dive into the sand and lay there, face downward, arms stretched out. "Are you afraid?"

" Of what? "

" Of the dark? "

" No."

" Sleepy? "

" No. I was. I feel a little heady now. The altitude . . ."

" Yes. I feel that way, too. Sit down."

Jimmy sat down beside her, and she raised herself on her elbows. " Of me? " she asked.

" What? "

" Are you afraid of me? "

" What do you mean? "

" I want you to kiss me."

At the base of his spine, a feeling started, spread, travelled. " I think we'd better go back," he said huskily.

" Why? "

" Blazer is my best friend." The words sounded hollow, childish.

" You're stuffy," she said. " But you're nice. I like you. You're a very nice boy indeed."

" Thank you."

Quietly, she put her hands on his shoulders and kissed him. " There," she said, drawing back. " My! "

" I'm sorry you did that."

" Why? I have a wanton streak in me, didn't you know? What's wrong with it? You'd never tell Blazer . . . and certainly I never would. Why shouldn't we? "

" Why shouldn't we do what? "

" Have an affair? It would be sort of an experiment. Do you think it would be hard to love me? "

Jimmy was silent, looking at her. Her head was thrown back, her blonde hair brushing the sand. Her lips were parted in a half smile, and her eyes, in the shadows, glowed bright and dark. " No," he said. And it would not, he knew, be hard. Wouldn't it be very easy now to take her face in his hands, and forget that she was Blazer's wife? Why not? Mentally, he shattered the Seventh Commandment, hovering between kissing her and not kissing her, kissing her lips and hands and forehead, tangling his fingers in her long gold hair. " But I feel loyal," he said slowly. " And I want you to be loyal, too."

" Loyal to what? To our Puritan ancestors . . .? "

And then, as though something suddenly snapped into focus inside his mind, he knew why, the real reason why he wanted to kiss her. It was not Claire he wanted; it was revenge, against Helen. As though, by taking Claire, he could put to rest the ghost of Helen. " You see," he would be able to say to her spectre, " you have hurt me; I will repay you this way; I will profane your image." The thought sickened him. He closed his eyes. *Be careful of that lighter, it will throw out sparks.* Like this. He knew he had to say something.

" Look," he said. " We're not making any sense, are we? We've both had quite a bit to drink to-night . . . we're just two people who are very fond of each other. Let's not get carried away."

She turned away sharply. " You're making me feel like a tramp! "

" I don't intend to. It's wonderful. I'm very flattered—you should be flattered, too." He stood up. " Let's get back."

She was silent. He wondered if she was going to cry, but she was not. Presently she gave a little shrug and stood up. They walked back together in silence. The moon disappeared when they reached the trees. With a little trouble, they found their beds.

Claire said, " Good night," and her voice—he could not see her face now—sounded cold and distant. They separated.

For a long time Jimmy lay looking up into the blackness. A slight wind came up, stirring the leaves, tossing up sparks from the dying fire.

6

In the morning, he was the first to wake. The sun was coming brightly through the trees, and he had to spend a moment or two locating himself, remembering that he was on a mountain, on a hard sleeping-bag that had become wadded and uncomfortable beneath him.

He stood up. Claire and Blazer were still asleep. On their bed of pine boughs, they had rolled apart. He fished inside his knapsack for his bathing-trunks, found them, and slipped off his trousers. For a moment he stood there, tall and naked, wondering what they would say if they should suddenly wake and see him. Then he stooped, pulled on his trunks, and walked down towards the water. The footprints were still there in the sand. Carefully, he walked up and down over them, erasing them. For what reason, he didn't know. Perhaps, he thought, by erasing the footprints, I can erase the incident from my mind. For a long time, he stood looking out across the water. Then he turned, and saw that Claire was standing farther back, on a rock, watching him. She turned quickly and moved away. Had she had the same thought, he wondered? To erase the footprints in the sand? The glimpse he had of her, in blue jeans and a sweater, standing there, her blonde hair tousled and loose, printed itself on his mind, then dissolved. He went to the water's edge, leaned over, and splashed cold water in his face.

He walked to where the rocks formed stepping-stones out into the lake, and he tried to step out to the farthest one. He lay flat on his belly on the final stone and looked over its edge into the water. With his fingertips, he drew slow angel-wing patterns on the smooth surface. Not far from him a snake darted along the top of the water. He followed it with his eyes until it reached the bank and hid among tall weeds and rushes. After a while, he got up and started back to the camp.

Claire was fixing breakfast. Blazer lay on his back on top of the sleeping-bag, still foggy with sleep. "We have cereal," Claire said brightly. "No eggs . . . I told you I was afraid eggs would break. And I've made coffee. I don't have any idea how it is."

Blazer looked up. "Been in the water?"

"No," Jimmy said. "It's not too good for swimming."

"Why the hell not?"

"Well, the bottom's pretty mucky," he said. "It's the kind of bottom that you step into, and your foot sinks. And a lot of bubbles come up. Besides, I saw a snake."

"Coward," Blazer said, and rolled over.

"I like to swim where I know what's on the bottom."

"I think I'll go in," Blazer said. He stood up and began unbuttoning his shirt.

"You're not going to change *here*, are you?" Claire said quickly.

"Why not?"

"Well——"

"Jim's a man and you're my wife. You've both seen me in the raw separately, for God's sake. Why not together?" He pulled his trunks out of his knapsack and started off into the shrubbery, swinging them by the draw-string.

"It sounds like a sensible argument," Jimmy said.

"Yes, I suppose so," Claire said absently.

Jimmy stooped over the fire and picked up the bubbling pot of coffee. "Mind if I pour myself a cup of this?"

"Go ahead, please do."

He poured coffee into a paper cup. "Smells good," he said. "Any cream?"

"Evaporated milk . . . there, in the can."

He poured milk into the cup and tasted the result. "Good," he said, "very good."

"Thank you."

"Can I pour you some?"

"No, thank you."

"About last night——" he began.

"Please," she said sharply. "Never mind."

"O.K.," he said. "That's just the way I feel. Never mind."

Blazer came out of the woods in his trunks and headed towards the water.

"Cereal?" Claire asked.

"No, thanks." Jimmy looked hard into his cup.

"Aren't you going to have any breakfast?"

"I'm not too hungry . . ."

"I can make some toast . . ."

"No, thanks." He drained his cup. "I'll see what Blazer's doing," he said.

He found Blazer standing on one of the rocks, studying the water. "What's the matter?" he asked. "Aren't you going in?"

"I don't know," Blazer said. "You're right about the bottom. It doesn't look too appetising. I saw a turtle over there—a snapper. How'd you like to step on one of those things?"

"Now who's the coward?" Jimmy asked.

Blazer leaped back on to the sand and laughed. "Well, let's all go in later," he said. "There's safety in numbers."

"Well . . . perhaps."

The two of them stood side by side, looking at the lake. It was one of those increasingly rare moments, Jimmy realized, when the two of them were actually alone together. Ordinarily, he would have thought nothing of this; to-day, it made him feel awkward and embarrassed.

"Christ, I wish we didn't have to go back to-day," Blazer was saying. "We really should have given ourselves more time—say a week. Then it would have been worth all the trouble getting up and getting down."

"Yes, a week would be good."

"Look," Blazer said, "let's do it again some time. Could you take a week off from work? I could, and probably Claire could take some time off from her charity cases. Later in the summer—and the four of us can come up here together."

"Four?"

"Sure, with Helen." Blazer looked at him. "What's the matter between you and Helen anyway? You don't seem to include her——"

"Well, the fact is," Jimmy said slowly, looking away, "we've—we've separated. I told Claire yesterday, on the lift. I'm sorry—I haven't been telling you the truth, I know. But that's the way it is. I wasn't going to tell you, but you'd have known sooner or later——"

"What happened? She walked out on you?"

The abruptness of the remark startled him. "Yes," he said. "She left. She—she went home. It's—well, it's just one of those things."

Blazer was silent. Finally, he said soberly, "I'm sorry to hear that, Keefe-o. I really am."

"Well," Jimmy said rapidly, "you never think that it will happen to you. I never did. And then it does happen to you, and you don't know what to do. I know I'm not unique, it's happened to lots of people. But—well, I just didn't have the guts to tell you before."

"Forget it. It's just a hell of a shame." He put his hand on Jimmy's shoulder. It was a spontaneous gesture—and, for Blazer, a boy not given to physical displays of affection, it was a singular one. "You're too nice a guy," Blazer said.

"Thanks," Jimmy said. His chest reverberated with gratitude, suddenly, and joy. They started back.

"Didn't you go in?" Claire asked.

"No, we lost our nerve," Blazer said.

"You're both cowards."

They sat around the little fire, the steaming coffee pot. "Jimmy just told me about Helen," Blazer said.

"Oh, did he?"

"Yes."

"It's a shame, isn't it?"

"What do you think he should do?"

"What?" Claire asked.

"Do. What should he do?"

Jimmy wanted to stop the conversation. "You've both been wonderful to me," he said. And, quickly realizing the vacuity of the remark, he added, "I mean you're both very therapeutic."

"We—well, we want to help you in every way we can."

"Sure," Blazer said. "But how?"

His joy, in the moment by the rock, had disappeared. Instead, he felt a dry sickness in his throat. This was why he hadn't wanted to tell them. He knew they would begin entwining themselves in his problem, making it their own. And after all, it was his, his to decide.

" Look——" he began.

But all at once Claire and Blazer were deep in a conversation about him.

" Of course we've never met her . . ." Claire said.

" She was damned good-looking in that picture . . ."

He began hearing them from a distance, and, for a minute, it seemed as though they were actually moving away from him. " Of course she's probably one of those *determinedly* California girls . . ." " Yes, but Jimmy's a little New England, too, don't forget . . ." " But didn't he come out *here*? Didn't he try? "

Their words had no meaning now, heard through such layers of air, with what seemed like trees and water and finally mountains in between. He had retreated from them now, into his familiar trough of self-despair, and he wondered if they would miss him if he should actually stand up and walk away. Presently he stood up and walked towards the woods. They went on talking—two conspirators, mapping strategies, laying plans. Why don't they try to straighten out their own marriage? he thought angrily.

He walked slowly into the trees, along the path they had taken yesterday. Of course, he thought, they were only trying to be kind. Perhaps even last night Claire had only been trying to be kind. Was that possible? Well, he thought bitterly, he didn't want their kindness if their kindness came in these odd spurts. Claire, for instance. Yesterday, they had climbed up the mountain, and she had fallen. He had reached for her, and she had cried, " Don't touch me! " and she had meant it. Then later, in the night, she had begged him to touch her, and meant it, too. She was off and on. He was out of their sight now. He heard them calling him. He stopped, but didn't answer them.

And yet, he remembered, when Claire had asked him, " Would it be hard for you to love me? " he had answered no, that it would not be. Hadn't he meant that, too?

What is happening to me? he wondered. And he thought, perilously, that perhaps there was some subtle ingredient in himself, some substance that, when it came into contact with others, precipitated unhappiness. Had this been what had destroyed his own marriage? And was it now destroying Blazer's?

" Jimmy! " Claire's voice called.

" Coming," he answered.

Hadn't he perhaps known, when Claire woke him in the night, that going with her would lead only to one thing? And hadn't he gone with her, knowing? And if that were the case . . .

He turned and started back. If that were the case, if he was to blame . . . he tried not to think what it would mean if he was to blame.

" Where've you been? " Claire asked when he reached them.

" Just exploring," Jimmy said, smiling hard.

" You didn't like us talking that way, did you? About Helen —we're sorry."

" Oh, that's all right."

" We promise not to do it again."

" I know you must be pretty broken up about it," Blazer said.

" No."

" Sure. You must be. I'm sorry."

" Please," he said, " let's not talk about it. I'm not broken up. I've just got to the point where the subject bores me a little."

" Sure, that's understandable."

Claire said, " While you were gone, I did have one thought. Not that I'm an expert on broken homes or anything, but I *do* do that sort of thing in San Francisco . . ."

" I'm not a charity case," Jimmy said.

" No—but what would you say if I were to try to see Helen? If I tried to talk to her. Would that help? "

" I'd say——"

" What? What do you think? " She looked at him searchingly.

" I'd say for God's sake let's shut up about it," he said.

They were both silent.

Jimmy looked around. " Do you mind? " he asked. " I mean, would you think it was awful if I had a sip from that Thermos? I feel in the need of something, and I'm afraid a drink is it."

Claire said softly, " It's hardly the cocktail hour—ten-thirty in the morning."

Blazer looked at him. " Yeah, why don't you hold off? " he said casually. " We'll have to start back in three or four hours."

" Oh, don't worry about me," Jimmy said. He picked up the Thermos, tilted it, and drank deeply. Putting it down, he said, " That warms me up fine. Just fine."

It was a large Thermos, and he looked at it, over the lip, inside. It was half-empty. Three hours? They would be starting back. Four hours, perhaps, and there would be enough. He patted the jar carelessly, and said, " I drink, you know." They said nothing. Furtively he thought: Four hours? Would there be enough for four slow hours of time?

7

THE opening scene, the earliest part, was vivid enough. It was the end, the weeks they had spent in the apartment on Capitol Avenue, that was the hardest to remember. He moved his mind back into this shadowy area of disjointed greetings and good-byes, trying to isolate the scenes, establish the sequence. Sitting by the rock in the warm sun, holding the cool yellow drink in his hand, he tried to put things together, one by one.

First there was that night, that first time, in the borrowed apartment on Sixty-eighth Street, when her love had seemed almost terrifyingly urgent. "Hallelujah!" she had cried, and afterwards, as he held her in his arms, she had sobbed long, deep, grateful sobs. And then, that December night in the motel outside Reno, after they had been married for the first time, then it had been wonderful, too, with no hint of what was to come later. The next day they had driven south, intending to go to Las Vegas, but they had changed their minds and driven to Yosemite instead.

He remembered Yosemite. How many days had it been? Less than a week, but it had been their one true honeymoon. The other one, the longer one, that they called their honeymoon, had been a different story. Somewhere, he thought, between those days at Yosemite and the trip to the West Indies, then home to the apartment, everything had changed.

He remembered Yosemite Valley covered with snow, cold and jewel-like, the tall cliffs rising abruptly from the valley floor, frozen waterfalls sparkling in the sun. He remembered Inspiration Point, Mirror Lake—poetic names—and the huge old Ahwanee Hotel, where they had sat, with their shoes off, in front of the fire. They had taken long walks in the snow every afternoon, and once, when a swift flurry of snow descended, it had blinded them and they had stood very still in the centre of it. He had been able to see only her eyes. Laughing, thinking that they were lost for ever in the snowstorm, he had pulled his heavy coat around her and they sank down together in the snow. "We're invisible," Helen had whispered, and he had kissed her with the snow blowing in her hair. The snow continued to fall. Later, she said, "If the Donner party had done this, they wouldn't have died crossing the Sierras. They could have kissed each other warm. Are you cold?"

"No."

"Neither am I. Isn't this a wonderful way to freeze to death?"

And they laughed as they pictured how they would look if a rescue party should happen to stumble upon them. ("I shall insist they put us in a single stretcher," Helen said.) After a while, the snow stopped, and they stood up and walked back to the hotel, cold now, and wet, but happy.

In the mornings they slept late. "Isn't it marvellous to think that no one knows where we are?" Helen said. They had no idea, during this time, that on either side of them, in California and Connecticut, plans were spinning out, arrangements were being made for a dignified wedding, a dignified honeymoon, a dignified life. The Keefe and Warren families were busily deciding how to deal with their erring children, figuring ways to make the best out of a bad situation.

In the evenings, they ate dinner in the big high-ceilinged dining-room and went to bed early. "No two people deserve to be as happy as we are," Helen had said, and the words echoed now, prophetically.

But it had to end. They couldn't stay in Yosemite Valley for ever; they had to go back to face whatever had to be faced with their families. On the last afternoon, walking in the snow, they talked about it.

"Well, we're big enough, aren't we?" Helen said. "We can stand right up to them—and tell them. Tell them how much we love each other, the things we plan to do. We can convince them, can't we, that we're old enough to know what we're doing?"

"It won't be easy," Jimmy said. "Remember how they acted on the phone. They still think of us as children."

"It will be easy if we just stand side by side and refuse to be cowed by them!"

"I ought to warn you about my family," Jimmy said.

"What about them?"

"Well, it's hard to explain. They're Yankees—they don't make mistakes. At least they don't admit to making mistakes. There's only one member of the Keefe family who ever made a mistake—and that was the end of her."

"Who was that?"

"My Cousin Harriet—my father's brother's daughter. Her picture has been turned against the wall!"

"What in the world did she do?"

Jimmy laughed. "Promise you'll never tell a soul? Everybody knows about it, of course, but it's just never mentioned. She married a cop."

Helen was silent. "What did they do?" she asked, after a moment.

"They were noble. They're always noble! They tried to reason with her, and when she wouldn't be reasoned with, they cut her off."

"Cut her off?"

"Yes. Severed relations. Pretended she was never born. Oh, my mother tried—she had them to dinner once, Harriet and her policeman. I remember the only thing she said about him."

"What was that?"

"She said, 'I imagine he looks quite *natural* in his uniform!'"

"Ah——"

"You see, that's the way they are. No mistakes tolerated. They have misfortunes, of course, like when somebody gets bumped out of Yale. Things happen that inconvenience them. But when those things happen, it's a sort of challenge. To see if they can turn the misfortune into an advantage. Do you see what I mean? Right now, they may be terribly distressed about you and me. We didn't get married the Keefe way. They'll have to figure out a way to make it a good thing."

"You mean," Helen said slowly, "that you marrying me is like—Harriet, marrying a policeman?"

"Oh, no, it's not that bad." Jimmy took her hand. "They'll like you. But they'll have to go through this 'working-things-out' process first. They'll have to get together, like a grand jury—all of them, all the cousins and uncles and aunts—and work it out. The next step will probably be a party. You'll have to be introduced to Somerville. Mother will have a tea for you, and you'll have to shake hands with Aunt Marian and Aunt Celeste and the Hartford cousins and the upstate cousins and my Great-aunt Kathleen, whose name—don't laugh—is Mrs. W. W. Doubleday . . ."

Helen giggled softly. " I *do* want to meet Mrs. W. W. Doubleday," she said.

" You will." He smiled at her. " You'll meet all of them. I'm afraid you'll sort of have to go along with it."

" Why? " she asked suddenly.

" Because "—Jimmy laughed—" because they never make mistakes. They haven't made a mistake for four generations. That's why." He swung her hand in his and they started back to the hotel.

That night, after dinner, instead of going directly upstairs, Jimmy suggested that they go into the bar for a drink. Helen had hesitated at first, but when Jimmy urged her, she consented. After all, he said, they were leaving in the morning to go back and face the music. He needed something, a drink, to strengthen him for that ordeal. Sitting in the bar, which was decorated to resemble a Western mining town, they talked about it some more. He tried again to explain about his father, who lived by rules laid down by his own father, and by his grandfather before that. And about his mother, Melise, who fancied herself a free agent, but who had lived long enough with the unwritten family laws to obey them always, and about Turner Ames, the lawyer, who counselled James Keefe, Sen., on everything, and about Miss Maitland, his father's secretary, who understood the intricacies of the Keefe family operation far better than Jimmy's mother did.

" But we're *ourselves*," Helen had said. " We can make our own rules, can't we? Do we have to abide by theirs? "

" We can lead our own lives," Jimmy said. " But we can't fly in their faces too much. We ran off and got married—we broke a rule there. But we can't do that sort of thing often. That's all I mean." He smiled at her, but her face remained worried.

" Can we live where we want? " she asked.

" Of course—as long as we can convince them that it's the right place for us to live."

" But why do we have to convince them? "

" Why should we antagonize them? "

" I don't mean antagonize them," Helen said. She stopped then, and smiled. " I don't know what I mean," she said. " I guess I just don't want anyone to interfere with us, darling."

" Don't forget that I'm an only child . . ."

" Does that make a lot of difference? "

" Yes. It does, to them." Then he told her what he had somehow not wanted to tell her before, though he had known that he must tell her some time. He had been trained to speak of wealth with modesty, or not at all. The richer you were, the poorer you pretended to be. It was known as " treating money tastefully." If you could afford to buy a Cadillac, you bought a Ford, because it was more economical on gasoline. " There's quite a bit of money involved," he said slowly.

" Oh? "

" Yes. We can ignore it for a while. But some day, I suppose, it will pull us back."

" Back to where? "

" Back to Somerville—where it is." He sipped his drink thoughtfully.

" Is it—that much? "

" Yes."

" How much? "

" I don't know——"

" A million dollars? "

" More than that, I think."

" *Two* million? "

" Well," he said, " of course I really don't know. But when my grandfather died, the figure they printed in the paper was four and a half million. . . . That was in 1946."

" Oh, my God," she said. " That's a lot. And it's all—all going to be yours some day? "

" I'm the only child, you see . . ."

She was silent. " Oh, dear! " she said finally. " It scares me! It terrifies me. I wish you hadn't told me."

" Let's have another drink."

" No, no . . ."

" Come on. I'm sorry I told you if it worries you."

" You have a drink. I'll wait."

" All right." He signalled the waiter.

" I'm beginning to see what you mean," Helen said later. " I suppose they'll think I'm a gold digger . . ."

" No, they won't. Not when they see how nice you are."

" Harriet's policeman," she said. " Is that what they thought about him? That he was a conniver? "

" Well——"

" They did? "

" I guess some of the family thought that."

" But she was—as you put it—' cut off.' "

" Yes."

" Poor Harriet," she sighed. " Poor policeman! " She smiled a weary smile. " I feel I know them both so well already. Especially him. He and I are in the same boat."

" Now, don't say things like that. It's not true."

" If they don't like me——"

" They will," he said. " Of course they will! Darling, you're the most wonderful girl in the world."

" Am I? "

" Yes," he said. " And do you know what I love most about you? "

" What? "

" It's—well, it's your *niceness.* You're so different from any girl I've ever known. You've got this wonderful thing—this niceness. It's everywhere—all about you, like a very nice perfume."

" I love you, too," she said softly.

He smiled broadly. " Then cheer up," he said. " Have another drink, quick. Let's have a party."

" Let's go upstairs now——"

" One more——"

" All right."

It was always with the third drink that his spirits rose. That night in Yosemite, drinking the third drink, he began talking gaily, confidently, about the future. " I only told you about the money to explain why they take a proprietary interest in what I do," he said. " And to explain why they'll take the same kind of interest in you. Which you mustn't mind. They're really quite nice people when you get to know them. Dad's a little Solomon Sobersides sometimes, but he's a good sport. But don't get the wrong idea," he said earnestly. "Don't think that I'm just going to sit around all my life and wait for that money. I want to get a job of my own and make my own way. I've got to—in order to prove to myself that I can. Do you see? That's why I married you."

"And I'll help you all I can," she said softly. And then, as he lifted his glass and drained it, she said, in a breathless voice, "Please don't have another drink!"

"Why not?" he said lightly. "Clears my head. Makes me see stars in your eyes."

"My eyes don't have stars!"

"Yes, they do," he said, holding his face close to hers. "They do, they do! There's the Pleiades, Electra, Merope . . . the Southern Cross . . ."

"Please, Jimmy."

"'Please, Jimmy,'" he mimicked. "Just one more. So I can see the whole damn' Milky Way . . ."

Much later, when they got up to leave, he knew he was a little tight. But he felt extravagant and courageous. Helen seemed nervous and withdrawn, and he laughed at her and circled her waist with his arm. When they got to their room, he closed the door, and pulled her to him quickly and roughly in the darkness. For the first time, she drew away from him. He reached for her again. "Please. No," she whispered.

"Helen——"

"Please, Jimmy—I'm afraid."

"Of the money? Forget about that."

"Not that!"

"Of me?" He held her tightly, laughing softly, searching for her mouth with his lips. Finally, she seemed to submit to him, let him kiss her and pull her down beside him on the bed. "Isn't this better than a snowdrift?" he asked her.

Then, all at once, she had cried out sharply. She gripped his shoulders hard with her fingers and began to sob. He held her as her whole body shook violently against him.

"What's the matter?" he had asked her. "Darling, what's wrong?"

She didn't answer him. He turned on the light then and sat

there, stroking her hair. " Please, darling," he said. " I'm sorry. Did I hurt you, Helen? "

" I don't know! " she cried.

" Please tell me what it is."

He stood up and lighted two cigarettes. He gave one to Helen and sat down again, in the chair, while she lay, huddled forlornly on the bed, still sobbing and holding the lighted cigarette in one trembling hand. " What is it? " he asked again. " What's happened? "

" I saw a ghost," she sobbed. " Forgive me. I saw a ghost . . ."

" What do you mean? "

" A boy," she said. " A boy I knew."

Then she told him. She had known a boy at Cal—she wouldn't tell Jimmy his name. She had been in love with him. At least, she had thought so then. They had been unofficially engaged—he had given her his fraternity pin. To celebrate, they had gone to a dance—a big dance at the Mount Diablo Country Club. He had got quite drunk, and afterwards they had gone for a drive in his car. She had worn a blue scarf around her head, and they had driven, very fast, through the night in the open car. All at once, in the quiet hills above Alameda, he had stopped the car, opened the door, pulled her from the seat into the darkness, held the blue scarf tight around her throat, and raped her.

No one had suspected anything. He brought her back to the Pi Phi house and let her out at the door. She got out of the car, went up the steps, into the house, and went to bed. For nearly a week, she went to her classes as usual. He did not call; she did not see him again. Then, one morning, she didn't wake up. Her room-mate became alarmed and called the house-mother; the house-mother called a doctor. The night before, quietly, automatically, after brushing her teeth and putting her hair in pin curls, Helen had swallowed twenty sleeping-pills, one by one. Helen's mother had rushed over to Berkeley from the valley; when Helen recovered, she refused to give her mother any explanation. Her mother took her out of college, and, because she seemed anxious and preoccupied, decided that Helen had been studying too hard. Mrs. Warren wrote an indignant letter to the dean of women, complaining that the courses were too rigorous. Then she planned pleasant things for Helen to do—things that would get Helen's mind off school. It had been Mrs. Warren's idea for Helen to take a trip to New York. It was on that trip that she had met Jimmy.

Helen tried to explain it to him. "I don't know what happened," she said desperately. "All of a sudden, for a moment, my mind went back! Suddenly it wasn't you any more. It was him! It was that night! It was like a vision, it was so real. I know you're not like that——"

He didn't answer her, but sat there, smoking. "I've never told anyone but you," she said. "Please forgive me." And then she said urgently, "It will be all right, won't it? It won't happen again, will it? Will it, Jimmy? Will you help me, Jimmy? It won't happen—if you help me!"

She held out her hand, and he took it, feeling a small shiver run through her arm. She lay back and closed her eyes. How young we both are! Jimmy thought suddenly. Helen was only twenty-one; he was not much older. The hotel room all at once seemed immense and empty, strangely impersonal, and a great tug of loneliness gripped him—loneliness, homesickness, a feeling of being lost in an unfamiliar place. Of being a little boy again, lost, frightened, running down a dark street, and being faced with the task of caring for another lost and frightened human being. Ashamed, he recognized the little-boy urge—to run away and leave her there.

But he sat there, holding her hand, smoking, knowing that if he got back into bed he would be unable to sleep. Knowing nothing else.

Claire and Blazer were clambering across the rocks. "I'm the king of the castle!" Claire chanted. "And you're the dirty rascal!" She stood on tiptoe on top of the first boulder that began the giant stepping-stones into the lake. "Dethrone me if you dare!"

Blazer climbed after her. At the top, he tussled with her a moment before she leaped to the next rock. He followed her, and, as she tried to leap to the third, she landed short of it, in the water, and began swimming and splashing and screaming. Blazer dived in after her.

Jimmy sat on the shore, his back against the rock, watching them. "Come on in!" they called. "It's wonderful!"

Jimmy gestured to his glass. " I'm having too much fun sitting here getting tight," he said.

" Lush! " Claire called.

The sun shone down brilliantly and caught every splash they made, reflected and pounded the glittering reflections back against the trees and rocks, and into his eyes. His eyes glistened; he felt warm, hazy. He sipped his drink. This made remembering pleasant, remote and effortless. He could watch the scenes as they flashed before him, like slides from a magic lantern, without involvement. He and Helen moved quaintly, curiously, figures in a faraway pantomime. He remembered driving back to Rio Linda in the rented car, becoming aware for the first time of the flat, broad Central Valley, brown now and winter-burned.

" I'm afraid my family's house won't be very grand by your standards," Helen had said as they entered the little valley town.

" What difference does that make? " he asked her.

" I'm worried," she said, " about what your family might think—if they came out here."

" Don't be silly," he said.

The Warrens' house was a two-story white colonial, but built, in the manner of many California houses, on a narrow lot so that the houses on either side of it pressed their windows close against it. In the back, Mrs. Warren had a patio and garden surrounded by a high ivy-covered fence. From the living-room, through the french windows, Jimmy had seen tubs of winter-blooming camellias.

The Warrens greeted them affectionately, if a little distractedly. There was a great deal of nervous laughter as Walker Warren showed Jimmy the front-yard sprinkler system he had recently installed, and explained that he planned a similar system for the back yard. Mr. Warren was a small, friendly man with smiling blue eyes behind rimless glasses. He was in the hardware business. He owned the largest hardware store in Rio Linda, and also two smaller stores in neighbouring towns. It was quite a coincidence, he thought, because he had stocked Keefe hinges, bolts, and valves ever since he had started the business. " You make a good product," he told Jimmy. " They're good sellers. I never thought I'd meet the man that made them, though."

" Oh, it's not me, sir," Jimmy said. " It's just the family."

" But you'll go into the business, won't you? "

" Well—perhaps," Jimmy said.

Then Mrs. Warren, a slim, handsome woman with blue-grey hair, took Jimmy by the arm and led him through the garden, pointing out beds that would soon blossom with tulips, lilies, and tea roses. " I always wanted a summer wedding for Helen," she said, " so that we could have it here—in the garden. But " —she smiled—" I'm sure this will work out for the best." Then Mrs. Warren looked at him. " I'm putting you both in the guest room," she said, and she laughed nervously. " After all, you are married! "

That night a special-delivery arrived from Jimmy's mother. It was full of elaborate plans. She was sorry, she said, if she had been a little bitchy on the telephone. It was only that it was such a shock, such a blow, so sudden. Could he really blame her? However, it was too late now to worry about things like that. They were working things out. Daddy and Turner Ames had been busy on it; the Warren family, she thought, were being most co-operative. She and Jimmy's father were flying to California in a week for the " nice " wedding.

Everything would be lovely, she was sure, and just to show him there were no hard feelings, she was buying Jimmy and Helen a honeymoon trip to the Caribbean. She enclosed the itinerary. She had made all the reservations, bought all the tickets, supplied the fat booklet of hotel coupons. She had planned the date of the trip so that it would allow Jimmy and Helen a visit with the family in Somerville. Finally, she had enclosed a cheque, signed in her firm, round hand, " Melise Kimball Keefe," for a thousand dollars.

That night, in the Warrens' pink and white guest room, Jimmy told Helen about it. Helen had not liked the idea of the trip. After all, she pointed out, they had decided to stay in California—for a while, at least. Jimmy was going to find a job. They were going to find a place to live. It seemed silly to fly back to New York just to take Melise's trip. But Jimmy wanted to go. He thought it might be good for Helen, and also he knew his mother. He knew she wanted the Caribbean honeymoon because she had been cheated, like Mrs. Warren, out of a proper marriage.

But the difference was that Melise Keefe could afford to do

something about it. If she could not have an Eastern marriage with her friends present, a marriage with crew-cut Eastern ushers, Eastern bridesmaids, and an Eastern bride, she would have a satisfactory, if not perfect, social substitute with the glamorous six weeks' trip to the West Indies. If she could not have a wedding with a reception held in a huge tent on a high terrace overlooking Long Island Sound or the Connecticut River, with champagne, red-jacketed waiters, an orchestra imported from New York, she would have the next best thing.

Besides, Jimmy argued, since his mother was paying for it all, why should they refuse? Why shouldn't they have the trip? It had been their first quarrel, although it had been conducted in whispers and had ended with Helen saying, "Quiet! Quiet! They're in the next room—they'll hear us!"

He remembered his parents' arrival. He remembered his father, chatting with forced geniality to Walker Warren about the hardware business. He remembered his mother, murmuring, "Charming . . . charming," as Mrs. Warren showed her through the house and garden. And, the night before the wedding, he remembered going alone to his parents' suite at the St. Francis Hotel in San Francisco—summoned there on the pretext of going over some business papers with his father. His mother had greeted him at the door in a long pale-blue robe; they had had cocktails sent to the room.

"This is the craziest business," Jimmy had laughed. "Getting married all over again. Are Helen and I supposed to act like a blushing bride and bridegroom to-morrow?"

"Well, well," his father had said, "you know how women are. Your mother wanted it this way, Jim. I guess she just didn't think you'd be really married if you weren't married in a church." He winked at Melise.

"I don't think it's crazy at all," Melise said. "It's the only nice way to do it. Thank heavens Mrs. Warren agrees with me." She sat down and arranged her long skirt about her feet. "Of course," she said, sipping her martini, "I suppose you and Helen have been—living together—all along." She shook her head. "Goodness, how could you help it—in that house?"

"What do you mean, Mother?" he asked her.

"I mean—well, there's hardly enough *room* in it for you to have had separate bedrooms!"

" That's a little unkind, Mother," he had said.

" I'm sorry," she said, " but I mean it. Honestly, Jimmy, couldn't you have looked into things a little bit before you took this step? Really, when I first saw the way they lived—well, it was the kind of house where I was afraid to ask where the bathroom was! For fear there wouldn't be any! "

" Now, Mellie——" Mr. Keefe said.

" Mother, that's not fair. You're not that much of a snob, are you? "

" I'm sorry. I guess I am! "

" I think the Warrens are very nice," Jimmy said. " They've been very kind to me. I love Helen, and—well, I think her parents are very nice! "

" Oh, they're *nice*," Melise said wearily. " They're very nice! I just don't *like* them, that's all. I'm sorry, but I don't! I've said it, and I never intend to say it again, but there it is. I don't like them."

Jimmy remembered sitting, flushed and angry, as his mother sat opposite him, silently sipping her martini.

He remembered the wedding and the reception afterwards in the Warrens' house. He remembered his mother inspecting the wedding present that Mrs. Warren had displayed in her dining-room. " I suppose you'll need lots of things like this," his mother had said, looking at a set of copper-bottomed pans that a cousin of Helen's had sent. And, a few moments later, " Goodness, what will you ever do with this? " she had asked, pointing to an enormous silver epergne which had been sent by Jimmy's Great-aunt Kathleen. " Oh! " Melise had said, accepting a glass. " I don't believe I've ever tasted California champagne." She sipped it. " It's *delicious*! " she had said. But Jimmy had noticed that she never took another sip throughout the whole reception, but carried the full glass with her, lifting it to her lips without drinking whenever toasts were proposed. And Helen noticed it, too.

Just before they were to leave, Helen had come to him and whispered, " Please—I don't want to go to New York! I don't want to take that trip. Couldn't we sneak away for a trip by ourselves? "

" Oh, I'm afraid it's too late to change plans now," he had said. And that night they had boarded the plane for New York

—for a week at the Plaza while the senior Keefes motored to Santa Barbara for a week of golf.

Remembering it now, Jimmy wondered if it had been the conflict between his mother and Helen that had been responsible for the unhappiness that came later. Certainly there had been a conflict; he had been aware of it, and yet, at the time, he had tried to push it far back in his mind. In New York, they had found theatre tickets waiting for them, paid for by Melise. Melise had paid for the hotel, including a substantial deposit for room service. When his mother and father returned from California, Melise had spent two days with Helen, shopping in the city, buying Helen dresses, charging them to her account. He remembered Helen, in their room, unwrapping a box that had arrived from Bergdorf-Goodman containing a short black evening-dress. Helen had thrown the dress across the bed. " I hate it! " she had cried.

" Why didn't you tell her you didn't like it? " Jimmy asked.

" How could I? She made me try it on. She said, ' It looks pretty on you '—and told the girl to wrap it up! Jimmy, I can't take much more of this! "

" She's only trying to be kind," Jimmy said.

" She's not! She's not at all. Do you know what she's doing? She's trying to embarrass me. She's trying to prove that I'm a gold digger! "

" That's not true——"

" It is! Jimmy, please let's go back to California. Don't make me go through Somerville with her! "

" Helen, we've got to. I told you we'd have to go through this sort of thing, didn't I? Can't you put up with it for a few more days? In a few more days we'll be on our own—off to the West Indies——"

" We'll never be on our own—not as long as she's around! "

" Helen," he said softly, " I know she has faults. But she's still my mother! "

" I'm sorry, I'm sorry," she said.

They had gone to Somerville, and Melise had given a huge party for them. Although it was winter, dozens of Chinese lanterns had been strung from the branches of the trees in front of the big white house. Inside, an orchestra had been hired for dancing, and extra servants. And friends and relatives had begun arriving from all over the East. Jimmy remembered standing in the doorway with Helen, watching as cars appeared in the drive, passed slowly under the porte-cochère, and stopped. Coloured chauffeurs hopped out, opening doors for new arrivals. In the winter night, under the great globes of light that glowed beneath the porte-cochère, the long black cars from Detroit seemed to have a special sparkle and a special shine. And the couples, too, seemed glittery as they emerged from the cars, the jewelled wrists of ladies catching the garish lights of the paper lanterns in the trees. The whole effect of Melise's party was queerly exotic, and, to Jimmy, moving trance-like through it with Helen at his side, wearing the black dress Melise had bought for her at Bergdorf's, the party, and the people, and the things that happened seemed unreal. And yet he felt he should make it seem real to Helen. He wanted to say to her, " See, this is what our life will be like, this is what my life has been like, this is what we must some day return to. See how everything is? See my grandmother's crystal—there are twenty dozen of those champagne glasses, bought in France. See that painting of my mother and father? It was painted, after they were married, in the summer-house of my Grandmother Kimball's place in Sachem's Head." He had wanted to explain to Helen that, somehow, the scene, the graceful people moving in it, had a certain significance to him, and a meaning, since it was part of his past, a part of the tradition and the pattern that had shaped him, good or bad, for what he was. He wanted her to understand it, to feel it as he felt it. But every time he looked at her, and began to tell her, her face seemed closed to him, her eyes to withdraw from his. " Everything is very pretty," she said.

And his mother had been very little help. He remembered her airy remarks, floating out over the room. " This is French champagne," she had said to Helen once. " Do you like it as well as your California kind? " And then, to a group of guests, she had said, " Isn't she pretty? It was such fun shopping with her. She came totally unprepared for our New England winters." And, when someone remarked to Helen that she was wearing a pretty dress, Melise had interjected, " Yes, isn't it? It was a little present from me! "

At one point, one of his Hartford cousins had cornered Helen.

" Did you see any shows while you were in New York? " the woman asked.

" Yes," Helen answered.

" What ones, dear? "

" The ones that Mrs. Keefe picked out," Helen said quietly.

The cousin hesitated. " Well," she said, " you must have enjoyed them. Mellie has excellent taste."

But the last scene that evening had been the worst. It had happened after the last guests had left, and the four of them —Jimmy, Helen, and his mother and father—were standing at the foot of the stairs, saying good night.

Melise took Helen's hand. " I hope you won't mind making your bed to-morrow morning," Melise said. " It's Sunday, and I have no maid until six o'clock. But then," she said, smiling, " I imagine you're used to making your own bed, aren't you? "

" I'm used to it," Helen said. And then she said, " I'm surprised you have no maid on Sundays, Mrs. Keefe. I should think, with four million dollars, you could afford one! " She turned and ran up the stairs.

" Well! " Melise gasped. " Well! "

" Why don't you leave her alone, Mother? " Jimmy asked angrily. " Do you have to keep picking on her? "

" She's got a lot to learn, that's all I can say! "

" Come to bed, Mellie," Jimmy's father said.

Jimmy turned and followed Helen up the stairs. In the darkness of their bedroom, he found her huddled on top of the covers, still in the black dress. " Helen," he whispered. " Helen, don't pay any attention to her! It will be all right when we get away by ourselves——"

" No, no——" she cried.

" Please, Helen——" He tried to lift her shoulders.

" Don't touch me! " she sobbed. " Don't! Don't touch me! "

He had gone downstairs again, to the library, and, as the last servant cleared the after-party disarray of heaping ash-trays and empty glasses, he sat with the whisky decanter, splashing the brown liquor over dissolving ice-cubes in a glass, and drinking it down. Much later, he became conscious of a shape in the doorway and looked up. His mother stood there, in a green satin robe, her hair in curlers. She came and knelt on the floor beside him, resting her cheek on his black-trousered knee. "I'm sorry, darling," she said. "I'm a bitch, I know. It's just that I had dreamed of so much *more* for you, Jimmy! So much more! Forgive me!"

They had talked for a while. But he had been very drunk. He could not remember now whether he had forgiven her or not. He could only think of Helen saying, "Don't touch me!" and pushing him away.

He had promised her that when they got to Nassau, the first stop on their Caribbean trip, things would be better. But they had not been. In Nassau, he tried to recapture the slim dark-haired girl who had said, "Hallelujah!" and who had fallen, laughing, with him into the snow at Yosemite, but she eluded him. He remembered watching her coming across the palm-fringed terrace of their hotel towards him, a small figure in a red cotton dress, a white lace mantilla about her shoulders, her short hair combed smoothly back, her chin lifted, her face and arms brown from the sun. An immense, aching longing had filled him; it was as though her very inaccessibility made him love her more. What was it that made him love her? he wondered. At first, he had thought it was a freshness, a simplicity, an ingenuous niceness about her—so different from the brittle girls, the somewhat haggard girls, the house-party girls he had always known. But now it seemed to be more than that. There was something child-like and woundable in her face, in the tilt of her chin. Loving her, he wanted to hold her and shield her, and yet, at the same time, he felt he needed her to shield and protect him from something in himself.

She sat down beside him on the terrace and said, "Shall we go inside for dinner?"

"So early? Oh, no, it's much too much fun out here."

He had ordered another drink.

Then, a little later: "Jimmy—shall we go in now?"

"Oh, no—not yet. I think I'd like another drink."

When, at last, they had gone in, they had had a swift, terrible quarrel in the dining-room.

In the morning, they lay on the beach. "Why don't you ever say anything?" he asked her. "Why do you look at me that way? Don't you realize that I'm your husband?"

Resistlessly, she let him stroke her toe with his finger.

" We talked last night," she said. " You said a great deal."

He withdrew his hand. " What's the matter with us? " he asked.

" I'm married to a man who's becoming an alcoholic at twenty-three! " she said. " It's true. You are! "

He stood up abruptly, picking up his towel. " Do you realize why? " he said softly and coldly. " Do you? "

" I know you blame it on me! "

" Because I'm married to a woman who gives me nothing—or next to nothing! Who makes me feel dirty and ashamed. Can you understand how I might feel? You say I'm becoming an alcoholic. Instead of admitting that there's something wrong with you, you say there's something wrong with me."

" Oh, my God! "

He looked at her. She was crying. " And now what? " she asked. " You must know that this can't last. We'll end up like pieces of kelp or rockweed, drifting—to and fro. Drifting in your family's money! Drifting in drink! I wish I'd died in California! I wish I could die now, in the sea! I wrote your name in the sand to-day. The tide came in and washed it away . . . and I wrote it again, wondering how I would feel, and the tide came again. And I couldn't feel anything! Not anything! " She stood up, pressing her bare arms tight against her sides, her fists clenched, her head bowed.

" Sit down," he said. " Just sit down, Helen, please."

She was sobbing uncontrollably. " Is there something wrong with me? Is there? "

Faces were turned towards them now, from beneath several umbrellas.

" Please, Helen," he whispered. " Please sit down. I'm sorry."

" Oh, I can't! I can't! "

But she did sit down, and, gradually, her sobs stopped. He sat down beside her and tried talking to her; they talked, in little spurts, for a while—a series of apologies followed by accusations and accusations followed by apologies. That afternoon they had flown to Montego Bay.

So many hotels. So many long, carpeted corridors. So many islands. It was hard for him, now, to remember them all in their proper sequence. St. Thomas, St. Croix, Martinique,

Antigua—the islands clouded into one. With a strange, purposeful malice, he drank too much in every one of them. Love, when it came, was brief and terrible; it was almost better when it was blurred with alcohol, and the remorse afterwards could die in swirling sleep. He remembered one evening, at one of the hotels, he had walked out in fury and left her in their room. He had stood for a while, smoking, looking around the deserted lobby of the hotel. He remembered seeing a chameleon scurrying across the white stone floor—the chameleon, pale as death, the colour of his thoughts. On a blue floor—he remembered thinking—the chameleon would turn blue. On green, green. He wondered, idly, what it would do on varicoloured tile. Would it die trying to match its background?

He went out on to the terrace and down the walk to the pool. It was very late, and there was a moon, reflecting on the still surface of the water. The hotel and the music from the dance floor were far away, and, after looking around, he suddenly stripped off his clothes and stood naked in the moonlight. When he dived in, silently, and the dark cold water was all around him, there was a kind of release from everything. It was as though the water, pressing all around him, kept all the other things out, pressed him into one burning, living entity that swam one length, then back, then half another length without coming up for air, the way he had swum at college. He swam slowly back to the edge of the pool then, and resting one of his forearms, looking into the blackness of the hibiscus and bougainvillaea, he saw her emerge suddenly from the shrubbery and stand. She had changed her clothes. She wore Bermuda shorts and a suède jacket, and she stood there with her hands in her pockets, a slim, lonely figure, looking at the ground. He was struck with the thought that somehow she had known where to find him. She had come straight to the pool. Happy or not, their minds were wedded. One could not move without the other knowing or caring. He leaped out of the water and ran to her, naked and shivering. " Helen! " he said. " Helen, for God's sake, I love you. I love you. Let's begin again."

" Let's go inside," she whispered. " Hurry! Take me inside. Let me try! "

Later, in the room, she had whispered, " Darling! Oh, my darling! "

"Was it me then?" he asked her. "Was it me?"

"Oh, it's you *now*——"

"What do you mean? Was it him again—even for a minute?"

"Yes," she said, and she began to cry softly. "But it's you now! That's all that matters now—it's you now!"

Then, angrily, he had said, "What are you trying to do? Turn *me* into him?"

"Oh, no, no, no——"

"Into a damn' rapist? For Christ's sake, are you?"

"Oh, Jimmy—please! No! Please!"

When he woke in the morning, she had already gone down to the beach. Looking around the room, he had seen a slip of paper propped against his hairbrushes on the dresser. It was a note, written on hotel stationery:

DEAREST DARLING,

Is it because I am such a naughty girl, I wonder, or is it because you are such a naughty boy that somehow we can never seem to cope with things like Somerville or last night—and I cry, or one of us says an unkind thing, and both of us are hurt immeasurably? I thought when I left college I had been hurt by a boy for the last time, but now sometimes the boy is my husband, whom I love of course. It is so hard to explain. And yet writing a letter is easier than talking somehow. Do you understand? I want us to live with dignity and grace. I know what you think—that I am a frigid woman—but all I can say is that I am a woman and all women are different. You are different from that other boy, I must believe this . . . if I stop believing this, it will be *both* of our faults!

So will you be kind and tolerant of me when I digress (sp?) and will you try to think of me sometimes as a person who needs to be helped a little? Just once in a blue moon?

Once in a blue moon you do . . .

Remember that morning before we were married for that silly second time when we sat pasting newspaper clippings of the wedding in our scrapbook, that morning in Rio Linda? You read them aloud in a funny voice and we laughed? Or Yosemite. I am glad we are going home soon. When we get home, I will buy another scrapbook and we will sit and paste in it all day and not even have one tiny drink! I will try to be better, I promise. But you must promise too

I love you,

HELEN

Claire and Blazer came out of the water. Blazer was in his trunks, but Claire was in blue jeans, sweater, and sneakers, all of which clung to her wetly. Her hair was plastered back across her head, and she looked more like a little boy than anything else. " Are you *still* drinking those martinis? " she asked gaily. " Really, I think you'd be ashamed of yourself. Remember, we have to climb back to the lift this afternoon."

" Look at this mountain," he said. " Look how far we've come to get up here." He gestured vastly around him. " Do you realize—a hundred years or so ago—Indians roamed all over these hills with bows and arrows? The Indians probably called this place Laughing Water. The young braves brought their maidens here in the moonlight and courted them with feathers and stone beads, and performed fantastic leaping feats here on the rocks, to show off. Can't you see them? Standing on that farthest rock? Shaking their headdresses? " He paused. " Do you realize that as we sit here, civilization is pushing on—that some day this lake will be drained, and the last arrowhead will be extracted, and the mountains will be flattened to make the earth turn faster? " He looked up and his eyes fogged. The outer branches of the fir trees caught the sun and glittered. " Some day, all these trees will be trimmed with Christmas ornaments," he said.

She looked up. " Oh, yes! " she said. " Blazer, did you hear that? Why can't you say things like that, darling? " She smiled at Jimmy. " Ah, Jimmy, you're wonderful! " she said. " Though loaded, you're wonderful."

" I wish it could be for ever."

" Here? For ever? Oh, no, I'd get bored. So would you. We couldn't stand anything as peaceful as this for ever."

He looked at her. Blazer had gone back into the water. " I want to apologize for last night," he said. " For whatever part of it was my fault, I want to apologize."

" Jimmy, please——"

" I do. For my part——"

"What makes you think it was your fault?"

"Some of it must have been."

"You underestimate me."

"There must have been something that I said or did——"

"You've always underestimated me," she said. "Everyone has. No one knows the many things little Claire is capable of." She looked at him, smiling a small, defiant smile.

He flushed. "Well, I'm sorry, anyway."

"Don't be absurd. Is that why you're getting drunk?"

"One reason."

"And the other reason is—Helen, I suppose?"

"Perhaps."

"Oh, Jimmy," she said earnestly. "What are you trying to do to yourself? What are you trying to prove? Let me talk to Helen. You're a nice boy, Jimmy! Why do you try to convince yourself you're a bastard?"

"I'm not——"

"Will you let me talk to Helen?"

"No."

"All right." She turned and walked quickly away, towards Blazer.

Jimmy sat there. He felt stunned. He felt he couldn't get up. The last drink stirred within him.

Helen. Was it possible that in some odd, involuted way Helen had wanted him to ruin himself? No, that was not fair. They had flown home, first to New York, then on to San Francisco. Jimmy had started looking for a job and had found the one in Sacramento. They had moved into the apartment on Capitol Avenue. He had kept his promise; for several weeks, he had nothing to drink, and—though it was hard to remember—perhaps things had got a little better. But then he had broken it—broken it deliberately, in anger and despair.

It was a warm Sunday in May. The Warrens had driven up from Rio Linda for dinner. Mrs. Warren had been enthusiastic about the apartment, and, as Jimmy remembered it, it had looked rather pretty, with bowls of fresh flowers on the tables and the windows open, a soft breeze blowing in. Helen had worked busily in the kitchen, fixing a turkey. He remembered her standing in front of the stove, frowning slightly, tiny beads of perspiration along her upper lip and a damp lock of brown hair falling across her forehead. The mood had been cosy and domestic, and Jimmy had fixed old-fashioneds for Mr. and Mrs. Warren and a gin-and-tonic for Helen. He had sipped a Coca-Cola. After dinner, Helen's father had kicked off his shoes and stretched out on the sofa. (" Goodness, Walker, do you need to make yourself *that* much at home? What will Jimmy think! " Mrs. Warren had said. " Can't a man be comfortable? " Mr. Warren had replied.) Jimmy and his father-in-law had talked for a while about the hardware business, and Mr. Warren had asked Jimmy several questions about the organizational set-up of the Keefe Company—a subject that Jimmy did not know too much about. Mr. Warren was still puzzled as to why Jimmy hadn't gone into his father's business. " I should think there'd be quite a future for you there," he said.

" I guess I don't want to do it, because it would be the easiest thing, sir," Jimmy said. " I mean, it seems a little lazy. And if I ever did go into the business, I'd be trapped there—it would be almost impossible to leave. I guess I just want to see whether I can do something on my own—see if I've got it in me."

" Well, I think that's very admirable," Mr. Warren said. But he did not look convinced.

They talked a while longer and suddenly Mr. Warren fell asleep. Jimmy sat opposite him, uncomfortably watching the older man's heavy breathing. Mrs. Warren came in from the kitchen, where she had been helping Helen with the dishes. " *Walker!* " she cried. " Walker! Wake up! Goodness me, is that any way to behave on our first visit here? " Mr. Warren sat up and rubbed his eyes. He smiled. " I guess Helen's dinner was just too good for me," he said. " Well, I guess we'd better be starting back, Arlene."

There were pleasant good-byes, promises to do it again soon, handshakes and kisses. They left and Jimmy and Helen were alone again. Helen sat on the sofa, her face troubled.

" Well, that was a lot of fun," Jimmy said easily.

" Was it? " she asked.

" Sure. We were just like—like old married people, weren't we? "

" I suppose we impressed them that way," Helen said.

" What do you mean? "

" I mean we put on a good act. You especially——"

" I wasn't acting, Helen."

" What do you mean? Do you mean to say you enjoyed it? Well," she said defensively, " they're my parents and I love them very much! They mean—everything in the world to me! I don't care how dull you think they are."

" I don't think they're dull——"

" Of course you do! I saw you—talking to Daddy—wishing you were somewhere else—a thousand miles, three thousand miles away from here! Back at one of your elegant Connecticut parties! Drinking French champagne! "

" Helen, that just isn't true."

" Of course it is! " She stood up. " Oh, why did you marry somebody like me! What in the world did you see in me? "

" Listen," he said, " you're absolutely wrong. Helen, I want to be married. *Married!* Like—like your mother and father. I want things to be homey and comfortable and friendly. I don't insist on everything being expensive and exciting. That's why I married you."

" That's what you thought you wanted, perhaps," she said bitterly. " But now that you have it—now that you see what it's like—you're bored to death! I know it."

" Well," he said finally, " what did I do wrong? What should I have done? Wasn't I nice to them? "

" Oh, you were nice! You're always nice, but I could tell that you were dying of boredom inside. When Daddy talked to you——"

" For Christ's sake, what was I supposed to do? "

" Do? Oh, I don't know, I don't know." She put her face in her hands.

" I don't get it," he said. " I'm sorry, but I don't."

" I mean, you were superior! " she said, looking at him. " Superior—and snooty and condescending—and stuffy! Calling my father ' sir ' all the time—and did you see how my mother acted? All in a dither—nervous—trying to match your so-called Eastern polish! You made both of them feel uncomfortable! "

Suddenly he was angry. " Uncomfortable! " he said. " I made them feel uncomfortable? Your old man didn't look so damned uncomfortable when he pulled off his shoes and lay down and started to snore! "

" You see, you see? " she said. " Just as I said! "

"You're right," he said, standing up. "I was bored to the ears. Bored to the God-damned ears, sitting around listening to a lot of dull, middle-class platitudinous crap!"

Helen sat down hard in the chair and Jimmy marched into the kitchen and poured himself a drink from the whisky bottle. He stood there, drinking his drink, his hand shaking. He wished he hadn't said that. It was not just the harshness of the remark that disturbed him. It was the fact that he wasn't sure whether he had meant it or not. He just did not know. Once upon a time, he had thought he knew what he wanted. He was no longer sure.

The days went on. It was as though some mutually destructive force compelled them now, drove them on, forced them to continue hurting one another. They were on a road by then that carried them down, wound them under, and it was too late to stop, to let it end; they hurtled along it, faster and faster. It was no longer possible to tell whether anyone meant anything that was said; the sudden, unkind remarks were always a mixture of truth and gratuitous cruelty.

As summer approached, the apartment was often oppressively hot. It was difficult to keep cool. In the Central Valley of California, hot days and nights can continue, relentlessly, from April. They slept under pink linen sheets—wedding presents from the East, from Mosse's, with gigantic pink *K*'s monogrammed on them—but soon threw them off and slept naked, perspiring. Jimmy bought an electric floor fan. It was the only real purchase he made for the apartment. Its whirring breeze lulled them to sleep.

Sometimes they went out, to a movie or to dinner. Sometimes they stayed out late, sitting in an air-cooled bar, drinking, talking, trying somehow to figure things out. The last act of the play had begun; it was too late to alter the scenes that had gone before, the churning months between the hushed, snow-covered valley of Yosemite and the apartment in Sacramento.

Returning to the apartment, late at night, was hard. For no reason, the light switch was across the room. They groped towards it together, forgetting where the furniture was placed, suddenly finding a chair, set like a trap to spring on moving prey. A whisper: "*Did you put this here?*"

Angrily: "No, it wasn't I——"

And then, perhaps later: " Darling——"

" Yes? "

" Would you——? "

" What? "

" Oh, never mind . . ."

One night, after playing tennis poorly in the park, they sat up very late with three bottles of red wine, talking, feeling that they must talk, feeling that somehow, by talking, they could pin it down, clarify and spread out on the table everything that had gone wrong. Helen had a phrase. " We are emotionally unsuited for each other," she had said.

" Why won't you see a doctor? " he asked her.

" What kind of doctor? "

" Someone—a psychiatrist—who knows about these things."

" You still think that, don't you? "

" What? "

" That I'm crazy . . ."

" No," he said hopelessly. " But it isn't getting any better—don't you see? "

" If you had helped! " she said.

" How could I help? "

" Ah——" She reached for the wine bottle. " Does drinking make you forget? " she asked. " Is that what it's supposed to do? It doesn't work for me."

" It makes me remember," he said.

" What? What is there to remember? Quarrels . . . scenes . . ."

" Don't you remember those first few days—when we were all by ourselves in Yosemite? My God, Helen, I'd never been so happy as I was then! But then it changed, all at once."

" You were a different person in Yosemite," she said. " In the beginning. Then you frightened me."

" What do you mean, I frightened you? "

She looked at him steadily. " You frighten me often," she said. " You frighten me right now."

He turned away from her angrily. " You're right. I do think you're crazy! "

" You frighten me when you drink."

" And why do you think I drink? Because of you! "

" Is everything my fault? " She stood up with tears in her

eyes. She went into the bathroom and stood in front of the mirror, brushing her hair. He followed her. " What about that night? " he asked. " By the pool—do you remember that? We were happy for a while. We can be happy, can't we? "

" Such a waste! " she said.

" What? "

" The honeymoon. How much do you suppose that honeymoon cost? Three thousand dollars? Just so that we could go from island to island, drinking and torturing ourselves . . ."

" But we're in our own apartment now. I've got a job, we're settled—or we should be! Why do we have to keep harking back to that honeymoon? "

She didn't answer him, but stood there, brushing fiercely, counting the brush strokes silently, under her breath.

" You should be grateful that there's money," he said.

" Not when it's helped to do this to us——"

" Look," he said, " I don't want to rely on the money. I want to do things on my own. I've told you that. That's why we're here, in Sacramento, and not back with the Keefe Company making hinges and staples! I want to be independent of that——"

" I know, I know . . ."

" Do you love me? " he asked her.

She stopped brushing and leaned forward, resting her forehead on the mirror. " Yes," she said.

" Then can't we be happy? "

" I want to be! I do want to be! "

" Then——" He put his hand on her arm.

" Then give me time! " she sobbed. " Give me time to forget things, and help me. Be considerate and patient, and help me! "

" I try," he said gently. " But there's some sort of curtain between us now. Something's stopping us——"

She bowed her head further, letting her forehead slide down along the cool glass. " Please . . . please don't talk to me any more. Please just leave me alone."

He went back into the kitchen and poured himself another drink. It was like all their quarrels—aimless, oblique, beginning nowhere, ending nowhere.

Later, she came into the kitchen in her robe. " Do you mind

if I drive home to-morrow for the day? " she asked him. " I'll drive you to work. Then go on in the car."

It was a short drive to Helen's home, forty miles down the valley. " All right," he said. With her short brown hair loose, in her light cotton robe, her tanned face and small body had a frail, sculptured look. She stood there, swaying a little—the way a few drinks always made her do—and smiled at him with a strange apologetic smile. " Are you sure you don't mind? "

" No. Why do you want to go? "

She looked away from him. " I want to think. I want to go home and think things out."

" Sure."

He took a cigarette from his pack and reached for the kitchen lighter.

" Be careful of that lighter," she said. " It throws out sparks."

" I know."

He smoked his cigarette, then put it out and followed her to bed. After he had switched out the light, he pulled the pink sheet tight around his throat. " Good night."

" Good night."

He huddled there, afraid to move, afraid that moving the slightest inch would start the shivering, the trembling he felt inside him. When, much later, he did move, the trembling started, but by that time Helen was asleep.

The next morning, she had driven to Rio Linda, but that evening she did not come back. Around seven, the telephone rang. " Jimmy? " she said. " I'm still here. Daddy's sick. We're a little worried. Would you mind if I spent the night? "

" No," he said, " that's all right."

He had suspected that she was not telling the truth, but the next day, at his office, she had telephoned him again. " Daddy's much worse . . . he's had an internal hæmorrhage. The doctor's terribly worried. Jimmy—I'm afraid he's going to die! "

" Would you like me to come down? " he asked.

" Could you? Could you come down to-night on the bus? "

" All right."

That night when he arrived at the Warrens' house in Rio Linda, Helen met him at the door. " He's upstairs," she said. " Go up and see him."

Mr. Warren lay in bed in the half-darkened room. He was

not a large man, but in the big bed he seemed even smaller, shrunken. In sleep, his face was fallen and old. Mrs. Warren sat beside him with a pile of yellow knitting in her lap. " Hello, Jimmy," she whispered. She reached up and brushed his cheek with her lips. " He's still asleep . . . he had a pill."

" What is it? " he asked her.

" It's a duodenal ulcer. Dr. Manger says he must have been suffering from it for years. They're afraid to operate—his heart. Poor Walker! He never mentioned anything to me."

Mr. Warren opened his eyes once, closed them, then opened them again.

Jimmy took his heavy, veined hand. " Hello, sir," he said. " How are you feeling? "

" Me? " Mr. Warren said. " I'm feeling fine, just fine. Did somebody tell you I wasn't? It's just these women—Helen and her mother—trying to make an invalid out of me."

" Don't let 'em do it, sir." Jimmy smiled.

" Yes," Mr. Warren said. " It's tough to live in a houseful of women. Was that the way your house was, Jim? "

" Well, there was my dad, sir——"

" Oh, yes. Do I sound fuzzy? I'm running a little temperature. Your dad's a fine fellow, Jimmy, a smart man——"

" Thank you, sir."

Mr. Warren closed his eyes. " Arlene! " he said. " Arlene! Are the children in? "

Mrs. Warren rose and stood beside him. " Yes, Walker, everything's fine."

" It's going to rain——"

" There, there, you're just having a dream."

Mr. Warren opened his eyes once more and looked at Jimmy. " I'll be up and around to-morrow, wait and see," he said. " Just running a temperature, that's all."

Mrs. Warren placed her hand on his forehead. " Hush, Walker," she said. " You need rest . . . lots of rest. Go back to sleep."

When Jimmy got downstairs, he found Helen curled on the sofa, weeping. She was close to hysteria. " He's going to die! " she sobbed. " He's going to die! I know he's going to die! "

" Don't talk like that," he said gently. " He's not going to die. He said he feels fine now . . ."

" Don't you know him? He says he feels fine—but he's in terrible pain. Oh, oh, oh! He's going to die! Daddy's going to die! "

" Please, Helen," he said. " You mustn't think that——"

She turned to him angrily. Her face was white and streaked with tears. " *He is going to die!* " she screamed. " Can't you understand that? Don't you have any feeling? Don't you even care? "

Later, he had gone for a walk. He walked aimlessly, up and down the lighted streets of Rio Linda. Finally, he went into a bar and had a drink. When he got back to the house and opened the door, Helen stood at the head of the stairs. Her face was expressionless as she started down. " Well," she said, " he's dead."

He couldn't believe her. " That's not true——"

She ran down the stairs and across the hall to where he stood and slapped him. " What do you mean, it's not true? " she cried. " Of course it's true! He's dead! And where were you? Getting drunk! "

Mrs. Warren hurried down the stairs after her. Helen turned to her mother. " He says I'm lying! He says Daddy isn't dead! " She turned away from him and ran into the living-room.

" What? " Mrs. Warren said. " What do you mean, you dreadful, dreadful boy? " Her pale eyes blazed at him. " I suppose, in your house, death is nothing! Well, in our house, it's not like that! My husband is dead. Now get out of my house! Go back where you came from! Get out of my house, you drunken wastrel! "

The little doctor came running down the stairs, carrying his bag. " Arlene," he said. " Now, Arlene! Be brave. He's out of his pain now, Arlene." He put his arm around Mrs. Warren's shaking shoulders and led her through the house, out into the garden.

Jimmy stayed in Rio Linda for the funeral. Afterwards, he and Helen drove back to Sacramento. They drove in silence.

Once he turned to her and said, " Would you like to take a trip? Go away somewhere for a few days? "

" To the Caribbean? Take another honeymoon? " she asked bitterly. " No, thank you."

It was about a week after the funeral. Jimmy went out alone

to a small neighbourhood bar a few blocks from the apartment, and had several drinks in rapid succession. Had he known then? Had he planned it that way, engineered the end himself? Perhaps. He rolled the bartender for another drink, won, and drank it. He remembered looking up at the Pepsi-Cola girl on the poster behind the bar—" Refreshing, but not filling," she said. He lifted his glass and drank to her. Someone, with a soft, stubby pencil, had indicated more explicit features on her body. " Here's to the girl who refreshes without filling," Jimmy said.

The bartender winked. " I could sure fill her up," he said.

Jimmy picked up the dice, dropped them in the can, and shook it. " Call it," he said.

" Odd."

" Even." The dice spun across the bar again. " Looks like this is my lucky night," Jimmy said.

When he got back to the apartment, Helen was standing in the bathroom brushing her hair. (Why was it, in every picture of her, she was brushing her hair—her short brown hair standing out about her head, snapping with electricity under the brush, lifting to meet the brush like a dark cloud of smoke?) She was wearing a full skirt and a light peasant blouse.

" Hello," he said.

" Hello."

He went to her and put his arm around her waist. " Here's to the girl who refreshes without filling—but the trouble is she's never willing," he said.

She stiffened. " Please let go," she said.

" Miss Pepsi-Cola——" He tried to kiss her.

" Let go! "

" Helen, please . . ."

She looked up at him. " Are you going to rape me? "

" Helen, for Christ's sake——"

" Are you? Just like him? "

" For God's sake, will you stop comparing me to him! I'm your husband! "

She tried to pull away. " No! You are him! "

" Shut up," he said. " Shut up, damn you! "

" Yes! " Her eyes were filled with terror. " Oh, help! " she cried. " Help! "

" Listen to me! "

She began pounding his chest with her clenched fists. " Let me go! " she screamed. " Hurting—oh, help! "

His arm slid up her back, and, as she twisted, struggling to get away from him, his fingers caught in the double strand of pearls at her throat. The beads snapped, fell, scattered and rolled across the tile.

His arms went limp. She turned and ran out, through the living-room and out the door. In the mirror was only his own face.

He remembered lying in bed in the darkened apartment, waiting for her. It was after midnight. Finally, he heard the key. The door opened and he saw her, framed in the light, her wide skirt swirling around her. Then the door closed. Saying nothing, she stepped towards him, and when she reached the bed, she looked at him, and, gradually, in the darkness, he made out the shape of her head, though her face was obscured.

" Are you awake? " she asked.

" Yes."

" I'm going home to-morrow."

" For good? "

" Yes."

Some sort of searchlight turned on his brain for a moment then, came out of a cloud, swirled in the protoplasm, and dissolved in darkness. " For a while," he said, trying to make his voice steady, " I thought you were going to stay for ever. Is the honeymoon over? "

" Yes."

She sat in one of the chairs and lighted a cigarette. Her hand, holding the match, trembled. " I've talked to Mother on the phone," she said. " We had a long talk. About everything. She wants me to come home."

" All right."

They sat in silence, on opposite sides of the room, Helen smoking, he sitting cross-legged on the bed, watching her. Intermittently, as she drew on her cigarette, her small, sculptured face was lighted with a yellow glow. Somewhere in the night then, he remembered, there had been a scream of tyres and brakes on the street outside, and a wild peal of laughter from a car, then the loud roar of the hot-rod engine. In the beat, the pause, that followed, he thought: I must think only of thunder, only of nothing. Or home. I could think of home.

Blazer stood over him in his dripping trunks and shook his wet hair. " Are you drunk, Keefe-o? " he asked.

" Yes," Jimmy said. " I'm afraid so."

Claire said, " Oh, Jimmy! What are we going to do? We've got to get back."

" I'm sorry," he said.

" I know how to sober him up," Blazer said.

" How? "

" Like this."

Blazer lifted his gun out of his knapsack. " This revolver is one of the best little weapons made," he said. He aimed it across the water. " Now listen to this! " He pulled the trigger.

Distractedly, in the disorder of echoing and re-echoing that occurred, Jimmy wondered if they had all been killed. For in the hollow of the mountains, the report refused to die.

They stood there—for with the sudden sound he had jumped to his feet—the three of them, like statues, marooned, fogged in by noise. The silence, shattered, lay about them like pieces of broken crockery. A ripple developed across the lake, expanded, sank, and disappeared. Another echo came, pounded, and came again. In Jimmy's head, everything seemed to rock. The trees seemed to shake their branches, their Christmas ornaments tossed off.

Claire's eyes were filled with tears. " Oh, Blazer! " she cried. " Why did you have to do that? *Why did you?* "

Jimmy tried to say something. " Well," he said finally, " that does it."

He knelt and was sick.

PART TWO

8

THE apartment on Russian Hill had a spectacular view. It was on the top floor, and, on three sides, it was solid glass from floor to ceiling. To the east, across roof-tops, was the Bay Bridge, stretching towards the white-dotted hills of Berkeley and Oakland. To the north, from the living-room, was the bay—the Marina, Alcatraz, and Tiburon in one direction, Mount Tamalpais and the Golden Gate in the other. To the west were more roof-tops, fringed by the trees of the Presidio. Everyone said that Claire and Blazer had been lucky to find it.

Actually, they had not found it. Junius Denison, Claire's father, had found the apartment for them, through a friend, Winston Applegate, an officer in the Crocker Bank. The apartment, and the building it belonged to, had been owned by Mr. Applegate's mother. After the senior Mrs. Applegate died, her son took over the building and managed it as part of her estate.

Originally, Mr. Applegate had planned to have his mother's furniture stored, but, under Mr. Denison's persuasion, he had agreed to leave it for Claire and Blazer to use. The furniture had been collected by Mrs. Applegate on a series of trips to the Orient; it was low, lacquered, ancient, and serene. Two painted Chinese screens separated the large living-room into two areas, one for sitting and one for dining; in this room, the only Western touch was the concert and grand piano in one corner. The floor was bare, highly polished wood. The bedroom floor was covered with thin sea-grass mats. Before Claire and Blazer moved in, Mr. Applegate took out considerable insurance on the furnishings in the apartment. This had proved wise. Already, at one of Claire's parties, a precious tea chest from an ancient dynasty had been sat upon and destroyed.

When Claire returned to the apartment that Saturday morning, it was still early. The heavy, blanketing fog—which is common to San Francisco summers—had not rolled in from the sea; the air was clear and prismatic. The drive back from the airport, along the bay, with the top down, had blown her hair and flushed her cheeks. It had also wakened her considerably more than her breakfast cup of coffee had. She had been up since six, getting Blazer to the morning plane for Los Angeles. Claire felt clearheaded and exuberant, and yet, when she entered the cool immaculate apartment, she felt somehow let down. Blazer would be in the South until Thursday. She had a long, uneventful week-end to look forward to.

She took off her coat and gloves, placed them in the closet, and closed the sliding doors. She went into the living-room, closed the drapes on the sunny side, and sat down on the sofa. She kicked off her shoes, put her feet up on the cushions, and lay back. She felt bored. She wished the telephone would ring. She got up then, went into the bedroom, unplugged the telephone, and carried it out and plugged it in beside the sofa. Then she lay down again. A friend from Smith, Diane Higbee, had written that she might be passing through. But, Claire thought, with a vagueness that was typical of Higbee, she had given no indication as to when. For a while, Claire concentrated on making the telephone ring, on making it be Diane Higbee on the other end of the wire, calling from the Fairmont.

On the way to the airport, she had suggested to Blazer that they have a party on the following Saturday night. They had not had a party for quite a while. The occasion for the party would be to welcome Blazer home from Los Angeles. She had thought of painting a banner and stretching it across the windows —a banner that said, " Welcome Home from L.A., Blaze! " It was a little silly, but perhaps some of their friends might think it was funny. Blazer had seemed agreeable to the idea of the party. She began making a little mental list of the people they would ask. She would have Sue and Alec Fry—she had known Sue in New York—and Arnold William and that girl, whatever her name was, that he was dating, and Bill and Phyllis Brower, Tweetums DeMay—Tweetums was older than the rest of them, but lots of fun, and could be counted on to bring an interesting man for herself—and she would have Diane Higbee if she showed up and Jimmy. Diane could more or less be Jimmy's date.

Had Jimmy ever met Diane at Smith? She couldn't remember. It was odd thinking about getting Jimmy a date; she had grown so accustomed to thinking of Jimmy as one-half of a married couple. Now she would have to make a mental effort to think of Jimmy as single again. Poor Jimmy. She wished he wouldn't drink so much. Was that the reason they had broken up? she wondered. Jimmy's drinking? No, probably he drank a lot because he was trying to forget all the unpleasantness. And besides, he didn't always drink too much, did he? Only sometimes, but still it was too bad. In college she didn't remember him that way. In college, he had been wonderful, funny, handsome Jimmy. Ah, she thought, he was handsome . . . and so proper! And so sweet. . . . She had often thought about him, wondering what he would be like, what would happen . . .

She let her thoughts wander deliciously off. The sun moved, came through the glass, and shone down upon her; dust motes swirled and floated in the air. Whom was it Zeus came to in a shower of gold? She tried to remember. But Jimmy wasn't Zeus. He was Hermes . . . Apollo. She imagined herself somewhere. Parnassus—and he, bronzed with the sun, in a shower of gold . . .

Poor Jimmy, she thought. Poor, sweet Jimmy. That morning on the mountain. He had looked so sad, so lost. It had been Blazer's fault, really, that he had started drinking like that. Blazer had started analysing his problem, saying to her, " Well, what do you think he should do? " Of course Jimmy had hated to hear them talking like that. What man wouldn't? Sometimes Blazer was so callous. She knew how Jimmy must have felt, but what could she say at that point? Well, she thought, it was a measure of Jimmy's manhood that he'd been able to climb back up to the top of that mountain, and across that ridge, after so much to drink. And he had.

Poor Jimmy. She wondered what he was doing now. Probably in his apartment, brooding, thinking too much. Instinctively, she disliked Helen. Though she knew nothing about her, she disliked her. She must be a fool, Claire thought, not to see what a good deal she had with Jimmy—handsome, sweet, and rich, too. She wished Jimmy had married someone like—like, for instance, herself. If she, for example, were married to Jimmy instead of Blazer . . . It was a tantalizing thought, and a darkly treacherous one; she let her mind tiptoe towards it, then moved away quickly. Blazer—why did she have, more and more lately, this odd twinge of misgivings when she thought about Blazer? After all, there was nothing wrong with Blazer. She loved Blazer—very much. It was not so much Blazer *now* that bothered her, but it was the thought of Blazer five years from now . . . or ten years from now. Blazer was like a fine, crackling fire that was dying down. Some day she would be left with the ashes, the grey ashes. The conceit pleased her; she thought about getting up and writing it down, but the sunlight on the sofa was too warm, too wonderful.

She would like to be able to do one specific, concrete, definite thing to help Jimmy. He needed help, no one had to tell her that. She remembered her mother's, the Mars Hill attitude when marital differences cropped up among their friends. It was, " Let's not see them for a while until it's settled, one way or another." Well, that attitude was wrong. Why shouldn't a person's friends gather around at a time like that? Why shouldn't they look for specific, concrete, definite ways to help? Why should they be afraid to get involved? Jimmy clearly still carried a torch for Helen . . . why shouldn't she, Claire, do whatever she could to help? If she went to see Helen, for example, if she talked to her, it might help Jimmy. And it might do another thing, she thought guiltily. It might help her soothe her own, vaguely troubled conscience.

She imagined going to see Helen. She was at her mother's, Jimmy had said, in Rio Linda. Where was Rio Linda? She could find it on the map—that was no problem. When she got there, she could look up Mrs. Warren's address in the phone book. Then, seriously, Claire began to explore her motives. Did she want to see Helen just out of curiosity? Did she, somehow, want to see Helen to satisfy herself that Jimmy's marriage was indeed permanently and irrevocably over? Was there a green-eyed monster? No, no. No to all three questions. Jimmy was an old friend—of hers, and of Blazer's. If Jimmy really did want Helen back, and she thought he did, and she could really do something to help—and who knew whether she could—then wouldn't she really be accomplishing something important in two people's lives? Sometimes her own life seemed so purposeless and meaningless, so selfish and ungiving. Even if she accomplished nothing, wouldn't it be something just to have tried? Was it really so maudlin and foolish—the way Blazer said? Perhaps she could explain it to Jimmy.

Claire picked up the telephone and cradled the receiver between her shoulder and her chin. She dialled Operator, and gave her the Sacramento number which she knew. She let it ring for several minutes. There was no answer at Jimmy's apartment. She replaced the receiver. Where could he be . . .?

Yes, she thought, my life is purposeless. Look at me, right now, lying on the sofa in my stocking feet with absolutely nothing to do for forty-eight hours, till Monday morning. At least on Monday morning there was a job to go to. All I need, she thought, is a pound of chocolate-covered cherries and a pile of movie magazines to complete the picture—the complete, indolent, parasitic life. She stood up abruptly and walked across the room to the desk. She rummaged through the drawers for the California highway map, found it, and returned with it to the sofa. She spread it out in front of her. After a little trouble, she found Rio Linda, and, suddenly, seeing it there on the map—not far from where she was, an hour, perhaps—she was filled with a swift flutter of excitement. All right, she thought, I'll go. It was now quarter-of-eleven. If she left, say, at twelve, she would be there by one. She would spend perhaps an hour, then leave, and be back well before dark. All right—I'll go.

She stood up and looked around the room. Already, instead of being bored, she felt as though all at once she had a million things to do. What would she wear, for one thing? Something simple, she decided, in dark colours—nothing extreme. And a hat . . . and white gloves. And what would she say? Well, she would go to the door . . . ring the bell . . . introduce herself, explain . . .

She went to her closet and began pulling out dresses. Then she remembered the party. If she were going to get anybody at home, she had better phone her invitations now. She ran through the list of names in her head. She would call them now, quickly, and then get dressed, fix a quick something to eat, then get in the car and go. She then remembered Scarlet O'Hara—the red Jaguar. It did not fit, exactly, into the picture she had planned to create with white hat and white gloves. Well, perhaps with the top up . . .

She went to the telephone and dialled Sue Fry's number.

" Susie? " she said when she reached her. " Hi! This is Claire. . . . Can you come to a party next Saturday night? Can you? Oh, wonderful! It's for Blazer—the poor guy's spending the week in Los Angeles on business. . . . Oh, come any time, Susie—you know our parties . . ."

By twelve-ten—miraculously, it seemed—she was ready to go.

Mrs. Walker Warren had three things to do that afternoon, and one of them, the most important one, was to water her garden. In California, watering the garden is a ritual, an almost daily one, as necessary as having a garden itself. But to Mrs. Warren that afternoon, watering the garden loomed up as just another of the heavy, unpleasant chores that life had lately been thrusting upon her. She dreaded it. Standing in her living-room on her shrimp-coloured carpet, with the chore ahead of her, she thought of her friends, her own contemporaries, who had either gardeners or husbands to do such things for them. She thought of Agnes Miller . . . Dorothy Widener. She looked out through the french windows at the garden, at the tall blue agapanthus, the tree roses bleeding at the end of thick woody stems, and felt sorry for herself. She turned and went upstairs to her room to change.

She spent a good deal of time finding a pair of slacks that would not reveal a panty line. Finally, she found a pair—soft blue denim—and put them on. To these, she added a short-sleeved pink cotton blouse and a large, wide-brimmed gardening hat. Looking at herself in the long mirror, she was pleased with the result. If it were not for the fluff of blue-white hair beneath the hat, she decided, she might pass for a woman of, say, forty. She turned sideways, sucked in her tummy, wishing she had not had quite so much lunch, and smiled wanly at her image. Thank goodness she had kept her figure. Thank goodness she dyed her eyebrows. She started down the stairs and noticed that Helen's door was closed.

She reminded herself of the two other things she had to do. One was to call her insurance agent about her fur-jewellery policy that seemed to have lapsed. The other was to find time, somehow, for a good, long, heart-to-heart talk with Helen.

Mrs. Warren's garden had been photographed many times by magazines—notably *Sunset,* which had called it "compact and care-free, making the most of every precious inch of a small city back yard." She had been pleased with the *Sunset* article, but her pleasure had not been undiluted. The article had reminded her that the garden was small. That it was not care-free. That it was, after all, only a garden on a city lot. It reminded her of so many of the unpleasant things about her life—the fact that the neighbourhood around her was disintegrating. Magnolia had once been the nicest street in town. But already, on her corner, was the Lucky Penguin Ice Cream Parlour. Though the Warren house still stood, trim, white, and dignified, at the end of a neatly tailored front walk, the house next door, just beyond her fence, bore a sign that said ROOMS TO LET. Mrs. Warren had often said that she couldn't understand why anybody would want to live anywhere but in California. And yet, as more and more people came to her way of thinking, and moved there from other parts of the country, she was dismayed. She deplored the rapid, haphazard growth of California towns; she yearned, nostalgically, for the days of the missions, the Spanish dons, private irrigation, and low taxes. She wheeled the garden hose to the centre of the terrace, turned on the water at the spigot, and began soaking the beds.

It was nearly two o'clock when she finished. She replaced the hose and sat down, exhausted, in one of the rattan chairs. It was getting hot. She felt that she would like a glass of iced tea, but it seemed like so much trouble—to go into the kitchen, make tea, crack open ice-trays, squeeze lemons. Doris, her housekeeper, had Saturdays off, and this was another thing that annoyed her. In the old days, even on the regular maid's day off, there had been another maid; there had been someone to fill in. A woman hadn't had to do everything herself. Mrs. Warren felt a familiar, slow ache rising from the small of her back. Arthritis. Old age. Loneliness. Fifty-seven years old. As old as the century. What good did it do to dye one's eyebrows, to have a garden, to diet and exercise to keep one's figure from thickening? She lay back in her chair, miserable, and fanned her face with her fingertips. Then, from the front of the house, she heard the door-bell.

She got up and walked across the terrace to the french windows.

She could see through the living-room to the front porch. There was a girl there—a girl she had never seen before. And what an astonishing-looking girl. . . . What an incredible shock of yellow hair. She opened the windows and walked through the house to the door, and opened it. " Good afternoon," she said pleasantly.

" How do you do? " Claire said. " I'm Mrs. Gates—Mrs. Stuart Gates—from San Francisco. I'm looking for Mrs. Keefe. Is this the right house? "

" Oh, yes," Mrs. Warren said. " Are you a friend of Helen's? Won't you come in? I'm Helen's mother."

Claire stepped inside.

" I'm afraid Helen's resting," Mrs. Warren said. " But I'll call her."

" Oh, I'm sorry," Claire said. " I don't want to disturb her. I should have telephoned."

" Oh, I know Helen will be glad to see you. Were you at Berkeley with Helen? "

" No," Claire said, " I'm a friend from the East."

" Oh, I see," said Mrs. Warren. " Won't you come out and sit in the garden? I'll call Helen . . ." She led Claire through the living-room and opened the french doors. " I think it's a little cooler out here," she said.

" My, what a lovely garden! "

" Oh, it's in sort of a *state* right now," Mrs. Warren said. " I have to apologize for it. It's just too much *work* for one person. Why don't you sit right over there and I'll send Helen down, Mrs.——"

" Gates," Claire said, " Mrs. Stuart Gates."

" Oh, yes . . ."

" I do hope I won't be disturbing her."

" Oh, I'm sure not. . . . I'll send her down."

Claire sat down in a rattan chair and placed her gloved hands in her lap. She felt hot and overdressed. Her light blue wool had been the wrong choice. She had forgotten, idiotically, the temperature change that occurred when you left the bay area, drove over the mountains, into the valley. The heat descended on her in a smothering blanket; her wool dress was warm and prickly. She felt a thin tricklet of perspiration form along her spine. She felt the trip was doomed already. What had she been thinking of, anyway, coming all the way up here? Well, it was too late now. Helen appeared at the doorway.

Claire's first thought was: My God, she's tiny! Such a small, small face. But pretty. . . . Helen wore shorts and a light cotton blouse; below her shorts, her slim legs were darkly tanned. She was barefoot. Her short brown hair was tied back with a yellow ribbon. Claire stood up. Helen approached her with a puzzled look, and held out her hand. " Hello," Helen said.

" Hello," Claire said, " I'm Claire Gates." She decided she had better come straight to the point. " My husband and I are friends of Jimmy's," she said. " Very old friends, from Connecticut."

Helen looked startled for a moment, then she smiled a little nervous smile. " Oh," she said, " I wondered——"

" Yes . . ."

" Well—won't you sit down? "

" Thank you." Claire sat down and Helen pulled a chair close to her and sat opposite her.

Claire laughed nervously. " Well," she said, " I suppose you're wondering why I'm here. Well, it's sort of a labour of love."

" Oh? "

" Yes," Claire said. " You see, we're terribly fond of Jimmy. We've been seeing quite a bit of him in San Francisco, Blazer and I——"

" Blazer? "

" Yes, Blazer. My husband——" She laughed again. " His name is actually Stuart, but everybody calls him Blazer——"

" Oh, yes," Helen said. " I remember now. I remember hearing Jimmy speak of Blazer. He roomed with Blazer, didn't he? "

" Yes," Claire said, " that's right—all through college. We're all—Jimmy, Blazer, and I—from more or less the same town. Jimmy and Blazer lived in Somerville, and my family lives near there."

" Oh, I see," Helen said.

" Well," Claire said, " of course this whole trip up here—to see you—may be just a terrible waste of time. It was my own silly idea to come. Jimmy has absolutely no idea I'm here. Neither does Blazer—he's away. But this morning I got to thinking——" She began talking rapidly, and as she talked, she brushed back her hair with her hand. " I thought, well, you know when two people—a couple—has, have—difficulties—it's customary for their friends to adopt a sort of hands-off attitude. You know—people say, ' Stay out of it! ' Well, it struck me that this was *wrong*. I mean, why shouldn't someone, a friend, pitch in, intercede, and do what she can to help? So that's why I came—and if it's all a waste of time, please tell me, and I'll leave."

" Why, I think that's very nice of you," Helen said.

" Thank you. I don't want to be Miss Buttinsky, but it's been so sad for me—for both Blazer and me."

" Sad? "

" Yes—sad to see Jimmy. He—he *loves* you, Helen. May I call you Helen? He really does. He can hardly bear to talk about it, but I know he does. Last week-end the three of us went on a hiking trip—up in the mountains. We drove up Friday night and stayed in Jimmy's apartment . . ."

" Goodness," Helen smiled, " how did you all fit into that apartment? "

" Oh, we had our sleeping-bags—for the trip. But Jimmy did the saddest thing when we were there! "

" What? What did he do? "

" He didn't want to tell us—about the two of you. Which is so like Jimmy—wanting to keep his problems to himself. So when we were there, the whole evening, he pretended—he talked—as if you were just away for a few days, and were coming back. He sort of set the stage—trying to keep us thinking that nothing was wrong. Of course I noticed, the way a woman would. I knew, or anyway I suspected. And honestly it broke my heart to watch him, to listen to him, talking as if you were still there, or were coming back."

" Poor Jimmy——" Helen said. But her face, as Claire studied it, showed no emotion.

" Yes, it broke my heart. I knew that he wouldn't pretend that way—so elaborately—unless really, deeply, he *wanted* it to be that way. Wanted you there. Do you see what I mean? Am I making any sense? Please stop me if I'm talking too much——"

" Oh, no, please. Please go on."

" He loves you, I know he does. This—this separation is hurting him tremendously, more than he could possibly say. Sometimes, he drinks too much——"

" Yes," Helen said. " I imagine so."

Claire wished she had not said that. " But he never *used* to," she said defensively. " I've known him—I don't mean to sound smug, but I *have* known Jimmy for a long time, most of my life. Longer than you have—and I just know, I just feel so certain that——"

" That what? "

" That the two of you should go back together again. Try again."

Helen smiled a tight-lipped smile. Oh, *dear*, Claire thought, oh, God, why did I get into this, *why*! Why hadn't she guessed it would be like this—this girl was impenetrable, stone! The palms of her hands, in her gloves, were damp. She stroked furiously at her hair. She longed for a cigarette, but she had left her pack in the car.

" Well," she said defiantly, " that's what I think! "

" Well," Helen said, " it was very nice of you to come. I appreciate the thought."

" Oh, I wish you would! " Claire said. " I wish you would get together for lunch, or for dinner or a drink—just the two of you, and talk it over! Jimmy has so much to offer! He does! Why, at home, Jimmy Keefe was always our hero—so popular! "

" I've gathered that," Helen said. " Jimmy is——"

" What? What is he, do you think? "

" He's—well, it's nothing, really. I can't remember what I was going to say."

" Isn't there any chance? " Claire asked. " Isn't there any chance at all? "

" No, I'm afraid not."

" Oh, I'm sorry . . ."

" And there's another thing——" Helen looked towards the house.

" What? "

" I haven't told Mother yet," she said. " I wasn't sure when I left Jimmy, but I am now, quite sure. I'm going to have a baby."

Claire sat back. " Oh, my dear! " she said.

" Yes, I'm quite pleased, really. In November."

" And even that—even with that, don't you think that's all the more reason why you should try? "

" Oh, no," Helen said quickly. " No, especially not with that."

Claire stood up. " Well," she said, " well, I'm sorry——"

" Not at all. As I say, I think it was a very nice gesture to come. Most people—as you said—wouldn't do it." She followed Claire to the french doors.

" Thank you." Claire walked through the living-room with Helen behind her. She was conscious of Mrs. Warren watching, from the head of the stairs, but she did not turn. At the door, she said, " Well, good-bye. And good luck——" She held out her hand.

Helen took it. " Good-bye," she said. She opened the door. " Oh, what a pretty car! "

Claire laughed. " Yes! Its name is Scarlet O'Hara! Well . . . good-bye! " She turned and ran down the steps.

In the car, she struggled to light a cigarette. The lighter kept popping out, unlit. She tried to push it in, couldn't, and threw it angrily on the floor. She clawed through her purse for matches. When she found some, finally, and had her cigarette going, she clenched it in her lips and started the car, backing it jerkily out of the drive. At the corner, she speeded through the yellow light. She had a sudden, wild impulse to go the other way—to Sacramento, to tell Jimmy. But no, she thought, she couldn't tell Jimmy. What would *that* do to him? No, no. Home! She had to get home!

On the freeway, a car pulled out of the opposite lane, swerved towards her, and narrowly missed her. " Oh, God damn you! Damn you! " Hot tears streamed down her face. " Damn you! " she sobbed. She couldn't see, her eyes fogged. She pulled the car over to the side of the road, stopped it, pulled on the hand brake, and lay down across the leather seat and cried.

Jimmy Keefe had been out of the apartment most of the day. He had had a series of small, bothersome chores to do. There had been an appointment with Harrington, the Sacramento lawyer, at ten that morning. (" There has been no complaint filed yet," Harrington said. "We'll keep our fingers crossed on the alimony question till then.") After that, he had had to retrieve his shirts from the Chinese laundry, and his sheets, socks, and underwear from the laundromat. He had also had to do some marketing. After that, he had taken his car to have it washed.

He got back to the apartment around five o'clock, and, for a while, he lay on the sofa, reading the evening paper. At about six-thirty, he got up and went into the kitchen to fix himself something to eat. From the window, Capitol Avenue was quiet. It looked cool and peaceful in the slanting sunlight. The telephone rang.

He picked it up. There was a click as the long-distance connection was made, and presently Claire's voice came on the other end of the wire.

"Jimmy?" she said. "What are you doing? Right now?"

"Right now?" he said. "Well, right now I'm standing here talking on the telephone."

"No—be serious. What are you doing this evening?"

"Nothing. I thought I might go to a movie."

"Come down here," she said. "Will you? Come on down and take me out to dinner."

"Where's Blazer?"

"In Los Angeles."

"Is something wrong?"

"No—but can you come? Get in your car right now."

He looked at his watch. "My God, Claire," he said, "it'll be almost nine when I get there——"

"That's all right. *Please?* We'll go to India House or somewhere."

"Well——"

"Please?"

"But look—I'll have to drive all the way back——"

"I'll make a reservation for you," she said. "You can stay in the city, can't you? I'll make a reservation at the Clift or some place."

"You mean, pack a bag?"

"Oh, for goodness' sake! If you need a bag, you can borrow one of Blazer's when you get here! Put a toothbrush in your pocket—and come!"

" All right——"

" Come right now."

" Are you sure nothing's wrong? You sound a little——"

" It's important. Come! "

" All right."

" You're a dear. Good-bye."

9

It was after nine o'clock when Jimmy arrived in San Francisco. He drove to the top of Russian Hill and circled the building several times in his green convertible, looking for a parking place. Finally, he found one, on the steep, uphill side of Hyde Street, and parked, cutting his wheel sharply until his right front tyre dug hard into the curb—the rule for hillside parking in the city. He turned off the motor, climbed out, and locked the car. The night was clear and chilly. A slight wind chattered the leaves of the magnolia trees along the street.

Claire's apartment was on Lombard Street, a slim, handsome building of white stucco and glass with jutting terraces above the street. He entered the building and started up the long series of steps to the top floor. At the top he stopped and rang the bell. Above it, a small enamelled calling card read, *Mr. and Mrs. Stuart Beckwith Gates, II.* Claire opened the door almost immediately.

She greeted him in a swirl of pale blue taffeta, rhinestones, and perfume. " My hero! " she exclaimed gaily. " I knew you'd come! " She brushed his cheek lightly with her dark red lips, and his nostrils were suffused with a variety of scents—soap, powder, toothpaste, lipstick, cologne. The apartment, as he followed her inside, smelled of nail lacquer and new luggage.

" My God," he said, looking at her. " Is all this just for me? " He gestured at his own clothes. " I'm ashamed to be seen with you. This suit is three years old."

Claire laughed. " Oh, I just thought it would be fun to dress up. I've been so darn bored all day——"

The apartment looked immaculate and spacious. On the low tables, lamps sent out wide round pools of light. In one of these, Jimmy saw a stack of brown cowhide suitcases in graduated sizes, from a vast wardrobe case down to a small overnight case. "Taking a trip?" he asked.

"Of course not—those are for you. Take your pick. I have a reservation for you at the Clift."

He looked at the luggage, amused. "You went out to Malm's and bought it, didn't you? Just for me!"

"It looks that way, doesn't it? It's my wedding present to Blazer. His own luggage was a disgrace. But he won't use any of this. When he travels, he still takes that disreputable Val-Pak!"

"I think I'll check in with all of it," Jimmy said. He picked up the largest suitcase. It rattled with empty wooden hangers.

"Can I fix you a drink?" Claire said. "Scotch?" She moved behind the small bar.

"Let me," Jimmy said.

"I'll mix the first and you can mix the second," Claire said. Jimmy heard the rattle of ice-cubes and the clink of bottles.

He set the suitcase down. "We'd better go soon if we're to find any place open," he said.

"Oh, no hurry."

Claire crossed the room, carrying two brown drinks in low, fat Mexican glasses. Jimmy took one. "To you," he said.

"No, to you," Claire said.

They touched glasses. Jimmy looked into Claire's eyes. She smiled brightly. They sat on the low white sofa.

"God, this is a terrific apartment," Jimmy said. The drapes were pulled wide open all around the room. In the black glass, the room was reflected back at them, and, beyond it, the lights of the city sparkled and shone—hill after hill. On the two great bridges, the sulphur lights created double strands of orange beads. "The city of gold," he said.

"Does it unnerve you?" Claire asked. "Shall I close the curtains? It unnerves me sometimes."

"No, I like it," Jimmy said.

"Sometimes there's such a thing as too much view," Claire said. "When I'm up here alone, I get to feeling uneasy—naked and self-conscious. I realize it's the view that's doing it. The people downstairs did a clever thing—they enclosed a whole room with redwood, so they'd have a place to go and get away from the view!"

"Well, it's a pretty place to live."

" Yes, I suppose so."

They sat in silence for a moment. Jimmy sipped his drink. " Where did Blaze go? " he asked.

" Oh, off on one of his wretched trips. Selling sheets! He went to Los Angeles. How he hates it."

" Does he hate it? "

" Oh, I don't know," Claire sighed. " I guess I just wish he hated it. I guess he likes it all right, actually. It's a good job."

" Oh, I know that." He paused. " Well, why did you want me to come? " he said. " You said on the phone that it was important."

She hesitated. " Well," she said, " it was important. I was just lonesome. I was going view-crazy. I wanted to hear a friendly voice. It was like when you phoned Jeep Tanner—I wanted to bend a sympathetic ear."

" Well," Jimmy smiled, " that's me. Father Confessor Keefe. Bend away."

" Oh, don't make me talk," Claire said. " You talk."

" Me? What shall I talk about? "

" Well——" They were silent. Then they both laughed.

" Here," Claire said, handing him her glass. " Stiffen my drink, will you? That will loosen our tongues."

Jimmy rose and went to the bar, carrying their glasses. As he splashed whisky on top of the drinks, Claire slipped off her shoes, raised her feet, and tucked them beneath her on the sofa. " Did you ever meet Diane Higbee? " she asked.

" Blonde? "

" No, brunette."

" Fairly tall? "

" No. Short. You didn't know her. Well, she may be coming through town."

" Oh? "

" No special reason. She's quite cute and fun. If she comes, I thought you might like to meet her."

" Could be," Jimmy said noncommittally. He returned, carrying the drinks. " Skoal," he said.

" Skoal." She sipped. " Ah, much better."

" Has Blazer forgiven me about last week-end? " Jimmy asked.

" Forgiven you? Why should he forgive you? "

"For getting stewed—up there on the mountain."

"Oh, heavens, Blazer didn't mind. You know Blazer—I think he thought it was kind of funny, actually. As long as he didn't have to carry you down or anything."

"Well, I'm sorry," Jimmy said.

"You were fine. You were perfectly fine. It was only—well, it upset me a little."

"I'm sorry."

"You—you get stewed so quietly. So privately. That's what worries me. I'd enjoy it much more if you got roaring drunk and smashed up furniture, I think."

"Would you?"

Claire laughed. "I remember one time," she said. "I remember one funny, funny time. Do you remember the time——" She laughed again, remembering it. "Remember? It was when we were all in college. We went down to New York, you and Blazer and I—and Lucy somebody was your date—such a prim little thing in a Peter Pan collar. And we went way down around Delancey Street. Remember?"

"Oh, yes. Lucy Simms."

"Simms! Yes—and do you remember the drunk sailor?"

"Oh, yes . . ."

"The Shore Patrol came along and picked him up in the paddy wagon, remember? They tossed him in the back, closed the door, and went around to the front of the truck. And you"—she laughed—"you simply went over, opened the back of the paddy wagon, and let him out! He tipped his cap, said thank you, and went reeling off. The paddy wagon started up and went barreling away without him!" She laughed a long, giggly, tinkly laugh and lay back against the cushions. "Oh, that was funny," she said mistily.

"Just tipped his hat and said thank you—I remember," Jimmy said.

"Blazer and I are having a party next Saturday," Claire said. "Can you come?"

"Hey," he said, "don't you think these week-ends with me hanging around might be getting to be too much of a regular thing?"

"Don't be silly," she said, sitting up. "If they were, we'd tell you. I'd tell you. Can you come down?"

"Sure," he said. "You know me—my social calendar is empty all the time."

"Good," she said. "I'm having Sue and Alec Fry, the Browers, Arnold Williams plus date, Tweetums DeMay plus date——"

"Ye gods," he said. "Tweetums DeMay!"

"Oh, I know," Claire said. "She's a funny old thing, but she's got a heart as big as a mountain. She always fits right in."

"How old do you guess she is? Forty?"

"Oh, at *least*!" Claire said.

"It strikes me kind of odd," Jimmy said. "A woman that age—running around with people so much younger . . ."

"I think it's kind of sad. She's divorced—she's lost. She's like so many——" She stopped short. "Present company excepted," she said. "Your case is different."

"Ha!" he said. He swirled the ice-cubes in his glass and looked down.

"Those men Tweetums brings!" Claire said. "I don't know where she finds them."

"I know," Jimmy said. "She finds them at the Mare Island Naval Training Station. Anything from an ensign up."

"Yes, and at Jim Dolan's."

"What's that?"

"Jim Dolan's? That's that creepy, crawly place on Sutter. Haven't you ever heard of that? It's a hangout for queers."

"Oh."

"Tweetums took Blazer and me there one night. Brrr!" She shivered. "Jimmy," she said suddenly, "what do queers *do*?"

He laughed. "What do you mean?"

"I mean, what do they *do*? You know."

"Use your imagination," he said.

"I have—I often have. I can't imagine."

"Well, ask Blazer——"

"I did. Blazer just laughed at me!"

"Well, read Krafft-Ebing."

"Oh, I've read that. All the good parts are in German . . . or is it Latin?"

Jimmy looked at his watch. "Look," he said, "it's nearly ten. Don't you think we ought to be going?"

" Oh, there's no hurry, is there? " Claire said. " It's Saturday night—places stay open. Fix me another drink."

Later, as they talked, Claire rested her shoeless feet on the marble top of the coffee table. She had placed a glass ash-tray on her stomach, into which she periodically tapped her cigarette. Jimmy lay back into the cushions, legs crossed at the ankles, feet out, with a drink in his hand. Claire had placed a Harry Belafonte record on the phonograph.

I peeked in to say good night,
And I heard my child in prayer—
' And for me, some scarlet ribbons—
Scarlet ribbons for my hair.'

Claire put her head back, listening to it. They were talking about places where they would like to live. " Anywhere but Somerville," Jimmy said.

" Arizona——" Claire said. " I'd like to live in Arizona. In the winter, anyway. The desert in bloom! Century plants . . . pipe-organ cactus . . ."

" Yes," Jimmy said. " That's nice—or Colorado . . ."

" Too wild, too many mountains. How about Santa Fe, or Taos? There you can have mountains and desert, too. I think I like the South-west. The air is so clear! It's so clear it has a colour to it—a brilliant purple colour! "

" I'd like to live by the sea," Jimmy said. " Would you ever like to live in Italy? "

" Oh, Italy . . . of course. I'd love to live in Italy! Portofino . . . or Spain? Along the Costa Brava! "

" I've never been there . . ."

" Estoril . . . Portugal. The sea is green . . ."

" Or the Vale of Kashmir," Jimmy said.

Claire laughed softly. " The snows come so early in Srinagar," she said. " ' Pale hands I loved beside the Shalimar——' " She extended the fingers of her right hand in demonstration.

" There you could live on a house-boat, floating in the lotus blossoms . . ."

" I could take that," Claire said. " That I could take, as they say in California."

" Or how about Tahiti? "

" Tahiti I would absolutely adore," she said. " Let's go. I want to go where the wild goose goes."

He smiled at her. " Why? "

" Because," she said softly, picking up her glass and stroking its frosted side with the tip of her finger, " because my heart knows what the wild goose knows." She looked at the glass, frowned at it intently.

" Which is? "

" Ah! " She put her feet on the floor and stood up a little unsteadily. " Do you mind if I close the curtains? " she said. " I've had enough view, haven't you? " She went around the room, pulling the cords and closing the heavy white drapes silently across the windows.

" That's cosy," Jimmy said. And the closed curtains made the sound of his voice quiet and muffled. It drew everything, suddenly, inside the room. " Hey! " He laughed nervously. " Hey, speak up. I can't hear you."

Claire padded silently across the room to him. " Fix my drink," she said.

" Look," he said, " it's after eleven. Don't you honestly think we'd better eat? "

" I have an idea," Claire said. " Let's eat here. I'll fix something."

" That doesn't seem fair," Jimmy said. " I promised you a dinner."

" Oh, let's just stay here," Claire said. " Fix me a drink and leave me alone in the kitchen for a minute."

Later, she came out with a tray of sandwiches. " Scrambled egg," she said, placing the tray on the coffee table.

" There's something wrong with this picture," Jimmy said. " A glamorous apartment—a beautiful girl—and scrambled-egg sandwiches! "

" Oh? Do you really think I'm beautiful? "

" Sure," he said cheerfully. " Of course I think so. So do you."

She pouted. " You're mean," she said. She sat down beside him on the sofa. They ate in silence. Claire finished a sandwich and licked her fingers. " Isn't this better than the India House? " she said.

" Sure is." Jimmy glanced at his watch again. " God," he

said, " it's after midnight. I've got to get over to the Clift or they won't hold a room."

" Oh, don't go yet."

" Well—don't you think I'd better phone? "

" No, they'll hold it—I told them you'd be in late."

" Well, I've got to go soon," he said.

" Oh, no—don't."

Jimmy glanced at her. She sat looking straight ahead at the opposite wall. He looked away. The air was suddenly tense and charged between them. " What do you mean? " he said slowly.

Up to that point, Claire had not actually decided whether or not to tell Jimmy about her trip to Rio Linda. In her mind, she had run the gamut between not telling him at all and blurting the whole story out, rehearsing all the gentle, graceful ways of telling him in between. When he said, " What do you mean? " that way, in that tight, strained voice, she had decided instantly to tell him—gently, gracefully, which ever way it came out. She had to tell him, she figured, if the thing she had done were ever to make any sense, or have any meaning or purpose. To justify what she had done—to justify it to herself—she felt she had to tell him.

" Because I haven't finished telling you what I want to tell you," she answered him.

" What? "

" Jimmy," she said, " I've been thinking about you and Helen. It was all pretty dreadful, wasn't it? "

He paused. " Well——" he began, trying to make his tone sound cheerful and easy.

" I mean, there weren't *any* happy times, were there? "

" Oh, sure," he said. " Sure there were happy times."

" When? "

" Well," he said, " right after we were married, for example. You know we were married two times—once by a justice of the peace in Nevada, and then a church wedding. In between those times, we were off on our own—in the car—for about a week, just driving around. We went to Yosemite—and, well, that was a happy time."

" And after that? "

" Well, after that—you know, my folks got into the act. They made us get married all over again, and my mother—she sent us on a damned trip to the Caribbean. And—well, everything got all loused up."

" You're not telling me everything."

" No," he said openly, " I'm not."

" I don't mean that you should," she said hastily. " But what I mean is—your marriage, *most* of it was pretty unhappy, wasn't it? "

" Yes," he said. " But why? Why the third degree? "

" Because I think you're still carrying the torch for Helen! "

He shrugged. " Well, perhaps——"

" I think you should say the hell with her! "

" Hey," he said. " Come on. Lay off, will you? Let me ——"

" I saw her to-day! "

" What? What did you say? "

" I went to see her to-day."

He stood up abruptly. " What? " he said. " What in Christ's name are you talking about, Claire? " His hands shook.

" I went to Rio Linda . . ."

" God damn it! " he shouted at her. " Can't you keep your lousy nose out of anybody's business? Who the hell do you think you are—God? "

" Jimmy, please——"

" Look," he said. " You mentioned that last week—you asked me if I wanted you to go. And what did I say? I said no, didn't I? Damn it, Claire, if I ever need your help, I'll sure as hell ask you for it! And I won't ask you to go snivelling around like a God-damned sob-sister newspaper reporter or something, digging up smut and patching up people's lives. Leave me alone! "

" Jimmy, Jimmy! " she cried. " I didn't mean to make you angry! Please, please, Jimmy! I know it was wrong—I only wanted to help! " She looked up at him. There were tears in her eyes.

He looked at her for a moment, then turned away. " I'm sorry," he muttered. He walked to the bar, splashed whisky in a glass, and drank it down. " I'm sorry. What's done is done. What did she have to say? "

Claire fell forward on the sofa, her head buried in her hands and her shoulders shaking. " She's pregnant," she sobbed.

" What? " he said softly. He went to the sofa and sat down beside her. " What did you say? "

" She's pregnant! "

" Oh, no——"

" Yes, yes, yes! " Claire sobbed into the pillow. " Yes! Oh, Jimmy! She's a dreadful girl—I think! She doesn't deserve you! She's going to have a baby, and she doesn't plan to tell you, or let you have any part, or even be *considered* in it—or——"

" Hush, hush," he whispered.

" What kind of a woman would do that? What kind of a cold, unfeeling woman? " She sat up, her face streaked with tears, her mascara blurred. " Jimmy," she said, " let her go! Let her go, darling! Don't let her blight your life! Let her go —in your mind! You're too good for her, Jimmy—to let her destroy you! "

He put his head in his hands. " Hush—let me think——"

She put her hands on his shoulder. " Look at me! Jimmy, please look at me! Bury her! "

He looked at her. His mind reeled. Suddenly he was kissing her, deeply and hungrily, and she lay back beneath him on the sofa, her fingers gripping his arms. She whispered, " Oh, God! Oh, my God! Oh, darling! Darling—for ever——"

He half lifted her from the sofa. Her bare foot swung, striking her glass on the coffee table. The glass shattered, the contents spilling, spreading a dark stain across the polished floor. " Oh, God forgive us! " Claire said, as he carried her towards the bedroom.

10

THAT evening Blazer Gates returned to his room at the Ambassador Hotel fairly early. The kick-off meeting of the sales convention had been a success—he guessed so, anyway. As much of a success as those things ever were. The convention had been badly time-tabled, that was the main thing. Kicking off on a Saturday like that, with an empty day Sunday with not a damn' thing to do, well—it seemed like a lot of wasted time. The delegates would find plenty to do on Sunday, of course. By five o'clock in the afternoon the upper floors of the hotel would be clattering with cocktail parties. Movie starlets, so called, would be in giggling profusion and a large amount of cheap glassware would end up smashed on the floor or dropped from open window-sills into courtyards and light wells. Delegates, lipstick-smeared and wearing their plastic-coated convention badges, would charge out of the hotel in the early evening to investigate Olivera Street, Skid Row, or the glossier spots along the strip. Blazer had turned down three invitations to cocktail parties and one invitation to join a bus tour of the movie stars' homes. He didn't know why he turned them down; he wasn't trying to act superior to these people. He just didn't want to go. He planned to stay in his room on Sunday, and loll around and read.

He unlocked the door to his room, went in, flipped on the light, and hung his coat over the back of a chair. He turned, loosening his necktie, towards the closet, and noticed that there was a message envelope under his door. He stooped, picked it up, and tore it open. It said, "Please call Operator 60 in Somerville, Conn."

Blazer looked at his watch. It was now nine o'clock; it would be three hours later in Connecticut. But, well, it might be important. And who could it be? Who, at home, knew he was in Los Angeles? As far as he knew, Claire was the only one who knew where he was. But possibly whoever it was had called Claire first and got the information. He sat down on the bed, picked up the phone, and placed the call. He lighted a cigarette with his free hand.

Finally, at the other end of the connection, he heard a woman's husky, cultured voice say, " Hello? Hello? Hello? "

" Hello," Blazer said. " Who's this? "

" Hello? "

" Hello! " he shouted. " Who's this? "

" Blazer! It's Mrs. Denison! How are you, dear? "

" Fine, fine," he said. " How're you? "

" What, dear? I can't hear you! This is a terrible connection."

" Fine," he yelled. " I'm fine! How are you? "

" How's Claire-y? "

" Fine. How did you know where I was? "

" What? "

" How did you know where I was? "

" How's Claire-y, I asked."

" Fine," he roared. " Hey, let me see if I can get us a better——"

" Ju wants to talk to you. Hold on," Mrs. Denison said.

Junius Denison's voice boomed across the continent. " Can you hear me, Blaze? " it roared.

" Yes," Blazer said. " How're you, Pop? "

" Fine. Fine. What's new, Blaze? "

" Not much," Blazer said, and he added inanely: " What's new with you? "

" Oh, the same old treadmill, the same old treadmill," Mr. Denison said.

" Say, how'd you know I was down here? " Blazer asked.

" Had a letter from Claire. She said you'd be in the City of the Angels this week-end, and I figured you'd be at the ' Bass. First place I tried, anyway. Say," he said, " speaking of angels, you don't have any little angels in your room right now, do you? Eh? " He chuckled loudly. " Do you? "

Blazer laughed. " No, Pop," he said. " No little angels."

" Say, Blazer," Mr. Denison said, " the real reason I called —you ever bump into Harry Masterson out there? "

" No," Blazer said. " Can't say as I have."

" Ever hear of him? "

" No——"

" Well, Harry's an old friend of mine. Harry and I were in the Navy together, back in the dim, dark days beyond recall. He's with Monarch Mills now—president."

" Masterson, eh? "

" Yes. Well, Blaze, the reason I wanted to get you to-night was that Harry's in Los Angeles right now. Could be he's there for the same shindig you're at. I dunno—but what I thought I'd do, Blaze, was give Harry Masterson a buzz and see if he wouldn't like to get together with you. Maybe you two could have a little talk. Harry's been in that business of yours for a long time. You never can tell, Blaze, he might be able to give you a couple of good steers."

" Say, that would be swell," Blazer said. " I'd appreciate that."

" Well, then, I tell you what I'll do. I'll call Harry Masterson right now. Or, no, let's see—is it earlier or later out there, I never can remember? "

" It's earlier here—about nine-fifteen."

" Well, I'll give him a call—ask him to get in touch with you in the morning. He's at the Bel Air—they told me that yesterday at his office."

" I'd appreciate that," Blazer said. " Monarch Mills is a pretty big outfit."

" Yeah—well, I thought I'd just see how you felt about it, Blaze, before I did anything. Wouldn't want to do anything behind your back, you know—or make you think I was butting in or anything like that."

" Heck, no," Blazer said. " I appreciate your consideration —it was darned thoughtful of you, Pop."

" Well, I keep my ears open for you, Blaze. You know that. How's Claire-y? "

" Oh, she's just fine," Blazer said. " She's got a job."

" Yeah—so she wrote her mother. Well, she'll get over that. You know how these women are, Blaze—always feel that they've got to be doing something." He laughed. " Well, take care, boy. And, oh, before I forget, Claire mentioned that you two have been seeing quite a bit of Jim Keefe's boy, Jimmy."

"That's right," Blazer said, "he's been down a few times."

"How's he doing?"

"Fine, I think," Blazer said. "He's doing some kind of publicity work up in Sacramento."

"Oh? Well, I ran into his dad the other day at the club. He was a little worried. That girl he married, you know—I guess they've split up."

"Yes, that's right," Blazer said. "But I think he's taking it pretty well."

"Oh, that's good. He's a good boy. I'll tell Jim Keefe when I see him. He'll be pleased to hear. Well, good night, Blaze."

"Good night, Pop—take it easy."

"Good night."

Blazer replaced the telephone. Unbuttoning his shirt, he stood up and wandered across the room to the writing-desk. He pulled open the desk drawer, pulled out a sheet of hotel stationery and a pencil. He wrote "Harry Masterson" in big block letters on the paper, and placed the paper under the telephone by his bed. It was damned decent of Claire's old man to be on the lookout for him like that, he thought. Claire thought he was a pompous old fool, and, hell, maybe he was a little on the pompous side, but he had sure been nice to them. This Masterson thing, for instance—that was typical of the kind of thing Claire's old man would do. Monarch Mills was an important outfit. Masterson was president. That was the kind of contact you couldn't make every day of the week.

Blazer took off his shirt, wadded it up, and tossed it into the corner of his Val-Pak. He yawned. He was dog-tired. It would do him good to get to bed early. He would read himself to sleep.

He finished undressing, turned on the lamp by the bed, crossed the room, and turned out the overhead light. He returned to the bed, pulled down the covers, and crawled in. From above and below, in the hotel, he could hear muffled party sounds; the delegates to the convention were beginning the week-end in typical style. Blazer picked up his book and started to read.

Blazer was reading *Death in the Afternoon*, and enjoying it immensely. Blazer was fascinated by bullfights, the history of bullfighting, and the biographies of the matadors. In the clash of *el torero* against *el toro*, Blazer saw symbolized man's eternal conflict against the bestiality in his own soul. In the orgiastic " moment of truth " with the sword, he saw a deeper, more poignant meaning. He had seen bullfights in Mexico; they had excited and disturbed him.

But to-night Blazer's thoughts strayed from the book. He began thinking about Claire, and then about Jimmy. He thought of the week-end on the mountain. He had lied to Claire's father, telling him that he thought Jimmy was bearing up well in the business with Helen. Jimmy had acted like an ass up there on the mountain, getting silly-drunk. He didn't enjoy seeing people act that way, especially Jimmy. He thought of the three of them, up there.

There was this about Blazer. He was not a homosexual, certainly. In fact, the thought—anything connected with the thought—disgusted him, sickened him almost physically, revolted him to a degree that another person might have thought was unwarranted. And yet Blazer had a recurring fantasy, a fantasy of violence and aggression. He had experienced it in college, and even before; it was inevitably a fantasy of three. Three people—himself, a girl, and another man. It lurked so far back in his mind that he was seldom consciously aware of it, but sometimes it emerged, like now, and became hauntingly real. In college, it had sometimes involved Jimmy, since Jimmy was his room-mate—but it was not always Jimmy. Sometimes his co-assailant was a faceless man, a private creation of his own. Lately, however, with Jimmy around a good deal of the time—and Blazer wanted him around, there was no question about that—it was always Jimmy. Jimmy, himself, and Claire. In actual detail, the dream could become as elaborate as he cared to make it. It came now, and he stood back from it and watched it; it stopped, then came closer. It came and fluttered all around the edges of his eyes. He turned off the light and retreated into it.

He began a curious tap-tapping with his foot, his right foot moving in a rapid, steady rhythm. It was a habit, a carry-over from the cradle when he had jogged himself to sleep that way.

It was a conscious habit; it was a childish one, he knew. He knew it was probably not common in people of his age. But then he knew that he was not precisely like other men his age.

It annoyed Claire. Sometimes, in the night, she would struggle awake and kick him sharply to make him stop the tapping. But to-night he was all alone.

II

In her bedroom in Rio Linda, Helen Keefe was getting ready for bed. She sat at her dressing-table in a pair of light blue pyjamas, putting her short brown hair into a series of small, fat pin-curls. She stopped from time to time, lowered her hands and studied her reflection in the mirror. Then she continued, slowly twisting a strand of hair around her finger, holding it tight, and securing it with a pin, pressing the ends flat. Her room was on the south side of the house, and now—it was nearly ten o'clock—the day had cooled, and a breeze came in through her open window, stirring the curtains, bringing with it the sounds of the town celebrating Saturday night. She could hear radios from open convertibles as they passed by slowly on the street below, and down the street, in the park, she could hear music from the open-air band concert. The band was playing a medley of Sousa marches. Presently there was a soft knock at her door.

" Yes? "

Her mother opened the door and stepped inside. " Going to bed now, dear? " Mrs. Warren asked.

" Yes. I'm a little tired." Helen continued to look straight into the mirror. Mrs. Warren moved towards the bed and began turning it down. She removed the quilted coverlet, folded it carefully, and placed it over the back of the chair. Then she turned down the sheet in a neat triangle.

" You don't have to do that," Helen said pleasantly.

" Oh, I don't mind," Mrs. Warren said. She turned and studied her daughter. " Helen," she asked finally, " is everything all right? "

" What do you mean? "

" I mean do you feel all right? Are you worried about something? "

" No, not at all."

" You seem so—sort of withdrawn, dear. You've hardly said a word to me all day."

Helen laughed softly.

Mrs. Warren sat down on a corner of the bed. " Helen," she said, " I don't want to poke and pry. I thought possibly you might tell me yourself——"

" What, Mother? "

" Well, it may be none of my business—but I naturally *care*, dear. I have a natural interest in you, and seeing to it that you're happy."

" What in the world are you driving at? " She finished the last pin-curl and turned on the stool to face her. Her expression was amused.

Mrs. Warren fidgeted with a corner of the sheet. " Well, that girl who came to-day," she said. " I thought you might explain to me—what it was about——"

" Oh, that! " said Helen.

" Yes. Who was she, Helen? Don't you want to tell me? "

" Of course! I meant to tell you. I guess—well, I guess it must have slipped my mind. She's a friend of Jimmy's."

" Oh! " Mrs. Warren sighed deeply. " Oh! That's exactly what I thought."

" What? What did you think? "

" She's his—his new flame, I suppose? "

" Oh, goodness no! No, not that at all." She laughed again. " No wonder you were upset! No, she's the wife of his old roommate from college."

" But why in the world——"

" She came to state Jimmy's case. I guess that was the purpose of it. Jimmy may have sent her, I don't know. She insisted he knew nothing about it."

" What do you mean, state his case? "

" She thinks we should go back together again," Helen said simply.

" Oh? What did you tell her? "

" That it was out of the question."

" What an extraordinary thing," Mrs. Warren said. " What an extraordinary thing for someone to do! "

" Well, I guess he's an old friend of theirs."

" I know—but imagine interfering with someone's private

life like that! It seems extraordinary. She was an extraordinary-*looking* girl, didn't you think? That blonde hair . . ."

"Yes."

"Well, I'm glad it wasn't—the other thing. You know—some girl of his coming to talk terms with you! That would have been dreadful."

"No, I guess there isn't any other girl."

"Helen, you—you haven't been in contact with him, have you? Since you left, I mean?"

"No, you know that."

"It is still the only thing, isn't it? A divorce, I mean?"

"Yes, I'm afraid so, Mother."

"Of course," Mrs. Warren said, "I don't really know what the trouble was—I don't want to know. You've told me only a little, about all the drinking and his immaturity, but I trust your judgment. I'm sure you know what you're doing, dear, and if this is the only thing——"

"It is."

"It saddens me to have a divorce in the family, you know. Sometimes—well, sometimes I think we've had more than our share of unhappiness. Losing your father—everything. And of course I remember how dreadfully he behaved when your father died. Oh, I relive that terrible night in nightmares, sometimes!"

Helen turned back to the dressing-table. She arranged her comb, brush, and mirror on the glass-covered top. She reached for her cold-cream jar, opened it, and began slowly to cream her face with her slim brown fingertips. "Mother," she said after a moment, "do you have plenty of money?"

"What do you mean, dear?"

"You haven't really told me. Did Daddy leave you—you know, money enough to get along on?"

Mrs. Warren hesitated. "Yes," she said, "your father left me in comfortable circumstances. I'm not a wealthy widow, of course, but if I'm careful, I'll have plenty to take care of all my needs."

"I feel I'm such a burden," Helen said. "Just coming home like this—to live off you."

"Now, Helen, don't talk that way. You're not a burden—not in the slightest. You know that, dear. You mustn't think about it."

" I'm wondering if I should sue for alimony——"

" Nonsense! We don't need their money," Mrs. Warren said angrily. " Just make a clean break of it. Alimony would be just another way he could have a hold over you. We certainly don't need any of that."

" I may have to," Helen said quietly.

" What do you mean? Have to what? "

" Have to ask for alimony."

" Why, for heaven's sake? "

" Well—there's going to be another of us, Mother." Helen turned and faced her mother.

" What? What do you mean? "

" I'm going to have a baby."

Mrs. Warren was silent. Then she said, " No, no, that's not possible."

" It is, Mother."

" It isn't! It can't be! "

" I wish it weren't, for your sake, Mother."

" Oh, my God! " Mrs. Warren whispered. " Oh, my God." She buried her head in her hands.

Helen rose quickly and crossed the room to where her mother sat. She stood over her and put her hand on her mother's shaking shoulders. " Mother, Mother, please! " she said. " It isn't so terrible, is it? Is it? I'm not the first girl in the world to have a baby, am I? "

" Oh, it is! " Mrs. Warren sobbed. " It's terrible! Dreadful! "

" Why? Why is it? "

Mrs. Warren looked up at her. " Are you sure? Are you absolutely sure? "

" Yes."

" When? "

" Around the first of November."

" Oh! " Mrs. Warren clutched Helen's arm and pulled her down beside her on the bed. " Oh, my poor little girl! My poor baby! What are we going to do? "

Helen's voice was patient, gentle. " There, there," she repeated. " It isn't so terrible—it doesn't seem so to me! Oh, I was frightened at first. At first—when I first suspected—I felt the way you do. But when I thought about it, gradually it began to seem—well, different. It began to seem all very smooth and simple, and rather glorious! Do you know what I mean, Mother? I mean, sometimes, before—with Jimmy—I used to feel rather futile, as though my life didn't have any meaning or any purpose or function. But now—now it's as though I've been given this wonderful opportunity—to do something completely by myself."

"But his child!" Mrs. Warren said angrily. "How can you bear it?"

"It will be my child, too!"

"But *him*! Such a—a wastrel! A good-for-nothing——"

"No, no," Helen said softly. "That's not fair."

"What do you mean? He's a bum! You said so yourself!" Mrs. Warren's voice was shrill.

"Jimmy isn't *bad*!" Helen said. "He's—well, he's mixed up, maybe—and there was nothing for us, nothing at all, but he's not *bad*."

"I don't understand you! I simply don't!"

"I've had a lot of time to think about it," Helen said. "We were wrong for each other—but that may have been my fault, too."

"I won't listen to you trying to blame yourself for his shortcomings!"

"Look, Mother," Helen said softly, "I have to think like this. Don't you see? If I didn't—well, I just don't know what I would do. I have to reconcile everything in my mind now, and try to work things out on my own. I'm going to get my divorce and have my baby—and behave like a big girl!"

"I think you're insane," Mrs. Warren said. "I've never heard anyone talk like this. How are you going to tell him about it?"

"I don't know. I don't know yet. I'll have to tell him, of course."

Mrs. Warren stood up abruptly. "I've got to lie down," she said. "I've got to think. This is like a bad dream. I can't believe it—any of it."

"Please, Mother," Helen said. "Please let me handle it. I want to."

"Let's talk about it in the morning," Mrs. Warren said.

"I have a headache. I can't think——" She walked rapidly to the door.

"I really don't see why you should be angry with me."

"We've always been able to hold our heads up in this town," Mrs. Warren said despairingly. "Always! And now this has to happen, on top of everything else! What in the world have I done to deserve it!" Her voice broke. "Good night." She opened the door quickly and stepped out, closing it sharply behind her.

Helen stood alone in the centre of the room. After several moments, she went back to her dressing-table, sat down, and reached for the jar of cold-cream once more. Slowly, with her fingers, she pressed the pale, cool cream into her skin, along her cheeks, her forehead. Then, with both hands, she blended the cream, smoothed it under her eyes, along her throat. "I want to be a big girl," she whispered once, softly.

And then, as though the sound of her voice had touched a chord within her, or had reminded her of some inner dread, her hands began to tremble. She moved her face closer to the mirror and looked. Her reflection—hair in flat curls, her skin shining grotesquely—seemed unfamiliar, a weirdly grimacing mask that mocked and rebuked her. "You heartless bitch!" she whispered, and, as her hands continued to tremble uncontrollably, she clutched her throat as if to stifle a scream. Then she put her head flat down on the cool glass surface of the dressing-table. "Oh, dear God in heaven!" she prayed. "Dear God in heaven! Give me the strength, the strength, the strength!" She lay still for some time. Then the trembling seemed to stop. Her face, when she looked at it again, was wet with tears.

All at once, she stood up. She went to her closet and removed her robe from the hook and slipped it on. She went out of her room, across the hall, past her mother's closed door, and down the dark stairway. At the foot, she stopped. There was a telephone there, on a long cord. She picked it up and carried it into the dining-room—as far as the cord would reach. Then she picked up the receiver and placed the call.

When, after she had let the number ring for several minutes, there was no answer, she replaced the phone, almost with a sense of relief. She was not at all sure whether she would have had the courage to tell him, even to speak to him, if he had answered.

12

In the dark bedroom on Russian Hill, Jimmy Keefe sat on the low round ottoman next to the window. In an ash-tray on the table beside him, the end of his cigarette glowed. The curtains were closed; there was no other light in the room. Claire still lay on the bed opposite him. " Don't you want to turn on the light? " she asked him. He could feel her eyes, in the darkness, watching him.

" No, thanks," he said softly.

" Can you see? "

" Yes."

" Turn on the light, Jimmy."

" No, I can see fine. It's better in the dark."

" Jimmy? "

" What? "

" Nothing," she said. Then she said, " What time is it? "

" I don't know," he said. " Around three, I guess."

" Jimmy," she said, " I'll ask you once more. Don't go."

" Yes, I've got to."

" Why? Why do you have to? "

" I just do," he said. " It's better this way. Going in the night. I don't know why——"

" Jimmy," she said softly, " please. Please don't feel ashamed."

" God, I don't know what I feel," he said.

" Jimmy," she said urgently, " please listen to me. It was wonderful. That's absolutely all. Wonderful. One of the most wonderful things that's ever happened to me. That's all it was."

" Ah," he said.

" Don't feel guilty. Please don't."

" I said before—I don't know what I feel."

" I know what you feel," she said. " You have this loyalty. To Blazer. And Helen. You think you've betrayed them! "

" Haven't I ? "

" No."

" Oh, Claire," he said, " let's not talk about it. I've got to go."

" Don't you think I wanted it, darling? " she said. " Do you really think it was all your doing? Don't you think I've wanted it to happen all along? Planned it? Do you remember the night at the lake? "

" Yes."

" Even then. Even before. I don't remember when, exactly, it was that I knew it first. But it's been a long time. And I'm glad! I'm——"

" No, no——" he began. He heard the sheets rustle as she pulled herself up in bed and rested on her elbows, against the pillows.

" Yes," she said, " blame it on me if you must blame it on someone."

" I've got to go," he said, standing up.

" Light me a cigarette," she said. " Have a cigarette with me, at least, before you go."

He fished for the pack of cigarettes in his pocket, found it, and crossed the room. He handed one to her and fumbled with a match. He struck it, and in the sudden light he saw her face, very close, looking up at him. Her blue eyes looked black. She smiled, and laughed softly, taking his hand with the match and holding it to her cigarette. Then she blew out the match, but continued to hold his hand. " Darling," she said, " I don't feel guilty. Why should you? "

" My God, Claire, what are we going to do? "

" Do? Why do we have to *do* anything, for goodness' sake? "

" But look," he said, " there is such a thing as loyalty. And there is such a thing as honesty. My God, isn't there? "

" Of course," she said soothingly. She pulled him gently down to the bed beside her. " Sit here," she said. " Just sit here beside me for a minute before you go. I want you to."

His voice cracked. " I don't know," he said. " I just think this is the worst thing I've ever done in my life. The very worst."

" Guilt, guilt, guilt! " Claire said. " That's not very flattering to me, you know, to say that. When I just finished saying I thought it was all rather grand!"

"You and I are different, Claire," he said.

"No, we're not. We're exactly the same."

He was silent.

"Do you love me?" she asked finally. "Or do you love her—in spite of everything?"

"How can I answer that?"

"Just answer it!"

He stood up. "What difference does it make?" he asked. "What difference does it make at this point?"

Then it was Claire who was silent. "Well," she said after a moment, "I guess you'd better go."

"Yes." He went back to the ottoman where he had left his jacket, put the jacket on, and snuffed out his cigarette in the ash-tray. "I've got to figure this out," he said.

Claire's voice was almost angry. "Why? I don't see why, or what there is to figure out, Jimmy!"

"Well—what about Blazer, for instance? We've—I've—turned this into a real thing now. What are we going to do about him?"

"Nothing! We'll go on, just as always! Nothing's changed! Why should we revise our lives, just because you and I——"

"Look," he said. "Let's skip it! Just skip it!"

"I'm sorry," she whispered. "I didn't mean to get angry. All I want—is just for you to feel as clean and wonderful as I do."

"Well," he said, "I guess I'll have to try."

"Where are you going? To the Clift now?"

"No, I'm going home."

"Home? Back to Sacramento? It will be dawn before you get there."

"Probably, yes——"

"Why don't you stay at the Clift? To-morrow, you can take me to lunch."

He turned to her. "Claire," he said, "I don't know what's going to happen, I honestly don't. But I know one thing—I'm not going to see you again. Ever."

"But next Saturday," she whispered. "I'm having a party——"

"I won't be there."

" Oh, please! What will Blazer think? "

" Tell him whatever you want. Make up something."

" Oh, Jimmy! Please! "

" I'm sorry——"

" You're being a bastard! "

" I've already been, thanks."

" Stop it," she said angrily. " You have the most delightful knack of making me feel like a whore on Mission Street! Do you know that? "

" Again, I'm sorry." He went towards the door.

" Jimmy! " Her voice was commanding.

" What? "

" Do you——" Her voice softened. " Did you enjoy it at all? "

He paused, his hand on the door. " You know I did," he said. " But that doesn't make it any better. That makes it all the worse. Good night."

" Good night. And thank you."

He opened the door, and the light from the living-room flooded in. He didn't want to, but then did turn, briefly, and look at her. She sat on the bed, her bare shoulders hunched forward, her arms wrapped around her blanketed knees. She looked straight at him, seriously, thoughtfully. Her incredible hair fell long and loose about her arms and shoulders, across her breasts. He closed the door and stood for a moment in the living-room.

He saw the dark pool on the bare floor where the drink was spilled, and the pieces of green Mexican glass, and went over to it. He stooped and picked up the broken glass with his fingers, then mopped up the spilled liquor with his handkerchief. He carried the pieces of glass into the kitchen and placed them in the waste-basket. He rinsed his handkerchief at the sink, wrung it out, and stuffed the damp wad in the pocket of his suit. He turned out the kitchen light. In the living-room, he turned out lamps, one by one, as he went towards the door. Then he opened the door, pushed the lock, and went out, closing the door behind him. He went down the wide steps slowly, and out into the street.

When he got to his car, he saw a bright yellow parking ticket tucked behind the windshield wiper. He swore softly, under his breath, removed the ticket, placed it in his pocket, and unlocked the car.

Inside the car, he let the motor warm up for a while. The night was cool, but not cold. The air was clear, with the peculiar clean, salty pungency of San Francisco air. It made him feel clear-headed and refreshed, a good deal better. He started the car, drove to the corner, then slowly down the steep, winding twists of Lombard Street. He didn't know exactly where he was going. He turned and headed towards the centre of the city.

When he got to Market Street, he turned again, and headed south-west. The street was empty. The movie marquees were dark, the honky-tonk bars and amusement palaces were closed. A lonely, empty trolley clattered by.

He drove down Market, and soon he was climbing the road that crossed Twin Peaks, then down, and out along the wide boulevard past Stonestown, Park Merced, still heading south and towards the ocean.

When he got to Half Moon Bay, he drove a little way beyond the town and stopped the car. He looked at his watch; it was ten minutes past four. Behind him, a faint flush of dawn had begun to colour the sky. Below him, he could hear the Pacific crashing against the beach. He turned off his headlights and got out of the car. Beyond a short rise, he found a path leading steeply down towards the beach. He followed it down, and soon was on the sand. In front of him, the sea was black, but the crests of the combers glowed and glittered with sparks of phosphorescence before they broke, sped shimmering across the sand, pulled back with a deep sucking sound, and broke again. Suddenly, looking at this great dark sea, he remembered summers at Cape Cod, watching the sun rise. There, the sun rose out of the sea; here, it rose from across the mountains; the sun's rays touched the ocean last. He felt, all at once, unbelievably tired. He went back across the sand to a sheltered place against the rocks and sat down. Presently, he lay back, lacing his fingers together and resting the back of his head in his hands. Almost immediately, he was asleep.

When he awoke, the sun was shining brightly down on him from overhead. He stared at it briefly and blinked, trying to remember where he was. Then he remembered, and sat up. His head spun dizzily; his mouth was painfully parched and dry.

He rubbed his face with his hands, and his face was sticky with salt and sweat and rough with a stubble of beard. Like an absolute bum, he thought, just a bum sleeping on the beach. He stood up.

Then he kicked off his shoes, pulled off his socks, rolled up his trousers and walked down to the water. He waded into the surf, stooped and splashed handfuls of icy water into his face. He stood for a while, ankle-deep in the water. Then he noticed, also wading in the water, a figure moving towards him, along the edge of the surf. The man moved slowly, intent on the fishing line that floated a little way beyond him. Periodically, he stopped, reeled the line in, and, in a neat, clean arc, cast again, and moved on towards him. Jimmy watched him. He was young, about Jimmy's age or possibly younger, with a bright shock of orange-yellow hair and a wide sunburned face. He wore a pair of rolled-up khaki pants and a white T-shirt. He stopped, reeled in once more, made another long cast, and waited. He turned to Jimmy and waved. " No luck here to-day," he called.

" Yeah," Jimmy said.

The boy came closer and smiled a big, friendly grin. " Rough night? " he asked.

" That's right," Jimmy said dryly.

" I saw you there on the beach." The boy gestured with his head. " You were dead to the world."

" Ha! " Jimmy said, looking away.

" Is that your car up on the road? Green convertible? "

" Yes, it is."

Holding his rod in one hand, he reached deep in the pocket of his trousers. " I took your keys out," he said. " You know —you never can tell." He handed the keys to Jimmy. " I saw you down here and figured that was your car."

Jimmy looked at him. " Hey, thanks! " he said. " That was darned nice of you. Thanks a lot."

" Don't mention it." The other boy smiled.

" As you can probably guess, I didn't intend to sleep here on the beach," Jimmy said.

" Yeah—I guessed that."

Jimmy looked out across the water. " You catch much around here? " he asked.

" No, not a hell of a lot. Bass, sometimes, if you're lucky. Or yellowtail." He began reeling in his line once more.

" Say," Jimmy said, " you don't happen to have a container of water, do you? My mouth is like sandpaper——"

The boy grinned again. " No water," he said, " but I tell you what I do have—I have a couple of bottles of cream soda up on the beach. How about some cream soda? I know nobody likes cream soda but me."

" Cream soda sounds like nectar," Jimmy said. " Like the greatest thing on earth. May I? "

" Sure. Look "—he pointed—" there's my stuff—up there. Wrapped in my windbreaker. You'll find an opener there, too."

" You're saving my life," Jimmy said. " I hope you know that."

" Help yourself."

Jimmy waded out of the water and walked up across the sand. He found the blue windbreaker, unrolled it, and found two bottles of cream soda and the opener. He opened one bottle and rolled up the other again. He went back to where the other boy stood, taking deep, thirsty swigs on the bottle. " You don't know how good this tastes," he said.

" I bet it's kind of warm," the boy said, " but maybe it'll quench."

" Say," Jimmy said, holding out his hand, " I'm Jimmy Keefe. And I'm darned grateful to you."

" Mike Gorman," the boy said, shaking his hand.

" And I don't live on the beach, in case you wondered," Jimmy said. " I live in Sacramento."

" You're a long way from home," Mike Gorman said. " What are you doing here? "

" Oh, I was at a party in town last night," Jimmy said.

" Look," the other boy said, " it's almost noon. I'm not having any luck and you must be hungry. There's a place down the road. Want to grab a bite? "

" You've had a series of good ideas," Jimmy said. " I'd like that very much."

" Let's go," He began reeling in his line.

Together, they walked back across the beach. Jimmy stopped to put on his socks and shoes. Then they started up the path.

" This place isn't fancy, is it? " Jimmy asked. " I imagine I look a little disreputable."

" Just a hamburger joint."

They climbed up to the top of the bank, and Jimmy saw Mike's car, a battered red station wagon, parked close behind his own. " Hey! " Jimmy said. " What's this? New Hampshire plates? "

" Yes, I'm a long way from home, too," the boy said, grinning. " I'm from Portsmouth. I moved to San Francisco about a month ago."

" I'm from Connecticut," Jimmy said. " Somerville. Another Easterner, anyway."

" No kidding? Well, pleased to meet you again! " They shook hands once more, laughing. " You're looking at the world's lowest-paid banker," Mike said. " I came out here to take a job with the Bank of America. Banker, hell—I'm just a step above a messenger boy. What are you doing out here? "

" Same sort of thing," Jimmy said casually. " Job—public relations."

Mike Gorman tossed his fishing-rod in the back of his station wagon. " Look," he said, " I'll lead the way—I know where this place is."

" Fine," Jimmy said.

He got into his car and waited for the other boy to pull out ahead of him. After a series of coughs and roars, the red station wagon started. Jimmy followed it down the road for about a mile until they came to a small, shabby clapboard structure perched on the edge of a cliff above the sea. A sign in front of it said, simply, EAT. They pulled in beside each other and climbed out.

" This place doesn't look like much," Mike said, " but it has good hamburgers."

They walked inside and swung themselves up on two high stools. A counterman in shirt-sleeves and a greasy white apron came out from what was evidently the kitchen. " Hi, Mike," the man said good-naturedly.

" Hi, Al."

" What'll it be, Mike? The usual? "

" Yeah—two hamburgers, Al. And a bottle of cream soda." He turned to Jimmy, his wide face in a smile. " I'm sorry," he said, " but I've got this thing about cream soda. What'll you have? "

" I'll have two hamburgers, too," Jimmy said. " And coffee."

" How's business, Al? " Mike asked.

The counterman shrugged. " Tell you after the Fourth," he said. " Usually get a good crowd down here around the Fourth." He walked back into the kitchen.

Jimmy smiled. " I guess you come here often," he said.

" Yeah—quite a bit. Saturdays and Sundays. After fishing."

" You must like to fish."

The counterman arrived and placed Jimmy's steaming cup of coffee in front of him, then disappeared. Mike slid the sugar bowl towards him.

" Thanks," Jimmy said.

" Yes, I like to fish. New Englander in me I guess," Mike said. " There're three things I like to do: fish, ski—and you'll never guess what the third one is."

" What? "

" Play bridge. I'm nuts about bridge—a real bug on it." He turned to Jimmy. " Do you play bridge? "

" I've played some," Jimmy said. " But not for quite a while."

" I don't play for money, though," Mike said. " Just for the fun of it."

Presently the hamburgers arrived. The two of them sat forward, elbows on the counter, and began to eat. Jimmy realized that he had, indeed, been hungry. For no reason, he remembered Claire's scrambled-egg sandwiches last night; for a moment, his heart sank leadenly. Then he turned his mind back to the present. " Best hamburgers I ever ate," he said.

" Al does all right," Mike said.

They finished in silence, wiping their fingers.

" How do you like San Francisco? " Jimmy asked.

" I like it fine," Mike said. " I don't know whether I'd want to settle here, though. It's too early to say. Do you get down often? "

" Now and then," Jimmy said. " It's nice to get out of the valley this time of year."

" Look," Mike said suddenly, his sunburned face brightening, " what are you doing this afternoon? "

" I've got to get back," Jimmy said.

" I was thinking—if you like to play bridge, we could go back to my place. I can get us a third and fourth—guys from work that like to play."

" Well, thanks anyway," Jimmy said. " But I'd really better get back."

" Well, look," Mike said, " let's do it some time, okay? Come on down some time and I'll get a bunch together. How about it? "

" Sure, that might be fun," Jimmy said.

" I don't lead much of a social life," Mike said. " Can't afford it—I'm usually free. Say, how about next Saturday? "

" Saturday? " Jimmy weighed it. " Well," he said slowly, " sure. Sure—that would be fine. I'd like to."

" Great! " Mike said. He smiled a big, open smile. " You don't meet a fellow Easterner every day of the week, you know," he said. He reached in the pocket of his windbreaker and pulled out a stubby pencil. He scribbled an address and phone number on a paper napkin. " Here's where I live—down by the gas-works." He handed the paper to Jimmy. " Call me next Saturday when you get to town." Jimmy looked at the paper, folded it, and placed it in his pocket. Suddenly he sat back on his stool and laughed broadly. He continued to laugh, shaking his head back and forth, rocking his whole body on the stool. " Christ! " he said. " Oh, Christ! "

" What's so funny? "

" I don't know," Jimmy said, still laughing. " Christ, I don't know. It just seems funny, that's all. I just thought—Mike Gorman, Jim Keefe, a couple of Irishmen. I don't know why it's funny—meeting each other on the beach, I guess——"

Mike Gorman began to laugh, too. " Yeah," he said, " I see what you mean." He leaned forward, his hands wrapped around the soda bottle. They both laughed, their shoulders shaking.

" I don't know why it's so damn' funny," Jimmy said. " It just is."

Driving back across the Bay Bridge, in the slow, crowded week-end traffic lane, Jimmy still shook with small bursts of laughter. The afternoon was cool, balmy. In the rear-view mirror, the white crystalline city reflected clearly. Jimmy caught a glimpse of his own face. " I look like hell, but I feel great," he said. Ahead of him, in the afternoon sunlight, the white dots of houses caught the sun as they marched, tier on tier, up the Berkeley hills. It was a vision of gardens and green, sprinkled with jewel-like houses of white stucco and glass; he was swept with the sensation that he must hold his eyes on it, keep watching it, or else, in a moment, it would all disappear.

13

On the wide terrace beside the pool at the Bel Air Hotel, the sun filters through broad, drooping palmetto fronds on to the tops of umbrellas, on white-jacketed waiters, and flashes in the blue water. At the tables under the umbrellas, even though it is a Sunday, business is being conducted. A well-known producer sits with a well-known movie star whose hair is wrapped in a white silk scarf; the two of them sip tall pale-green drinks —grasshoppers. At another table, an actor, in swimming trunks and a boldly monogrammed terry robe, munches a sandwich as he reads a script that his agent has just handed him. A crimson-haired girl with a white sealyham on a leash stares boredly, through dark glasses, at her escort, a nobody like herself, who wears a crimson jacket to match her hair. Three television writers from New York spread out story boards in front of them, pass them back and forth; the story boards are commercials for a well-known tooth paste. A woman, older, in brilliant orange slacks, considered at the moment to be the wisest woman in Hollywood, tells the fortune of a budding starlet; she sorts the tarot cards in front of her. " I see happiness for you within a three, baby," she says, and the starlet looks at her with deep, grateful eyes. The white sealyham barks as a little boy—a little boy nobody knows—runs by. The air smells of alyssum, for there is an entire lawn planted with alyssum beyond the pool. All the sounds are glass-like; glasses chink at the tables. Even the conversation sounds like glass.

In this milieu, even Mr. Harry Masterson, president of Monarch Mills, a short, stout man in a vivid sport shirt, had no real confidence. He strutted importantly, nevertheless, as though he belonged there, reminding himself that he, too, had a house with a pool, though the house was not in Bel Air; it was in Scarsdale. He followed the head waiter across the terrace to a table beneath an umbrella and ordered a Scotch-and-soda in a commanding voice. He looked around, recognizing several celebrities instantly, and stared at them while pretending to stare through them. He crossed his feet, looked at his watch, and began an impatient tapping on the table-top with his fingertips; presently he saw a slim, curly-haired young man standing at the edge of the terrace, looking from table to table. The young man was dressed so differently from the others—in a dark grey worsted suit with a white shirt and striped tie—that Mr. Masterson knew instantly that this was Stuart Gates, Junius Denison's, son-in-law. He waved. The young man saw him, smiled and came towards him. Mr. Masterson rose. " Stuart? I'm Harry Masterson. Sit down, Stuart."

" Pleased to meet you, Mr. Masterson."

" I've ordered myself a drink, Stuart. Would you care for one? "

" Why sure, thanks. Scotch-and-soda."

" Just what I'm having. Waiter! Hey, waiter! Another Scotch-and-soda here."

" It certainly is a great pleasure to meet you, Mr. Masterson. I've heard a lot about you."

" Have you? Well, not all bad I hope. Ha ha. Well, Ju Denison's an old buddy of mine. We were in the Navy together."

" So I understand."

" A great fellow. A prince among men, Stuart. You're a lucky fellow to have a man like Ju for a father-in-law."

Following this exchange, there was a moment of silence. Blazer looked around. He'd certainly worn the wrong thing for a poolside conference, he decided. He felt hot and uncomfortable; even in the umbrella's shade, the day was hot. He looked back at Mr. Masterson. Mr. Masterson was frowning intently, waiting for his drink. Presently the drinks came. " Well, here's to you, son," Mr. Masterson said, lifting his glass.

" Thank you, sir."

Mr. Masterson sipped his drink. " Quite a few cuties here, eh? " He winked.

" Yes, sir, there certainly are."

" Notice that redhead over there? Now, who's she? I wonder. Ever seen her before? "

Blazer followed his glance. " No, I don't think I have," he said.

" Well, that's Hollywood for you," Mr. Masterson said. " That's really Hollywood for you. Lots of beautiful girls. How's your own bride, Stuart? "

" Claire's fine," Blazer said.

" Haven't seen her since she was yea high." Mr. Masterson lowered his palm towards the ground. " Yea high. Cute little yellow-haired kid."

Blazer smiled.

" So," Mr. Masterson said, " I understand you're in the soft-goods business, Stuart."

" That's right, sir. I'm with Norden-Clark. Sales."

" Norden-Clark, eh? That's a good outfit. Competitor of ours, of course, in certain areas. But, like I always say, Stuart, competition is a healthy thing. A very healthy thing."

" You're absolutely right."

Mr. Masterson sloshed his drink gently back and forth. His eyes narrowed as he looked across the table. " You know Bob Clark? " he asked.

" No, not personally. No," Blazer said. " I'm still in the lower echelon, you see."

" Well, Bob Clark's a funny fellow," he said. " A very funny fellow. I could tell you a few stories. Remind me to tell you of the time——" He broke off. " Well, that's water over the bridge. I mean under." He looked at Blazer suddenly. " How much do they pay you? " he asked.

Blazer hesitated. " Forty-eight hundred," he said.

Mr. Masterson studied him intently, saying nothing. Blazer gulped his drink. " Forty-eight hundred," Mr. Masterson repeated, finally. " Well. That's not a hell of a lot, is it? "

Blazer felt his face reddening. " I've only been with them seven months," he said.

" Young fellow like you ought to earn more than that," he said. " I'll tell you why I ask. How old are you? "

" Twenty-four," Blazer answered.

" No kids yet? "

" No." Blazer laughed nervously. " Not yet."

" And none—ah—on the way? Ha ha! "

" No, sir."

" Well, I'll tell you why I ask," Mr. Masterson said. Then he retreated abruptly into silence, staring at his half-empty glass.

Blazer was silent, too. Then, finally, he asked, " Why? "

" Well, I'll tell you," Mr. Masterson said musingly. " You know why I'm out here? "

" No."

" Well, our West Coast manager has been giving us a little trouble. He—well, to put it frankly, he doesn't quite have it. He doesn't quite have it on the ball. Sales are slipping. But the market is good. Something's wrong."

" I see," Blazer said.

" Well, this is all by the by but anyway I came out here to take a look-see. We've got a trouble area here, no doubt about that. Something's wrong." He continued to stare at his glass.

" Contact? " Blazer ventured.

Mr. Masterson looked up quickly. " Contact! " he bellowed. " Contact! That's it. You've put your finger on it! " He jabbed his finger at Blazer's chest. " Contact! That's where we're falling down. Personality. My motto is personality makes contacts—contacts make sales."

" I sure agree with you on that," Blazer said.

Mr. Masterson looked at Blazer appraisingly. " I like you," he said. " I like the cut of your jib."

" Thank you, sir."

" Cut out this sir stuff. Call me Harry."

" All right, Harry."

" Now, look. Are you married to Norden-Clark? "

" Well——"

" No, don't answer that. Foolish question. Skip it. Sorry I asked. What I meant to ask you was, do you—do you, Stuart Denison——"

" Gates," Blazer murmured.

" Gates, sorry. Do you, Stuart Gates, think that you could manage a division here in L.A.—a division with fourteen salesmen working directly under you, reporting only to our general sales manager in New York? Do you? " He looked at Blazer closely, and repeated, " Do you? "

" Well," Blazer answered slowly, " frankly—I don't know."

" Good! " Mr. Masterson yelled. Heads turned from several tables to glance at him. " Good. If you'd answered yes, I'd have laughed in your face." He clapped Blazer on the shoulder. "Of course you don't know! And—what's more to the point—I don't know either. But," he added steadily, "I could find out, couldn't I? Yes." He nodded slowly, up and down. "I like you. Contact. I like what you said about contact. I like that very much." He reached for his glass and swallowed the remainder of his drink. "Well, look," he said, and he sing-songed, "I-tell-ya-what-I'm-gonna-do. We'll forget we had this little talk. For the time being, see? It's strictly *entre nous*, as the fellow says. But I'm going to bear it in mind." Mr. Masterson looked at his watch. "I've got to meet a chap here in a few minutes," he said. "But you just may be hearing from me. Okay?"

"Harry," Blazer said, smiling, sure of his ground all at once, "I certainly appreciate all of this. I certainly do."

"Don't mention it." Mr. Masterson stood up. "Contact," he said. He held out his hand. Blazer jumped to his feet. Mr. Masterson smiled at him; they shook hands.

Harry Masterson watched the slim young man as he moved away, through the tables, towards the edge of the terrace. He liked him, yes. It might work, who could tell? And if not—well. Well, he thought, there could be worse things than bringing the son of a man like Junius Denison into the business, or rather the son-in-law. Who knew when he himself might like to ask a favour of Junius Denison? Didn't one good turn always deserve another? He drummed his fingers on the table. In Mr. Harry Masterson's world, one good turn did.

14

THERE is a secret area of a man's mind from which he can view himself objectively. From this place, this platform, it is possible to see each motion and each action in a clear, chilly light. It is not always possible to reach this platform. That is, it must be reached voluntarily, and with some effort. But when a man does reach it, and can stand far off, observing himself, events seem orderly and sequential, in a way almost justifiable, if you figure that effect follows cause, and that every happening in life follows a pattern of action and counteraction. Jimmy tried to view the events of the past two days from this impersonal region as he lay, feet up, in his stocking feet, on the sofa in his apartment that Sunday evening. He was deliberately not fixing himself a drink, because he knew that drinking would cloud the process and blur the image. But, try as he might, he could not reach the plateau of candid objectivity that he wanted to reach. Some odd, interior jeering interrupted him and pulled him back. Back to the hot, close apartment, the tasteless furniture, the spot on the rug, his shoes on the floor, himself lying on the sofa. He was being pulled back to the knowledge that something terrible had happened, and was happening, and to the haunting fear that he was making it happen. He had crossed a barrier that he had sworn never to cross. He had defiled a sacred image. He had defiled Helen. But he had defiled an image that he treasured even more: the image of himself.

And yet it was curious. Claire managed to break the Seventh Commandment and observe the breakage as casually as she might observe a broken fingernail. It was an attitude that, to Jimmy, was hard to understand. Was he being too Puritanical? No, because it was he who had finally brought the episode to a finish. Not that Claire hadn't wanted it to finish that way. She had wanted it, he had recognized that, all along. And how about himself? Had he wanted it, too? Ah, he thought, there was a question, there was indeed a question. Yes, he had wanted it, too. He thought about Claire.

It was hard to imagine what went on in that mind of hers. He thought he understood her. A girl—young, beautiful, foolish—a girl who was easily bored with things. She was vain, wanted to be the centre of attention—she was all those things. But underneath, was there something else? Was there some deep unfathomable reservoir that waited, empty, waiting to be filled? Was he falling in love with her, falling in love with Blazer's wife?

It was curious, too, to think about Helen. Helen, in Rio Linda, with his child growing inside her, a child that she evidently never planned to let him see. A totally unfounded thought floated to the surface of his mind. He had had it before, even last night, afterwards. He rejected it, but it persisted. Could it be, he wondered, that this had all been a part of Claire's plan? If it had been, it had certainly worked marvellously for her. For that had been what had set him off. Surely, he knew, he would not have gone to bed with her if she had not told him about Helen and the baby. He had been fairly drunk, yes. But even so—even so, if it hadn't been for that, the final barrier wouldn't have fallen. Was it possible that Claire had made the whole thing up? That she had not gone to see Helen at all, that she had no information and no knowledge, but simply told a quick, effective lie? It was part of the whole question mark that was Claire's character that it *was* possible, quite possible. It would be the sort of thing she would do. Or rather it was the sort of thing she could easily be suspected of doing. Why, for example, would she go to Rio Linda? Why should she care whether he and Helen got back together or not? Yes, it was not only possible, it was quite probable. She had deceived him because in some uncanny way she knew ahead of time what his reaction would be. So that was that. So there was no baby coming.

He felt relieved at this. And, at the same time, angry and lonely.

To hell with it. He would have a drink. He leaped off the sofa, went into the kitchen, opened the refrigerator, and pulled out ice-cubes. He clattered the ice-cubes roughly in a glass, reached for the whisky bottle, and splashed whisky into the glass until the ice-cubes rose and swirled. Standing there, he drank. He thought suddenly, sorrowfully, of the night on the mountain when he had poured out the drink, promising himself to stop, stop for ever. But it was too late now to stop. He had gone by the stopping point, it seemed. From now on it was downhill. The thought frightened him, and yet, as the first rush of whisky flowed through him, there was a certain heady fascination in the downward path, wondering what odd, degraded torments lay at the very bottom.

A tremulous picture of the inevitable slime came to him. It was like the time, as a little boy, he had stood at the head of the cellar stairs. The cellar below was dark and alive; there was a light switch within reach—he could turn it on and the cellar would appear, whitewashed, clean, and familiar. But he would not turn on the light. He crept down the stairs, one by one, into the forbidding darkness, the rustlings, the shadows of strange shapes. He must go down. He must not turn back. He must not reach for the light switch. He must meet the phantoms of the cellar on their own terms.

He shook his head free of these thoughts and carried his glass back into the living-room. Well, he thought, perhaps he should go home, back to Connecticut. What was there to keep him here, in a city that he didn't love, at a job that satisfied him only because it was the merest sort of a challenge? To hell with it all. What was he trying to prove? There was no chance that Helen would come back, no chance at all. He was living in a dream of foolish hopes and self-deception, fondly presuming that he was fighting some sort of inner battle. The battle seemed suddenly insignificant. And, for that matter, he had already lost it. He remembered with a shudder how he had gone through the elaborate business of pretending Helen was still around when Claire and Blazer came. Christ, he thought, he'd been a fool! A damned fool! He flung himself down on the sofa. The drink in his hand splashed on his trouser-leg, but he ignored it. He took another deep swallow and lay back, resting the drink on his chest.

As he saw it now, he could choose one of three courses. He numbered them and ticked them off in his mind. One. One was to stay right here, where he was, and let the affair with

Claire take whatever turn it might. If she wanted it to go on, okay, it would go on. (Oh, you're a nice boy, Jimmy old boy, he thought, a real nice boy, a high type!) And two, he could go home, back to Somerville. Three—three was impossible. Three was get Helen back, but that was hopeless, that was idiotic. So there were really only two choices. It was simple. It was the simplest God-damned thing in the whole world, and to hell with everybody!

All at once, he couldn't stand it. He stood up. The drink spilled again in his hand, ran down his wrist and arm. Frantically, he looked around the room, wanting somewhere to go, somewhere to drive into the night—the way he had driven to the beach. He had driven to the beach because he wanted to drown himself, because he was through with himself, hated himself. He wanted that again. Just death! Just silence! He wanted that now, and with a wild clarity, Helen came back, stood in the room, and he knew that he would never be happy without her. He had to have her back, that was all, if he was to go on living. He saw her sharply, at Yosemite, in the snow, that brief wonderful week, the week in which they had shared some great improbable secret thing that filled their lives and thoughts every single moment. And the time at the pool, when she had found him and he had run to her.

Had the trouble been all Helen's fault, as he had imagined? Did she really need psychiatric help, or had he simply reached for that as an excuse? Hadn't he, in fact, consistently betrayed her? Why had some times been happy and others not? "Something happens to you when you drink," she had said to him. "Something happens to your eyes that frightens me, and reminds me of that other boy. He was drunk and raped me. He told me that he wanted to kill me. When you are drunk, you rape me. You want to kill me. I see it in your eyes. It makes me fight you, don't you see? I feel my scarf tighten at my throat..."

It was true. Last night, with Claire, it had been the same. But with this one difference: the quick fury and the violence, the brutality were what Claire enjoyed. The sudden, dark, drunken attack was what was wanted.

Then perhaps there was still a third course. He put the drink down on the coffee table and stared at it. In the evening light from the window, filtering through the eucalyptus branches, the glass seemed to swell and glow voluptuously. " Pick me," it seemed to say. " I am like a flower. I am the end of all desire; I hold hope and warmth, and the comfort of death; I am everything that you want to be, but cannot be . . ."

He gazed at it for a long time, unblinking.

Then he knew he had to move. He needed help. He moved about the room and thought of calling Mike Gorman, the boy who had helped him on the beach.

Then he thought of calling Helen.

He had thought of calling Helen before, but he had not done it. He had written letters, but letters were cowardly forms of communication. He needed her voice.

He had wanted to call her. He had been afraid to call her. The inner jeering was beginning again.

He went to the kitchen and reached for the telephone.

Then a surprising thing happened: the telephone rang in his hand.

He lifted the receiver and heard Helen's voice. " Jimmy? "

" *You knew*——" he breathed. " *You knew where I was!* "

" What? "

He collected himself. " It's just that—well, I was just about to pick up the phone and call you."

" Oh." There was a pause. Then she said, " How are you, Jimmy? "

" Fine, fine," he said. " How're you, Helen? "

" I'm fine, too," she said.

" It's so funny," he repeated. " I had the phone almost in my hand——"

" What were you going to call me about? "

" I don't know. I'd been sitting here, and I started thinking——"

" Well," she interrupted him, " how's everything going? How's the job? "

" Oh, fine, fine . . ."

" Jimmy——" she began, and he thought he detected a catch in her voice. " Jimmy, this is sort of a business call—no, I don't mean that. It's not that—but I do have something to tell you."

" Yes? " he said softly.

" Jimmy, I want you to take this like a man. It's very serious news——"

" What is it? "

" I'm—I'm going to have a baby."

He was silent.

" Jimmy? Jimmy? Are you there? "

" Yes . . ."

" Jimmy, now please—before you say anything—let me say —I'm very happy about it! "

" I'm glad."

" I am! " She had begun to cry. " I had to tell you, Jimmy, because I'm sure now, and I made a mistake yesterday. A friend of yours came to see me—Claire Gates, your friend Blazer's wife—she was here, and I made the mistake of telling her. I didn't want you to hear it from her first. I wanted you to hear it from me. I tried to call you last night! I did, Jimmy——"

" Yes, yes," he said. " I was out——"

" Jimmy," she said, " now it's nothing to worry about. It'll be a wonderful baby, I know—and I want you to share it, of course, as much as is possible—if you want to, I mean——" Her voice trailed off.

" Helen," he said, " can I come down to see you? "

" No, no! No, please—not now. It wouldn't do any good. It would just upset me, I know. After the baby—of course. But not now."

" Look," he said, " Helen, listen to me. I love you. I'm willing to try it again. Are you? Will you? "

" Oh, no! No, there's no use—there's no use talking like that——"

" But now—for the baby's sake."

" No, that's wrong. That's very wrong, Jimmy. That's the worst thing in the world. They all tell you that——"

" Who does? "

" The books. It isn't fair for the child—if the parents are, well, if they don't get along, it's wrong for them to—to go back together—for the baby's sake."

" All right—for our own sakes then."

" Jimmy, please—please don't talk that way. There isn't

anything for us! Really, there isn't, Jimmy—I wish it weren't true, but it is!" Her voice broke.

"Helen," he said deeply and urgently, "oh, Helen . . ."

There was no sound.

"Helen!"

"I had to tell you. That's all. That's why I called——"

"Helen. Do you remember Yosemite——?"

"No. Yes! That's all I have to say, Jimmy, truly——"

"Listen. Listen to me, darling, don't hang up. Please listen to me——"

"I've got to go now!"

"Let me come down."

"No. I don't want to see you——"

"Can I write to you?"

"Yes. No . . . I don't care. Work through Mr. Gurney—my lawyer."

"Don't hang up, Helen. Don't——"

"I must——"

"No!"

There was a click, and then silence.

He stood there, holding the phone. Then he put it down. He felt hot, painful tears in his eyes, but he blinked them back. He went quickly to the refrigerator for ice-cubes and fixed himself another drink. He drank it half down before he remembered that he had left the first drink in the living-room. It was beginning to get dark. From the kitchen window, he could see Capitol Avenue filling with long shadows. Across the street, at number 3360, the woman appeared from around the corner of the house to collect her evening paper. She stooped, picked it up from the front steps, unfolded it, glanced at the headlines, put it under her arm, and disappeared again around the house. It was a ritual. Did she realize that he watched her, night after night, picking up her paper? In her back yard, as in all California back yards, there would be a barbecue and the smell of charcoal smoke, and people would be sitting around the brick terrace in canvas chairs, drinking cocktails, ushering in the evening. He had a crazy desire to wander over, drink in hand, and join them. But he stood there.

Later, he took out a piece of stationery and a pen and wrote a letter, sitting at the kitchen table. He wrote:

DEAR HELEN,

You said just now that you were happy, and I want to tell you that I hope the baby will make you as happy as I have made you unhappy. I hope that you will have people to take care of you, to give you books to read, and a comfortable chair. . . . *Sic transit.* Amen. The curtain is drawn. The book is closed, put down . . .

I have a certain brilliance, he thought, reading it over, before he stood up and ripped it once down the middle, once down the side, into four strips, and eight strips, and sixteen. He went into the living-room, where his other drink was.

15

On Wednesday night, Claire called Jimmy from San Francisco. " Darling," she said, " how are you? "

" Hi," he said casually, " how are you? "

" I'm wonderful," she said, " but worried."

" What about? "

" You—are you coming Saturday? "

" No," he said.

" Darling—why not? "

" Look," he said, " I thought I explained that before——"

" Guilt feelings! " she said teasingly. " I want you to stop having them, just stop."

" Look, let's not——"

" Jimmy," she said, " you've got to come. You really do."

" Why? "

" For obvious reasons. What would Blazer think? "

" I don't know."

" He'd want to know why you weren't coming. He's coming home to-morrow, Jimmy. I want to come down Saturday and we'll both behave as though nothing has happened. Because nothing really has."

" Is that the way you feel? That nothing has happened? "

" Oh, you know I don't mean that. A very exciting thing has happened—but it's all between you and me; it doesn't involve anybody else, don't you see. Jimmy," she said, a trace of anger creeping into her voice, " you were a man last Saturday, please be a man now. You've got to, darling. Even if you don't think you owe it to me, you owe it to Blazer—not to let him suspect——"

" Look, Claire," he said, " I'm fond of you—I won't deny that. Last Saturday was—well, maybe it was inevitable, but anyway I'm rather sorry it happened. There's a name for it, you know. Adultery——"

"Oh, Jimmy! Don't be such a prig. Are you sober?"

"Yes, as a matter of fact, I am."

"Well, then for goodness' sake get drunk. You're no fun at all when you're like this. You sound like a minister or something and it's hardly becoming. As far as Saturday night goes, it doesn't have to happen again, does it? If you don't want it to happen, then I don't either. And it won't happen again."

"But that's just it," he said. "I'm afraid it will."

There was a silence. Then, in a changed tone, she said, "Well—I wouldn't mind. You should know that, darling. I've thought about it—ever since. A great deal. It was—well, it was one of the most wonderful things that's ever happened to me, darling. So different from—from anything else. I thought about it all day to-day," she said softly.

"That must have helped you with your charity cases."

"What? Oh, I forgot to tell you," she said gaily, "I quit. I quit Monday. I decided I'm not a do-gooder"—she giggled—"I'm a do-badder, I guess. So I quit. It was all a sex substitute, I think. And, for some reason, Monday morning I didn't need a sex substitute . . ."

"Oh, Claire, Claire," he said wearily.

"Don't be despondent! Go fix yourself a big fat drink, will you, and make up your mind that you're coming down here Saturday."

"I've got another engagement, actually," he said.

"What do you mean? What kind of engagement?"

"I promised a guy I'd play bridge with him."

"A guy—what guy?"

"A fellow I met on the beach——"

"On *what* beach?"

"Look, it's too complicated——"

"Do you mean to say you're going to spend Saturday night playing *bridge*—with some guy you met on a *beach*? Don't be absurd!"

"I promised him——"

"Well, dear, I wouldn't be so vehement about it if it weren't so important. Right at this point, I mean. With Blazer."

He was silent.

" What did you do after you left here? " she asked. " Did you drive back? "

" No," he said. And then he said, " Oh, my God! "

" What? What is it? "

" God, I almost forgot. Look, Claire, could you do me a favour? "

" That depends. What? "

" I got a parking ticket Saturday. It was there when I came out. I'm supposed to appear on Friday——"

" Goodness, is *that* all? "

" If I mail you the ticket with a five-dollar bill, could you run over to the traffic court on Friday and pay it? It will only take a minute—as long as you're not working."

" I'll do it on one condition," she said.

" What? "

" If you'll come down Saturday."

" All right," he sighed, " I'll come."

" Good. Mail me the ticket, and I'll go storm the halls of justice for you."

" Without telling Blazer, naturally——"

" Naturally."

" Thanks," he said. " Thanks a lot, Claire."

" Thank *you*," she said. " And cheer up, darling. It's really not as dreadful as you think it is."

" I'll try."

" Have you stopped thinking about Helen? Have you been trying to push her way, way back into the farthest corner of your mind? "

" I guess that's what I've got to do," he said slowly.

" Well, keep pushing. You know what I think. She had a wonderful thing in you, and she let it go. So let her go."

" Yes——"

" I'll see you Saturday," she said. " Bring your friend if you want to. Diane Higbee *is* coming."

" Who? "

" Diane Higbee."

" Who's she? "

" Just a girl. Originally I thought of having her for you, but if you bring your friend, he can have her. I'll positively thrust them together! As for you, I just want to be able to catch your eye—one or twice—across the crowded room . . ."

"I'll see you then, Claire," he said.

"Good-bye," she said. "My darling!"

Jimmy hung up the phone and went to the closet. In the jacket of his grey suit, he found the yellow parking ticket and the crumpled paper napkin on which Mike Gorman had written his address and telephone number. He took both of these back into the kitchen with him. It was funny. He felt as though he had known Mike Gorman all his life. He felt pretty sure that Mike wouldn't want to go to Claire and Blazer's party. Somehow, Mike's easy, sunburned face didn't belong with Claire and Blazer and their friends. He was too relaxed and healthy; their friends would look wan and brittle in comparison. But there was no harm in asking him. He'd have to call him anyway, to beg out of the bridge game. At that moment, to Jimmy, the prospect of playing bridge seemed a lot more pleasant than going to a party. It was such a simple, unhectic way to spend an evening. But he'd promised Claire now. He picked up the phone again and gave the operator the San Francisco number.

After a few rings, Mike's voice answered drowsily, "Hello?"

"Hi," Jimmy said. "This is Jim Keefe."

"Oh, hi," Mike said. "How're you doing?" He yawned. "Sorry—I was asleep."

"Hey, it's only nine o'clock," Jimmy said.

"Yeah, but I was reading this book and I fell asleep in a chair."

"I'm sorry I woke you."

"Don't mention it. What's on your mind?"

"Well, look," Jimmy said, "about Saturday—I think I'll have to take a rain check on the bridge game——"

"Oh, that's too bad. Something come up?"

"Well, more or less," Jimmy said. "These friends of mine in San Francisco are having a party. I'd promised them I'd come. I forgot about it when I told you."

"Sure, I understand. Well, maybe some other time, huh?"

"Yes," Jimmy said. "Because, you know—I'd really been looking forward to it. I haven't played bridge in a long time."

"Well, we'll do it some other time," Mike said.

"These people—the fellow was my room-mate in college, and

his wife—they're quite an experience. They really are. I told them I met you and they asked if you'd like to come to the party. There's going to be an extra girl, I guess. Would you like to go?"

"Well," Mike said slowly, "I don't know. I'm not much for parties. What kind of a party is it going to be?"

"God knows," Jimmy said. "It could be anything—you never can tell what their parties are going to be like. They have this terrific apartment up on Russian Hill with a view that makes you airsick, and the usual idea is to see how many people they can pack into three and a half rooms . . ."

"Russian Hill? Sounds a little rich for my blood——"

"Oh, it won't be fancy—nothing like that. Just people—people from the East, mostly. Hell, you might bump into some long-lost friend, you never can tell."

"I'm the kind of guy that feels choked in a necktie," Mike said. "It's about all I can do to wear one through the day, at work. But sure, I'll go. Why not? It ought to be fun."

"I really ought to warn you about these people—Claire and Blazer Gates. I mean, they're apt to throw you at first—they throw most people. They have a way of talking—I don't know, as though everything was a great big act. But underneath it all, they're—well, they're darned nice."

"Sure, I'd like to go," Mike said. "Probably do me good to get out of this place. Everywhere I look there's a pile of laundry. Where'll I meet you?"

"Why don't I meet you at the Mark around seven? In the lobby. How's that?"

"Fine. See you there then."

"Okay, Mike. You might just have a good time, I don't know. So long."

"So long."

Jimmy hung up the phone. He went into the living-room, found an envelope in the drawer of the chest, and hurriedly addressed it to Claire. He took a five-dollar bill out of his wallet, placed it in the envelope with the parking ticket, licked the flap and sealed it. He put a stamp on the envelope and looked at his watch. He would have time to make the ten-o'clock mail collection if he took it to the box on the corner. He went out of the apartment and down the steps to the street. Perhaps, he thought, going to the party was the best thing. It would help get his mind off Helen. Push her back, Claire had said, into the farthest corner of your mind. Well, that seemed like the only thing to do. He had not written to his father yet, about the baby. That would be a tough letter to write, he knew. He could picture his father's face when he found out. He would be stern and stony. He would summon the members of the clan —first his mother, then Turner Ames, Miss Maitland. Grimly, methodically, they would begin to fortify themselves against this new disaster. But they would rise above it; they had risen above every other disaster. All things—death, divorce, federal taxes, children that turned out badly, diseases, labour disputes —these were merely bothersome details of living. They could be overcome, settled, filed away. And they rather enjoyed the bother. It gave them something to do; it reaffirmed the Keefe family status. Bother went with being rich.

Jimmy was glad Mike Gorman was going to the party, too. Just talking to Mike on the phone cheered him up. Without knowing exactly what it was, he recognized an ingredient in Mike that he himself lacked, a sort of quiet optimism. Mike would be a good friend to have.

At the corner, he dropped the letter in the letter-box. He turned and walked back along the dark, quiet street, under the trees.

16

WHEN Jimmy and Mike Gorman arrived at the apartment on Lombard Street Saturday night, Claire met them at the door and greeted them gaily. She stood in a slim, metallic, gold sheath dress, with her hair pulled tightly back and wound into a bun at the back of her neck. Silver ear-rings, fashioned to resemble mobiles, danced from her ears. They were a little early, she explained breathlessly, but that was all right, they would have a little time to visit. Most of the people hadn't arrived. She had invited lots of new people. She didn't know how they were going to get along with the old people. But Tweetums DeMay was here already. Tweetums was doing the funniest thing—they must come in quickly and see her do it. She brushed Jimmy's cheek lightly with her lips. Jimmy introduced her to Mike, and Claire said, " How do you do? " and looked at him appraisingly. She led them into the living-room. " Do it again for Jimmy, Tweetums," she urged.

Tweetums DeMay, a plump, animated little woman, older than the rest of them, sat on the white sofa. " Lookee," she cried. She held a nylon stocking in her hands and suddenly popped it over her head, pulling it down hard across her face. The stocking forced her face into a grimacing, distorted leer. " Isn't it dreadful? " she said beneath the stocking. " Doesn't it do the most ghastly things? Try it." She yanked the stocking off and offered it to Jimmy.

Jimmy laughed. " Wait till I've had a drink," he said.

" Blazer's out there mixing the most ferocious daiquiris," Tweetums said. " Bla—zer! " she called. " Another guest—two more guests." She smiled at Mike. " Who're you? " she asked.

For a moment, Claire remembered her Madeira manners.

" Mrs. DeMay," she said, " I'd like to present Michael Gorman. Mr. Gorman, this is Mrs. DeMay."

" Oh, skip that ' Mrs.' part," Tweetums said. " Just call me Tweetums. Everybody does." She gave Mike another bright smile. " You're cute," she said.

Mike reddened. He turned to Claire. " You have a great place here," he said.

" Oh, do you like it? " Claire said absently. " If the view gets too much for you, let me know and I'll close the curtains. What *is* Blazer doing? " She looked towards the kitchen.

Presently Blazer arrived from the kitchen, carrying a trayful of drinks. " Hi, Keefe-o," he said. He put down the tray and shook Jimmy's hand.

" Hi, Blaze," Jimmy said casually. " How was L.A.? "

" Oh, just the same. Hot as hell."

" Mike Gorman—Blazer Gates, our host."

" How are you? " Blazer said, shaking Mike's hand.

" Pleased to meet you," Mike said.

" Say," Tweetums said, " you two didn't see my date lurking around downstairs, did you? He's supposed to meet me here, but he's half an hour late already—the dirty dog."

" No, I didn't see him," Jimmy said.

The door-bell rang and Claire rushed to answer it. " *Higbee!* " she shrieked when she opened it. " Sweetie! You came! I knew you would! " Claire and Diane Higbee clutched each other in a quick embrace.

" I had the rudest taxi-driver," Diane said. " He insisted there was no such address." She came into the living-room and Blazer took her coat. She was a small, dark girl with a quick, nervous mannerism of brushing at her hair with her fingertips. She was introduced, and flopped into a chair. She opened her purse, removed a flat gold cigarette-case, extracted a cigarette, and screwed it into the end of a long gold holder. When no one immediately lighted it for her, she removed matches, and lighted it herself. She inhaled deeply and blew out a thin, sharp stream of smoke. " What're those? " she asked rudely as Claire held the tray of cocktails in front of her.

" Daiquiris," Claire said.

" And they're ferocious, so watch out, honey," Tweetums said.

" I'm ready for another." She put her empty glass on the tray and took a full one.

Blazer was putting records on the phonograph. " Jazz? Does everybody like jazz? " he asked.

For the next half-hour or so, the door-bell rang steadily. There were more effusive greetings, introductions, drinks passed. The room began filling with smoke and people and voices. Many of the people Jimmy had never seen before. " Where did they all come from? " he asked Claire as she hurried by.

" I don't know. Isn't it marvellous? " she answered.

Tweetums DeMay took hold of his sleeve with one hand. " I think I've been married to everybody in this room," she shouted over the noise. " Everybody except you, that is. My first husband just walked in! Isn't that a scream? "

" Did your date show up? " Jimmy asked her.

" Yes, he's here somewhere. He's a football player. You can't miss him."

The door-bell rang again, and the jazz record on the phonograph suddenly blared out loudly. " Turn that thing down! " Claire's voice shrieked.

" I don't think your friend likes me," Tweetums said.

" Sure he does, Tweetums," Jimmy said. He had lost sight of Mike Gorman.

Diane Higbee joined them. Her cigarette, in the gold holder, was bent, and her eyes were brightly glazed. She held a daiquiri in one hand. " It's fabulous! " she said to Jimmy. " Perfectly fabulous to meet you. I didn't realize you were the fabulous Jimmy Keefe. I'd have been furious if you hadn't come."

" You're going to have the pleasure of meeting my first husband to-night," Tweetums said to Diane. " I don't know how he got here, but there he is." She pointed. " Ed! " she called. " Eddie! "

The man turned and gave her a friendly smile. " Hi, Tweetums," he said, waving. " Fancy meeting you here! "

She turned to Diane. " I think I've been married to every man in this room," she said. " Except Jimmy. Aren't these ferocious daiquiris? I've been drinking since two o'clock."

Diane Higbee ignored Tweetums. " We've been having rather a ridiculous time on the other side of the room," she said to Jimmy. " Did you know Harriet Webb at Smith? Well, she's here, and she's brought a Chinaman! Have you seen him? He doesn't speak a word of English. Have you seen him?" She looked around. "Oh, there he is. See, over there by the couch." Jimmy followed the direction of her finger. Through a clearing in the people, he saw the young Chinese. "There! Imagine! I don't know where she finds her friends. Anyway, we're all going down to Chinatown later to celebrate Chinese New Year. It isn't Chinese New Year yet, of course, but we thought we'd go down and celebrate it anyway. I want to find an opium den. Don't you *love* opium dens? I do." She called across several heads. "Ching Chong!" she called. "Sing Foo! C'mere!" The Chinese turned his head, gazed at her blandly, then looked away. "He's terribly snobbish." Diane giggled. "You notice he won't speak to a soul except Harriet."

"You're a scream, honey," Tweetums DeMay said. "An absolute scream."

Diane and Tweetums eyed each other coldly for a moment. Then, with a toss of her head, Diane turned back to Jimmy. "I'm sailing on the Lurline Tuesday," she said. "Just think—I'll be gone six solid months. Isn't it *dreadful*?" she said sadly.

Jimmy tried to extract himself from the group, but Diane held his arm.

"Claire told me you'd had a tragic, tragic marriage," she said.

Jimmy took another daiquiri as Claire appeared, holding the tray. She smiled up at him. "Having fun?" she asked.

"Sure, sure——" He sipped the drink.

Claire handed the tray to Diane Higbee. "Sweetie," she said, "would you be a dear and finish passing these?" She turned to Jimmy. "Now follow me, I want you to meet all these other people."

The party was out of all proportions. New people kept coming in, and the ones already there were forced farther and farther back into the room against the glass walls. Silhouetted against the lighted backdrop of San Francisco, they resembled a crowd on a precipice; they were jockeying for positions at the edge, to see who would be the first one over. Corks popped. Someone had brought champagne. Endlessly the party seemed to grow, the talk rose, drowning itself in a roar of laughter, screams. Someone fell down, and as Jimmy pushed through the room behind Claire, a tall pale girl came up to him and said, " Will someone take me home? I want to go home in a *car*! " " My sombrero! " someone shrieked. " Look where you've put it! Oh, God! "

" Let's escape," Claire whispered. " Just for a minute." She led him quickly into the bedroom and closed the door. The bed was piled high with coats. Claire leaned against the door and laughed weakly. " Oh, dear," she said, " I had no idea I'd asked so many people."

" It's quite a mob," Jimmy said.

" Are you happy? " she asked him.

" Sure," he said. " What's happened to Mike? Have you seen him? "

" Oh, he's around somewhere," Claire said. " Don't worry about him. Everybody's having fun."

" Nice guy, don't you think? "

" Who? Oh, what's-his-name, Mike. Yes. Hardly says a word, though. Come here."

" We'd better get back."

" I paid your parking ticket," she said. " I went down to traffic court in my oldest, shabbiest dress, looking like Mrs. Miniver——"

" Thanks," he said. " But we'd better get back."

" All right," she sighed.

He turned towards the door, and noticed a picture on the dresser in a narrow silver frame. It was a picture of a little yellow-haired girl. " That's me," Claire breathed, close to him. " Five years old. I haven't changed, have I? I'm still a little girl——"

He pushed gently past her and opened the door. " I'd better see how Mike's getting along," he said. " I feel kind of responsible."

As he opened the door, the sounds of the party flooded around him again. Suddenly there was a crash. Alec Fry had toppled over one of the ceramic lamps by the sofa, and one side of the room was plunged into darkness. " Thank God everything's insured," Claire murmured, behind him.

He found Mike; Diane Higbee was pressed close against him, holding his hand outstretched in hers. Mike looked across at Jimmy and winked. " She's telling my fortune," he said.

" Look at this hand," Diane said. " It's so enormous, it could simply crush a person, don't you think? "

Tweetums DeMay whispered in his ear. " He's her uncle," she said.

" Whose uncle? "

Tweetums pointed across the room. " The man with the moustache. Look at him."

" Whose uncle, Tweetums? "

" Aren't they a howl? Isn't this a howl? "

" Yes——"

" We're all going to Chinatown. Can I go with you? "

" Well——"

" We'll take the cable car."

More drinks came. " Where's your date? " Jimmy asked.

" What? " said Tweetums.

" I said——" Jimmy began, then laughed. " What's the use? I can't yell loud enough."

" What? "

" I said I can't yell! "

" There's my date," Tweetums said, as though she had heard him all along. " Over there." Jimmy saw a tall, broad-shouldered young man in a bright blue sport jacket. He looked in his twenties, or, Jimmy guessed, roughly twenty years younger than Tweetums. " He's a football player from Cal," Tweetums said. " Isn't he a caveman? " She headed in the young man's direction.

Mike Gorman was at his shoulder. " Had enough? " he asked pleasantly.

Jimmy turned and smiled. " I told you it would be an experience," he said.

" It is that, all right."

" Want to go? " Jimmy asked.

" I don't care, whenever you're ready."

" Well—in a minute, okay? I'm sorry your date turned out to be Diane Higbee."

" Yeah, she's a character, all right."

" Have a drink! " Blazer yelled, pushing his way towards them. " Hey, Keefe-o, c'mon! You're not oiled yet! " He grabbed a glass and handed it to Jimmy. He offered another to Mike, who shook his head.

"What's the matter?" Blazer asked him. "What's the matter with these drinks, huh?" Jimmy realized, suddenly, that Blazer was very drunk.

"I've had my limit, thanks," Mike said.

"Oh, yeah?" Blazer said, staring at Mike with half-closed eyes.

"C'mon, Blaze," Jimmy said quickly.

Blazer turned to him. "Hey, Keefe-o," he said, "I know what let's do. Let's go find a fairy and beat him up, okay? How 'bout it? I know a place over on Sutter——"

"Now, c'mon, Blaze," Jimmy said.

"I mean it. Find a fairy, beat him up. Fun, huh?"

"Yeah," Jimmy said. "Sure. Go have a cup of coffee, Blaze."

All at once the phonograph blared loudly again, drowning out all the other noise. Claire rushed by. "The police!" she said. "I think somebody's called the police! Oh, my God!" Blazer turned unsteadily and followed her.

Jimmy heard a woman's laugh behind him. "We found the most wonderful little place," the voice said. "In the Caribbean. Just ourselves, nobody else. And native boys! Built like—like little castles, every muscle. So perfectly formed——"

"Do you have a cigarette?" Claire asked, coming back. "It was a false alarm. No police, thank God!"

Jimmy offered her one and reached for his lighter. Claire held her face down close to his hand, and clutched it with her own. "Do you believe in me?" she asked, hovering over the flame.

"What?"

"I mean, do you?" She released his hand, but her cigarette was not lighted. "You stand here so quietly, and I think perhaps—you——"

She lowered her face again to try for the light a second time, and the woman behind him said, ". . . the most wonderful hotel, with the most beautiful terrace, and a pool. In the morning, the beach! What I wouldn't give——"

The room, the lights seemed to spin as he tried to close his ears. "Be careful of this lighter——" he began.

"Hold still," Claire said. "I can't get this damn' thing lit!"

He steadied his hand, and she drew in on the cigarette. "Let's get another drink," he said.

" All right."

Later, Mike Gorman came up to him. " What do you say? " he said, smiling. " Had enough yet? "

" I sure have," Jimmy said. " Let me say good-bye to Claire and Blazer and I'll be right with you."

" I was just thinking—want to drive out to the beach and go for a swim? "

" Sounds like a great idea," Jimmy said. " Be right with you." He started across the room towards Claire.

Half-way across the room, the broad-shouldered man in the blue sport jacket stopped him, grabbed his arm. " Hey," he said. " You're a lone wolf here, too, aren't you? "

" Well——" Jimmy began.

" Tweetums, the old bag I came with, has passed out in the can. Let's you and me scoot out and grab a piece of tail."

" I'm sorry, not to-night——"

" C'mon."

Jimmy looked at him. He was tall, blond-foreheaded. His eyes were lake-blue and Nordic; he was smiling a big, friendly smile.

" I didn't get your name," Jimmy said.

" Stan Erickson—went to Cal. What's yours? "

" Jim Keefe." He took his outstretched hand.

" What d'ya say? I know a good place, south of Market. Let's beat it out of this joint."

" I can't, no kidding——" Jimmy said. From the other side of the room, he could feel Claire watching him.

" C'mon," he said. " I'm feeling real horny. How about you? And I've got funny tastes—I like to rough 'em up a bit——"

" Oh? " Jimmy said. Something buzzed, far back, inside his head.

The man went on talking. ". . . girl back at Cal, about a year ago. I got loaded and took her out in my car after a dance. Raped hell out of her—but she was a good sport, never breathed boo——"

What happened then, or whether it was then, or whether the man said some more, and Jimmy hit him after that, he couldn't remember. But all at once, in a terrifying, blinding whir of sounds that drowned out every other sound in the glass room, he went off. He was hitting him, and tears were running down his face. He was not striking another man, he knew that. In that blond, blue-eyed face, he was striking himself, who had now betrayed Helen as thoroughly and as permanently as this man had.

And with the hate, the private, unspoken hate that each man reserves for his own being, he went at him, to kill him.

The man rose from the floor, and, sobbing, Jimmy hit him again. The man rose again and came forward. Jimmy watched him. Then, with a sound like the tinkling of a breaking glass, he stopped thinking.

When he came to, he was on the sofa, and Claire was bending over him. " Oh, Jimmy! " she cried. " Oh, Jimmy! Why did you do that? What's happening to you? Jimmy, we can't have you around here any more! We can't! Now go. Oh, why! Why would you do such a thing at my party! "

He closed his eyes again.

" Come on, old trooper." It was Mike Gorman's voice.

After Jimmy and Mike had left, Claire felt she should say something, make some sort of explanation to the guests who remained, and try to put together the shattered pieces of the party. Everyone had gone except the Frys, the Browers, and Diane, but she felt she should make the effort anyway.

" If you had only known him *before*," she said. " If you had only known him before, as we did. He was—oh, I don't know, the most wonderful guy! The most wonderful guy in the world. Full of fun, and I mean real fun, not just silly things like to-night. Why, he—he used to throw these fantastic parties at his family's place, and everyone, but everyone, came to them—from New York, from Philadelphia, from everywhere. 'Jimmy's having a party——' the word would start, all over town. People would do anything for invitations, and they usually came anyway, without them, and brought all their friends. His family have a beautiful place in Somerville—they're very rich." Claire's eyes grew misty. " I remember one night someone brought a ladder and we all climbed up on the roof, and someone set off fireworks in the chimney, skyrockets, Roman candles, and things—you should have seen us! And one time there was a terrible drink we made in a huge glass—it had everything in it—gin, whisky, liqueurs, brandy, milk—awful! The Flaming Mame, we called it, after the song, and because it was inflammable, to say the least. We floated a gardenia in the centre of it, and everyone that came through the door had to take a sip of it, before they could come in! He loves people so. He never wanted them to go, never wanted the party to end. He'd do anything to keep the party going. He was never like this. A couple of weeks ago, he and Blazer and I went up to the mountains—behind Squaw Valley. Jimmy brought a huge Thermos of martinis! That's the sort of funny, wonderful things he always used to do . . ." She turned to Blazer, who sat on the sofa, gazing stonily into space. " Remember at college, Blazer? " she said. " Remember Jimmy's twenty-first birthday party, when everyone rode bicycles down the stairs of the Zeta Psi house, with toilet-paper streamers, and for hors d'œuvres we ate empty ice-cream cones, and there were balloons filled with helium all over the ceiling, and oh—just fabulous! He was always organizing things—wild, crazy, fantastic things. He'd get that look in his eye one day and say, ' Let's have a party,' and then off we'd go, only every party had to be the party to end all other parties . . ."

" Where did it all end? " Sue Fry said.

" Here. To-night, in this living-room. Oh, no, not really, of course. Because he's been through a lot—that's why he flew off the handle to-night. He'll be the way he used to be again, I know. I have too much faith in him. I know he won't be like this always——"

" Well, no wonder his poor wife——"

" No, you don't understand," Claire said. " Poor wife indeed! I met her——" She stopped abruptly. " I mean, I never met her," she went on quickly. " Neither Blazer nor I have ever met her. They were married only for a short time, but when I think of what that bitch has done to him——"

" It is a shame."

" He used to stand in the middle of the room, like a god or something. Like Adonis or Apollo—he didn't use to be so thin, and everyone in the room would converge upon him, and he'd talk—he would say the most wonderful things. There was a group of friends he had—Pat Berry, the Caldwell twins, Elizabeth and Mary Lewis, Joanne Furness and whoever her current beau would be, myself, Blazer, Scrib Newton, Harry Gerische, and Lou Bonner and his girl, Carrie Henderson—they were the nucleus of it. Really, he was the nucleus, because there never was a set group before he came along—and we flamed—oh, how we flamed! The roaring twenties had nothing on us. Not only had we all had our first drink before we were sixteen—we'd done more than that. We'd been drunk, and been sick, and been taken out to the car, and we'd been crazy in love and cried on some strange boy's lap all the way home, we were so in love with someone—usually him. He created a kind of fiction out of our lives for a moment—giving us wonderful tales to tell, all this before we were even *in* college. And then of course college——" Claire stopped, wondering if she was weaving too much of a fiction around Jimmy's life.

The last people yawned. " It all sounds very exhausting," Phyllis Brower said. " Too bad we can't keep up that pace any more ourselves." She looked at her husband. " Remember we have to get the sitter home, Bill," she said.

" There was no pace! " Claire said desperately. " It was just —well, *interest* was what it was to keep up. Of course we all knew that nothing we did was—important, or even very worthwhile, but we loved him just the same. We still do! "

She excused herself and went into the bathroom. She found Tweetums DeMay sprawled, face downward, on the white tile floor, a pathetic figure with her black faille cocktail dress twisted around the backs of her knees, above her stocking tops. Her arms were outstretched, embracing the toilet bowl. Claire sat down on the edge of the bathtub and burst into tears.

When Jimmy awoke the next morning, he had to spend a minute or two figuring out where he was. He was in an unfamiliar room, on a lumpy sofa; the walls of the room were hung with assorted fishing prints and snapshots secured with pieces of Scotch tape. On a cluttered desk in the corner stood a pile of books, phonograph records, and newspapers. In another corner was a pile of athletic equipment, hockey sticks, lacrosse sticks, ski poles, tennis rackets, and fencing foils. Jimmy sat up, swung his legs over the side of the couch, and shook his head, trying to clear it. Mike Gorman appeared from the kitchen carrying coffee in an aluminium percolator. He was wearing a white T-shirt, khaki pants, and a pair of woolly bedroom slippers. " Hi," he said easily. " How're you feeling? "

" Rotten," Jimmy said, rubbing his jaw. It was swollen and tender. " What happened? " he asked. And then he said, " Never mind. Don't tell me."

" Want some coffee? " Mike asked.

" Thanks."

Mike poured some of the black steaming liquid into a cup and handed it to Jimmy. Jimmy took the cup with both hands and sipped it. " Is this your place? " he asked.

" Yeah—how do you like my view? " Mike gestured towards the window. Beyond it was a smooth grey steel tower. " Best view of the gasworks in the city, I bet." He smiled. " How's your jaw? "

" Great. I'm in great shape," Jimmy said.

" I don't blame you for wanting to clobber that boy," Mike said. " He and I had a few brief words earlier in the evening."

" Yeah," Jimmy said. He sipped his coffee.

" I thought you had him at first," Mike said. " He outweighed you by about thirty pounds, that's all. Still, he didn't look so pretty when he left."

" I'm sorry," Jimmy said. " You must have had a pretty lousy time. I guess you don't think very much of my friends."

" Heck," Mike said, " I didn't mind them. I've met people like that before. They're just a little young, that's all."

Jimmy looked at him. Mike smiled his broad, sunburned smile. " Thanks for taking me out of there," Jimmy said, humbly.

" Don't mention it."

" I guess that's the end of them. I guess I'm glad."

" You could do a lot better."

" I know."

Mike Gorman sprawled in the chair opposite. " If you feel up to it," he said, " we could drive out to the beach and go fishing. I usually do on Sundays. I've got an extra pole."

" Okay." Jimmy looked into his empty cup. " Christ," he said, " I wasn't drunk, was I? Never mind—I know I was. I must have been a little drunk, or I wouldn't have hauled off at him. Christ! Why do I keep on drinking so much? " He stroked his tender jaw again.

" Well, why do you? " Mike asked.

Jimmy shook his head. " I don't know," he said.

" Why don't you stop? "

Jimmy looked at him. " Well——" he began. And then, a little defensively, " What do you mean, stop? "

" Stop. Quit. Swear off. Or——"

" Or what? "

" Or I don't know. Some people have a—a habit of drinking, which makes it harder. Look, I'm not trying to criticise——"

" I know, I know," Jimmy said. He reached for the percolator and poured himself another cup of coffee. " Stop," he said softly.

" Sure. Why not? "

" You're referring to last week, I suppose," Jimmy said. " Sleeping on the beach? Well, that was different——"

" I'm not referring to that," Mike said, smiling. " Hell, I've slept on beaches."

" I suppose I could stop," Jimmy said. " I could just stop, like that. Like you said. But what would be the use? It would mean the end of Claire and Blazer . . ."

Mike Gorman sat way back in the chair and stretched his legs forward. He put his thumbs in the top of his trousers. " What did that guy say to you, anyway? " he asked. " Why did you clobber him? "

" Oh, it's a long story," Jimmy said. " Do you want to hear it? "

Mike swung his long legs over the arm of the chair. " Sure," he said, " if you want to tell it."

In the valley, the day was warm. It was a Sunday, and, in a religious community like Rio Linda, it was a churchgoing Sunday. Bells, from the seven churches in the town, sounded periodically, some close, some far away. It was a church-going Sunday and a car-washing Sunday, Helen thought as she walked down Lime Street by the park. The gutters trickled with water from the car washers, busy in driveways with their garden hoses. The sidewalks were decorated with churchgoers, in their church-going best, singly, in pairs, some with children. You could almost tell, by the way the women were dressed, which church each was attending. The High Episcopalians wore cool linen suits from Magnin's, white gloves, pastel shoes, small, expensive straw hats. The Methodists looked hot in dark hats, dark shoes.

From Okey town, came women in damp dark cotton dresses, often hatless, with bare legs, leading their children, who were uncomfortably crammed into grown-up-style hats and collars, going to the Church of the Foursquare Gospel. From the distance, a faintly discordant carillon began. " Rock of Ages, cleft for me . . ."

Helen was not going to church. Her family had never been churchgoers. (" There's no sweeter sound," her father used to say, " than the sound of church bells ringing across the golf course on Sunday morning.") She was dressed simply, in a cotton skirt and blouse, and she walked slowly, with her hands in the pockets of her skirt, under the trees that bordered the park, smiling hello at people she knew, stopping to chat with others.

" Good morning, dear, how are you? "

" Fine, thank you. And you? "

She walked on. She had no particular destination. She was walking for exercise, for relaxation, for something to do. She wished, in a way, that she was going to church. She wished religion compelled her, moved her the way it seemed to move some people, comforting them, giving them something to feel. Rosary beads in their hands, a silver cross, the feet of a statue, a shaft of sunlight through a stained-glass window, the smile of a saint's face, the swinging censer, murmurous chants and benedictions, signs and radiances—faith. Something to feel. Religion, to her, existed in terms of these unrelated feelings; she did not understand them, she had never tried. It was shameful, really, she thought, to know so little about what went on inside a church. Was it only feeling, impressions, emotions swelling from songs—or was it also something thoughtful, intellectual, reasonable? She didn't know. It would be a worthwhile thing to do, she thought, to get some books on religion, read them, and acquire a little authoritative knowledge. Perhaps she would.

Spending her time until the baby came would be a problem, she could see that. Life, which had been so tumultuous for a few months, had slowed abruptly to a great, calm quiet. A quiet of mornings in the garden, talking with her mother, napping in the afternoons, sitting in the sun. She could not live this way for ever. Soon, but perhaps not yet, things must be decided. She would have to take some course. Perhaps she could take a job, get a nurse for the baby, move away from home, find a little apartment.

It was not an exciting prospect, but then nothing seemed to be these days. Was this the divorce doldrums? This irresoluteness, uncertainty, a feeling of being neither this thing nor that thing? Rock of Ages, she thought, cleft for me. Let me hide myself in thee. Ah, at least that would be something, a quiet place in the cleft of a great rock with no thinking, no wondering about the future. She tried to lift her thoughts out of this channel of despair. She tried to think that having the baby would give her life purpose. After the baby, she told herself, everything would be all right. But that was hard to believe. It was even hard to believe that there would be a baby. What would it be like?

At least she had told Jimmy, she was glad of that. At first, she had planned not to tell him, but that would have been too cruel. She remembered the shocked expression on that blonde girl's face when she told her. She had not realized until then, really, that she was being unfair, trying to keep everything private, within herself.

But I am a private person, she thought. I am afraid to be known, to be seen, to expose the horror within me, afraid to confide in people until I am sure that they love me. . . .

That girl, Claire—what a surprising thing that had been, what a strange visit! She was certainly pretty. She had an emphatic prettiness that Helen herself lacked, a positive, movie-star prettiness. She was Jimmy's type. He should have married someone like Claire, Helen thought, instead of someone like me. They would make an attractive couple—Jimmy so dark and tall, Claire so gold-coloured and tinkly, like a pretty ornament—and gay. Jimmy liked things gay. He liked the party to go on. He hated to see the guests go home, or to see the bar close. She laughed bitterly. Had Jimmy found her dull? she wondered. Was that it?

If only . . . if only . . .

Why did you keep on hurting me? she asked him now, almost aloud. Why didn't you stop, or pause, just once? Couldn't you see that I was capable of love in my own way, in my own quiet, private way? How could you think I was cold, when I tried to explain at Yosemite, when I asked you——? Didn't you ever understand what I was trying to tell you? A secret about me . . . and about yourself—or did you understand the secret and decide it was far too dull to live with? I know I'm not perfect, she said. I am not smart. I am not beautiful, or gay—or even inspired! But you could love me, and you seemed to once. And I. I love you!

What was he doing now? His life involved Claire, she was sure. A party here, a party there, this one or that one for dinner, this group of friends now, another group later, never any finish. Something new, some new place, some new, nice person he could laugh with—that was what he lived for, wasn't it? They loved him, she was sure, for his impression, the impression he made with them. Not for anything true or fine or honest within him, things she had glimpsed once upon a time, or thought she had. They loved him for his money. In their eyes, he could afford to make any mistake he wished. "The Keefes never make mistakes," he had said. How much does a mistake cost? A hundred dollars? A thousand? Pay for it. Go on to another.

I'm thinking crazy again, she thought.

She had come to the corner of Oakdale Avenue. The park ended there, and Lime Street continued on, downtown, past the hospital, the courthouse, the movie theatre, to the railroad station, out to where it joined Route 99. She turned and started back.

She didn't feel well. She felt a little dizzy. It was the heat, the terrible valley heat. She turned under the trees and found a bench and sat down. She felt breathless. Then she felt a curious flutter, soft and inward, like butterfly wings. That was all.

She had felt life. Her child. It had gone as quickly as it had come, but of course that was what it was. She pressed her hands below her breasts, wondering if it would come again. It did not, but she waited for it anyway. And with a strange preknowledge, she thought: It's a boy and his name is Billy. She began to laugh, as though the rock she had prayed would open had opened, sucked her inside, and pressed its hard warm sides about her, in ecstasy, mother and son.

PART THREE

17

In California, the approach of winter is not distinct. There is no true autumn, no real foliage change. Leaves fall, and all at once the elms and sycamores are bare. But the palm trees remain the same, and the rhododendron and boxwood, and, except for a damp chill in the air, it is possible to believe that nothing really has occurred. Winter begins with a rain. Suddenly, the long, dry summer is drenched with a great downpour. Streets run with water, rivers rise in their banks, and dry creek beds become slowly moving, muddy ponds with eucalyptus and poplar trunks rising in the middle of them. Swimming-pools rise to their gutters and turn murky green with algae. In the valley, the ditches and canals from the great dams in the north run swiftly. After this first rain, every day seems to have more rain, or heavy fog, or cold wind, and, for a period, the land of eternal sunshine seems lost in a damp, swirling cloud.

A true Californian respects the rain, and this curious half winter. For Californians never lose their awe of water, the water that made the desert bloom with peaches, apricots, artichokes, lettuce, tomatoes, and grapes. This great source of life returns to California each year, sometimes as early as September, sometimes as late as November.

This particular year, the first rain came on Columbus Day, a Monday, in the evening. Jimmy was sitting on the terrace of the Maguires' house in Fair Oaks, sipping coffee, listening to Bob Maguire tell about the trip he and Margie had made to Pyramid Lake the week before. It was summer weather, the flies buzzed in the air. They had finished dinner, and there was still a charcoal smell and a steak smell from the barbecue, and from other back-yard barbecues along the street. There was a soft, warm wind that tinkled the Chinese wind chimes Margie Maguire had hung in the branches of a lemon tree. Suddenly a drop of rain fell. Jimmy put his hand out, and all at once the downpour came. " Winter's here! " Margie Maguire laughed, and there was a great scurry as they carried cushions, magazines, cigarettes, dishes, and linen from the terrace into the house. By the time they had finished, the three of them were soaking wet. Then Jimmy remembered that the top was down on his car, and raced out into the driveway to raise it. As he opened the door, a waterfall rushed out from the floor of the car. " Damn," he whispered. " Damn! " He struggled with the clamps on the convertible top.

Back in the house, Margie Maguire offered him a towel and a dry shirt of Bob's. Bob had a tray of cold beers on the coffee table, and the television set was glowing. It was time for *I Love Lucy*. Jimmy said no to the shirt, the beers, and the television. He explained that he'd remembered leaving the windows open in the apartment, and he'd better get back to close them. " I've never known it to fail," Margie said. " Whenever I plan a party for this time of year, it starts to rain."

" I thought it never rained in California," Jimmy laughed.

" Thank God it does," Bob Maguire said.

At the door, Margie Maguire took his hand. " Thank you for the box of chocolates, Jimmy," she said. " You didn't need to do it."

It was what she always said.

" I wanted to do it," Jimmy said. " It was a great dinner. The steak was perfect."

" Thank the chef, Monsieur Robert, for that! " Margie said, smiling. She had a wide, expressive face, full of wrinkles and laugh lines. " Come again soon."

" Some day I'll repay your hospitality," Jimmy said.

" Nonsense. How's your avocado doing? "

" Fabulously," Jimmy said. " It's got three honest-to-gosh leaves. How long has it been? Six months? "

" Give it plenty of water," Margie said.

Bob Maguire clasped his hand. " See you to-morrow, boy. Bright and early! "

" Drive carefully," Margie said. She opened the door. " Look at it rain," she said. " Oh, lord, look at it rain! "

" Good night—and thanks."

" Good night."

Jimmy ran across the lawn to his car.

After he had left, Margie Maguire said, " He's such a nice boy, isn't he? He looks happier these days, don't you think."

" He's filling out a bit," her husband said. " This California sunshine is good for him. He's lost a lot of that Eastern whatchamacallit. That paleness."

" Too bad about his wife."

" He's getting over her. This summer was good for him."

On the tiny lighted television screen, Lucille Ball flummoxed across the room. Margie Maguire hugged her skirt around her knees and laughed. " I love it when it rains," she said.

Jimmy drove slowly back through the rain. The streets were flooded, and a high north wind blew leaves from trees across his windshield. He had not left his apartment windows open, he was quite sure, but it had given him a good excuse. He liked the Maguires. It wasn't as though he had genuinely wanted to get away from them. Normally, he would have stayed with them, talking quietly and easily, until eleven o'clock or so. But somehow, with the rain coming as it had, so suddenly, and Margie exclaiming, " It's winter! " he had felt the need to go home. If this is going to be my first winter in California, he thought, I'd better face it alone. He thought of Somerville at this time of year—clear October skies, bright foliage, his mother bringing armfuls of chrysanthemums in from the garden, beginning to talk, expectantly, of " the holidays." What did Californians do at this time of year? Just move indoors out of the rain, he supposed. On Saturday, he and Mike Gorman had talked about driving up to Stinson Beach for fishing. Would it be raining on Saturday, or would it be summer again to-morrow morning?

He and Mike had spent a lot of time together over the summer. It was a curious friendship, in a way, because it was such a quiet one. Often, when they were fishing, for example, hours would go by when they would not speak to each other. There seemed to be no need to. It was as though each knew the other's thoughts so well that conversation was unnecessary. It was a strong friendship, though, perhaps even stronger in its wordlessness. For Jimmy, it was a new kind of friendship, like having a brother. Mike was a quiet boy who was happiest when he was doing something which required a great intensity. One of these was bridge playing, and, at this, Jimmy could equal him.

They competed at this, but with a mutual warmth and understanding that each one trusted completely. They laughed at the same things, hummed the same tunes from *My Fair Lady* as they played.

They had played a great deal of bridge that summer. Al Whalen and Dex Pratt, two friends of Mike's from the bank, played with them as a rule, but sometimes new people turned up. Mike had begun taking out a girl from San Francisco, Cathy Williams, whose tastes, Mike admitted privately, were a little rich for his blood—she liked being taken down to L'Omelette's and Dinah's Shack on the peninsular—but sometimes Cathy and her sister, Margaret, joined them in Mike's Laguna Street apartment for a bridge game. Jimmy and Mike played wonderfully well together, as partners. Their bids always conveyed exactly what they had and wanted, and their hands, by some good fortune, always seemed to blend. They became legendary as they headed for slams with speed and self-assurance. Sometimes, Jimmy spent the night on Mike's couch, and in the morning they would drive to the beach for fishing or swimming, or sometimes they would begin a gin-rummy game, and eventually, by Sunday afternoon, the Williams girls or someone else would come by and another bridge game would start. Jimmy drank only Coca-Cola. He had had nothing to drink since Claire's party. He and Mike never discussed this; again, there seemed no need to. Jimmy was proud of himself, and, he felt, Mike was proud of him, too.

He had had no word from Claire or Blazer since that June night. Evidently, they would not forgive him for the fight in the apartment. This saddened and yet, in a way, relieved him. He tried to push Claire out of his mind. He tried to push Helen out of his mind. He tried to keep everything out of his mind except the present, his job, his new friends. It was not always easy to do, but when he was successful, he achieved a kind of high, lonely satisfaction.

He drove down Capitol Avenue, turned, and put the car in the carport behind the apartment house. He got out and went up the back stairs. Then he remembered his mail—he had gone to the Maguires' straight from work—and went back down the stairs to a row of mailboxes in the courtyard. There were several letters. He carried these up the front stairs with him and let himself into the apartment. He groped his way across the darkened living-room to the light switch. He found it, turned on the light, and started unbuttoning his wet shirt. He looked down at the letters. On top, was a letter addressed in a neat, round, schoolgirlish hand. He picked it up, flipped it over, and saw Claire's Lombard Street address. He studied the envelope a moment before opening it, torn between reading it and not reading it. Then he opened it. "Dearest Jimmy," it began:

I kept hoping that I would hear from you, of course, remembering your manners and "bring-upping" enough to apologize to me, but since so much time has elapsed and you have *not*, I shall eat humble pie and write to you. You *were* a beast, and *not* at all funny, but live and let live, say I. I hope you have spent the last few months in perfect agonies of remorse, and knowing you as well as I do, darling, I wonder: have you?

I hope not, because time heals all wounds, even mine, and I am asking you, begging you, to call or come see us. You see, I am forgiving you all on my own.

Blazer blames me for saying what I did that night, ordering you out, and says I am a complete and utter bitch, that I have destroyed his best friendship. Have I? I hope not. You see, I just kept hoping that you would write or call!

Jimmy dear, *please* come back. We miss you a great deal, really. I guess we got so used to you being around, we didn't appreciate you until you stopped being around. I apologize 1000 times for saying what I did, and you, I know, are sorry, too. It was just a too bad thing, as they say out here.

If it makes you grateful, Stan Erickson wanted to have you arrested for assault and battery, but I prevailed. He is really a nice guy. You were just both a little buzzy. So call. *Please?*

Love,

C.

He folded the letter and put it back in the envelope. He flipped through the other letters—a fraternity newsletter, a couple of bills, a letter from an insurance company. Suddenly he saw that one letter was not a letter at all, but a Western

Union telegram in a yellow envelope. He ripped it open. It was very short.

> YOUR FATHER HAD A FALL. CONDITION MOST SERIOUS. IMPERATIVE YOU FLY HOME AT ONCE. ADVISE FLIGHT NUMBER BY RETURN WIRE AND I WILL MEET PLANE. TURNER L. AMES

Jimmy stood up abruptly. A fall? And why had Turner Ames sent the wire? What was the matter with his mother? He stood in the centre of the room, holding the telegram. Then he went to the kitchen and picked up the phone. He gave the operator the Somerville number.

While he waited, he realized that it was three hours later in Connecticut—past midnight. The number began to ring, and surprisingly, it was answered almost immediately. He recognized the voice of Milly, his mother's maid.

" Milly? Is Mother there? " he asked.

Milly's voice was choked and strange. " Yes," she said.

" Can I speak to her, Milly? "

" She's not supposed to speak to you. You're supposed to come home."

" Milly, what's the matter? "

A pause, then slowly: " Your father—he fell."

" Fell? What do you mean? "

" Down the stairs."

" Is he all right? "

There was silence, and then, at the other end of the wire, Milly sobbed.

" *Milly?* "

" He's dead! " she cried.

" What? "

" He was going up the stairs—and—just like that! Oh! I wasn't supposed to tell you! Please don't tell them I told you! You're just supposed to come home! Oh, please, Mr. Jimmy! It was his heart . . . it just stopped! "

" How's Mother, Milly? " he asked softly.

" Oh, she's terrible! She's taking it so bad! Oh, just come home," she sobbed. " Just come home as fast as you can. Don't talk! Come home! "

18

The next few days blurred and clouded into one. The next morning, he took the plane from San Francisco, and, by evening, he was watching the lighted towers of New York below, the pattern of street lights throbbing up at him through layers of air. Turner Ames was waiting for him at the airport and soberly told him what he had learned already from Milly. (" Be a brave soldier," he said, " just as he would want you to be.") They made the long drive to Somerville in Turner Ames's big car, in silence. As they drove in the drive, and turned under the porte-cochère, Jimmy saw that the white house was ablaze with lights. His mother ran down the steps to meet him and threw her arms around him. " Oh, darling! " she cried. " You're the head of the house now! You're the head of the house! " Tears ran down her face.

Later, they sat in the green living-room, with the curtains drawn, talking—Jimmy, his mother, and Turner Ames. They talked in little sudden spurts, followed by long silences. Melise Keefe wore a long, pale dinner dress, and she held a glass of sherry in her trembling hand.

" Do you want to see him? " she asked once.

" I don't know . . . not yet," Jimmy said.

" We can go now, if we want, can't we, Turner? I haven't seen him yet. But—no. No, we mustn't see him," she said quickly. " I remember something he said once—about how awful it must be, to have people *looking* at you! He'd hate it, Turner. We must have the casket closed at the services."

" Well, Melise, that's a little out of the ordinary . . ."

" Never mind," she said commandingly. " That's the way he'd want it. Will you take care of it, Turner? "

" Very well."

There was another silence. Jimmy could think of nothing to say. He still couldn't believe that his father was dead. At one end of the room, there was a painting of the two of them, his mother and his father. It was a curious painting. It had been done after their marriage, late in the twenties. It showed his father as a young man, in slim trousers and jacket and white shoes, standing in a romanticized garden bower, or pergola; his mother, a girl in white chiffon, sat on a stone bench, looking up at him. It was a Maxfield Parrish mood, full of foliage and sunshine, frankly a sentimental picture of love. And it was a huge painting, the figures nearly life size. How many times he had looked at it, searching the young, unfamiliar faces for things he knew. They were dream people, in a dream garden, strangers in a land where time was frozen. He had never known his father in that painting. He was struck now with the thought that he had never known his father at all. He was filled suddenly with pity for this unknown young man, tall, smiling, and handsome, one hand raised and holding the latticed arbor, dressed like a silent-movie star.

After the funeral, the chauffeur drove James Keefe's black Chrysler slowly back from the cemetery. Jimmy's mother held his hand. " He was so worried about you," she said softly, rubbing his knuckles slowly between the soft fingers of her glove. " He didn't say much, of course, but he was worried just the same—about you and Helen. There's never been a divorce in our family, you know. He was so upset when he heard about the baby; it bothered him to think of her child bearing the Keefe name. When is she to have the baby? "

" I don't know, Mother, I try not to think about it . . ."

" He was proud of you," she said. " So *very* proud of you! For being so brave, and so grown-up, through all the trouble she's caused. Oh, sometimes we used to think about it—about you, all alone out there, having to go through so much. It's a shame! I wish—I wish he had lived to see you married again, happily, to some nice girl. Not a——"

" Now, Mother," he said.

" I can't help it," she said. " I wish her dead! I've never wished that of anyone but her, but I do. I wish her dead! "

" Please, Mother," he said. " A lot of it was my fault."

" Nonsense! "

" Let's not talk about it . . ."

" I just hope he knew—before he went—that it was going to work out happily for you. Do you know what the last thing he said was? "

" No."

" He was in the hall. We were about to go upstairs, but I'd forgotten my sweater. I'd left it in the library. I went back to get it. He started up alone. I keep thinking—if I hadn't gone back for that sweater, if I'd gone up with him, beside him, perhaps I could have—but never mind. I went into the library—and he called, ' Do you think we should phone Jimmy to-night? See how he's getting along? ' And I didn't answer right away, and then I heard him call out, ' *Mellie!* ' like that, and then I heard—oh! " She released his hand and held her handkerchief to her eyes. " But anyway," she said, " you were last in his thoughts, you were last in his thoughts! "

Jimmy put his arm around her. The car turned into the driveway. The day was clear and cool. The house, when they entered it, was strangely quiet; the rooms stretched out emptily on either side of the wide hall. " People may come," she said. " But I can't see them. I've got to lie down. Will you take care of any callers, dear? " She started up the stairs, holding the railing in her gloved hand.

Late that afternoon, Turner Ames arrived at the house. He was dark and sombre in his black coat, black hat and shoes. His starched collar shone immaculately white, secured with a thin gold pin behind the black necktie. He and Jimmy sat in the library. The day was darkening outside, and as Turner Ames sat, he flexed his wrists, exposing a starched white cuff and small gold cuff link on each arm. Then he pulled the black sleeves of his jacket down, then back again, a mannerism Jimmy had noticed long ago. Turner Ames's tone was awed and reverent as he said, once again, all the appropriate things. " Your father died at a very inopportune moment, Jimmy," he said at last. " A very inopportune moment."

" What do you mean? "

" I've been going over his things, of course, as is my duty. Naturally, I haven't had time to go over everything thoroughly, that will take time, but what I feared seems to be true. It was a most inopportune time."

" I still don't see what you're driving at," Jimmy said.

" You see," Turner Ames said slowly, looking away, out the window, " your father expected to have many more good years ahead of him. He had every right to expect that, Jimmy. He was a young man. He was only fifty-three, still in his prime. He had every reason to expect many long fruitful years ahead of him." Turner Ames paused, then went on. " He had begun, as you know, to set things up for his estate. The stock-purchase plan, for example, that we discussed with you a few months ago. It was your father's intention to make certain gifts, in substantial sums—of property, securities, and other items—over the years, in your name, in your mother's name, and, in the event of your remarriage, in your children's names. This was all a part of his long-range plan." He extended the white cuffs again, and drew them back. " This would have the effect of lessening the tax burden on his estate, do you see? He planned to distribute the bulk of his estate before his death. Unfortunately—this plan has barely had a chance to begin. In fact, almost none of his intentions were accomplished."

" In other words," Jimmy said, " there is no money."

" Now, let me explain," Mr. Ames said hurriedly. " Perhaps I myself should take some of the blame for this situation. Perhaps I should have recommended that your father begin this plan years ago. Frankly, I thought there would be plenty of time to work it all out. He was such a robust man! Never the suggestion of ill health! I never imagined anything like this."

" Please," Jimmy said. " Get to the point."

" Well, the point is simply this. Your father's estate is now valued at a very high figure. And it is all in the estate. He had no life insurance; he didn't believe in it. There will be heavy taxes, Jimmy. Extremely heavy taxes which must be paid."

" Is there enough to pay them? "

" Jimmy, you misunderstand me. You and your mother will not be in the poorhouse—far from it. As the will now reads, the bulk of the estate goes to your mother, and, in turn, to you. But, because of this, the estate will now be doubly taxed—first, as it passes to your mother, next, as it passes to you. A very unfortunate thing. Your mother will have plenty to get along on. I shouldn't be surprised if she could continue to live in much the same manner as she has always lived. There are some properties already in your name, which you own, and these, of course, you will continue to own, and earn a small income from. The thing that I'm sorry to say is—that instead of your being, as your father hoped, a wealthy man—you will have to wait until your mother—ah, passes on, before you really will have any of this estate. And by that time——"

"By that time, there won't be much left. Is that it?"

"There will be some, of course. But the tax bite will be terrific. Do you have any idea of what the tax bite will be on your father's estate at present?"

"No."

"I can't give you the exact figures, of course. But it will be well over a million dollars."

Jimmy was silent. "Well," he said finally, "I guess there's nothing more to say."

"It's a terrible thing. If your father's plan had been worked out fully, why, within ten or fifteen years you would have had an income of forty or fifty thousand dollars a year, and a controlling interest in the Keefe Company."

"And now," Jimmy said softly. "Does it seem too crass to ask what I can count on now?"

Turner Ames hesitated. "Three—maybe four thousand dollars a year. You see, a lot of the income property will have to be sold to pay the taxes. Fortunately, there are things to sell—without selling the company. But whatever we have to sell will permanently deplete the estate."

"It's funny," Jimmy said slowly. "I never really believed I'd be rich. I used to hear about all those millions and millions of dollars. It was like millions and millions of balloons. It's as though I knew all along they'd never be mine. Perhaps—I don't know—perhaps it's because I never really wanted them."

"I beg your pardon?"

"Nothing." Jimmy stood up. "Well," he said, "thank you for being so frank with me. I appreciate it."

"I will have to tell your mother, I suppose," Mr. Ames said. "I don't know how she'll take it. I have a feeling she thought there would be unlimited money for her. She will have enough to live on, I'm sure, without undue economies—just as she has always lived . . ."

"What more should she expect?" Jimmy asked.

"I've known your mother for a long time. She likes—well, she is used to having large sums of money on hand all the time. I'm sure she imagined that—one day—she would be an extremely rich woman."

"And she won't now?"

"Comfortably fixed. Not rich. There's quite a difference," Turner Ames said. "Ah—if only your father had been given his full quota of years! Well, I expect I'd better speak to her."

"She's in her study upstairs."

Later, his mother came running down the stairs. "Jimmy!" she screamed. "Jimmy! What's Turner been saying? I don't understand! Jimmy! Where's all the money? *Where's all the money?*"

Turner Ames followed her down. "Melise, Melise . . ." he said.

She stood at the foot of the stairs in her long, pale gown. "*Where is it?*" she cried.

The Sunday after the funeral, there was a telephone call for Jimmy. He picked up the phone and heard a woman's husky voice at the other end of the wire. "Jimmy? This is Georgette Denison. How are you, dear?"

"Fine, Mrs. Denison. How are you?"

"I want to tell you—I want to express to you—my deep sympathy," Mrs. Denison said in her throaty, cultured voice. "I knew your father well, and loved him. It is a great loss to us all. I saw you at the services Thursday, but I didn't get a chance to speak . . ."

"You're very nice to call," Jimmy said politely.

"I was wondering," she said, "are you busy this evening? Could you possibly drive up to Mars Hill?"

"Why—yes, I think I could," he said.

"Could you? I'd ask you for dinner, but I'm cookles on Sundays these days. But I'd love—I'd really love to get a report on my children. Claire-y and Blazer. I know you've seen quite a bit of them out there. I just want to hear all their news . . ."

"Sure, I'd be glad to."

"Could you drive up after dinner . . . around eight-thirty?"

The road to Mars Hill wound along the edge of the river under huge trees, up steep rises, and around sharp curves. Jimmy drove slowly, at the unfamiliar wheel of his father's Chrysler. At one turn of the road, Mars Hill appeared silhouetted against the night sky, towers and peaked roofs, chimneys and high, buttressed walls. A few windows glowed with orange light. The house disappeared, and at the next turn he came to the high, arched gate. He entered the drive, past the empty gate-house and the no-trespassing signs, and drove up the hill to the house.

Mrs. Denison came to the door herself; the front door of Mars Hill was huge, made of oak, and banded with large, iron spears, and as she pulled it open and stood there, in the lighted arch, she looked curiously small. She kissed Jimmy lightly on the cheek, and whispered, "Dear boy." Her breath, behind the heavy perfume, smelled faintly of cigarette smoke and Scotch whisky. "Come in," she said. "I'm just sitting down to have a little after-dinner drink."

She led him across the huge black and white marble foyer, through another archway, into an enormous living-room that had been copied from the Great Hall of Warwick Castle. The walls were hung with tapestries from the high vaulted ceilings, and, resting on an expanse of crimson carpet, the furniture that filled the room seemed miniature, dwarfed. A few lamps were lighted, but the corners of the room were dark and shadowy. In front of a white sofa, on a marble coffee table, was a silver tray that held two crystal decanters, a bowl of ice-cubes, tongs, and heavy crystal glasses. One glass glowed brownly with Mrs. Denison's drink.

Mrs. Denison was a short, rather plump woman, and she wore a dress that was much too ornate for her figure. It was made of dark green silk, and, at the sides and back, it was gathered in huge folds and swags. She sat on the sofa and arranged the dress about her. Her small plump hands flashed with chunky emeralds, and two more emeralds glittered at her ears. Jimmy sat down opposite her., " Now you must tell me everything," she breathed in her throaty voice. She crossed her ankles, and Jimmy noticed that she wore elastic stockings. " Will you have Scotch or bourbon? " she asked. She reached out and fingered the heavy silver medallions that hung about the necks of the decanters; the huge emeralds—there were three, on three fingers of her left hand—caught the light.

" Nothing, thanks," Jimmy said.

" Nothing! " she gasped. " Nothing at all? "

" No, I'm on the wagon these days." Jimmy smiled.

" What on earth *for*? " she said, giving him a long, horrified look. " Won't you have one little drink? "

" Well—I'll have a Coke if you have one," Jimmy said.

Mrs. Denison looked annoyed. " Oh, dear," she said, " I don't think—well, there may be some in the kitchen."

" Please don't bother——"

" Oh, it's no trouble." She stood up again. " I'll see what I can find. I'm absolutely servantless Sundays," she sighed. " Aren't servants *dreadful* these days? Does your mother have the same problem? " She started across the room.

Jimmy stood up. " Can I help you? "

" No, no."

She was gone for what seemed like fifteen minutes. Finally she returned, carrying a bottle of Coca-Cola. She handed it to him. " Will you fix it with ice-cubes and things? " she said. " I'm sorry to be so informal, but you understand."

Jimmy put an ice-cube in a glass and poured the bottle into it. " Where's Mr. Denison? " he asked.

" In Washington," she said, sitting down again. " He's always in Washington these days, it seems. Poor Junius. He works too hard."

" Then you're all alone? "

" Yes. Well, America is upstairs. America is my cook; isn't that a wonderful name? But she refuses to do a thing for me on Sundays. If I rang for her now, she wouldn't come down." She laughed. " America is one of Father Divine's angels. I don't know what she does in that room of hers. Polishes her wings, I suppose! " She picked up her drink and looked through it. Then she drank. " Now tell me all about my children," she said.

"Well—what would you like to hear first?"

"Tell me about the apartment. Is it pleasant? Claire-y's no housekeeper, I know. Does she have anyone?"

"I think she has a cleaning woman that comes in once a week," Jimmy said. "It's a wonderful apartment—all glass. A marvellous view of San Francisco—both bridges."

"Oh, I'm so glad it's nice. It belongs to a friend of Junius's. He assured us it was nice. The address sounded all right. Russian Hill is pleasant. I haven't been to San Francisco in a long time. We always stayed at the Fairmont, which is a pleasant hotel. Tell me, have Claire-y and Blazer made any pleasant friends?"

"Oh, they have quite a few friends. A lot of people from the East seem to pass through from time to time, of course. Claire gave a—a very nice party this summer."

"I've been trying to get them to join the Burlingame Country Club," Mrs. Denison said, "but they don't seem interested in it. I should think they'd enjoy getting out into the country once in a while, after being cooped up in the city. But they have minds of their own, don't they?" She smiled and sipped her drink. "There's no arguing with them. I wonder—when do you think they plan to start working on a family?"

Jimmy flushed. "I—I really don't know," he said. "I guess they're too busy having fun right now."

"Oh. Well, I hope they don't postpone it *too* long. You see, I'm quite sure that once they start on a family, they'll have to come back East. They couldn't continue living there with children, could they?"

"It's not a large apartment," Jimmy said.

"Yes. We're trying—Junius and I—to persuade Blazer to come back and work for Junius. We're trying to persuade without letting Blazer know we're persuading. We'd really like it. We'd prefer to have our little Claire-y a *tiny* bit closer. After all, San Francisco is not a place where one lives."

Jimmy laughed softly.

"I mean, why should they want to?" Mrs. Denison looked at him searchingly. She reached for the medallions on the decanters again, studied them, and lifted the bottle designated "Scotch." She splashed some of the liquid into her glass. Mrs. Denison's hands moved slowly, carefully, replacing the decanter on the silver tray gingerly, as though she feared it might fly out of her hands. Jimmy realized suddenly that the drink she had when he arrived had not been her first. Even her speech was slow and cautious, each word pronounced with care. "Now tell me," she said, "have they made any pleasant friends?"

It was the same question she had asked him a moment before and Jimmy fumbled a moment for a different answer. "There was a girl at the party," he said. "Diane Higbee——"

"Oh, I know Diane," Mrs. Denison said. "She's from New York. I mean, San Francisco people."

"Well, there's Tweetums DeMay . . ."

"*Tweetums* DeMay! Goodness, it sounds like a chorus girl or something! Who is she?"

He moved uncomfortably in his chair. "I don't really know," he said. "I just met her that evening."

"And Blazer? How is he doing?"

"Fine. Working hard . . ."

"Yes. Blazer is a hard worker. But he does have a mind of his own, doesn't he? He's a very determined boy, don't you think?"

"Of course, I've known Blazer most of my life," Jimmy said.

"Oh, of course. I'd forgotten that. You were both at Taft, weren't you?" The glass in Mrs. Denison's hand trembled slightly as she raised it to her lips. "Junius and I have great hopes for Blazer. But of course Junius could do so much more for him if only he'd come back East. He needs things to be done for him, we both agree."

"Why do you say that?" Jimmy asked.

"Well, for obvious reasons," she said, looking at him with heavy-lidded eyes. "He has no money. You know all about that."

"Not exactly . . . I thought . . ."

"Goodness, didn't you know that? Of course you knew about his parents."

"That they're both dead, yes."

"Yes, they were both killed in a terrible auto accident in Florida, when Blazer was just a baby. Blazer's father, Billy Gates, was—well, sort of a ne'er-do-well, really. He was what we called a playboy in those days. He played polo, and liked to drive foreign cars. Blazer's mother was a giddy little thing —they used to race around. Billy Gates came out of the crash in '29 with a little money, but he squandered it all, poor dear. By the time he died, he was monstrously in debt. Poor little Blazer was left all alone in the world."

" But his uncle——"

Mrs. Denison put down her glass emphatically. " Oh, his uncle is quite a different story. Stu Gates managed his money and bounced right back. Oh, Stu Gates is one of my favourite people. He's done everything for Blazer—educated him, brought him up—but Stu Gates has children of his own. None of Stu's money will go to Blazer. Not more than a token, anyway."

" Oh, I see."

" That's what I mean by helping Blazer." Mrs. Denison lifted the decanter carefully once more, and poured. " Would you like another whatsis? Coca-Cola? " she asked.

" Thanks, I still have some."

Later, Mrs. Denison's eyes grew bright and sparkly; she was talking more rapidly, and, as she talked, she gestured with her glass. The drink sloshed inside it. " Oh, I'm glad they're happy! " she said. " And that they're having fun. Let them sow a few wild oats, I say. Let them have their fun. There's time enough for the other thing, the other business. Keep telling me things," she said.

Jimmy told her about the week-end on the mountain, riding up the ski lift from Squaw Valley, climbing across the rocks and nearly falling, climbing down the other side, and sleeping, under the stars, in sleeping-bags. He told her about swimming in the lake, Claire cooking breakfast over a fire. As he talked, Mrs. Denison's eyes wandered, over his shoulder, about the room. He had the feeling that she was not really listening. She interrupted him from time to time. " What did Claire have on? " she asked. And then, " I hope she's watching her weight."

And when he said that Claire was wearing blue jeans, Mrs. Denison said, " When we picked her trousseau, we didn't know about San Francisco. Does she ever wear the blue lace? "

Jimmy returned to the party, but Mrs. Denison interrupted him again, this time talking about Blazer. " He's a wonderful boy, isn't he? And kind to Claire-y, isn't he? He never does anything unkind to Claire-y, does he?"

"Oh, I'm sure not," Jimmy said.

"Some men are not kind," Mrs. Denison said, and reached for the decanter once more. She started to lift it, then put it down. She put her drink down, and then reached for the decanter with both hands. "Oh, I think Blazer is more like his father than Stu. No. I mean he's more like *Stu*. Not like his father, Billy. Blazer is named for Stu. And he's more like him. Billy was wild. I knew him in the old days. But Stu is my favourite people. Oh, yes. Stu is the Rock of Gibraltar. When they made Stu Gates, they broke the mould." She laughed gaily, swinging the drink in her hand.

"I've got to be getting back soon," Jimmy said.

"Oh, don't go yet!" she exclaimed. "Tell me more. Is Blazer kind to Claire-y? I hope so. We watched Blazer through the growing-up process, Junius and I. We had him sort of picked out—for Claire. He was a beautiful child. We didn't care that he had no money. Goodness, Claire-y will have plenty of her own. He was such a nice, well-mannered boy. He used to come over here to play tennis. He played beautifully! Don't you think that boys when they reach their puberty are at the most beautiful state? Something happens to them around the hips and around the eyes and shoulders, and their faces become a little bit grave and enchanted!" She smiled and her eyes glistened with tears. Then she put her head back on the sofa and closed her eyes.

"I really must get back, Mrs. Denison," Jimmy said.

"No, no." She straightened up once more. "It's so wonderful to talk to you, dear," she said. "It's wonderful to know you're out there—with them. Part of home."

"They've been very nice to me," Jimmy said.

"Have they? Oh, yes, I heard. I'm sorry. About your wife. Well," she sighed, "we all make mistakes. But they are happy, aren't they? Blazer and Claire?"

"Very happy."

"Happy!" She laughed suddenly. "Happy! Thank God somebody's happy! What do you think of a man who strikes a woman?"

'I beg your pardon?"

Her eyes closed once more. "Junius! He's a brute. He struck me, knocked me down. Oh, I suppose there are some who think he's God. Down at the plant, they all think he's God! I've heard that. Junius is God. Well——"

Jimmy put down his glass. "I'm sorry, but I've got to——"

"Little Claire," Mrs. Denison said. Her voice was deep and rattling. "Little Claire-y. '*Clair de Lune*'!" Once more she opened her eyes, her head back, looking upwards at the dark rafters above. "Did I ever tell you why I named her Claire? When I was a girl, Claude Debussy played it for me on the piano! It must have been 1910 or 1911. I was just a child. Mother and I were in Paris and we were having dinner with the President of France. What was his name? I don't remember now . . . such a nice, funny Frenchman. It's on the tip of my tongue—his name. But Mother knew him. She knew Debussy. She called him Achille—I remember that. He was Claude Debussy, but Mother called him Achille—he went to the piano after dinner. I was sitting on the knee of the President of France—I had long, long blond curls! But Achille Debussy went to the piano and played and played! Then he said, 'This is for you,' only he said it in French, and looked at me. And it was the most beautiful song I'd ever heard! '*Clair de Lune*'! Just for me!" Her eyes widened and brimmed with tears; she reached for a lace-fringed handkerchief and dabbled her nose. "Oh, dear! To think that I've come to this . . . my little girl . . . and Junius! Everybody's gone!" Tears ran down her face.

"You know," she went on. "You know my misery. You know death. You've just come from death . . ."

"Please, Mrs. Denison," Jimmy began.

"No. Quiet. Don't talk. Listen to me about Junius, what he's done to me. He's God, they say. He's the most hateful, the most horrible——"

"Please——"

"Quiet. Leave me alone. Can't you see I'm unhappy?"

"I'm sorry, Mrs. Denison——"

She took a long, endless swallow from the dark brown drink and hunched forward on the sofa, rocking slowly back and forth, sobbing, a small, round, fat figure in green folds and festoons of silk, her grey hair rumpled, the pins falling out. She raised her small veined hands, heavy with the three emerald rings, and pressed them against her face. "Go away!" she moaned. "Go away! Leave me alone! Leave me to my misery!"

He hesitated, then stood up, turned, and left her sitting there. He walked across the enormous living-room—the room so huge that the furniture in it seemed doll size, overpowered by the high walls, the dark tapestries, the curiously beamed and vaulted ceilings. It seemed to take an eternity to get across the sea of crimson carpet to the other side, through the archway, and across the black and white marble foyer to the door. Somewhere, in the empty house, a clock began to strike. It struck only four times, echoing hollowly in the night, although the time was ten o'clock. Jimmy lifted the iron latch on the great oak door that looked as though it had been built for a church, and let himself out.

On Monday, Jimmy and his mother had a quarrel.

"I never dreamed you were going back!" Melise Keefe said. "How can you leave me here all alone?"

"But you won't be alone," he said. "You've got your friends, you've got Aunt Marian, Aunt Celeste . . ."

"And I'll be penniless!"

"But that's not true, Mother!"

"You're supposed to be the head of the house now! How can you desert me?"

"I'm not deserting you! If you want me for anything, I can fly back in seven hours. Don't you understand? I've got a job. I can't just walk out on that——"

"You could get another job."

"I like this one, Mother. And I'm—I'm committed to it."

"You're committed to me! To your father's memory!"

"That's not fair, Mother——"

"What about the company? Are you going to let that go?"

"I never wanted to work for the Keefe Company. Father understood that——"

"But what will happen to it? There's always been one of the family at the head of it!"

"The Keefe Company will go on," he said. "They'll probably make Turner Ames president. We've got our stock in it. We don't have to work for it, too!"

"Oh, if your father could hear what you're saying!"

"Please, Mother. If he could hear—he'd understand——"

"*I* don't understand," she said.

"Look, Mother," he said gently, "I've tried to do something on my own. It isn't finished yet. Let me finish it first—if I can."

"Finish what?" she said angrily. "Finish making a mess of your life? You talk as though you were actually accomplishing something out there. What have you accomplished? All you've done is get some silly girl pregnant, and have her sue you for divorce! Are you proud of that?" She stood up. "You talk so *noble*! Doing something on your own! What have you done except fail at everything and bring shame on us all? Why don't you admit you've made a fool of yourself and leave that place—while you *have* an excuse!"

He was silent, staring at his open hands. Then he said, "I'm sorry, Mother."

She came to him and put her hands on his shoulders. "Forgive me, darling," she said. "I didn't mean that!"

He said nothing.

"Jimmy, I'm sorry. It's just that I should think you'd want to get away from that state—where she is. Where you've had so much trouble. I should think you'd want to come home now—where we can be happy."

"I'm sorry, Mother, but I've made up my mind. I'm going back. For a while anyway. I've got to."

"Jimmy, I *implore* you!"

"Mother," he said quietly, "what would you say if I told you that I still love her? That I want her back?"

"I would say," she said, her voice breaking, "that you're trying to break your mother's heart!" Melise Keefe turned and walked rapidly out of the room.

That night, in San Francisco, Claire and Blazer also quarrelled. Claire had put down the telephone after trying, without success, to reach Jimmy in Sacramento.

"He's just not answering the phone," Blazer said angrily.

" He knows it's us, and he's not answering. It's all your damned fault! "

" Why is it mine? Why? I wrote him——"

" You told him to get out. You threw him out. He was my best friend. You threw my best friend out! "

" I apologized . . . I did everything I could think of . . ."

" You've destroyed a friendship that meant a lot to me," Blazer said, his voice hard and even. " I'll never forgive you for that as long as I live."

She didn't answer him.

19

THE day was too cold for fishing. Jimmy and Mike sat in heavy sweaters and windbreakers on a rock above the beach and ate the hamburgers they had brought from Al's place, back on the cliff. There was a raw north wind that whipped the grey sea into white caps and sent mists of spray into the air. They ate in silence. They had talked most of the afternoon. Jimmy had told Mike about his father, about the funeral, about Turner Ames. He also told him what his mother had said. Mike listened quietly.

They finished the hamburgers and wiped their fingers on the waxed-paper wrappings. They wadded the paper and stuffed it back into the paper bag. Suddenly, the late afternoon fog bank came sweeping in from the sea. They watched it racing across the surface of the water, and all at once they were inside it. The sea disappeared. All around the rock where they sat the fog heaved and floated; the sound of the breakers on the beach seemed to come from far away.

"You know, it's really kind of beautiful," Mike said.

"What is?"

"This—everything. California."

"Yes," Jimmy said.

"Everything that happens out here is bigger than life. We have fog in New England—but it's nothing like this. This is the granddaddy of all fogs."

"Sure," Jimmy laughed. "It's California. It has to be the most magnificent fog on earth."

"Everything's that way. The mountains are bigger, the beaches are wider, the trees are taller . . ."

"The Golden Gate Bridge has the longest single span——"

"Ah, you're not taking me seriously. I mean it. I mean it's beautiful—nature."

" I know what you mean," Jimmy said. And then he said, " Mike, how come you're so grown up? "

" What do you mean? "

" I mean, how did you get to be? My God, you and I are the same age—but you're really years older than I am. How did you go about it? "

" Maybe I had to," he said. " Maybe you always had somebody else to jump in and take your side and help you out."

" I suppose you're right."

" Cheer up," Mike said. " I'm sorry about your father, I really am. But you know, in the long run, it may be the best thing that could happen to you. Because now you're really on your own. Don't take that the wrong way—but think about it."

" Yes."

" I forgot to tell you," Mike said. " She called me up."

Jimmy looked up. " Who did? "

" That girl—Claire."

" Really? "

" Yes, last week when you were away. She was trying to get in touch with you."

" I got a letter from her," Jimmy said. " I suppose I ought to call them up."

" She didn't know where you were. She acted like I was trying to keep you a prisoner or something. I told her I didn't know where you'd gone, but she insisted I was hiding something."

Jimmy laughed. " That sounds like Claire," he said.

" She's in love with you, old trooper. Did you know that? "

" Oh, no," Jimmy said quickly. " We're old friends, that's all."

" No, there's more to it than that where she's concerned. I warn you."

Jimmy was silent.

" How about you? " Mike asked. " How do you feel about her? "

" She's just an old friend," Jimmy said slowly.

" I'm not so sure. Have you—have you ever given her any reason to fall for you? "

" What do you mean by that? "

" I don't know. I just wondered."

" You mean, have I slept with her? "

" Perhaps . . ."

Jimmy opened his hands. " Well," he said, " you know everything about me anyway, so I might as well tell you. Yes. It was a damned stupid thing that happened when I was drunk, and I suppose I've got to live with it for the rest of my life. It's just one of a lot of things about myself that I'm ashamed of."

" I sort of suspected it," Mike said.

Jimmy laughed softly. " Damn you," he said, " you're clairvoyant! Do you know everything without being told? How in hell did you know? "

" Oh, at that party, that night we were there. It was just something that occurred to me."

" It was a noble thing to do, don't you think? Your old college buddy goes out of town for a day or so, and you go and call on his wife . . ."

Mike laughed. " I guess Frank Merriwell wouldn't do it," he said, " but the important thing is how you feel about her. Are you in love with her, I mean? "

Jimmy thought about this. " I won't deny there's an attraction," he said. " Maybe I could fall in love with her. But too many other things keep coming in between—like Blazer, and Helen. It would never work. Not in a million years."

" You still carry the torch for Helen, don't you? "

" Yes, I guess so."

" Then why don't you go and see her? "

" No, I can't do that. I called her once——"

" I mean, go and see her. If you really want her back——"

" No, there's no use in that. It wouldn't do any good."

" Then forget about her."

" What? "

" Forget about her. Let her get her divorce. How come she hasn't got the divorce, anyway? "

" There's some mix-up on her residence," Jimmy said. " At least that's what they tell me. When we were married, she became a resident of Connecticut—because I was one. Now she's got to re-establish a California residence from the time we took the apartment."

" Oh, I see."

" But do you really think I should say the hell with her? "

" Do you really want to know what I think? "

" Sure. Tell me."

" I don't want to lead your life for you," Mike said. " But the only thing I think you've got to do is *something.* I mean, do one thing or the other. You've got to decide for yourself, but what you're doing now is—well, it's nothing. You're not getting anywhere. You've got a bad case of inertia, if you ask me."

" Hey, give me time, give me time," Jimmy said. " My God! I've been getting along—fairly well—without a wife. I've also been getting along without alcohol. Now I've got to get along without money. I might be able to get along without one of those things—but without all three? Hell, I just don't know."

Mike looked at Jimmy searchingly. Then he smiled his wide grin and clapped a hand on Jimmy's shoulder. " You'll be all right," he said. " Now let's get back to town and round up a bridge game."

They stood up and clambered down the wet, slippery rock. They walked slowly back across the beach through the thick, swirling fog to the path that led up the steep bank to the parked car.

In the little hospital in Rio Linda, the elevators were too small to hold the rolling beds. The maternity patients from the private rooms on the first floor had to be carried up the stairs to the labour rooms on the second. At six thirty-five, Helen was transferred from her bed to a stretcher, carried up the stairs, and placed in another bed, then rolled down the corridor. It was an awkward, uncomfortable operation, but Helen, actually, was not entirely conscious of it. She was aware of bright yellow lights passing over her head, and the changing sounds of voices around her. With her teeth clenched, she was most conscious of the pain inside her. Then, in the corridor, she heard her mother's voice calling, and above her she saw her mother's face. " Helen, dear! why didn't you call me? I raced over from the garden club as soon as Doris called me. Did you take a taxi all by yourself, you poor child? "

" Please, Mother, go away . . ."

" Helen, dear . . ."

" Please! Go away! "

"You'd better go, Mrs. Warren——" a man's voice said.

"But it's my own daughter! She's——"

"Will you wait downstairs, Mrs. Warren?"

"Helen! Speak to me!"

The man's voice, commanding: "Mrs. Warren!"

The rolling continued, and then a woman's voice said gently, "This is the labour room, Mrs. Keefe."

She was conscious of more bright lights, of shining chromium, of white sheets, and the sound of water running from a faucet. "I'm a little frightened," she said.

"There, there," the nurse said. "It won't be long, Mrs. Keefe."

"Will you call my husband?"

There was no answer.

"What is your name?" Helen asked.

"Mrs. Adams."

"Will you call my husband, Mrs. Adams?"

"No, my dear, the doctor says we mustn't."

"Please, Mrs. Adams!"

"There, there, dear."

She felt a cool towel pressed against her forehead.

"Is the doctor here?" she asked.

"Not yet, Mrs. Keefe."

"I can give you the number, Mrs. Adams."

"This is an injection, Mrs. Keefe," the voice said. "It won't hurt."

She felt a sharp pain in her arm. "Oh, God!" she screamed.

Then, later, she said, "Mrs. Adams! Will you please call my husband?"

"Mrs. Adams is off duty, dear," a voice said. "You'll be having your baby soon."

"Oh, please! Please!"

She felt herself being lifted once more, then lowered on to a hard, flat bed. "What's happening?" she asked.

"She's a little groggy still," a voice said.

Then a masked face bent over her. "Just relax, Helen," a man's voice said. "Put your hands here. Now just relax."

"I am relaxing." The pain came once more.

Then there was a long, shuddering silence. In this void, years passed blackly, and only in the very centre was some vaguely shining thing. Effortlessly, she was back in her mother's garden, walking under hollyhocks and tea roses and thick trumpet vine, and, even before that, she was naked on the sand somewhere, long ago. And then the shining thing—a candle, or a mirror held to the sun—beckoned flickeringly, then went out. In the total dark, she gave up, and curled lovingly in the womb. " I'm very tired now! " she said.

" Push down hard, Mrs. Keefe . . ."

" I can't, I can't . . ."

" You're doing fine."

" Did I make that noise? Oh, God! "

" There, there."

" Did I do that? "

" Can you push down very hard now, Mrs. Keefe? "

" I don't want to make any noise." And then, " Oh, it's not working! Help . . ."

" It's working nicely, Mrs. Keefe . . . you're doing nicely . . ."

" Give me that thing again! "

" There you are! "

She felt it against her face and sucked her breath in sharply. The flickering mirror went out again, and she was alone again in the sweet-smelling dark, surrounded by murmuring voices.

It was six o'clock, Wednesday night, the following week. Jimmy stood alone in the kitchen of his apartment, looking out at the street. It was almost dark, but not quite. Through the bare trees he watched the newsboy coming down the street on his bicycle, splashing through rain puddles on the sidewalk. The newsboy tossed a rolled newspaper deftly on to the steps of the big grey-shingled house across the street, then cut back towards the apartment house, bounced over the curb, and disappeared, momentarily, in the courtyard underneath. Jimmy watched the empty street for a while longer. Then, with amusement, he realized that he was waiting for a signal—for the woman at number 3360 to emerge from around the corner, from her back-yard terrace, to collect the paper, carrying iced tea in a fat, cherry-decorated pitcher. But to-night lights glowed palely inside the house from behind drawn shades. California had moved indoors. He turned away from the window and went to the refrigerator, took out eggs, milk, and butter. He had planned to make scrambled eggs for supper, but when he had the ingredients out on the counter top, he realized he wasn't very hungry. He replaced the eggs in the refrigerator, removed a slice of bread from the loaf, and placed it in the electric toaster. When it popped up, he spread the toast with butter and stood there, in the centre of the kitchen, eating it. He looked around the apartment. The place was a mess. He hadn't really cleaned it since he got back from Connecticut. There was dust everywhere. The sink was filled with sticky coffee cups. It would take, he figured, a full evening to clean it. Perhaps he would do it to-night. He had nothing else to do. Halfheartedly, he ran hot water in the sink over the coffee cups. The water came out in steaming, scalding gasps. He turned off the faucet and wandered into the living-room. The appearance of things there was no better. The hell with it, he thought. He would go to a movie instead. He flopped down on the sofa and stretched his legs in front of him, staring despondently at the opposite wall. On nights like this, when he was alone with nothing to do, he became more aware than ever of the oppressive ugliness of the apartment with its motel-like furniture, its garish attempts to be " modern." Perhaps, he thought, it would do him good to move to another place. Perhaps rent a little house farther out of town. But he reminded himself that he had to keep an eye on his pocket-book.

He jumped off the sofa and went to the door. He opened it and went down the redwood steps to the courtyard to pick up his paper. He opened his mail-box, pulled out the paper, and then saw that there was a special-delivery letter inside. He picked it up and saw that it was from Eldridge Gurney, Helen's lawyer.

He was almost sure, as he ripped it open, standing there in the chilly courtyard, that he knew what it said. He had been expecting it. He had tried not to think about it, but knew that sooner or later it must come. He unfolded the letter and read it. It was very short. It advised him that a son, William Warren Keefe, had been born Sunday morning, November third. Mrs. Keefe and the child were doing nicely. That was all. It did not say how much the baby weighed. It did not give the name of the hospital. It said that his son, William Warren Keefe, had been born November third, and that was absolutely all it said. He folded the letter carefully and placed it in his inside jacket pocket. He turned, with the newspaper in his hand, and mounted the steps again, slowly.

At the door of the apartment, he stopped. He stood there with his hand gripping the door-knob. He had a sensation now that he knew. It was a feeling that went everywhere within him. It was behind his eyes, in the corners of his mouth, in his stomach, and in his fingers. Mostly it was the aching dryness in the corners of his mouth. He wanted a drink. It was very simple. He smiled, examining this feeling vicariously, exploring it. He had not had it for a long time. With a peculiar excitement, he felt it spread. He released the door-knob and reached slowly towards his back pocket for his wallet. He had plenty of money, really. He thought of the little bar nearby. There was a package store on Fourteenth Street. His heart pounded. A pale, floating shape passed before his eyes, then vanished: a drink. He half turned towards the steps.

He was not aware of resisting. He was not aware of fighting anything. But looking down the shadowy steps, he knew that he was not going. He was not going yet. It was not strength, not fortitude, he knew. But he was not going yet. There was too much to think about. He turned back to the door, opened it, and let himself in. He pushed the door closed behind him and leaned against it, not with a sense of triumph, but of despair.

20

WHEN he opened his eyes on Saturday morning and looked out at the grey, rain-filled sky, he thought suddenly of Squaw Valley. He felt like getting away, out of Sacramento, going somewhere alone in the car, driving a long way with the radio going. He thought of the mountains in winter. All at once, the prospect of seeing snow again excited him. He decided to go. He ate breakfast hurriedly, tossed warm clothes into a suitcase, and was on the road by nine-thirty.

It was one o'clock when he arrived at the lodge. He checked in, changed his clothes, and went down to the ski shop, where he rented skis, boots, poles, and bindings. By two o'clock, he was on the chair lift, swinging up the side of the mountain, his ski bottoms brushing the soft, powdery snow underneath.

The mountains looked different now. Shielding his eyes from the glare, he searched the white slopes for the shale-covered trail they had climbed across in June. The wind had carved sharp ridges that concealed the old landmarks. The mountain was new and strange, the summit hidden in a cloud of swirling snow. Then, as the wind dropped momentarily, the cloud vanished and Squaw Peak appeared. At the very top, the wind had swept a clean scar where the black rocks showed through. At the top of the lift, he swung himself off.

Jimmy had been a fair skier in college, but had done little since then. That afternoon, he felt some of his old form coming back. He skied by himself, taking a long cross-country run to keep away from the more popular trails. By five o'clock, it began getting dark, and he skied towards the lodge in the twilight with the sun at his back. He took the last slopes with speed and ease, watching his long shadow race in front of him.

That evening, after supper, he went into the bar and had a

Coca-Cola. There was a week-end college crowd there, from Berkeley, Mills, and Stanford, and the room was bright with ski clothes and noisy with voices, laughter, and tinkling ice-cubes. Sitting on the bar stool with his elbows on the bar, Jimmy felt drowsy and self-contained. His muscles ached pleasantly, and his face was hot and burned from the sun and wind. The rise and fall of sounds in the room seemed far away, and then, this time almost lazily, the phantom of a drink passed before his eyes. The glass he held contained ice-cubes, tinged pale brown with dregs of the Coke, and he stared at it, letting the cubes swirl slowly about inside the glass. In front of him the dark brown bottles glittered behind the bar.

He realized that he had always thought of drinking in terms of things that sparkled, like the glittering parties of his youth. He thought of cocktail parties on south-facing patios in New England, girls in long white dresses holding champagne glasses at débutante parties in New York. Perhaps, he thought, it was the sound of the voices in the room, college voices that sounded the same everywhere, that seemed to pull him back to this shining oblivion of crowds gathering in Yale fraternity houses after the game, of headlong rides into the night in open cars.

He saw himself in white flannels standing in the grass on Derby Day, waving to a crowd of people with a silver cocktail shaker. A couple came running towards him, a girl in a beaver coat and a slender, crew-cut boy who wore a blue jacket with brass buttons—Claire and Blazer. "Jimmy! We've been looking all over for you," she said. And then, on the Yale boat at the crew races in New London, Claire had suddenly for no reason at all kicked off her shoes and thrown them overboard. Jimmy had dived into the water after them and had been pulled aboard, soaking wet, holding the shoes.

At that moment, someone did cry out, "Jimmy!" but it was a second or two before he separated the sound of the voice from his thoughts. Then, turning on the stool, he saw Claire, threading her way through the crowd towards him. "Jimmy!" she cried. "Jimmy!" She reached him and took his hand impulsively. "What in the world are you doing here?" she asked, her eyes shining brightly. She laughed a little hysterically. "Wonderful," she said, "wonderful to see you! I can't believe my eyes!" She stood there, wearing a full black velvet skirt and a black jersey top that glittered with rhinestones. Her bright hair was pinned back with two rhinestone clips in the shape of angel wings. " I drove up for the week-end," Jimmy said. " But what are you doing here? Where's Blazer? "

" Blazer's in Honolulu," she said. " I came up Thursday. I was going view crazy—*really* view crazy. I was opening and shutting the curtains . . . talking to myself . . . oh, Jimmy! " she gasped. " I'm so sorry! "

" What about? "

" I heard—about your father. I had a letter from Mother. Oh, I can't tell you how sorry I am! "

" Oh, that's all right," he said.

" Dreadful——" she whispered. And then she said, " Ah, Jimmy, it's wonderful to see you. You look wonderful. Have you forgiven me for saying what I did that night? I didn't mean it, honestly I didn't. I wrote you a letter——"

" Yes, I'm sorry, I meant to answer it——"

" Then am I forgiven? "

" Of course. There's nothing to forgive."

" Oh, I'm glad. Blazer will be glad, too. He thought—well, he and I wondered, when we didn't hear from you again. Goodness, it's been months since we've seen you. Let's find a table. I'd like a drink."

They pushed through the crowd.

After a little trouble, they found a table in a corner and sat down. Claire rested her bare elbows on the table top. The angel-wing clips in her hair caught the light and sparkled. " I can't believe it," she said. " It's really kind of funny—both of us coming up here alone."

" Was the view really getting you? "

" Oh, yes. And boredom. Nothing to do. I shouldn't have given up the social work. On Thursday I suddenly looked at Scarlet O'Hara all parked and lonesome and thought I must get away. I was going to take ski-ing lessons, but I haven't. I've just been sitting here for two solid days relaxing." She smiled. " Now tell me why you came here."

" Pretty much the same reason," Jimmy said. " I was getting kind of bored with California winter—I thought I'd see what real winter looked like."

" You see," she said, " we're just alike! You can't change

us. But you know," she said seriously, " even this isn't real winter. Have you seen the pool? "

" What pool? "

" The swimming-pool—outside. I went swimming this morning. Isn't that incredible? You walk to it through snow-drifts, and there it is—all heated, carved out of the snow. Isn't it preposterous? But then everything's preposterous in California, isn't it? Preposterous on purpose."

Jimmy smiled. " Ready to go back to Mars Hill? " he asked her.

She looked at him intently. " How was Mars Hill? " she asked him. " Mother said you came by. That was awfully nice of you, Jimmy, to go by. How was everything? Was it just the same? "

" Just the same. Big—overwhelming. The biggest damned house in the world."

" Oh," she sighed wistfully, " but I love it so! It sounds silly, but I do. Do you know that house has a secret room? At least it's supposed to be a secret room. Daddy tells guests about it and tries to make them find it. Very few people can. I know where it is, of course, but it does have a secret panel leading into it. During Prohibition, they kept it filled with liquor Daddy had shipped down from Canada . . ."

A waiter approached them.

" Will you buy a girl a drink? " Claire asked brightly. " I'd like Scotch-and-water."

" One Scotch-and-water," Jimmy told the waiter.

Claire looked at him. " Aren't you having anything? " she asked.

" No, thanks," Jimmy said, " I'm off the stuff."

" Why? "

" Well—I guess it was getting to be a habit."

" Oh, no! " she said. " Really? When did all this come about? "

" Well, I actually haven't had a drink since your party."

" What was that you were drinking at the bar? "

" A Coke."

" Why, Jimmy! " She reached out and covered his hand quickly with hers. " Was it because of that party? Was it because of what I said? Were you afraid you'd hurt me? "

" Well, that was part of it, I guess."

" Poor Jimmy! "

" Why do you say that? "

" I must have hurt you terribly that night. But I didn't mean to. It was all—it all happened so quickly that I really didn't know what I was saying . . ."

" No, it wasn't that," he said. " It really wasn't that."

" Stan is really a nice guy," she said.

" Yes," he said dryly.

" Well," she said defensively, " at least he's somebody for Tweetums. Tweetums needs somebody like that, poor thing. She has a heart as big as a mountain, you know that—but, well, I guess she thinks she's past her prime, and he's been very kind to her, taken her out a lot. Even though she's years older than he is."

" Let's change the subject," Jimmy said.

" Well, I like Tweetums," Claire said emphatically. " I like everybody. Don't you like everybody? "

Claire's drink arrived. She picked it up and held it in front of her eyes, staring through it. " Well," she said, " here's to—here's to Squaw Valley." She gestured around the room. " This is a house-party crowd, isn't it? All these well-scrubbed faces! I feel old already. Does it bother you to see me drink? "

" No. Not especially, no."

" I—I think it's very strong of you," she said. " Not to drink, I mean. You make me feel like a weakling. But then, you always have." She looked up at him and smiled. " You look absolutely wonderful," she said. " You've put on a little weight—but that's good. And you're sunburned and healthy. Just wonderful."

" Thanks."

" Which is your cue," she said, " to tell me I look positively ravishing. Do I? "

He laughed. " Yes," he said, " you do."

" Blazer never compliments me, you know. Or if he does, he does it in such a way——" She broke off, sipping her drink.

" What's he doing in Honolulu? "

" Blazer? " she said, looking dreamily across the room at the crowded tables. " He's gone there to write a long epic poem. He's gone there to paint beautiful pictures of brown-skinned girls bathing in waterfalls with hibiscus blossoms in their hair." She laughed. "He's gone there to sell sheets. What else would he have gone there for? It's almost—obscene, isn't it? Native huts by blue lagoons—furnished with hundred-and-eighty-count percales. But he may take a new job."

"Really?"

"Yes. Have you ever heard of Harry Masterson?"

"No, I don't think I have."

"Well, he's a friend of Daddy's—also in the textile business. He's interested in Blazer. Oh, I just dread it."

"Why?"

"Well," she said, "I suppose it's a good deal for Blazer. It's a West Coast managership. But it means we'll have to stay in this dreadful state."

"You're really fed up with California, aren't you?"

"You know," she said slowly. "You know where I'd like to go . . ."

"I've forgotten——"

"Never mind." She looked up brightly. "Buy me another drink, will you? It's so wonderful to have you to talk to again."

Jimmy signalled the waiter.

"You didn't really need to cut yourself off from us, you know," she said. "Really, it did upset us—not hearing from you, never hearing a word."

"I should have called, I guess," Jimmy said.

"Yes."

Claire's drink arrived, and she said, "I think it's wonderful you've gone on the wagon. I couldn't do it. To me, it would be like—like giving up Arpège, or giving up baths! Oh, I'm being silly, aren't I? But what I mean is, was it really that bad? I mean, I always thought you held your liquor awfully well—you never went off the handle or anything. You always became—well, more *you*. Laughinger, gayer—the way you always were." She looked at him, her eyes clouded, lifting the glass to her dark red lips, then looking away.

Jimmy laughed nervously. "Don't tempt me to fall off again," he said. And the shining thing came again, hovered in his vision, and he watched it inwardly. He reached for a cigarette. He remembered, *be careful of that lighter . . .*

"Am I forgiven?" Claire asked.

" Forgiven for what? "

" For the thing I said. That night . . ."

" Yes, of course."

" Good! Whatever happened to that friend of yours—Mike somebody? The one that came with you to the party."

" Oh, I see him now and then. We went fishing last week-end."

Claire smiled a small, pinched smile. " So you have a new set of friends. What kind of a person is he? "

" Well," Jimmy said, " he's quite a remarkable guy, really. He's—well, he's just one of the few really nice people I know——" He stopped, wondering if this had been an unkind thing to say, but Claire appeared not to notice it.

" What does he do? " she asked.

" He works in a bank."

" How fascinating! " There was sarcasm in her voice. " Rather prudish, though, isn't he? At least I'm quite sure he didn't approve of me."

Jimmy didn't answer her, but looked down at the table.

" But then," she went on, " I suppose there are a lot of people who don't approve of me." When he said nothing, she said, " I'm sorry. I'm being unkind about your friend. It's just jealousy. I'm just jealous because he's seen you and we haven't." She sipped her drink slowly. " Do you remember your Ibsen? Do you remember *A Doll's House*—I think it was *A Doll's House*. The old doctor who lived upstairs. And when he went away, Torvald, or whatever his name was—Nora's husband—said, ' I shall miss him. He was like a dark cloud against our sunlit happiness.' I don't know what made me think of that, except that's sort of what you were—only the other way around—to Blazer and me. A sunny spot in our cloudy happiness." She laughed. " Oh, I'm getting silly! You must stop me when I get silly! "

" That's very flattering," he said lamely.

" Dare I? " she said, rattling the ice-cubes in her glass. " Dare I have another *eau de vie* . . .?

" If you'd like——"

" Tell me," she said earnestly, " how are—things? "

" What things? "

" With Helen. Have you seen her? "

" No."

" Are you divorced yet? "

" No."

" What on earth is taking it so long? "

" I guess these things take time," Jimmy said.

" Why doesn't she go to Reno? "

" I don't know. Maybe she doesn't want to go to Reno . . ."

" I think she's stalling it," Claire said. " She's heard about your father's death. She thinks she's going to get all that money somehow."

" Claire——" he began.

" You forget I've met her," she said. She hesitated, stroking the rim of her empty glass with a polished fingernail. " Has she had the baby? "

" Yes."

" When? "

" Last week."

" Is it—a boy or a girl? "

" A boy," he said.

" Have you seen it? "

" No."

" Do you plan to? "

" I don't know, Claire."

The vision was not vanishing this time as it should. It stayed in front of him everywhere he looked, beckoning. Voices rose and fell in the room, and somewhere, from a nickelodeon, a woman's voice sang, " Love is a simple thing, love is a silver ring . . ." He rubbed his eyes with his fingers, thinking that the curious floating shape would be gone when he opened his eyes again, along with the dry, aching feeling in the corners of his mouth. He felt, all at once, that it was touch and go.

" Jimmy," Claire said, " take my advice. Don't go to see it. Don't ever go to see it. Just pretend it isn't there."

He didn't answer her. " It's important," she said. " You simply mustn't ever see it."

He forced a smile. " Again, do you mind if we change the subject? "

" Poor Jimmy! You've taken it hard, haven't you? Why were we born with New England consciences! We suffer so from the things we bottle up inside us! " She looked away, and he looked at her, wondering if there were tears in her eyes. But she turned and smiled brightly. " Aren't you going to buy me another drink? " she asked.

" You're drinking those things pretty fast, aren't you? " he said.

" Why shouldn't I? " she asked him. " Let's face it, I drink for the effect. I like being a little tight. It's fun. I think everybody should be a little tight all the time . . ."

He rubbed his eyes again. The sounds in the room—voices, laughter, and music—seemed to grow louder. He tried, now, not to look at Claire. He studied the crowd that stood around the bar. With the exception of the way they were dressed, in bright ski clothes, they could have been a crowd at a Yale house party. It made college seem very real and recent. He remembered the self-assurance and swagger and the smell of the streets of college towns, and the smell and sound of college drinking places—always different from drinking places of any other kind. He remembered term papers and midnight candles and sudden bursts of destructiveness that overtook whole groups before exam time, that led young men in wild, spontaneous marches through quadrangles, into streets with pillows flying, riots that ended with someone being depantsed on Chapel Street. He remembered long, wonderful parties that followed the course of a summer's day and ended in a happy twilight of romance.

" Jimmy," Claire said, " are you feeling all right? "

" Yes," he said. " Sure."

" You seem so—you look a little odd," she said.

" Do I? "

" Have a drink——"

" No, no . . ."

" Oh, why not? You deserve one—after what you've been through."

" No, thanks."

" Who would know? I won't tell a single, solitary soul, I promise! "

" That's not the point——"

" What *is* the point? I like you better when you've had a few drinks," she said. " You're not so solemn. Don't look at me that way—so solemn! " She laughed. " Here, let me show you how you look." She reached in her purse and pulled out a jewelled compact, flipped it open and held it in front of his eyes. He smelled the heavy perfume of face powder. " Look at yourself! How solemn you are. You used to be so funny and gay."

" Funny and gay," he said.

" See what I mean? " She withdrew the compact, glanced at her own reflection briefly, and replaced the compact in her bag. " Have one little drink."

He laughed. " No, Claire, no."

She sighed. " Well, please let me have one."

" All right." He turned and signalled the waiter once more.

He couldn't get over the feeling of drifting backwards, in time, to an older place. It was dangerous, he knew, to be sitting here with Claire like this. He felt, once more, the sensation of looking down the cellar stairs, the challenge of going down without turning on the lights.

" You're being positively morose! " Claire said. " Talk to me."

" What shall we talk about? "

" Anything. Talk about thunderstorms. Do you miss thunderstorms as much as I do? I don't think they ever have them out here. Remember the thunderstorms in Connecticut? Remember the way the day gets, just before the storm comes? Oh, I adore thunderstorms! I think I miss them more than anything else."

The waiter arrived, and Claire said, " I'll have another Scotch-and-water. The gentleman is a teetotaller." She smiled brightly. When the waiter left, she said, " The only thing that bothers me is that it's so unnecessary! You didn't need to quit drinking. You didn't need it any more than Blazer, or I—or anyone. Why you feel you must put yourself through this sort of thing, I just don't know. It's masochistic, if you ask me."

" It's sort of a challenge," he said.

" Why do you have to challenge anything? You're more of a man than anybody else I know. Yes, I mean that. You're more of a man than Blazer."

" Don't say that," he said.

" Why shouldn't I? It's true." She leaned forward, speaking with soft intensity. " Do you remember on the mountain? Do you remember going up? Remember—I fell, and you reached out to help me? You offered me your hand. And I said no—I said I'd make it by myself. I think of that so often. I said it because of Blazer—it was what he would have wanted me to say. He wants me to be independent, to survive by myself. He can't have anyone trying to reach for him. If I tried to reach for him, he'd run away . . . he wants me to climb my own mountains. After all, I have the money, he says. But you reached out. You're big enough to—to carry another person! And that's what I want to be—I want to be carried." As she leaned forward, a strand of yellow hair fell across her face, and with the back of her hand she brushed it away. " You're the one who said, ' Hold still, I'll pull you up.' "

He looked at her. " You're really quite an amazing person, Claire," he said. " You're so——"

She reached across the table and took his hand. " Ah, Jimmy," she said. " I do love you! I just do, I can't help it. I've thought about you so much . . ."

" Don't say that . . ."

" Look," she said, staring at him, her blue eyes seeming to grow bluer, " you can drink! You can do anything you want. You can say the hell with Helen. Why don't you have a drink, and drink to—to the hell with Helen? Drink to the hell with the lousy way she's treated you, making you eat dirt, having a child that she'll hold over your head as a weapon—like blackmail. A child that she'll simply use to create more misery for you! "

He felt all at once very limp and tired. " Oh, my God," he said. " Why did I have to run into you? "

" It was fate," she said, smiling. " You see, we're just alike. We're tougher and stronger than other people. You and I are people who tell other people what to do! " And then she said almost angrily, " Jimmy, you're a man. Next to you, who is Blazer? Just a handsome loafer who married a rich girl! Oh, for God's sake, don't let me down! "

" All right," he said quietly, " I'll have a drink."

" Will you? "

" Yes."

" Then let's do it right," she said quickly. " Come back to my room. I have a bottle of Scotch in my suitcase."

" All right."

" Let's hurry! " She stood up, and suddenly giggled. " Oh!

I'm fairly buzzed already! Come on. Let's make it a party. Cancel that order! " she called to the waiter, who was already moving towards them with a drink on a tray.

Jimmy fumbled in his pocket for money to pay the check.

Then he followed Claire across the smoky, crowded room. " My room's in the other building—the annex or whatever they call it," she whispered. " Follow me."

At the door, she took his hand. " Oh, darling! " she said. " Are you scared? "

" Of what? "

" Of this—this affair of ours? "

" I don't know . . ."

" We can cope with it, can't we? "

Then they were outside, coatless, in the clear, frosty night, and she clung to his arm, leading him along the path towards the annex. " It's Johnnie Walker Black Label," she whispered, and laughed again.

They entered the annex and went up the flight of stairs to the second floor. Claire led him down the corridor and stopped in front of a door, fumbling in her bag for the key. She unlocked the door, stepped inside, and turned on the light. Inside, the familiar smells greeted him—perfume, soap, and luggage. The room was strewn with clothes, shoes, and cosmetics. " Don't mind the mess," she said. " I told you I've been relaxing."

She moved quickly about the room, scooping up little armfuls of debris and depositing them in the closet. Then she opened one of the suitcases and extracted the Scotch bottle. She placed this on the crowded dressing-table and disappeared into the bathroom. He heard water running and presently she emerged with two tumblers half full of water. She placed these on the dressing-table and splashed Scotch generously into each glass.

" For ice," she said gaily, " we use this! " She went to the window, threw it open, reached upward and snapped off a large icicle. She showed it to Jimmy triumphantly. " Break it in two for me, will you? "

He snapped the icicle in two pieces and placed a piece of ice in each glass. Then Claire picked up the glasses and swirled them in her hands. " Oh, isn't this fun! " she said.

She handed him his drink.

He carried it to the window and looked out. The mountain

was only a dark shadow now against the stars; above the summit, the stars seemed to throb in the thin air. Well, he thought despairingly, this was as good a place to end it as any other; to end it darkly and dirtily in this untidy room, far away from home, against a backdrop of heavy snow. He thought of the snow at Yosemite when he and Helen had huddled in the drifts, waiting for the blizzard to pass. ("If the Donner party had done this, they wouldn't have died crossing the Sierras," Helen had said. "They could have kissed each other warm.")

He remembered coming down the mountain, in the summer, with Claire; drunkenly running, leaping. He remembered thinking that the mountain looked as though it had tried to reach something, but had failed. It had tried to touch one particular portion of sky, and, failing, it had fallen into a heap of stone. He remembered saying this to Claire, and she had looked at him, mystified, and said, "What else would you have it do? Why would a mountain want to reach the sky?" And, after all those Martinis, he had seen—or thought he saw—something vaguely shining in the things she said. And he had almost loved her then.

She didn't shine now. Would a drink make her shine?

Claire came and stood just behind him. "Darling," she said, "I know it sounds terrible, but I don't love Blazer any more. And do you know when it happened? It happened up there. After that, what happened in the apartment was inevitable. Do you remember how Blazer fired that gun of his? That was when it happened, when I realized I didn't love him. That was so typical of Blazer. He needs things like guns and axes and knives—all those props! I think it's Freudian. I think he needs things like that to assert his masculinity."

"Claire——" he began.

"You don't. That was when I realized I loved you," she said.

"What's going to happen to us?" he asked her.

"Well," she said, "do you really want to know? Because I've thought it all out. First, you must get your divorce. Then I'll get mine."

"And then what?"

"Then——" she said, "then the rest is up to you."

He set his glass down on the window-sill and turned to her.

"Listen," he said gently, "I want to make a speech. I want you to listen to everything I say and remember it. It may be that I'm in love with you, but I don't know. I don't want you to say you love me, because I'm still not sure I feel the same. I'm very fond of you. I think you're one of the most exciting and delightful girls I know, and I think I could be in love with you very easily. But I can't be yet. I came back here to finish something. I don't know how it's going to end, but it hasn't ended yet. Do you see what I mean? I've got to see Helen first, that's one thing. Maybe it is all over with Helen. Maybe there's nothing left. But right now she's still my wife. I owe her something. Some day maybe I'll wish I'd said I love you right now—to-night. But I can't. That's why I stayed away from you and didn't answer your letter. A minute ago, I almost thought all right, to hell with her. But I'm afraid I can't. I can't give up now."

She was silent for a moment, standing there, swaying slightly. Finally, she said, "That doesn't give me much to go on, does it?"

"It's all I can give you."

She turned and walked slowly across the room. "That was —quite a speech," she said. Then she turned to him and he saw that her eyes were filled with tears. "Do you mind if I say you're being a fool?"

"That may be true."

"Oh!" she said. "You look so stern!" Her voice broke. She went towards the door. "I guess you'd better go," she said.

He went towards her. "I'm sorry, Claire."

She leaned with her back against the door, her hand on the knob. "Well," she said, "I'll just have to be patient, won't I? If I ever want to be happy!" She moved away from the door. "Kiss me," she said. "Just once. For courage." She closed her eyes tightly.

He went to her and kissed her gently on the lips.

"Oh, Jimmy," she sobbed, "I can't help loving you, even when you hurt me so!" Then she pulled away from him. "Good night," she said.

"Good night, Claire."

"Let me know," she said. "Keep in touch."

" All right. Good night."

He let himself out the door.

Alone, in her room, Claire wandered aimlessly about for a moment or two. She kicked off her shoes. Then she saw her drink on the dressing-table, went to it, and picked it up. She drank it rapidly. Jimmy's drink, untouched, was still on the window-sill. She drank that. Then she returned to the dressing-table and began removing the rhinestone clips from her hair. All at once she lowered her hands, leaned forward, towards her blurred image in the mirror, and kissed the glass. She pulled back and there, on the mirror's surface, was the imprint of her mouth in lipstick—a round, perfect Cupid's bow.

On the way back, Jimmy stopped to look at the pool. It was, as Claire had said, an incongruous sight, a warm black rectangle in the snow. He walked slowly around the pool's perimeter, looking at the water. From inside the lodge, he heard the college voices at the bar raised in song—

Each morning at dawning birdies sing—
And everything!
A sun-kissed miss said, " Don't be late! "
That's why I can hardly wait—
Open up, open up, open up that Golden Gate!
California, here I come!

He squatted on his heels beside the pool and trailed his hand in the water. The water was warm, and suddenly there was a moon. For the stillness of a moment, the pool was a moon, glittering and shimmering all around. And whether it was this sudden transition, or whether it was the words of the song, he felt he saw a dawn breaking. Right there. At the tip of his hand.

21

He was in the same mood of quiet elation when he awoke the next morning. He dressed quickly, and, deciding not to risk seeing Claire in the dining-room, repacked his suitcase and went downstairs to the desk and checked out. It was still quite early, and a sleepy, ski-clad young man who served as a bell-hop carried his suitcase out to his car.

"Aren'tcha going to ski to-day?" the boy asked grumpily, tossing the bag in the back seat of the convertible.

"Not to-day," Jimmy said. "Got to get back."

He tipped the boy and climbed into the car. He started the cold, sluggish motor, and then got out of the car again to scrape the thin layer of ice from the windshield. When he had it clear, he got back into the car, raced the motor, and, with a curious thrill of excitement, decided to drive to Rio Linda. He backed the car out of the parking lot. Then he stopped to light a cigarette. He realized that his hands were trembling.

He stopped in Truckee to have breakfast, and sat at the small, grimy counter rehearsing in his mind the things he would say. For a while, he debated telephoning Helen first, but he decided against it; he knew what she would say. He paid his check at the restaurant and started out again.

It was nearly two hundred miles to Rio Linda, but, once he had crossed Donner Summit, the downward road was fairly fast. There was very little traffic, and when, towards noon, he entered the flat, broad valley, the road straightened ahead of him; he held the car at a steady sixty miles an hour. It was not raining, but the day was damp and chilly. From far off, a heavy cloud hung over the Mokelumne River. Even in the grey winter, the fields that stretched limitlessly on either side of the road showed promise of green. Here and there a palm tree rose and flapped incongruously in the cold, sunless day. Here, in this vast Central Valley, he had heard, lay California's true wealth, the wealth that sprang from the black earth. He wondered if the Western settlers had previsioned this as they looked across the Sierras, imagining somehow the desert irrigated, seeded, harvested. He flipped on the car radio, and for a while listened to the inevitable, twangy hillbilly music that was transmitted daily from valley towns.

It was almost two when he arrived in Rio Linda, and for a while he drove around the town, noticing the changes, trying to place things he remembered, getting up his courage. He drove past Helen's house three or four times, afraid to stop, and then he stopped driving around it, afraid that someone in the house would notice him. Finally he parked the car on the other side of the park, got out, and walked through the park past the empty tennis courts, then stopped, looking across at the white house that showed through the trees opposite. He thought: No, I can't do it. I haven't got the courage. I can't go there. Then he asked himself the question: What do you want from her? More scenes and recriminations, more bitterness? You've satisfied yourself now; you've seen the house again. Go back.

He turned back towards the car, but he realized now that he had to do it. He had to see her. He got back into the car, lighted another cigarette, then drove the car around the park and stopped it in front of the house. He got out and walked quickly up the walk to the front door.

Mrs. Warren answered the bell. She looked, he thought, a little frightened. "Jimmy!" she exclaimed. "What do you want?" And then, before he had a chance to reply, she said, "Did you come to see the baby?"

He realized, with a start, that he had really not stopped to think about the baby at all, but he answered, "Yes."

She stood in the doorway. "Is this what they told you you could do?" she asked. "The lawyers and everything, I mean?"

"No," he said, "but I'd like very much to see him. If it's possible and you don't mind——"

She seemed undecided. "Well—it's a little——" she began. "I think he's asleep right now."

"Shall I come back later?"

"Yes. No. No—come in, Jimmy. Come in and sit down. I'll—I'll tell Helen you're here." She held open the door and he stepped inside.

"You've redecorated," he said. "Doesn't it look nice?" He realized he was smiling inanely and talking too rapidly. "The curtains are new, aren't they? When did you do all this?"

"Well, we had to do *something*," she said, looking around distractedly. "And Mr. Warren left me the money to do it with—with those specific instructions—for what he wanted me to do with it—to do something to the house——"

"Very nice——"

"I'll get Helen," she said. "Sit down, Jimmy, won't you? Excuse me——"

She started up the stairs and Jimmy went into the living-room. He sat down on one of the small French chairs. For several minutes, the house was silent. Then he heard Helen's footsteps coming down the stairs.

He stood up. She came into the room. "Hello, Jimmy," she said.

"Hello, Helen."

She stood a few feet away from him, not moving closer. She was wearing a pale yellow dress that was cut loosely, and leather-thonged sandals. Her brown hair was brushed smoothly back, and he noticed, irrationally, that she had on fresh lipstick. As he stared at her, she averted her face from him. "Sit down," she said.

"I'm sorry, Helen," he said simply. "I had to come."

"You *had* to come?" She looked at him briefly, then away again. She moved to the sofa and sat down, placing her hands in her lap. Jimmy sat down in the chair.

"Yes," he said.

"You could hardly have picked a more inconvenient time," she said. "Mother's having guests in about half an hour."

"I'm sorry . . ."

"Couldn't you have telephoned? Or written? Did your—your attorneys tell you this was what you could do?"

"No. It was my own idea, Helen. I felt I had to see you."

"I'm sorry," she said, "it's sort of a shock——"

"If you want me to go now, I will," he offered.

"No, no," she said quickly. "No—you've driven all the way from Sacramento."

"From Squaw Valley, actually——"

"Squaw Valley?"

"Yes, I went up there yesterday to ski."

She didn't answer him or seem interested any more. She put her arm on the arm of the sofa and looked into the corner of the room. He watched her. Her slim legs were bare below the full yellow skirt, and her feet, in the curious Indian sandals, were small, placed firmly on the floor. He studied her as she sat with her face turned away from him, averted, turned to the shadow. He thought that her sculptured face seemed pale; her features, too, seemed to have attained a sharpness, an angularity. There was an expression, too, that he couldn't recognize. He wondered whether it was time or pain or suffering.

"How have you been?" he asked her.

"Fine, just fine," she said.

"You look——" he began. "You've lost weight, haven't you?"

She laughed sharply. "Yes," she said. "I've lost a little. I've just had a baby, remember?"

"Oh, yes," he said quickly, "yes, I'm sorry, of course that's it." And he added, "Is he much trouble?"

"All babies are trouble."

"Midnight feedings—that sort of thing?"

"Yes. That sort of thing." She looked up at him. "But this one's worth it," she said.

"I'm glad."

There was another long, full silence, and she looked away from him once more. "I'd like to see him," Jimmy said.

"Well—I don't want to wake him up just yet. He's due for a bottle soon. I'll give him a little while longer."

"Tell me about him."

"There's really not much to tell," she said. "He's not much to look at either—only a week old. He doesn't do any spectacular things like walk or talk or sing. He has a cute little——" She stopped. "But you heard everything from Mr. Gurney."

"Mr. Gurney supplied me with his birth date and his sex. That was all."

She gave him a quick, worried look. " Was that all he told you? "

" Yes."

" Oh. I'm sorry. His name is Billy——"

" Forgive me, he did tell me that."

" And he weighed seven-thirteen——"

" Is that about average? "

" Yes, that's a good weight. And his eyes are—oh—an indistinguishable colour! " She laughed. " And he has long fingers —I'm sure he's going to play the piano—and he's bald——"

" And family resemblances? "

" Oh, yes, he looks just like you! " She smiled at him, and then stopped smiling. " I guess he looks just like a baby," she added, looking away again.

" And was it—easy for you? "

" Yes—so they tell me. I thought it was ghastly at the time, but everybody tells me I was terribly normal about it."

" I'm glad to hear that." There was another silence, and he asked, " Where did the Billy come from? "

" From nowhere. I thought it was a pretty name, that's all."

" It is," he said. " I like it. It's a nice name."

" I'm glad you approve."

" I'm glad you approve that I approve," he said.

" How have you been? " she asked

" Fine."

" And the job? "

" Just fine. Bob Maguire is——"

" What? "

" He's a nice guy to work for," he said. " I'm not getting rich at it, of course, but I'm enjoying it. I got my first raise when I got back from the East."

" Oh, have you been East? "

" Yes, I was back about a month ago for the funeral."

" What funeral? "

" Didn't you hear? "

" Hear what? "

" My father died."

" Oh! Oh, no! " she gasped.

" Yes, he had a heart attack. I'm sorry, I thought you knew."

" No! " She stared at him, tears welling in her eyes. " Oh, Jimmy! " she said. " I'm so sorry! "

" It was very sudden. It was all over very quickly."

" Oh, Jimmy! Of course I hardly knew him, but——"

" Yes. He was a nice man." Hearing the words come out, they sounded vacuous. And yet, in a way, they didn't.

" How is your mother? "

" Well, she took it a little hard at first, but she'll rally. You know Mother. She's busy rallying now."

" Poor Jimmy! " She brushed at her eyes with the back of her hand. Then she leaned forward towards the coffee table, opened the glass cigarette box, and extracted a cigarette. She searched for matches.

Jimmy stood up and reached in his pocket for his lighter. He walked over and offered it to her. As she lit the cigarette, her eyes fluttered up to him for a brief moment, then, frowning, she concentrated on the cigarette and the flame. " This isn't that kitchen lighter," he said softly. " No sparks."

She inhaled deeply and blew out a thin stream of smoke. Then she stood up. " I'll get Billy now," she said.

While he waited, Mrs. Warren walked through the living-room carrying a tray of hors d'œuvres towards the little sun parlour in the back of the house.

" Isn't it a dreary day! " she said.

" Yes, it certainly is," he answered.

" But of course," she said, looking about her with an odd, distracted look, " we need rain this time of year." She disappeared into the other room.

Presently Helen came down the stairs again with the small blanket-wrapped bundle in her arms. " Well—here he is," she said in a strained voice. " You don't have a cold or anything, do you? " she asked.

" No . . ."

" Would you like to hold him, then? "

" All right."

He accepted the small bundle gingerly. " My God, he's little! " he exclaimed.

" Yes, isn't he? " She laughed, a little wildly. " Don't—there, that's the right way to carry him! "

Jimmy carried the baby slowly across the room towards the

window, looking down at the small, pinched face. It was a curious sensation, encountering his child for the first time. It was the sensation that, for months, he had wondered how he would cope with, and yet now he couldn't define his feeling at all. He felt only a kind of wonder. Love, he supposed, would come later. He began talking to the baby in a soft voice, and Helen picked up her cigarette from the ash-tray and stood on the other side of the room, smoking, saying nothing. " Do you like it here? " he asked. " Do you like it here in this pretty house? Do they feed you enough? I don't think they feed you enough —tell Mommy that you're nothing but a bag of bones." He laughed then, to let her know that he wasn't serious.

" Where did he get the blue bonnet? " he asked her.

" I think it was a present," she said. " Someone gave it to him."

" Who? "

" I don't remember."

" Well, it's very handsome," he said. " Hey—look, he's smiling."

Helen laughed a small, tight laugh.

" He looks like an Irishman," Jimmy said.

" There's enough Irish around," Helen said.

" He's not scared of me, is he? I think he knows who I am. I think he knows—by instinct. Do you believe in instinct? "

Her voice choked. " I don't know," she said.

" I do. I think we know our fathers and mothers by instinct. Does he act this friendly with everyone? "

" I'm afraid so," she said.

" Well, I'm glad to hear that, anyway," he said.

" I think I'd better take him now," Helen said.

" Oh, let me hold him a few minutes—he doesn't mind."

" All right."

He went back to the chair and sat down, placing the small bundle on his lap.

" Don't scrunch him up so! " Helen said.

" Like this? "

" Yes, that's better——"

" I'd like to make these Sunday afternoons a regular thing," he said slowly, not looking at her. " That is—I'd like to if you have no objection."

She seemed to think about this. " I have no objection," she said finally. " Of course he's—he's your child, too. But I—I may be busy on some Sundays and——"

" Oh, I don't mean it would be like clockwork or anything like that," he said quickly. " No rigid schedule. Just on Sundays when it's convenient for you."

" I'd need to have some notice of when you're coming," she said seriously. " Some notice in advance."

" Or perhaps," he ventured, " perhaps we should wait until —after the divorce."

" Perhaps."

There was a pause, and, still looking at the baby, not at Helen, he said, " How is that coming along, anyway? "

" Oh, you know," she said, " there's this residence mix-up . . ."

" Why don't you go to Reno? "

" We were married in Reno," she said, and then she added quickly: " Well, that's hardly practical, is it, with a tiny baby? "

" No, I guess not," he said. And then he said slowly, " I suppose there's no chance—of us, you and I——"

" No," she answered quickly. " No chance at all."

" I thought not," he said. " That's why I thought we could make it more or less a standing date. Sundays, I mean. So there wouldn't be a lot of bother or fuss ahead of time. You could drop me a line . . ."

" No," she said.

" Or I could telephone," he said quickly.

" Yes, you could telephone me—or Mr. Gurney," she said. " That is, unless you want to make it a standing date, as you said."

" Well, yes, yes," he said. " That's what I mean. Then I could let you know what Sundays I'm *not* coming—that would be better. Just one or two hours every Sunday afternoon."

" Very well," she said. " I suppose I have no objection to that."

" And if you're busy," he said, " I could take Billy out with me in the car——"

" No, not in the car! " she said sharply.

" I mean when he's older," he added hastily.

" Well, we'll see."

" Or I could take him out in the carriage . . ."

" He doesn't have a carriage."

" I'll buy him one."

" Well, we'll see."

He decided not to press this any further, to let it drop. He was on tenuous, fragile ground. They were both silent. Then in the distance, he heard the door-bell, and Mrs. Warren's footsteps going through the hall to answer it.

The voices, outside, in the hall:

" Arlene! What's happened, dear? Are you all right? "

" Yes, yes. Jimmy's here to see the baby, that's all."

" Oh, we've come at the wrong time. We'll come back later——"

" No, no—come in. We'll sit out here——"

" Are you *sure? Positive?* "

" Oh, yes, yes. I've got everything set up . . ."

Jimmy felt his face reddening. In the distance, in the little sun parlour, he heard the sound of glasses, the swirl of ice-cubes in a pitcher. " Scotch for you, Edrita? " Mrs. Warren's voice said. " And Bert—I know you're a Martini type, like me." She laughed.

" Are you going to Santa Barbara after Christmas, Arlene? " a man's voice asked.

" Goodness knows! " said Mrs. Warren.

" You're getting to be an expert bartender, Arlene," the woman's voice said.

" I'm learning," Mrs. Warren replied.

" I suppose you'd like one," Helen said suddenly.

" What? " Jimmy asked.

" A drink. You can have one if you'd like——"

" No, thank you," Jimmy said.

" It wouldn't be any trouble."

" No, thanks." He hesitated, then said, " I don't drink any more."

" Is that true——? "

" Yes. I stopped. About four months ago."

" Oh——" she breathed.

" Yes. That was one of the things that ruined us, wasn't it? My drinking? "

" I always thought that was the only thing," she said softly.

" Yes. That's why I stopped."

" I'm glad," she said. She looked at him as though now, for the first time since he'd arrived, she was genuinely interested in what he was saying. " Are you an Alcoholics Anonymous or something? " she asked.

" No, it was something I did by myself."

" Oh, I think that's wonderful, Jimmy! "

" That's why," he said, " that's why—I thought possibly we might try again."

She looked away again. " Look," she said, " we're not children any more. There's no point in fooling ourselves, is there? You can't just ask me to forget—just like that. There were other things—like the night Daddy died—and you were nowhere to be found—and——"

" I know, I know," he said. " I'm sorry I mentioned it." He turned again to the baby. " Diddle-diddle dumpling, my son John," he said cheerfully, " went to bed with his breeches on—how does the rest of it go? "

" I don't remember," she said absently.

" And what was the story about the princess who woke up and found that the frog had turned into a prince? "

" What are you talking about? "

" I'm just trying to remember some of the stories I used to be told when I was little."

" I'm afraid he won't take much of it in at this stage," she said.

" Well, I'm really just trying to make conversation," he said, " just trying to prolong the visit." He held the baby's head between his two hands. " I'm glad I met you," he said. " I'm glad I came. Do you realize it took a lot of courage to come down here? Did you know that? "

" A lot of what? " she asked.

" Courage."

" It's almost time for his supper," Helen said. " You'd better give him back to me now." He rose and handed her the baby.

" Helen——" he began.

" Yes? "

" If you're going to feed him, could I watch? "

" It's not very interesting to watch him have his dinner,

actually," she said. "He spits the formula up sometimes, and——"

"I don't want to interfere."

"Perhaps some other time. I think he's had enough excitement for one day."

"Yes, yes. I agree. Perhaps the next time I come."

"What? When will that be?"

"Next Sunday?"

"Well—I think—no. I don't think so. Not next Sunday, I really don't think so. I think you'd better work through Mr. Gurney, Jimmy."

"There once was a fellow named Gurney, who decided to be an attorney," he said.

Her eyes flashed at him. "I don't think it's very funny," she said. "He's getting a divorce for me."

"Do you want a divorce?"

"That's a silly question!"

"I don't want one either," he said.

"Please, Jimmy. It's time for you to go."

As they talked, she was slowly and surely walking him towards the door. In the hall, he stopped.

"Do you mean I can't come down again?"

"No, I don't mean that. But not next Sunday. Jimmy, this was a bit of a surprise—your coming to-day. Give me a chance to think about it. We'll work something out, some arrangement. But don't rush me."

"Let me hold him again," he said. She handed him the small, almost weightless bundle again. "Hey," he said, looking down at the small face, "you and I will spend a lot of time together when we're older, you know that? We'll take trips and go fishing together. You'll spend at least half your life with me—because you're half mine, anyway."

"Don't hold him so close," she said. "Here, let me have him——"

Suddenly, as she lifted the baby from his arms to hers, the baby began to cry a thin, despairing wail. And Jimmy held on to him almost roughly. For a brief moment, they swayed together, the baby between them. She held the baby then, and he put his hands on her elbows and kissed her lightly on the forehead. "Do you believe in change?" he asked her. "Do you believe that people have the ability to change? That's what it all hangs on, doesn't it—whether you believe or not that in the last few months I might have changed? "

She didn't resist him or try to pull away, but lowered her eyes and shook her head sadly. " I don't believe in fairy tales," she said. " Frogs turning into princes——"

" I'm talking about the future, too," he said urgently. " I don't give a damn about the past. But this is the future, right here——"

She looked up at him with tears in her eyes. " I want to believe," she whispered.

" Then say it. Say, ' I believe! ' "

" Oh, I can't, I can't. I know I can't." She drew away from him and he let his hands fall to his sides.

" You know it wasn't really Billy I came to see," he said. " You know why I came. You know it was you——"

At the door at the end of the hall, Mrs. Warren appeared. " Helen," she said pleasantly, " the Kerrs are here, dear. Won't you bring the baby in to show them? "

" Yes, Mother." She held out her hand. " Well, good-bye, Jimmy," she said.

" Will you let me know when I can come again? "

" Yes—or rather Mr. Gurney will, I think. Good-bye."

" Good-bye." He took her hand briefly. Then he turned quickly, opened the front door, and let himself out.

After he had left, Helen stood for a moment in the hall.

" Coming, dear? " her mother asked. And when she said nothing, Mrs. Warren said, " Helen? Helen? "

Helen turned sharply to her. " Why do there have to be so many *others*! " she said. " Why are there always people who have to *intrude*, who have their own ideas and keep telling me what to do! Did you ever think that this was a problem for the two of us—the three of us! Did you? " Her voice broke. " I mean, we *do* have things to say to each other, and we do have to be alone, don't we? Don't we? " Holding the baby in her arms, she ran sobbing up the stairs.

A week later the weather suddenly broke, and, as occasionally happens, California became balmy and tropical again for several days. The sun shone, the thermometer climbed to eighty, and Californians flocked to the beaches. The California Bureau of Commerce took photographs and sent long, jubilant Press notices back to Eastern cities that were at that moment shivering under sleet and snow. Convertible tops were lowered. Swimming-pools that had been allowed to stagnate were hastily refiltered. Outdoor living began again.

Jimmy and Mike lay on the beach at Half Moon Bay, soaking up the sun. The tide was pounding in. They debated whether or not to go in the water.

" It's cold as hell," Jimmy said.

" Look, I've got to do it," Mike said. " I want to write my folks back in New Hampshire that I went in the ocean in November."

They walked to the water's edge. The waves were crashing in heavily now, sweeping the sand in front of them, tossing kelp and bits of rockweed into the air. " We'd better stick close to shore," Jimmy said. " There'll be a terrific undertow."

Then they dived into the surf. For a while they splashed about, shouting and laughing. The water was cold, but the air was warmed by the western breeze. After a while, wet and salty, they came out of the water and flopped on the hot sand again.

Jimmy lighted a cigarette. The smoke, in the salt air, tasted clear and sharp. " Well," he said, " I went to see her."

" Who? Helen? " Mike asked.

" Yes."

" I thought probably you had," Mike said.

Jimmy roared. " What do you mean, you thought I had? "

" I just figured you had. I figured you were close to it, anyway."

" My God," he laughed, " are you *always* clairvoyant? Do you have a crystal ball or something? "

" No, but it's logical, that's all."

" All right," Jimmy said, " then tell me how it went. How did I do? "

" How did you do what? "

" How did I get along with Helen? "

Mike thought about this. He lay on his stomach with his arms out, scooping up handfuls of white sand and letting them trickle through his fingers. He frowned. " Well," he said at last, " I'd say it went pretty well. Considering. I mean you've got to give these things time. You can't expect her to come flying into your ever-loving arms the minute she sees your face. She's been through a lot, too, don't forget. She has to think things out, too, the way you did. By herself. I think you've made a good start. The girl was only a baby when you married her and so were you. You were both all mixed up. Give it time. Don't be impatient. That was the mistake you made before."

Jimmy said nothing. He lay there, looking straight ahead, up the beach, at the great grey cliffs that rimmed the coastline as far as the eye could see.

22

A WEEK later, the weather changed and winter returned. It returned with a cold, damp wind that blew steadily from the north and ruffled whitecaps in the bay. Claire got back to San Francisco on Monday—the Monday before Thanksgiving—and, in the apartment on Russian Hill, she was immediately depressed. The apartment was immaculate and cool; she had had it cleaned while she was away. But for some reason the cleanness and orderliness of it, with the low, handsome Chinese tables waxed and polished, the great glass walls freshly washed, made her feel out of place and rather purposeless. She had absolutely nothing to do, that was part of it. Ordinarily, there was some small housekeeping chore that could occupy her, but now, wandering from room to room, everything was perfect. She had left Squaw Valley out of boredom, too. The ski-ing lessons had turned out badly. She had begun, in the evenings, to drink much more than she was used to. She had sat, night after night, in the little cheerful, noisy bar and got herself pleasantly tight. Then, in the mornings, she had lain in bed for hours, wrestling with giant hangovers, hating herself, improvising elaborate and futile ways to relieve her tedium.

And now she was back. She was all alone. Blazer would not be back from Honolulu for another week. Norden-Clark had considerately planned Blazer's sales trip so that he would be away over Thanksgiving, and Thanksgiving was a holiday that had always had a great sentimental meaning to her. She thought, miserably, of spending it alone, in this chilly, unfriendly city. She thought, nostalgically, of Thanksgivings at Mars Hill. They were always huge, warm, bustling family affairs that began in midmorning with cousins and uncles and aunts arriving from all over the East, their long black cars filling the driveway and the circle in front of the huge front door. She remembered that her mother always ordered at least two extra turkeys for the chauffeurs, who were served a banquet identical with the one that the family was served, in the servants' dining-room. She remembered the huge, long table set up in the family dining-room—set up sometimes for as many as forty—with the long, white banquet cloth, the silver place plates, and, in the centre, her mother's traditional Thanksgiving centrepiece—a group of three stuffed pheasants with brightly coloured feathers and long, drooping tails in a lifelike arrangement of wheat sheaves, Indian corn, and artificial fruit. She remembered the chatter of servants in the kitchen—extra girls, brought in for the day, and her mother, in a long dinner dress, hurrying about, arranging last-minute details, greeting relatives, lighting the tapers that rose from the four five-branched silver candelabra. Dinner began with cocktails in the drawing-room, children curtsying and bowing to their elders as they helped pass bowls of nuts and trays of hors d'œuvres. Then it proceeded into the dining-room for course after course of dinner, with the magnificent turkeys, the wines. The mood was cheerful, warm, and intimate. They were all family. They were Denisons and Walthours and Merrimans and Sloats on her father's side, and Chases, Hockings, and Van Camps on her mother's. Daughters, home from college, brought their fiancés—smooth-faced, cheerful, polite young men from Yale, Dartmouth, and Williams. After dinner the party spread out, lazily and informally, throughout the house at bridge tables, chess tables, billiard tables. There were always an energetic few for ping-pong. The sky darkened, lamps were lit. Soon the whole house glowed with light. Then, some time during the course of the early evening, her father would propose a Thanksgiving toast. Everyone stood quietly to hear him utter it, and the servants were brought in from the kitchen and were given drinks, to join in it. It was a solemn moment, and Junius Denison raised his glass. The toast was always the same: "We live in an anxious, troubled world," he said. "A world that, at times, seems to have lost its standards. Standards of dignity and humanity. But at the very centre of the world stands an institution—the family. If this institution is lost, then the world is lost. But as long as there are families who stand together and work together in kinship and in love, there is hope for mankind. So I drink to the family!"

The toast was drunk in silence, and, in the silence following it, Georgette Chase Denison moved towards her husband and kissed him lightly on the cheek.

Claire knew it would be the same this year. It would be the same, except she would not be there. She had considered, actually, flying home for Thanksgiving. In fact, she would do it without any hesitation at all if it weren't for the fact that she had spent rather mountainous sums of money at Squaw Valley. She thought guiltily of the balance in her cheque-book. Blazer would be annoyed, she knew. For Blazer cherished the illusion—even though it was nothing more than an illusion—that the two of them lived within the limits of his salary. Or at least practically within them. Whenever he was reminded of the number of dividend cheques which Claire endorsed and deposited in his account (Claire collected cheques as they came and placed them in the bottom of her jewel-case in her bureau drawer, and withdrew them when they were needed), Blazer was apt to become angry. So there was nothing for her to do but spend a lonely, quiet Thanksgiving Day in the apartment.

Claire now went to the window and looked out. There was the view, sifting through fog. Alcatraz, Angel Island, Belvedere, Tiburon . . . Mount Tamalpais and the Golden Gate. She stood there, a slim figure in tight black toreador pants and black sweater, her yellow hair falling over her shoulders. She crossed slowly behind the sofa to the side of the room which hung, cantilevered out over the story below, towards the east. Standing there, she had the sensation of falling through airless space slowly, the way one falls in a dream. She felt dizzy and ill. She pulled the heavy curtains closed.

She went back and stretched out on the white sofa, stomach down, with her feet, in black ballet slippers, hanging over the edge. She put her cheek on the white nubby upholstery and lay there for quite a while. She thought about Jimmy. Jimmy was a bright, shimmering spot of hope. It all seemed so simple, and yet, in a way, it all seemed terribly complicated. It should be simple. Jimmy loved her, she was sure of that. Anyway, he would love her as soon as he got over feeling guilty about it. Jimmy's wife had left him. They had been separated now for over six months. Obviously, she was never going back to him.

Obviously, she would get a divorce. And yet everything seemed to have come to a curious standstill. That night in Squaw Valley had been suddenly nothing—nothing. He had appeared, then disappeared. Well, she thought sadly, a lot of that had been her fault. In fact, most of it. If she wanted Jimmy, she had hardly played her cards well. She had been impulsive, demanding, hasty. She had tried to back him into a corner. After all, Jimmy was a man. No man liked to be pushed around by a woman, she should have known that. She had literally thrown herself at him. Tears of shame came to her eyes. There was no other way to describe it. She had thrown herself at him.

And yet, she felt, he did need help. He needed to be manœuvred, helped to make up his mind. Yes, but manœuvred with a little subtlety! She had practically lain on the bed and pulled up her dress. What every woman knows, Claire thought, I don't seem to know. Or practise, anyway. What would happen, she wondered suddenly, if she were to go again to see Helen? She knew what to expect now. She wouldn't be frightened as she had been before. She could go to Helen, meet her on her own ground, and have it out with her, woman to woman. "I am the other woman," she would say pleasantly. "Jimmy and I have grown fond of each other in recent months, and my own marriage, unfortunately, seems to be disintegrating due to my husband's——" No, she wouldn't go into that. "My own marriage seems to be disintegrating." Period. "And I would like—I would like to ask you exactly how soon you plan to release Jimmy." That would be simple enough. Blunt and frank, not possibly misunderstood. There was certainly no reason why she couldn't do that. If she wanted Jimmy. And now she asked herself, did she want Jimmy? Analysing herself in a cold, impartial light, Claire realized that she had always yearned for unobtainable objects, simply because they were unobtainable. It was a game. She remembered it from college. See that young man over there with Kathy Squiers? Watch me take him away from her. And later, in what she called her Bohemian period, living in the Village, wanting to be an artist, had that been part of the game, too? She had believed it to be sincere at the time.

Oh, yes, she thought, it must have been sincere! It was the

only thing I ever tried to do! More tears came. Am I a nice girl? she wondered. And then, despairingly, she thought: It isn't my marriage that's disintegrating, it's me.

She pushed herself up on her elbows, and, urgently, for something to do, she seized her yellow hair with her hands. She pulled half the hair to one side, divided it into three strands, and began, rapidly, to braid it. When she finished one braid, she held the loose end with her teeth as she began to braid the other side. It's the weather, she thought. It's California. It's living in this dreadful fish-bowl room that's putting me into these morbid emotional states. I'm being subjected to a peculiar Oriental torture, known as view torture. It was like living in a room completely surrounded by mirrors, only this was worse. With mirrors, at least you could look at yourself. With clear glass, the whole world was looking at you. She finished the second braid, and, holding both ends in her teeth, she jumped up and went into the bedroom to look for elastic bands. In the mirror, she caught a glimpse of her reflection—two thick yellow braids clenched in her teeth. She grimaced at her image. There, she thought. Do I look like all the other damn' fools from Smith now? Do I?

By five o'clock, she was in a cheerful mood. She felt almost gay. She placed a stack of records on the phonograph and turned the volume low, to the barest whisper of music. She went to the bar and mixed herself a small, crystal, jewel-like martini. It was really rather fun being alone. It was like her New York days when she had enjoyed cooking for herself, and setting the table for herself, and sitting down to eat by herself with candle-light. She sipped her martini slowly and then went to the telephone and called Jimmy.

When he answered, she laughed a small, tinkly laugh. "Well!" she said. "What have you been doing?"

"Hi, Claire," he said. "Where are you?"

"In Squaw Valley," she said.

"Still up there?"

"Yes. I'm having too much fun to leave. Parties—a simply wild round every night. Throngs of fascinating people."

"How are the ski-ing lessons coming?"

"Marvellously! I'm schussing and slooshing and whooshing everywhere. My instructor says he's never seen such progress!"

" Well, that's great! " he said. " I'm glad you're learning to whoosh. Can you do it on one ski yet? "

" Oh, yes. Tell me, Jimmy, is entering the Olympics terribly time-consuming? "

" Well, it would take some of your time, I suppose."

" That's what I'm afraid of. I think I'll tell them no. My time is simply too valuable."

" Before you go much farther," Jimmy said, " I should tell you that before I heard your voice, the operator said, ' San Francisco is calling.' "

" Beast! "

" I'm sorry."

" Well," she said, " let me tell you why I really called."

" Yes."

" Well," she said, " the darndest business has come up."

" What's happened? "

" Well," she said, taking a quick sip of her cocktail, " do you remember what I told you about Blazer—about that new job with Monarch Mills? That Harry Masterson character? "

" Yes."

" Well, of course Blazer's in Honolulu, and this is all strictly *sub rosa* with Norden-Clark, but anyway, this Masterson character telephoned me to see if I could locate some papers of Blazer's, some sort of vital statistics on him or something, and I've discovered they're on file in Sacramento."

" In Sacramento? "

" Yes. You know, in the capitol or in some sort of state office building or something, so I have an appointment to go up there and pick them up on Friday."

" What kind of papers are they, Claire? "

" Oh—vital statistics things, I guess they're called. His birth certificate and everything——"

" Blazer wasn't born in California——"

" No, not his birth certificate actually, but things like that."

" So you'd like me to drop over there and pick them up? I'd be glad to."

" No, no! I have to be there. Myself. It requires my signature and everything. I have the appointment and everything, with the legislature or whatever it is——"

" The legislature? "

" Yes."

There was a silence on the other end of the wire. " Now, let's get this straight," Jimmy said finally. " You have to go up to the state legislature to put your signature on some vital statistics of Blazer's like his birth certificate so he can get a job with Monarch Mills."

" Yes, exactly."

There was a muffled sound on the other end of the line that resembled coughing.

" Oh, damn you! " she said. " Look—Thursday's Thanksgiving, and I've got nobody to spend it with. I thought I'd come up Thursday night and let you take me out to dinner."

" Gosh, Claire——"

" Please! " she said. " I know how you feel, how you want to wait and everything. But is there any harm in our having dinner somewhere? Just a nice, quiet Thanksgiving dinner? You came down here for dinner one time, and now it's my turn to go up there! "

" The thing is, Claire, I've got a date already. Bob and Margie Maguire—the fellow I work for—have asked me to their house for Thanksgiving dinner. I'm awfully sorry. Really."

" Then Friday night," she said.

" Friday? "

" Yes. Please! "

" Well——"

" *Please!* "

" Sure, Claire," he said. " I'd love to."

" Good," she said quickly. " And I've turned over a new leaf. I'm not going to try to coax you to drink, and I'm not going to try to seduce you. You won't be able to get me inside your apartment if you try. Just to show you my intentions are absolutely pure, I'll blow my horn outside your building at seven o'clock."

" All right."

" You'll hear Scarlet O'Hara blow her horn at seven," she said. " Good-bye."

" Good-bye, Claire."

She hung up the telephone and gulped down the rest of her drink. Then, because she still felt like talking to somebody, she picked up the phone again and called Tweetums DeMay.

"Tweetums," she said, when the other woman answered, "I'm home again. Come on over and have a cocktail with me."

When Tweetums DeMay arrived, about half an hour later, Claire had closed the curtains all the way around the room; the whole apartment seemed now to be upholstered with thick white cloth. And Claire, in the middle of it, still in her slim black toreador pants and black sweater, her hair still in pigtails, created a single decorative accent. Tweetums noticed it right away. "You should always wear black in this room," she exclaimed. "It looks perfect!"

Claire laughed. "One thing I can't ever wear is white," she said. "In white, I simply wash out."

Tweetums arranged herself comfortably on the sofa, tucking her short, plump legs underneath her. "How've you been?" she asked. "Did you have a wonderful time at Squaw Valley?"

"Oh, yes," Claire said, "but I've decided I'll never be a skier." She went to the bar and mixed another pitcher of pale martinis.

"Ah, *merci*!" said Tweetums, when Claire handed her a glass.

"Now tell me what you've been doing," Claire said. She put her glass on the coffee table and sat, tailor fashion, on the floor opposite Tweetums.

"Oh, nothing very exciting," Tweetums said. "Stan and I have been to a few football games. At Berkeley and San José. You know how crazy Stan is about football."

"Oh, I know."

"He's just like a great big kid! I think he wishes he were still back in college . . ."

"Is he working yet?"

"Well, that's a sore point," Tweetums said. "He's not. Not yet. I want him to get a job downtown, in one of the investment houses. I know some people at Schwabacher's. But Stan says he wants to sow a few wild oats first."

"Say, is it getting serious between you and Stan?" Claire asked.

Tweetums let out a whoop of laughter. "Oh!" she said. "Oh, no! No, no, no! Goodness me, I'm thirty-seven. I'm almost fifteen years older than he is. Give me credit for a little sense. I know I don't have much, but I have that much. No, he's just—well, he's a lot of fun, that's all."

" I just wondered," Claire said.

Tweetums put her head back against the sofa cushions and looked up at the ceiling. " You know how it is," she said. " No, you probably don't know how it is, but when a girl reaches my age——" Her voice trailed off. " Well," she said, " I've had three marriages, all flops. I'm thirty-seven. I've lost my figure and most of my looks—I don't kid myself. And at this point, the only thing I want out of life is to have fun. Stan thinks—he probably thinks he's being pretty daring, running around town with an old jade like me! " She laughed gaily. " I mean it. His friends probably kid him about it, and he gets a kick out of that. Oh, a couple of times he's told me he's in love with me. I take it with a grain of salt. He likes me because I know the ropes, that's all. My God," she said, " if there's one thing I am, it's aware! "

Later, after another cocktail, Tweetums said, " What are you doing for Thanksgiving? "

" Nothing," Claire said glumly, " absolutely nothing! Blazer won't be back till a week from Wednesday. I'm going to spend Thanksgiving sitting right here in this apartment . . ."

" Oh, what a shame! " Tweetums said.

" What are you going to do? " Claire asked.

" Oh, it's all up in the air at this point," Tweetums said. " Stan is immobilized at the moment. He's without wheels. His car is on the blink. We were going to drive down to Carmel for dinner, but now I guess we'll have to stay in town."

" I guess we're both in the same boat," Claire said.

" Oh, no. Not you. At least you have a husband, dear. Even if he's thousands of miles away, at least you have a husband."

" Yes, I suppose you're right. I should be grateful."

" Oh, you should, you should. Why, you're the happiest two people I've ever seen—you and Blazer. What difference does it make to you if you miss one little old Thanksgiving dinner together? "

Claire laughed.

" You'll have so many more," Tweetums said. Then, sadly, she said, " I'm quite aware that Stan will get tired of me pretty soon. It's bound to happen. I'm prepared for it, but it'll be a blow just the same. Then I'll have to get myself another beau." She gazed despondently into her glass.

"Let's have another cocktail," Claire said.

Much later, when they were both quite tight, Claire stood up unsteadily and went into the bathroom. When she came out, Tweetums had kicked off her shoes and lay on her back on the sofa. She had rested an ash-tray on her bosom into which she periodically tapped her cigarette. Tweetums had finished recounting, in elaborate detail, the story of each of her marriages, and, in this mood of easy confidence, like two college roommates, Claire had been tempted to tell Tweetums about Jimmy. But she had caught herself, and, instead, had talked aimlessly about Blazer, her parents, Mars Hill, and her Bohemian period in New York.

Claire stood in the centre of the room, her feet planted wide apart. "Look," she said suddenly, "why don't you borrow Scarlet O'Hara to go to Carmel?"

"What?"

"Borrow my car, the Jaguar. I'm not going to be using it."

Tweetums sat up. "Oh, no, honey, I couldn't do that," she said.

"Why not?" Claire asked gaily. "There's no earthly reason why you couldn't. It'll just be sitting here. Why don't you two take it?"

"And go to Carmel?"

"Yes!"

"Oh, no. You're sweet to offer it, but——"

"I mean it," Claire said.

"Well——" Tweetums said tentatively, looking at Claire, and then quickly away. "Well, we were planning to spend the night there."

"Oh," Claire said. "Well——"

"Oh, it's perfectly all right," Tweetums said hastily. "I have an aunt in Pebble Beach; we were going to stay at her place. I mean——"

"Well," Claire said, "I do need the car on Friday. I have to—I have some things to do Friday night. I'd need it back by five."

" Oh, we'd be back by five," Tweetums said.

" Well, then——"

" Oh, no, it's too much of an imposition, really," Tweetums said. " I couldn't think of borrowing Blazer's car——"

" It's my car really," Claire said.

" Well, even so——"

" I must have it back by five o'clock, that's all," Claire said.

" Well, you're terribly sweet——"

" Do you want to take it? "

" Oh, we'd love you for ever—if you're sure you wouldn't mind——"

" Take it then," Claire said. " Take it overnight. Only have it back by five on Friday."

" Oh, you're a lifesaver, honey! " Tweetums said. " Wait till I tell Stan! " She jumped up and ran across the room to Claire in her stocking feet. " You're wonderful! " she said, hugging her quickly. " You're a real friend! "

Claire squeezed Tweetums affectionately. She felt warm and happy. She felt she was helping the course of true love. And she was fond of Tweetums. In her innocent, cheerful way, Tweetums reminded her of her mother.

23

On Wednesday afternoon, Helen had an appointment with her lawyer. Mr. Gurney sat at his roll-top desk in shirt-sleeves and galluses. Outside, from the street below, Helen could hear the midafternoon traffic sounds, but inside the office she was back in the gold-rush days. The office was cluttered with dusty books, papers, and odd mementoes. Fading photographs and yellowing calendars lined the walls. On top of one ancient filing cabinet was the whitened skull of a steer; in another corner was a huge, garishly painted safe. Above it, in a glass case, were a pair of crossed pistols. On Mr. Gurney's desk, serving as a paperweight, was a chunk of crusty, glinting gold ore from the Mother Lode.

Mr. Gurney had always terrified her a little. He sat there now, pushed back in his swivel chair with his thumbs in his trouser-tops, squinting at her critically through his spectacles. " Well, Helen," he said, " I think we'd better get this show on the road."

" Yes, I expect we'd better," she said.

" In a few more weeks, you'll have satisfied the residence requirement. Then we can file your complaint." He went on, talking about the possibility of a cross complaint, or a motion for change of venue. " In view of the fact that you have the child," he said finally, " I think we will ask the court for permanent alimony. I don't anticipate any difficulty on that score. Now, you're more familiar with the young man's circumstances than I am. What would you say would be a suitable figure? "

Helen thought about this. " Is it necessary to ask for anything? " she said finally.

Mr. Gurney rearranged himself in the chair. " Didn't you say he comes from people of considerable means? " he asked.

" Yes, but——"

"Well, I don't say it's necessary. But I think it's rather foolish of you not to. After all, you have his child. The court won't expect you to feed, clothe, and educate the child all by yourself. Is there any reason why he shouldn't share his burden?"

"I just don't want any unpleasantness about money," Helen said. "I think his family always thought I married him for his money, and I don't want to have them think——"

"Why should you give a hoot what they think?"

"Well, I just do, that's all."

Mr. Gurney looked at her crossly. "Sentimental!" he snapped.

"Perhaps——" she began.

"Perhaps what?"

"Mr. Gurney, Jimmy came to see me a couple of weeks ago."

"Is that so?" He didn't sound particularly interested.

"Yes, he came down to see the baby, and—I guess—to see me, too."

"Did he behave himself?"

"Oh, yes . . ."

"Well, what about it then?"

"Nothing. It was just that—well, it was the first chance we've really had to talk together for a long time."

"Well?"

"Well—I've been thinking. Do you suppose he could have changed?"

Mr. Gurney slammed forward on the swivel chair. "My dear young woman," he said, "I have not met the man. How should I know?"

"Well, I was wondering," Helen said, "if we could wait awhile—before filing the complaint, I mean. I mean, do we have to go right ahead with it, or can we postpone it for a while?"

Mr. Gurney scowled at her, but in his eyes there was a twinkle of amusement. "My dear," he said, "you are getting the divorce, not I. You may do whatever you wish."

"Well, frankly I'd like to talk to him again."

"I think you might very well do that. I think if people weren't so ashamed of talking to each other, there'd be far fewer divorces."

"I don't mean a reconciliation," Helen said. "I mean just a talk—a sensible talk."

" Of course you've been pretty cagey about why you wanted a divorce in the first place. What was it you said? He got drunk and abusive? "

" Yes, but he doesn't drink any more——"

" Well, get in touch with him then. Tell him you'd like to talk to him again."

" Yes," Helen said. " I thought perhaps you might write to him."

" Why should I write to him? He's not my husband! "

" Yes, Mr. Gurney, but I thought—well, I thought that would be the right way to handle it."

" *I* write to him? Don't be absurd, woman. I've got more important things to do than that."

" I keep thinking," Helen said softly, looking down at her white gloved hands in her lap, " that he might have changed. That I might have changed, too."

Mr. Gurney waved his hands. " Then run along," he said. " Do it. Don't bother me with all the details."

" All right," she said. She stood up to go. " I'll do it, and I'll let you know."

" Very well," he said crisply. " Good afternoon." He swung around towards his desk. Helen started towards the door. " Just a minute! " Mr. Gurney said. Helen turned. Mr. Gurney looked at her over his shoulder and scowled. " Just remember," he said, " nothing makes me happier than putting a divorce file in the back of the drawer."

" Thank you," Helen said. " Good-bye." Then, impulsively, she blew him a kiss with her gloved hand. " You're a dear," she said.

Mr. Gurney's face turned bright red, and he turned and bent over the papers on his desk as Helen let herself out.

On Thanksgiving Day, Tweetums DeMay drove the red Jaguar slowly up Telegraph Hill. She parked it in front of the grey frame building where Stan Erickson lived. She climbed out of the car, ran up the flight of steps to the front door, let herself in, and went up another flight of stairs to the second floor where Stan had a one-room apartment. She rang the bell. After a moment, Stan came to the door. He was tousled, unshaven, and still in his pyjamas. " Lookee! " Tweetums cried gaily, taking his arm and leading him across the untidy room to the front window. She pointed down at the car. " For us," she said.

Stan gave a long, low whistle. " Where'd you get it, Tweetums? " he asked. " Did you buy it or something? "

" No, it's Claire and Blazer's. Blazer's away and Claire let me borrow it."

" Terrific! " Stan said.

" So-o-o——" Tweetums said, extending the vowel, and turning to him and looking him up and down, " you scoot into the bathroom, shave, comb your hair, and get dressed. We're going to Carmel! "

" Great! " He squeezed her arm excitedly and started towards the bathroom; he chucked his pyjama-shirt on the unmade bed. Tweetums stood at the window, looking out. " And it's going to be a nice day, too," she said.

At the bathroom door, he stopped. " Hey, Tweetums," he called.

" Yes? " She turned.

" Fresh, young beauty! " He pulled the cord of his pyjama-bottoms and let them fall to his ankles.

" Oh, Stan! " She laughed, weakly.

He ducked into the bathroom and she heard the shower running.

As they drove down the peninsula, the sun kept appearing and disappearing. But the day was warm, and Stan had insisted that they drive with the top down. The Jaguar fascinated him. He studied the dials on the panel, practised double-shifting the gears. " Great little car," he kept repeating. " God, what a piece of machinery! "

Because he enjoyed driving the car, they took their time. They made several side trips. In Palo Alto, they made a tour of the Stanford campus. Farther down, near Los Gatos, they took a long, winding road that led up into the hills. When they got to Monterey, they stopped, parked the car, and took a stroll along the fishing-pier. It was close to dusk when they arrived in Carmel. They drove the car along the Seventeen Mile Drive, past Cypress Point and Pebble Beach as the sun, giant and orange, began setting into the sea.

They drove then to a restaurant south of Carmel called

Nepenthe for dinner. High on a cliff above the ocean, they had cocktails, and, after that, Pacific lobster. " What the hell does Nepenthe mean, anyway? " Stan asked her once, during dinner.

" It means ' forgetting pain,' I think," she said. She reached across the table and covered his hand with hers.

They left the restaurant, and, in the car again, Stan continued heading south along the high, winding highway that followed the coast line. Tweetums rested her head peacefully on the back of the seat and looked out into the night. Drifts of mist were floating in now from the sea, swirling about the rocks. The surf echoed far below. Finally, she said, " Don't you think we ought to be heading back? "

" Back where? "

" Back to Carmel——? "

He was silent. Then he said, " Hey, Tweetums, how much money have you got with you? "

She hesitated. Then she opened her purse. " I've got about a hundred dollars," she said.

" Good. I've got about thirty. Let's go to Tijuana."

" Tijuana! "

" Sure. Why not? "

" But, Stan—it's about six hundred miles! "

" I know."

" We wouldn't get there till to-morrow! "

" Sure. So what? I've never been there, have you? "

" No, but——"

" Then let's go. O.K.? "

" Oh, we can't! We really can't! I've got to have this car back by five to-morrow, for one thing——"

" She'd understand, wouldn't she? We'll phone her when we get there."

" But why? Why on earth do you want to go down there? Oh, Stan, it's just crazy, starting off for Tijuana at ten o'clock at night! "

" Hell, I think it would be fun," he said.

" Oh, it would be fun, but we can't. That's all there is to it. We can't."

Stan was silent. They continued driving south.

" Turn back now, Stan, please," Tweetums said.

" Why won't you go? " he asked her a little petulantly.

" Because, honey, it's silly. Why do *you* want to go? That's more to the point! "

He stared at the road ahead. Then he smiled a small, curious smile. " Because," he said mysteriously.

" Because why? "

" Because we could get married in Tijuana."

" Oh! " Tweetums gasped. She sat back in the seat, looking straight ahead. " Oh! " she said again.

" Are you game? " he asked her, teasingly.

Tweetums DeMay had a kind heart. Any touch of sentiment struck a great emotional chord within her, and she responded with a great outpouring of feeling. She longed, as she often said, to see people happy. It was seeing people happy that made her happy. In this unselfish longing, a kind of reckless giving, the surge of offering swept through her now, as the car sped on along the Coast Highway. She felt she must give Stan something now, in return for the ultimate flattery he had given her. The gift, which she intended only to be the gentlest, warmest kiss on his smooth blond cheek, she moved now to give. And the car, taking a sharp turn, threw her soft and generous body against his. His shoulder yielded with a jerk; his eyes had been intent on the curving strip of concrete that appeared through the swirling fog, and the wheel, in his hands, spun free. He grabbed for it, and in the tiny front seat of the red car, the two of them were thrown apart. Tweetums cried out once, sharply, as the car leaped, out of control, across the shoulder and the low embankment. At the edge, it seemed for a moment that it would save itself, but it did not. Too late, it fell, rolling now, down the black, jagged rocks towards the sea. Then the night was pierced with flame and the little red car flashed brightly, casting jagged rainbows into the waves below, rainbows that sparkled blue and gold, orange and crimson.

As five o'clock approached, Friday afternoon, Claire became increasingly nervous. She was dressed, ready to go. Where was Tweetums? Why on earth wasn't she back? Why, she wondered, had she been such a fool as to lend the car to someone she knew was irresponsible? She paced the huge glass room, smoking cigarette after cigarette. Outside, the afternoon fog thickened; the windows streamed. Soon there was nothing to be seen beyond the glass but a dense grey blanket of fog. Soon it was five-fifteen. Her nervousness changed to worry. Then her worry became anger. She flopped on to the white sofa, planning terrible, cutting things she would say to Tweetums. She was certain to be late now. Traffic would be slow over the bridge. In even the best driving conditions, it was a two-hour drive to Sacramento. She lighted another cigarette, wondering whether to phone Jimmy now or wait till Tweetums arrived. If she knew Jimmy—if the way he had acted in Squaw Valley was any indication of his present mood—she could not count on him to cool his heels for hours, waiting for her. If she didn't show up on time, it would be just like him to go to a movie.

Then the door-bell rang. Well, it was about time! She jumped up and walked rapidly across the room to the door. She pulled it wide open, angrily, then gasped suddenly to see two totally unfamiliar men. One was a state policeman. The other was a young, hatless man in a damp trenchcoat.

" What is it? " she said.

" Are you Mrs. Stuart Gates? " the trench-coated man asked.

" Yes . . ."

" We're from the police. May we come in? "

Claire stepped inside. The two men entered the apartment, and the patrolman politely removed his cap. " What's the matter? " she asked in a faint voice.

" Do you own a red Jaguar automobile, licence number——" The young man looked at a slip of paper in his hand and read the number.

" Yes. Yes, what's happened to it? " she asked sharply.

" Do you know a Mrs. Eleanor Spiers DeMay? "

" Yes. Tweetums DeMay. She had my car. Please tell me——"

" And a Mr. Stanley C. Erickson? "

" Yes! What's happened? "

" You say you lent Mrs. DeMay the car? "

" Yes. Oh, please——"

" I'm afraid there's been an accident, Mrs. Gates."

" An accident! "

" Yes. Perhaps you'd better sit down——"

" No, no! Tell me what happened! "

" The car went off the road on the Coast Highway, about

fifty miles south of Carmel. It wasn't spotted until noon to-day when Patrolman Flaherty here"—he nodded to the man in uniform—"noticed marks on the shoulder." He paused. "It's a drop there of about two hundred feet, Mrs. Gates. The car caught fire. I'm sorry to say both occupants—Mrs. DeMay and Mr. Erickson—were killed."

Claire pressed her fingertips hard against her temples, shaking her head back and forth. "Oh, no!" she sobbed. "Oh, no!"

"I'm sorry, Mrs. Gates."

"I had a date!" she cried. "*I had a date to-night!* Damn them!" She stopped abruptly, covering her mouth with her hand, looking at the two men in horror. Then she turned and walked stiffly across the room to the low white Chinese sofa and sat down hard on it. She sat there, like a little girl, knees pressed close together, hands clasped in her lap, head bent. "Oh!" she sobbed, tears streaming down her face. "Oh, oh, oh!"

24

HELEN's letter was waiting in the mailbox when Jimmy arrived home from work Monday night. He sat at the kitchen table reading it over and over. It was very brief:

> DEAR JIMMY,
>
> I have been thinking about your suggestion that you come down to see Billy and me again some Sunday, and I have decided it would be unfair to say no. Since we will be very busy with the holidays—Christmas, etc.—coming up, perhaps the most convenient day for us would be the Sunday after New Year's, January 5th. Around three in the afternoon would be a good time.
>
> Sincerely,
>
> HELEN

Coming as the letter did, so close after the news about Tweetums and Stan Erickson, Jimmy's first reaction was to wonder if there was any connection. If, perhaps, Helen had heard about the accident, and Stan's death had put to rest a ghost. Was it possible that this strange young man was continuing to influence his life, even in death? He remembered the peculiar feeling he had had that night in Claire's apartment that Stan was in some way his *alter ego*, that they were linked, like brothers, in some dark and terrible sharing. His reaction to Claire's hysterical telephone call Friday night had been a sudden feeling of freedom, and, at the same time, a deep twist of grief, a feeling that part of himself had bounced with the red car over the cliffs into the night.

Then he decided that Stan's death had nothing to do with Helen's letter. Helen probably knew nothing about the accident. It received only a small paragraph in the *San Francisco Call-Bulletin*; the other newspapers didn't carry it at all. In California, after all, violent highway deaths occurred so frequently that they were not hot copy.

The two funerals had been held that very day. Claire had telephoned him several times over the week-end, begging him to go to them with her, but he had refused. She dreaded going alone, she said, and yet she felt she must. It was her New England conscience, commanding her to do her duty to the dead. And she would always feel, in a way, responsible. For she had actually urged Tweetums to take the car.

He read Helen's letter once again.

It was certainly impersonal, cool, with its deliberately formal close, " Sincerely, Helen." And the date she had suggested was five weeks away. She purposely wanted to create the impression that she was not anxious to see him. She would be busy during Christmas, etc. She did not want his visit to coincide in any way with the sentimentality of the holidays. And yet, he thought, she had written. It was the first letter she had written to him in all these months. It was not a cold, legal communication from Eldridge L. Gurney, Counsellor at Law, Rio Linda, California. These were Helen's own words, written in Helen's own hand. She had been thinking about his suggestion. She had been thinking about him.

He stood up and went into the living-room for stationery and a pen. Then he returned to the kitchen table and sat down to compose a reply.

He worked on his answer for a long time. Unfinished pages fluttered, crumpled up, to the floor. He wrote letters that included words of endearment. He wrote others that seemed so cold as to be actually cruel. He wrote letters that mentioned Billy, their son, their future. He wrote letters that called back the past, the week at Yosemite. He told her that he could never live without her, and, at one point, told her he had fallen in love with someone else.

Finally, he had the only letter that seemed right. It said, simply, " January 5th at three o'clock is fine with me." And he signed it, " Love, Jimmy."

He stood up and rubbed his eyes. He felt exultant.

It was after midnight.

On Wednesday afternoon, Claire drove to the San Francisco

airport to meet Blazer in the new car. She was feeling miserable —tired and ill. That morning, in the mirror, her eyes had been sunken, and her face grey. She had done her best with cosmetics, but hadn't successfully been able to hide the ugly shadows under her eyes. Now she felt feverish; driving down Bayshore Boulevard, she gripped the steering-wheel tightly in her gloved hands.

It was a combination of things: the accident, the police, the funerals, and then—Monday, Tuesday, and even to-day—long, stormy sessions with the insurance company. She had insisted on another red Jaguar, identical with Scarlet O'Hara. And she had insisted, of course, that it be delivered before Blazer got back from Honolulu. They had told her that it was impossible; that it would take at least three weeks to locate an identical car. Finally, Tuesday morning, in desperation she had called her father. Junius Denison had taken up the cudgel for her. The new car had been delivered, with a vice-president of the insurance company at the wheel, at one o'clock this afternoon.

She drove into the airport and parked the car. She was a few minutes early, which was a good thing since Blazer hated to be kept waiting. She spent her time in the ladies' room, working on her face. She was determined not to let Blazer know what she had been through. When his plane was announced, she went to the gate and waited for him. She watched as the great silver plane came down, sped along the runway, turned, and taxied slowly back towards the gate. The ramp was rolled into place, the door was opened, and the passengers began streaming out. When she saw Blazer—at first she didn't recognize him; he was darkly tanned and, like the other passengers, wore a white *pikaki lei* about his neck—she called to him and waved gaily.

He made his way towards her and, when he reached her, gave her a quick, affectionate hug and kissed her on the cheek. " Hi, sweetie," he said. " Did you miss me? "

" Oh, did I! " she said. " Darling, you look wonderful! Is that the way you sold sheets—lying on the beach at Waikiki? "

" I did some of that," Blazer said.

" And what's that crazy thing? " she asked, pointing to the *lei*.

" Compliments of the airline," Blazer said. He reached up, removed it, and placed it over Claire's head.

" Thank you, kind sir! " She took his hand and they walked to the baggage counter.

Driving back to the city, Claire chattered about her trip to Squaw Valley, about the unsuccessful ski-ing lessons, about the dreary winter weather. " Boy, you're really wound up to-day, aren't you? " he said, laughing, and then, all at once, he rubbed his hand over the dashboard of the car.

" Hey——" he said. " What the hell? "

" What's the matter? "

" Is this—is this a new car? "

" Why—what makes you think——"

" I don't know. There's something different about it. It smells different——"

" Oh, Blazer! "

" What's happened? "

" This is Scarlet O'Hara the Second! " she said wildly.

" What do you mean? "

Then she blurted it all out.

They drove the rest of the way home in silence.

They entered the apartment and Claire moved about the living-room turning on lamps; it was beginning to get dark. She started to close the white curtains.

" Don't close them," Blazer said.

" Why not? "

" I want to look at the view."

Claire shivered. " I'm so sick of this view! " she said.

Blazer went to the window and looked out. " Poor Tweetums," he said. " I think I feel sorrier for Tweetums than for Stan. It must have been his fault. I bet he was driving like a bat out of hell."

" Please, let's not talk about it any more," Claire said.

" I only said, ' Poor Tweetums.' "

Claire sat down on the white sofa. After a moment, she said, " What about poor Claire? What about me? I'm the one who's had to live through it! "

" I'm sorry," he said gently. " I know. It must have been rough."

" Rough! Yes, it was! "

" Look, Claire——" he began.

" I'm sorry," she said, resting her head on the back of the sofa. " My nerves are absolutely at the snapping point. Don't pay any attention to me."

" Let me fix you a drink."

" Yes, please."

He went into the kitchen and returned, with a bowl of ice, to the bar. He stood, in silence, mixing proportions of gin and vermouth, swirling them in a pitcher with a long silver spoon. " No word from Jim, I suppose," he said.

" From who? From whom? "

" Jimmy."

" Oh. No. No word."

" No answer to your letter? "

" No."

" You did write to him, didn't you, like I asked? "

" *As* I asked. Yes. I wrote to him."

" Your grammar's as good as ever, that's for sure," he said. He filled two glasses with the pale liquid and carried them to the coffee table.

" What do you mean by that crack? " Claire asked him.

" Look, Claire," he said, " I know you're tired, but stop barking at me, will you? "

" Sorry," she said emptily. " I think I'm coming down with something. Virus X."

He sat down beside her on the sofa and picked up his glass. " Well," he said, " welcome home, Blazer. Nice to have you back, old boy, it sure is! "

Claire smiled faintly. Blazer sipped his drink.

" Funny about Jimmy," he said after a moment.

" His father died," Claire said.

" What? "

" His father died. Mother wrote me. He went back to Somerville for the funeral. He stopped by to see Mother."

Blazer stared at the drink in his hand. " Everybody's dying," he said.

Claire laughed bitterly. " Yes! "

They were silent again, and finally Claire leaned forward and picked up her glass.

" I'll have to write him a letter," Blazer said.

" That would be nice."

" He came back to Sacramento, didn't he? "

" Yes." And she added, " So Mother said——"

" Poor kid," Blazer said softly.

" Poor who? "

" Poor *whom*," he said crossly. " Poor Jimmy, naturally."

" You seem to feel terribly sorry for everybody else except me, don't you? "

" All right," he said, " give me one reason—just one reason—why anybody should feel so damn' sorry for you? You came out with a new car——"

Claire pressed her fingers to her temples. " Stop," she said. " Stop, stop, stop! I can't stand you screaming at me! "

" Nobody's screaming at you! "

" Stop! Can't you see I'm simply at a point of nervous exhaustion? Just stop."

Blazer hunched forward, resting his elbows on his knees, frowning at his glass. " Sorry," he said finally. Claire sipped her drink, saying nothing.

Finally, Blazer said, " Well, tell me what you did while I was away."

" I've told you everything. Went to Squaw Valley. Took ski-ing lessons . . ."

" Nothing exciting? "

" Nothing exciting."

" Masterson didn't call, did he? "

" No. There's a letter from him, though. On your dresser."

Blazer slammed down his glass. " Well, for Christ's sake! " he said.

" What now? "

He stood up. " You might have told me, that's all. This could be my job coming through, that's all. Hell of a lot you care! " He walked into the bedroom. He was gone for several minutes while Claire sipped her drink. When he came out, his expression had changed. He waved the letter at her. " This is it! " he said breathlessly. " I'm hired! Ten thousand dollars a year! "

Claire said nothing.

He sat down beside her again. " Hey, sweetie," he said. " Come on! Be yourself! Don't you understand—this is it! He wants me to be West Coast manager! This is what I've been waiting for! " He put his hand on her shoulder. " Claire? " he said. " You might say *something*! "

She stared bleakly in front of her. " Oh, Blazer! " she said at last.

" What? "

" I can't bear it! "

" What? What can't you bear? "

" This means—this means we'll have to stay in California! "

" What's wrong with that? "

Her eyes filled with tears. " Oh, we promised! We promised each other—a long time ago—that we'd go back East! "

" But that was before——"

She stood up and moved away from him. " Before what? Before all this misery and unhappiness, is that what you mean? Oh, I hate this place! I hate this apartment! I hate the God-damned view and the God-damned city and the winter—and I hate——" She walked to the glass and put her hands against it, sobbing. " I hate it! I won't stay here! I'm going home! "

He stood up and followed her. At the window, he tried to put his hands on her shoulders, but she moved away. " No, no, no! " she said. " I'm sorry, but I'm going home——"

" Claire——"

" No, no. What do you think it's been like for me—sitting here all day long with nothing to do, going crazy? Yes," she screamed. " Yes! I think I am going crazy! What about Thanksgiving? " She turned, went to the sofa, and threw herself across it. " Thanksgiving! What do you think it was like for me—here—during Thanksgiving? Thanksgiving at Mars Hill was always so—so wonderful! I almost went home! I almost did, but I knew you—I knew you'd—you'd punish me somehow if I did! If I had gone home, none of this would have happened!"

He knelt beside her on the sofa. " Claire," he said gently, " that's not true. That had nothing to do with——"

" It did, it did . . ."

" We've been happy here, haven't we, Claire? Haven't we? "

" No, no, no. Maybe you have—I haven't! "

" Don't you see? " he pleaded. " This is the chance I've been waiting for. This is a big step! West Coast manager! Claire, this is the biggest moment of my life! "

She turned, on the sofa, her eyes flaming. " Sheet salesman! "

she said cruelly. " And don't act as though this was some great accomplishment! Do you think you'd have got this if it hadn't been for Daddy? Do you? Where would you be if it hadn't been for me—and Daddy? "

Blazer stood up. He walked slowly over to the bar and stood there, gently sloshing the pitcher of martinis. Then he poured himself another. " All right," he said softly, " all right."

They were both silent for a long time as he drank his drink. Finally he said, " I'm going to take this job."

" All right."

" What are you going to do? "

" Go home."

" I see," he said steadily. And then he said, " I'm surprised. I should think you'd want to stay in California."

" Why? "

" Where your boy friend is . . ."

Her eyelids fluttered up, then she looked away. " I don't know what you're talking about! "

" Don't you? "

" No."

" Jimmy . . ."

" Jimmy! " She laughed sharply.

" He's staying here, isn't he? He's not going back East yet——"

" I haven't the vaguest idea——"

" I mean, he'd come back to see us, wouldn't he—if he knew I didn't mind? "

" Blazer, I don't know what you're talking about! "

" Look," he said, " I know why you're not happy here. You want Jimmy. Isn't that it? "

" Don't be absurd! "

" You know," Blazer said slowly, " it's a funny thing. It really is a funny thing——"

" What is? "

" I wouldn't mind."

" Wouldn't mind *what*? "

" Letting him—well, letting him share you——"

She was silent. " What do you mean? " she asked softly.

" I mean—what the hell? " He poured another drink in the glass and lifted it to his lips. " Why not? We have anyway—

he and I. Why shouldn't we go on that way? Only open and above-board?"

"Blazer—I really don't know what you're saying."

"I mean, why couldn't both of us—Jimmy and I—sort of share you? Then everybody would be happy."

"*Share*?"

"Yes, all three of us." Blazer's eyes brightened. "I wouldn't mind. You wouldn't mind. In fact, you'd like it, wouldn't you? If we worked out a mutual arrangement like that, if we all agreed, what would be wrong? Would you let me take this job then—would you stay here?"

"Sometimes——" Claire began, her voice the barest whisper.

"Sometimes what?"

"Nothing. Sometimes I wonder if I know you at all. Blazer, you're scaring me. You're just saying these things to scare me, aren't you?"

"You may not know me," he said, "but I know you, inside and out."

"You don't!"

"Sure I do. And what the hell—it's as good as done already, isn't it?"

"What are you trying to make me say?"

"Look, Claire," he said casually, "I know Jimmy screwed you. Why not? I would have if I'd been in his shoes."

"What makes you think——?"

"Look, sweetie, if you were trying to cover up, you did a pretty lousy job. Leaving that parking ticket in the desk—Jimmy's licence number on it—the time—two-fifteen a.m.—parked over here on Hyde the night I was in L.A.——"

Claire let out a short gasp.

"Neither of us are angels. You've probably seen a lot of him these past few weeks. So why not? Why not continue to see him—on this basis?" He came close to her and looked at her intently. "I'm not kidding. I think it might be—well, kind of fun. All three of us would have what we wanted——"

"*Quiet!*" Claire buried her face in her hands.

"I'm willing," Blazer said. His voice, which had been casual and even, all at once became intense, almost pleading. He knelt on the floor beside her. "Listen to me! I need you, you're right. I'll do anything you say to keep you here. You can call Jimmy right now and tell him it's all right with me, Claire. Because I don't mind, sweetie, I really don't. I just want us to be happy, sweetie, that's really all . . ."

" Please . . . stop talking . . ."

" It's because I love you! "

" Love! "

" Doesn't it prove I love you if I'm willing to go along with this? "

" Quiet, quiet . . ."

He reached out and touched her hair. " Claire! "

She spun sharply and struck him across the mouth with her hand. The fine edge of her diamond ring caught his lip, and a dark trickle of blood appeared from the corner of his mouth, glistened against his tanned cheek.

He dropped his hand quickly and stood up. For a long time, he looked down at her. His eyes flashed with storms of anger and grief. He seemed to tremble, as though his whole body wrestled with some inner force, terrible and deep. Finally, he shrugged, bent, and picked up Harry Masterson's letter from the coffee table. " Well, think it over," he said. " If you won't—well, maybe you've served your purpose. I've got the job." He turned and walked into the bedroom.

Claire said nothing. After all, there was nothing to say.

After all, there is nothing to say, she told herself, again and again. *There is nothing to say.*

She sat there, in the glass room, the white *pikaki lei* around her throat. She studied the view, as though she had never seen it before. She heard Blazer flop into bed. The bedroom light went out. And, after a moment or two, that curious rhythmic tap-tapping, that childish habit that refused to go, sounded from the bedroom.

Claire continued to study the view beyond her shadowy reflection in the black glass.

25

Jimmy had promised to play bridge with Mike and the two Williams girls, Cathy and Margaret, on Saturday. He got an early start from Sacramento and arrived at Mike's apartment on Laguna Street a little before noon. He felt lighthearted. The day was cool, but balmy, rather like a New England spring. He whistled happily as he ran up the steps to Mike's door and rang the bell.

Mike met him with rolled-up shirt-sleeves and a kitchen towel tied around his waist, apron fashion, over his tan trousers. "Hi," Mike said. "I'm just fixing myself some lunch. Come on in and join me."

"Ah, I can smell it," Jimmy said. "Broiled fillet of beef with mushroom gravy, French fries, and fresh peas!"

"That's right." Jimmy followed Mike into the little kitchen, where two hamburgers spat and sizzled in a frying-pan. Deftly, Mike shaped two more patties from the mound of ground beef, dropped them in the pan, and jumped back as the hot fat sputtered angrily. He went to the refrigerator and took out two bottles of cream soda from the clutter of bottles on the bottom shelf.

"Hamburgers and cream soda," Jimmy laughed. "Your menu never changes, does it?"

Mike grinned. "Yeah, I guess I'm in a rut."

When the hamburgers were done, Mike produced buns and a catsup bottle, and they carried their lunch back into the living-room.

"You know," Jimmy said, "I think you should marry Cathy Williams. At least she'd make you eat balanced meals."

"Maybe," Mike said between mouthfuls, "but that'll have to wait." And he added, "She'd feed me soufflés with truffle sauce. That girl needs a millionaire."

" What time are they coming? "

" Around two o'clock."

After a minute or two, Jimmy said, " I got a letter from Helen."

Mike smiled broadly. " Say, that's great," he said, " that really is! "

Jimmy's face flushed. " Yes," he said, " I think so."

" It had to happen, didn't it? Didn't I predict it? Didn't I see it in my crystal ball? "

" You and your damned crystal ball! " Jimmy laughed.

" I knew it would. But remember—don't rush things. Don't get hot under the collar and try to rush things too much. Take it in easy stages. Play it like—like a seven-no-trump bid."

" All right, teacher——"

" I mean it. You've got to make a slam this time."

" I'll hold on to my high cards——"

They both laughed. Mike sat back and wiped his sticky fingers on the towel that still hung around his middle. " Well," he said, " now that you've told me your good news, I'll tell you my bad."

" What's happened? "

" Oh, it's not really bad, I guess. I was expecting it. Uncle Sam."

" You mean—' Greetings——'? "

" Yep." Mike pushed his empty plate forward on the coffee table and stood up, clicking his heels together. " Ten-shun! Recruit Gorman reporting, sir! " He raised his arm and delivered an exaggerated salute.

" When do you have to go? "

" Three weeks. I'll be home for Christmas. My folks will like that, I guess. Then I'll see the New Year in at Fort Devens . . ." He walked to the window and stood there, looking out, his hands thrust deep in his pockets. " Just as I was beginning to like this city, too," he said. " Even the gasworks."

" Gee, that's tough, Mike," Jimmy said.

Mike turned and grinned. " Well, I'm philosophical," he said. " That's my philosophy of life, you know—be philosophical."

" They'll be calling me one of these days, too, I guess," Jimmy said thoughtfully.

"That's why Cathy—and all that—will have to wait."

"Have you told her yet?"

"No—I will, though."

"Well, that's too bad," Jimmy said.

"No, it's not, not really. I'll put in my two years, then I'll come back, get married, settle down, have a baby—like you."

"You mean, come back here?"

"It's funny," Mike said, "but I've really got to like this town. I never thought I would—but I have."

He walked across the room and clapped Jimmy on the shoulder. "Hey, cheer up!" he said. "It's not that bad." He picked up the plates and carried them into the kitchen. He returned and stood in the doorway. He ran his hand through his stiff orange-yellow hair. "Look," he said, "I've got to get a haircut before Cathy comes. I promised her. Will you guard the place from prowlers?" He unwound the dish-towel from around his waist, wadded it up, and tossed it to Jimmy. "And you can even do the dishes. O.K.?"

Jimmy caught the towel. He smiled. "Sure, Mike," he said.

In the apartment on Russian Hill, Blazer was trying to locate Claire. He had come home Friday night and found her gone. She had taken the car, and, as far as he could figure out, only her blue overnight case. Most of her dresses still hung in the closet, along with her mink jacket and most of her shoes. So he knew she must be planning to come back. He sat with the telephone cradled in his lap, calling one hotel after another, first asking for her under her married name, and then—in case she was in one of her melodrama-heroine moods—under her maiden name. He tried the Fairmont, the Mark Hopkins, the St. Francis, and the Palace with no luck. In between he tried to reach Jimmy at his apartment in Sacramento, where there was no answer.

It was possible, of course, that they had gone somewhere together. And yet he was fairly sure they hadn't. He couldn't believe they would be quite so obvious. Jimmy, he was sure, would be smarter than that. At eleven o'clock, he gave up and fixed himself a short, stiff drink. At eleven-thirty, he went back to the telephone, this time going through the list of hotels in the classified directory. He started alphabetically, skipping only the ones south of Market Street where Claire, even in her social-working days, had refused to venture. When he got to the Clift Hotel, he found her. Mrs. Stuart B. Gates had registered yesterday afternoon, but her room did not answer. No, he said, there was no message.

He had another drink and tried the Sacramento number again. There was still no answer. For a while he sat in the empty room, sipping his drink, staring into space.

Then he remembered Jimmy's friend—the fellow with red hair—whom Jimmy had brought to the party. Mike somebody. Mike Gorman. It occurred to Blazer then that Mike Gorman, perhaps, was the only person who could give him the complete story. He found a Michael Gorman listed in the book, on Laguna Street. He started to dial the number, then stopped. This was a situation that called for a face-to-face talk—he was a good enough salesman to recognize that. So he made a note of the address, stood up, and went to the bar and made another drink. He stood there, drinking it. On the exterior, Blazer seemed calm, but he was far from being so within.

After a while, he went downstairs and flagged a taxi. As the taxi entered the thirty-five-hundred block on Laguna, Blazer saw Jimmy's green convertible parked, and knew that he was on the right track.

When the door-bell rang, Jimmy was just finishing up the dishes. He wiped his hands hastily on the towel and went to the door.

" Hi, Keefe-o," Blazer said, smiling.

" Blazer! " Jimmy said. " My God, what are you doing here? "

" Can I come in? "

" Sure—come on in, Blaze." Jimmy stepped aside.

" It was an off-chance," Blazer said. " I thought I might find you here. How've you been? "

" Fine. Fine, Blaze. And you? "

" Just fine." Blazer strolled about the room, looking at photographs on the walls, at the random collection of athletic equipment that lay about. " Where's your friend Mike? " he asked.

" He went out to get a haircut. Sit down, Blaze."

Blazer kicked a lacrosse stick lightly with the toe of his shoe.

" What is this guy? Jack Armstrong or somebody? " He plunked himself down on the sofa, stretching his legs in front of him. " Well," he said lightly, " it's been a long time, Keefe-o."

" Yes," Jimmy said, " it has."

Blazer looked around the room. " Christ, what a dump! " he said suddenly.

" Look, Blaze——" Jimmy began.

" I'm sorry," Blazer said quickly. " I didn't mean that." He sat up. His eyes searched Jimmy's for a moment earnestly. " Look, Keefe-o," he said, " we're still friends, aren't we? "

" Sure," Jimmy said. He fished for a cigarette in his pocket, found one and lighted it. Then he sat down opposite Blazer. " Sure," he repeated.

" Do you mean that? "

" Of course I do."

" We've been trying to get in touch with you, you know—Claire and I."

" Yes," Jimmy said slowly. " Yes, I got a letter from Claire."

" I asked her to write."

" Yes."

" Why did you cut us off like that? " Blazer asked.

" I didn't mean to—to cut you off, really," Jimmy said. " But—well, a lot of things came up. My father died, for one thing——"

" Yes," Blazer said. " Claire's mother wrote us. I'm sorry."

" Thanks, Blazer."

" We really felt pretty bad about it. Especially since you'd cut us off your list, so to speak."

" Hell, it wasn't that, Blaze——"

" I know why it was, and that's one reason I wanted to see you. I wanted to apologize."

" For what? "

" For what Claire said—you know, that night you clobbered Erickson. She didn't mean it. She was tight, like the rest of us."

" I know she didn't mean it."

Blazer was silent for a moment. Then he said, " I don't want to make you feel badly or anything, but did you hear what happened to old Stan—and Tweetums? "

" Yes," Jimmy said quietly, " it was in the paper."

" It happened in our car. Did you know that? Tweetums

borrowed it." Blazer shook his head slowly back and forth. "You know," he said, "it's kind of queer . . ."

"What is?"

"Stan and Tweetums. In our car. That was how my folks died, you know. In an accident in a sports car."

"Yes, I know," Jimmy said gently.

"History repeats itself!" Blazer laughed bitterly. Then he shrugged. "Well, that's life, I guess."

"Yes . . ."

"So—are we forgiven, Keefe-o?"

"Really, Blaze, there's nothing to forgive."

"Will you come back and see us, then? You know—like you used to? Hell, we used to have great times, didn't we? Like that time on the mountain, remember? That was a great time, wasn't it? The three of us—camping out? We can have more great times like that, can't we?"

"Well," Jimmy said slowly, "sure. But right now—well, to tell you the truth, Blaze, I'm in the process of—what do they call it?—'effecting a reconciliation'—with Helen."

Blazer stared at him. "You're kidding!" he said.

"No."

"You mean—you're going back to her?"

"It's more like getting her to come back to me."

"What the hell do you want her back for?"

"Well," Jimmy said quietly, "she's the girl I married."

"You're a damn' fool! I mean, after the lousy way she treated you!"

"We both made mistakes . . ."

"Aw, you're a damn' fool, Keefe-o!"

Jimmy studied Blazer's face intently, the face he had known through school and college. It seemed unchanged, still smooth, rather handsome, with short-cropped curly hair, the thin, straight nose, the pale, almost impersonal, blue eyes. Blazer's clothes, although he wore them with an air of studied casualness, were still carefully pressed, neat, and selected with care. He remembered at Taft Blazer had been voted Best-Dressed Boy; he had the feeling suddenly, looking at Blazer, that he was looking at a posed, slightly smiling, year-book picture. Still, there was something in Blazer's expression now, or in his manner—he couldn't put his finger on it—that he didn't recognize. The too-pale eyes looked frightened, defensive. " I thought you'd be pleased, Blaze," he said finally.

Blazer shrugged and looked away. " I think you're a fool," he said. Then his expression changed. He brightened. " Hey," he said, " how about a drink? What kind of liquor does this guy have around here? "

" There's some beer in the ice-box. Mike says he's too poor to buy booze. Want a beer? "

" Beer! " Blazer said disgustedly. He seemed to sag again into the sofa. He put his head back and stared dully at the ceiling. " Keefe-o," he said.

" What? "

" I really came here to ask you a favour."

" What is it, Blaze? "

" Claire."

Jimmy paused. " What about her? "

" I want you to talk to her."

" What about? "

" She and I—well, we had a fight. A real free-for-all the other night. I'd just got back from a sales trip to Hawaii. I was dog-tired, and Claire had—well, she'd been through all the business with Tweetums and Stan. She was a wreck—nervous, looking like death warmed up. We were both played out. We had a fight—a real one this time. Not the make-believe fights we used to have. Yesterday, while I was at work, she walked out on me."

Jimmy said nothing.

" You know what she said? " Blazer went on. " She doesn't want to stay in California. She wants to go home. How do you like that? Just when things are looking up for me. You see, I'm going to take a new job—with Monarch Mills. As West Coast manager." He paused. " It's a pretty good deal. I mean, it's a hell of a good deal! Good salary—everything. But she's sore because it means we have to stay on the West Coast." He paused again. " You're staying on the West Coast, aren't you, Keefe-o? I mean—you don't mind it, do you? You're not planning to go back, are you? "

" No," Jimmy said. " I've got a job here."

" Sure, that's what I told her," he said rapidly. " I said, 'Jim's staying here.' But she's got the idea she can't stand it any more. She's homesick for that damn' creepy castle back in Connecticut—Mars Hill! My God, you should have heard her! She got all weepy over how wonderful things were at Mars Hill, how wonderful her mother was—Christ! Her old lady's nothing but a lush. She's been a lush for about fifteen years! And her old man is a pompous ass! " He stopped. " I probably shouldn't say that, because he's helped me out. I mean, he's taken an interest in me. He put this guy at Monarch Mills on to me, for instance, and I'm grateful for that. But I've got the job now. Why should I go back to Connecticut and end up working for her old man? I've got a good job now."

" Sure," Jimmy said, " sure——"

" I found out where she is. She's gone to the Clift. I've tried to phone her, but she doesn't answer. Maybe she's just not picking up her phone, I don't know. The thing is, I thought maybe you could talk to her."

" Me? "

" Yes." Blazer sat forward, his eyes flashing intensely. " Would you do it for me, Keefe-o? She'll listen to you, I know that. She's always—well, she's always worshipped the ground you walked on. Even back in college. She'll listen to you! "

Jimmy stood up and walked to the window. All at once he couldn't look into Blazer's face any more. He looked out the window, at the clean, silver-grey gas towers. Up the street, in the tennis courts, he could see white-suited boys playing; beyond the towers, in one small sliver of view, he could see the Marina. " Do you really think that would help? " he asked finally.

" I know it would! She thinks you're the greatest guy in the world——"

" Perhaps if you went over there, Blaze——"

" She won't speak to me! Honest, Keefe-o, I'm afraid I'm going to lose her. It's that serious. Look, I'm desperate. I really am. You're the only person who can help me out, I mean it. You may have got sore at us—but wouldn't you do it for old times' sake? We were room-mates in college—remember? "

" I remember——" Jimmy said softly.

" Then will you do it? "

Jimmy still looked out the window. " I think——" he began.

" What do you think? "

" I think you should talk to her, not me," he said weakly.

" Then do this much for me," Blazer said eagerly. " Come with me. Come on over to the Clift with me. Right now. The two of us will talk to her."

" What good would that do? "

Blazer stood up and walked over to the window. He stood at Jimmy's shoulder. His face was flushed and his voice, now, was a little hysterical. Jimmy noticed then the faint, sweet odour of whisky on his breath. Jimmy rested his arms on the window sash; he felt ill. " Hey, Keefe-o," Blazer said, " remember that night in New Haven when you and I were going to go out together—we had it all planned—to grab a little tail? Remember—I chickened out at the last minute? I was the cold-feet guy that night, remember? "

" What's that got to do with it? "

" I just suddenly remembered it, that's all. I remembered—you went out, but I didn't. And, you know you never did tell me what happened. Did you get any? "

Jimmy laughed, a little wildly. " My God, Blazer—you're still the same, aren't you? Always interested in the gory details . . ."

" Just curious," Blazer said defensively. " Sometimes I think I need a few lessons along those lines. Maybe you could give me a pointer or two."

" I doubt it——"

" But remember—in those days, at college, we were always Gates and Keefe Incorporated, remember that? Remember how we used to talk about going into business together, and how we used to argue whether it should be Gates and Keefe Incorporated? Remember all that——? "

" Yes, yes——"

" I chickened out on you that time. You're not going to chicken out on *me* this time, are you? Are you? "

At that moment, the door to the apartment opened and Mike Gorman came into the room. Blazer, hearing the door, spun around as if he had been shot.

Mike stopped, puzzled, seeing Blazer, then stepped forward, holding out his hand. " Nice to see you again," he said.

Blazer ignored the outstretched hand. " I'm talking to Keefe! " he said angrily.

" Oops, sorry," Mike said, withdrawing his hand. He looked at Blazer, his face faintly amused.

Blazer turned to Jimmy. " Coming, Keefe-o? " he demanded.

" I can't come, Blaze," Jimmy said.

" Why the hell not? "

There was silence in the room. Mike moved towards the sofa. " We were going to play bridge——" Mike said easily.

Blazer turned on him. " Honeymoon bridge? " he asked shrilly. " What are you two, anyway—a couple of queers? Is that what's happened to you, Keefe-o? "

For a long moment, the three of them stood motionless. The room was still. They stood in a triangle—Jimmy at the window, Blazer in the centre, Mike half-way between the door, which still hung open, and the sofa. Then Blazer's body seemed to quiver, his head jerked back. " Well? " he said. " Well? "

Finally, in a soft, even voice, Jimmy said, " Get out of here, Blazer."

Then Blazer's composure seemed to return. His face, which had been flushed and twisted in a sneer, became expressionless. Ignoring Mike's presence, he turned and walked past him to the door. He stopped and looked back. His pale blue eyes gazed at Jimmy for a moment steadily, then flickered slightly and gazed away. Blazer ran his tongue along the edges of his lips and shaped his mouth as if he were going to whistle. " Well," he said, " *comme ci comme ça.*"

Jimmy thought: Pieces of my youth keep dropping away.

" So long, Keefe-o," Blazer said casually, from his year-book face. " See you around."

Then he was gone.

If they had gone to see Claire at the Clift Hotel that afternoon, they would not have found her there. In the new red car, she had driven to Rio Linda. She sat now, in Mrs. Walker Warren's living-room, wearing a beige wool dress, her bright hair tied back in an orange scarf, waiting for Helen to appear.

Upstairs, Mrs. Warren begged Helen not to go down. " Haven't you had enough of this? " she asked. " They're trying to put some sort of pressure on you, can't you see? Let me tell her to go away . . ."

Helen stood in front of her mirror, applying fresh lipstick. " I can handle it, Mother," she said.

" It's some sort of scheme! " Mrs. Warren said desperately. " They're going to try to take Billy away from you or something! "

" Fat chance they'll have of that! " Helen said gaily. She turned and brushed her mother's cheek with her lips. " Look," she said, " this girl and her husband are old friends of Jimmy's. They want to help us get back together again. Is there anything wrong with that? " She went out the door and ran down the stairs. " Good afternoon," she said pleasantly to Claire.

" Hello, Helen," Claire said, rising. The two girls shook hands.

" Won't you sit down? " Helen asked. She went to the coffee table, lifted the crystal cigarette box and offered it to Claire, who at first shook her head, then changed her mind and said, " Thank you," taking a cigarette.

Helen lighted their cigarettes. Then both girls sat—Helen on the sofa, Claire on one of the small French chairs. " How have you been? " Helen asked.

" Fine, thank you," Claire said. " I hope I didn't disturb you."

" No, not at all," Helen said. " I was just giving Billy his bottle."

" Oh, how *is* the baby? " Claire asked.

" Oh, he's fine. Would you like to see him? "

There was a pause as Claire inhaled deeply on her cigarette, then dispersed the smoke with a wave of her hand. " No, thank you," she said.

Helen looked at the other girl quickly. Claire's face was composed, her mouth firm. She saw, all at once, that this was not a friendly visit. What kind of a visit it was, she didn't know. She prepared herself for it.

" My business won't take a minute," Claire said finally. " I've come to find out what your plans are."

" What plans? " Helen asked quietly.

" About your divorce. Are you going ahead with it? "

" I'm sorry," Helen said, " I don't quite understand——"

Claire smiled and tapped her cigarette resolutely in the ashtray. " I want Jimmy," she said.

" What? "

" I want to marry him."

Helen closed her eyes and pushed herself back into the sofa's depths. " I see," she said finally.

" I want to marry him, and naturally I want to know what kind of divorce you plan to give him."

" What *kind* of divorce? " Helen asked.

" Yes," Claire said. " There are different kinds. There are the nice, pleasant, speedy kind, the best kind, that take place very painlessly. Then there are the kind that drag on with lots of unpleasantness for everyone. Which kind is yours going to be? "

" You say that you want to marry Jimmy," Helen said. " Do you mean—he's asked you to? "

" I don't think that makes any difference," Claire said quickly.

" I think it does."

" Jimmy's too much of a gentleman to ask a girl to marry him while he's still married to someone else," Claire said. " But over the last few months we've seen a great deal of each other, and we've become very fond of each other. You see," she said pointedly, " Jimmy and I are just alike. Our—well, our backgrounds are similar, for one thing. And we like to do the same things."

" I see," Helen said.

" My own marriage was a mistake," Claire said. " Blazer and I have separated."

" I'm sorry to hear that," Helen said.

" Don't be! It's really going to work out for the best. I'm going back East. Then I plan to go to Florida to get my divorce. Then—depending on what you do—Jimmy and I will——"

" Depending on what I do? "

" Yes. You're—well, you're the only obstacle in the plan at the moment."

" You keep talking about the plan," Helen said. " Whose plan is it? "

" Mine. Ours," Claire said defiantly. " Jimmy's and mine."

Helen said nothing. Then she said, " Yes, I suppose I am an obstacle then." She laughed suddenly. " Forgive me, it's a little funny," she said.

" What's funny? "

"I thought——" Helen said. "I really thought when Mother said you were down here—that you'd come to try to help us get back together. Like the last time you were here. But now—now I find it's just the opposite!"

"The situation has changed," Claire said quickly. "That other time was before I—before I realized I was in love with him. I was sincere that first time. I really thought it would make him happy to have you back. Now I know that I am the only one who can make him happy."

"Oh, you're so self-assured!" Helen said. She laughed again, and there was a trace of hysteria in her voice.

"Why shouldn't I be?"

"Oh, no reason! It's a quality I've always lacked, that's all. Perhaps—perhaps that's what he likes in you!"

"Perhaps."

"Just tell me one thing and then go," Helen said. "Tell me—is this what Jimmy wants?"

"Yes."

"Then why hasn't he told me so himself?"

Claire blew out a sharp stream of cigarette smoke. "Because," she said, "he doesn't want to see you again. He doesn't want to get involved with you any more!"

"He asked you to come here?"

"Yes," said Claire, her eyes never wavering.

Helen was silent. Was it true? she wondered. Desperately, she tried to remember the things he had said when he had been down. For the life of her, she couldn't remember now, but they had seemed—he had seemed—so different. He had talked about the future. Had he meant something else entirely? Had something like this been in the back of his mind the whole time? All at once, nothing made sense any more. "Well, what do you want me to do?" she asked.

Claire leaned forward. "Go to Reno. Go to Reno, where you can get it done quickly. Don't go through this California process—waiting a year for the decree to become final. California is the worst place in the world to get a divorce, you must know that. And if it's a question of money——"

"How much are you offering me?" Helen asked, her face amused.

"I don't mean that," Claire said hastily. "But I'm sure

Jimmy would be willing to take care of all your expenses. It would be worth it to him. I'm sure you know his circumstances. His people are—well, quite wealthy."

"Yes, I know," Helen said softly. "But it's not money. It's——"

"What is it, then?"

"Nothing, I guess." She stood up.

"Then will you do it?"

"I wish I could talk to him——"

"There's no need for that. Jimmy and I have talked about everything. Everything." And she added, evenly, "Everything that two people in love can talk about."

Helen put out her cigarette. She raised her empty hand, her wrist trembling, and touched her hair. "All right," she said finally. "If that's what Jimmy wants, I'll do it."

Claire jumped up. "Will you?"

"Yes, yes . . ."

"Oh, he'll be so happy when I tell him!"

"Yes. Please tell him it's all right. I'll do it."

"I *knew* you'd be a sport about it!" Claire said. "Thank you! This means so much to us!"

"Don't mention it," Helen said wearily. "Now, if you'll excuse me——"

"Of course," Claire said. "And I hope you don't think I'm a dreadful bitch. I like you, really. I think you're a very sympathetic person. I can't help liking you. If I sounded hard-boiled in some of the things I said, it's because—well, I guess back East we're a little more sophisticated about things like this. And I don't mean that unkindly. But we are. Heavens, marriages break up all the time—nobody thinks a thing about them!" She laughed.

"Good-bye," Helen said.

Claire started towards the door. "I knew you'd be understanding," she said. "I knew you were that kind of person. I knew you'd see that this was the only right thing—for all of us."

At the door, she turned. "I don't know whether we shall ever see each other again," she said. "I know Jimmy wants to keep completely out of the picture where the baby is concerned——"

"Does he?"

" Yes," Claire said confidently. " He told me he never plans to see it. Not that he doesn't care about it, but he just doesn't want to get involved with it. He——"

For the second time that afternoon, Helen looked at the other girl with surprise, at the incredibly polished, animated face. " He never plans to see it? " Helen asked.

" Never." Claire chatted on. " Oh, Jimmy will be so pleased when I tell him this news. He's been so miserable through all of this. Poor guy—poor sweet guy! If you'd seen him during these last few months as I have, you'd have seen a completely different person. Gloomy, refusing to take a drink or have a good time, flying off the handle, taking punches at people! Oh, he'll be so happy to have this over with! "

" Taking punches at people? " Helen said.

" Yes, but it was nothing—it didn't mean a thing. Just an indication of the state he's been in——"

" It doesn't sound like Jimmy."

" Well," Claire said, " when a guy's going through a crisis, you can't blame him for flying off the handle, can you? Poor guy. For no reason at all—they were talking together, Jimmy and this friend of ours, and all of a sudden Jimmy went at him. Tooth and nail! Goodness, we thought he was going to kill poor Stan——"

" Stan? "

" Stan Erickson. But it was just an emotional thing, I'm sure——"

" Did he——? " Helen stopped. She moved across the room, away from Claire. " What a curious thing! " she said finally.

" Of course I think I know why he did it," Claire said.

" Why? "

" I think Stan must have said something—about me—that Jimmy didn't like. And Jimmy has such a crazy sense of honour! He probably thought he was defending me. At least," she said, " I like to think that's what it was! "

" Yes."

" Well," Claire said, " I must be going. Good-bye."

" Good-bye," Helen said softly.

" And thank you! " Claire lifted her hand and blew a kiss. " You're an angel! " She opened the door and let herself out.

Helen stood in the centre of the room for a moment. Then she went to the front window and watched as the blonde girl ran down the front steps to the sidewalk, then down the sidewalk to the red car. The girl opened the car door and slid gracefully into the front seat, behind the wheel. The motor started with a roar and the car pulled away from the curb. Helen watched as the car went down Magnolia Street, then turned at Lime and disappeared, beyond the park. She smiled; then she too raised her hand and blew a kiss to Claire. Then, all at once, she had so many things to do it was difficult to decide where to begin. Where had she put Jimmy's letter? she wondered. It had been so brief, so terribly brief! First, she wanted to read it again.

In San Francisco, the wind blew.

On the street, it scattered the dry leaves of magnolias and lemon trees. In the apartment on Russian Hill, it buffeted the huge, heavy panes of glass; the windows creaked in their frames. A portion of the glass room jutted out over the story below, and from this corner of the living-room, standing, looking out and down, one had the feeling of being surrounded by nothing at all; it was like being imprisoned within a huge glass paperweight far above the bright fairy-tale city. The effect was peculiarly insular; only the frail cobwebby strands of the two bridges, stretching to the east and north, created any feeling of escape. From here, the drop was easily seventy feet to the ground, which fell away below. Standing there, Blazer Gates contemplated it.

Then he went into the bedroom, placed his drink on the dresser top, and opened the drawer. He looked at the object inside; he had gone, like this, to the drawer and looked inside several times that afternoon. This time he picked the object up, curling his fingers around the hard steel butt, and, with his other hand, stroked the slim, cold barrel. Tentatively, he aimed through the doorway at the glass wall opposite. In his mind, he heard the great, thundering fall of shattered glass. He envisioned it all around him, stabbing him. He was a matador; in the arena, the bull came towards him, head lowered. He felt the dark upward thrust . . .

Trembling, he replaced the gun in the drawer among the handkerchiefs and closed the drawer.

It was a foolish wish. He would never do it. It was an untrue wish. He would never have the courage. The kind of destruction that he dreamed of for himself was always impossible in fact. Helplessly, he saw this now. He saw, stretching bleakly before him, all the rest of the years of his life. He went to the bed and threw himself across it. He lay there. Then he began to sob, lifting himself on his elbows and beating the bedclothes with his fists.

26

The wind was still blowing on Sunday afternoon. Jimmy and Mike stood on the sidewalk outside Mike's apartment building, feet apart, braced against the gale. It was almost five o'clock; the day was darkening.

" You sure you don't want me to help you move out? " Jimmy asked.

" No," Mike said, " I'm just going to throw all my stuff in the back of the station wagon next Saturday morning and head back over the Great Divide. Just the way I came . . ."

" Well," Jimmy said, " don't forget to drop me a line when you get assigned somewhere. Who knows—you might be shipped back to California."

" That would be just like the Army, wouldn't it? " Mike said.

" Well, we'll get together again some time," Jimmy said.

" Sure, and if you ever get back East——"

" I'll look you up."

" You might get back for a vacation or something."

" Well, drop me a line. And good luck——"

" Good luck to you, too," Mike said. " Let me know how things work out."

" Well, so long. It's been great knowing you. Thanks for everything."

" So long," Mike said. " Thanks for bridge games."

" It's a good thing we never played for money——"

" Too bad you can't play bridge by mail."

" So long, Mike."

They shook hands. " So long, trooper." Mike saluted.

" You're getting better at that," Jimmy laughed. He opened the door to his car. " Christ, what a wind! " he said. " Give my love to New England."

"I will . . . so long."

Jimmy climbed into the car and started the engine. At the foot of the block, he made a wide U-turn and started back up the hill. From the sidewalk, Mike gave a jaunty wave. Jimmy waved back. He blew the horn three short blasts.

Driving across the Bay Bridge, the wind tugged at the car. The convertible top slapped noisily against the metal frame. It was quite dark now. Thousands of tiny lights pierced the blackness from the Berkeley shore. The wind continued as Jimmy drove along the East Bay, then up into the hills. About an hour later, as he entered the valley, the wind turned to driving rain. In patches, he encountered low-lying tule fog—fog that formed in the tollin rushes along the river-beds and spread out across the valley floor. In each of these sudden swirling mists he had to reduce his speed almost to a crawl. It was after eight o'clock when he reached Sacramento. Crossing the bridge and entering the city, he discovered that over the week-end the streets had been strung with Christmas decorations, gaudy festoons that glowed red, green, and yellow. And all at once he was achingly lonely. It was not the sinking, despairing loneliness of a few months ago, after Helen had left, but a different kind. It was the loneliness of being in a strange city at Christmas time, with no place to go. Oddly enough, he had not thought much about Christmas until now. He thought, wryly, of sitting alone at his kitchen table eating Christmas dinner.

Driving under the bright street decorations, he thought suddenly of Claire Denison's début party at Mars Hill, coloured lights strung from trees in the garden, balloons floating in the lighted swimming-pool at the foot of the terraced lawn. Claire, standing in the garden, in a long white dress, white gloves, a bouquet of pink rosebuds in one hand, the other outstretched, being presented to the guests. At her throat, he remembered, hung a diamond lavaliere. *Give my love to New England.* He thought of home, of the white house in Somerville. It would be empty now. His mother had written, telling him that she was spending Christmas with Aunt Celeste Kimball in the Bahamas. The white house in Connecticut would be dark this year, though it, too, had been strung many times with coloured lights for parties, Christmases . . .

Was he cherishing some foolish, childish dream, this dream of accepting a challenge, fighting a battle, making his own terms with life? Was there anything, really, to look forward to with Helen? The assurances of a happy ending were certainly slim. Perhaps they had all been right—his father, his mother, Turner Ames, Claire—even Blazer. Perhaps he should simply forget her. They had all thought so, said so—everybody except himself and Mike. He remembered thinking once that the rich were never really troubled. They were only inconvenienced. Inconvenienced by death, federal taxes, disappointing children, divorces, Democrats, impudent servants. For no reason at all, he remembered a conversation with his mother when he was fifteen or sixteen. He was home from school and he and a friend, Scrib Newton, had been planning to go to a dance in New York. Scrib's father had promised to drive both boys into town, but at the last minute Scrib had telephoned to say that Mr. Newton couldn't take them, he was having trouble with his car. Jimmy's mother had been astonished. "Trouble with the car?" she had said. "Why would they have trouble with the car? Heavens, if you turn a car in at ten thousand miles, as we do, you never have *trouble* with a car!" She had probably not intended the remark to sound as vacuous as it did; to her, it was that simple. Cars might be late. They might be tied up in traffic; they might even, though one hoped they wouldn't, be smashed to smithereens in a ghastly accident. But they never had *trouble*.

"*If you do as we do . . .*" If one did as they did, life was graceful, polite, untroubled. He wondered now if, because he had been brought up in this tradition, he had set out in pursuit of trouble as a quaint, romantic adventure. He had thought of himself as fighting a lonely battle to save his marriage. But did he actually want to save it—or was it just the experience of battle that he wanted? He was not at all sure now. It would be easy—terribly easy—to end the trouble by going home, going down to the office to talk to Turner Ames, going to work for the Keefe Company. Some day, surely, he would be president. He could build his own house in Somerville. He could marry someone like Jessica Morton. No, not someone like Jessica Morton. Someone like—Claire.

He wished now that there were someone with whom he could

talk about it, but that was another trouble. There was no one. His father was gone, Mike was gone, Blazer was gone—all the voices he had once listened to with respect. Of course there was Claire. He could have Claire, he supposed, for the asking. There would be no trouble to that. When he got back to the apartment, he would only have to pick up the phone, call the Clift Hotel . . .

He turned into Capitol Avenue, drove slowly down it, and turned into the narrow alley behind the apartment house. He parked the car in the open carport, got out, and walked slowly through the courtyard and up the wide redwood steps. He fished in his pocket for the key and let himself in. As usual, he had forgotten and left the living-room lights burning—through the open door, the living-room was flooded with light. He would have to watch out for things like that, he thought. After all, he was not so rich any more. He started to go into the living-room, then changed his mind, stepped into the kitchen, and flipped on the light there. He went to the refrigerator, opened it, and took out a bottle of milk. He reached in the cupboard for a glass, and then, all at once, he noticed a strange scent in the air. Not strange, but familiar. He stopped, his hand frozen in mid-air, reaching for the glass, wondering if he was awake or dreaming, his heart pounding, because he knew that Helen was in the living-room.

It was several moments before he could move, go to the door, and look into the lighted room. She was sitting on the sofa, her brown hair brushed back, her small, sculptured face looking at him, smiling.

"Hello," she said. And then she said, "I hope I didn't frighten you."

He stared at her.

"Did you think you were being burglarized?" she asked. "I'm sorry——"

He sat down limply in the chair opposite her. "How did you——" he began.

"How did I get in?" She smiled again. "I still had my key," she said. "I've been here quite a while—hours, in fact. I came up this afternoon and rang the bell and thought: Darn it, he's not home—now I'll have to go all the way back. Then I remembered that I still had my key!"

"You've been waiting here—all afternoon?"

"Oh, I've kept busy," she said lightly. "Or don't you notice? Don't things look a little cleaner? Didn't you even notice that your dishes had been washed?"

"I'm sorry—I guess——"

"I was going to give you till nine o'clock. Then—well, by then I decided you would be—out with another girl."

He said nothing, simply stared at her.

"You saved my pearls, didn't you?" she asked. "I found them in a little dish in the kitchen. Why did you save my pearls?"

"I thought—you might like to have them restrung."

"They were only ten-cent-store pearls. But they could be restrung," she said. "I think I will have them restrung . . ."

"I think I've got them all," he said a little wildly. And then he said, "Where's Billy?"

"His grandmother's been dying to baby-sit."

"Is he—all right?"

"Of course. He's fine."

"Well——" he said, taking a deep breath, "I don't mind saying—well, I'm absolutely—I don't know what to say!"

"I'm sure I scared you out of your wits."

"I was in the kitchen, and I smelled—your perfume, I guess."

She laughed. "That smell isn't my perfume! It's Clorox!"

"You didn't have to do all that."

"I told you, I had to do something to keep busy!"

"I'm sorry, Helen. If I'd known you were coming——"

"I thought of telephoning," she said slowly. "But—I was afraid. I was afraid that if I telephoned, I'd lose my nerve. I wouldn't come . . ."

He forced a laugh. "Well," he exclaimed, "how does the old place look?"

"Exactly—exactly as I'd remembered it. I saw your avocado in the kitchen—I gave it a drink. It's beautiful——"

He laughed again. "The remains of a salad—you know, from my salad days——"

"It's big enough to be put into a pot. Yes," she said, "I think you could put it into a pot now and it would get bigger—*even* bigger, I mean."

" Yes, yes," he said seriously. " I suppose you're right."

Then suddenly they both laughed. Helen swayed forward, her hand on her bosom, choking with laughter. " Oh! " she gasped. " Oh, I don't know what's so funny, but——"

Jimmy rocked in his chair, holding his sides. " I don't know either, but it is——"

Then they stopped laughing simultaneously. Helen dabbed at her moist eyes. Finally, she said soberly, " I had to come."

Just as soberly, he said, " Why did you? "

" Because," she said, her eyes pleading, " I wanted to see you again."

" Oh," he breathed.

" I've thought——" she said, " I've thought a lot about the things you said. When you came down, I mean. About the future, and——"

" Yes? " he asked.

" And when you asked me—do you remember? You asked me if I believed in change, that you could change, that people could change . . ."

" Yes . . ."

" And I thought: Well, how can I ever know whether to believe in it or not unless I see? Because things can change, I know. Even I could change."

They were silent, looking at each other.

" Because," she went on softly, " perhaps it isn't necessary for one person to do all the changing. You, I mean. Am I making any sense? What I mean is, if I believe that you have changed, then I can believe that I've changed, too——" Her voice trailed off.

" I understand," he said.

" That's why I didn't bring Billy . . ."

" Why not? "

" Because Billy isn't important—no, no, I don't mean that. Of course he's important, but it's really you and me, first, who have to believe, isn't it? "

" Yes," he said.

" So—so I came . . ."

" My God! "

" What is it? "

"Nothing," he said. "It's just—nothing. I can't seem to——"

Helen stood up and walked to the corner window. "You said," she said, "that you thought perhaps we could work things out, didn't you?"

"Yes . . ." He studied her from the back, slim, almost frail in a simple black wool dress. He had forgotten how short she was.

"Did you mean that?"

"Yes."

"Well, I thought if you were willing—willing to try it, then I should be willing, too. After all, I'm not faultless . . ."

"I'm willing," he said softly.

She turned and faced him again. "Then so am I."

He stood up and went to her. She looked up at him. "I believe—that if you're strong enough to fight for me, then I am strong enough to fight for you."

He kissed her very gently, and she clung to him for a moment, then she buried her face in his shoulder. "It won't be easy," she said. "It's going to be hard. Good things are always hard to come by, aren't they? It may be the hardest thing we've ever done. No, I know it won't be easy. It will take a long time—a long time before we know whether we've done it or not! We may never know whether we've done it or not! But I'm willing to try——"

They separated, and Helen moved around the room. "You know," she said, "sitting here in this apartment—all afternoon, cleaning it—I wondered why we never *did* anything to it!"

"What do you mean?"

She laughed. "I mean—why didn't we do things, little things? Like take down the Venetian blinds! I suddenly thought this afternoon: Why, those windows might be rather pretty if it weren't for the Venetian blinds! And I thought—if we put the sofa there——" She pointed. "Oh, I just mean little things. Like hang some pictures! What was the matter with us, Jimmy? Were we too lazy—or what—not to try to make this place look a *little* less like a motel?"

"I never thought there was much you could do with it—except take it as it is!"

"Oh, just little things would help. Just little touches—I know the furniture's pretty dreadful, but——"

"I see what you mean," he said. "Like take down the Venetian blinds."

"Yes! Exactly!"

He went to the window and peered up under the cornices. Then he reached up. "Look," he said, "they lift right off——" He lifted the blind from its brackets and lowered it, placing it in a heap on the floor.

"There! Isn't that better?" She laughed. "Now do the other one!"

He repeated the operation with the other window.

"Isn't that better? Oh—I remember that pretty eucalyptus tree!"

He dusted his hands on his trouser-legs. "Of course we'd need a bigger apartment now—with Billy," he said.

She thought about this. "Yes," she said finally, "but I think we should wait—wait before we bring Billy into it. I mean, I want this to be you and me first. If the experiment works—I mean, if things seem to be working out, then we can bring Billy into it. But first it must be by ourselves——"

"What are you going to do with him?"

She turned and moved away from him again. "Let's not be hasty," she said. "Let's try—let's try visits. I could come up, or—yes, I could come up, like this, and Mother could baby-sit——"

He went to her again, put his hands on her shoulders and turned her slowly around. "Darling," he said.

"I'm scared, a little," she said, her eyes clear. "Aren't you? I think it's so important—that I'm scared."

"I'm scared, too."

"Oh," she said, "we had so many things against us, didn't we? That was part of the trouble, wasn't it? We had families fussing over us—making us get married again. We had Daddy dying—we had so much to contend with! Things from the outside—that we couldn't control. No wonder we couldn't seem to grow up!"

Slowly, thoughtfully, he kissed her again. Then, once more, they separated.

"Yes," she said emphatically, "this apartment could be

made attractive, it really could. It needs—oh, of course it needs a good cleaning. A better cleaning than I could give it in an afternoon. But wait and see—if we hung some pictures there—and moved the coffee table over there—why didn't we ever think of that? To move the coffee table over there, so it could cover up that hideous spot on the rug——"

"I can't remember," he said, "was that spot there when we moved in?"

"I can't remember either."

Together, they walked to the spot and studied it. "I've never been able to figure out what that spot was," Helen said. "Do you suppose it could be——" Together, they kneeled to examine the spot, and, kneeling, their heads cracked together. "Oh!" Helen said.

"Oh, God, I'm sorry, Helen . . ."

"No, it was my fault."

They sat, on their knees on the floor, rubbing their heads. Then they began to laugh, and, all at once, they were in each other's arms. "It won't be easy, darling," Helen said urgently. "It's going to be hard! The hardest thing! The hardest thing we've ever done. But it's worth it, isn't it? Isn't it?"

"Oh, darling! My darling!"

"Jimmy!"

Then a few moments later, she whispered, "Darling . . .? We're still married . . ."

Then, much later, in the total darkness of the room, with only the sound of rain falling on the courtyard below, and the sound of the eucalyptus branches scraping in the wind, Jimmy said softly, "I feel as if I've come out of a great noisy room suddenly to a quiet place. There's been a great party going on—a huge, noisy party with disreputable people letting their hair down and performing all sorts of noisy feats, telling noisy jokes, laughing at the noise, being their worst. And all at once, the door is closed on it all, and I'm in this curiously quiet place. The party is still going on somewhere—way over there—but nobody at the party misses me and I don't miss it. I'm far away on the other side of the house, on the other side of the world. Whole mountains in between me and the others. Perhaps somewhere in the party, someone will shriek, 'Where's Jimmy?' And there'll be a frantic, noisy search for me—under the sofa, in the closets—and when they don't find me there, they'll pick up and go on. I'll be back in a minute, they think. But the thing is, I'll never be back. My whole life has been in that crazy party, that never-ending nonsense. I've escaped from it into a very quiet room where the doors are open, leading out, where I can come and go, through the doors . . . through the doors . . . in and out . . . this quiet room. Thank God!" He began to laugh softly.

27

When Jimmy got home from work Monday night, Helen had fixed dinner. She had set the kitchen table with mats and napkins and they ate by candlelight. In the centre of the table, she had arranged a low bowl of Shasta daisies. She had also rearranged the living-room furniture. The coffee table now covered the spot on the rug. " I'd forgotten how much fun it is to keep house," she said.

" Tell me," Jimmy asked once during their dinner, " does your mother have any idea where you are? "

Helen laughed. " No," she said. " Or rather she has an idea—but it's the wrong one. I told her I was going to San Francisco to stay with friends."

" Are you going to tell her? "

" When I get back, yes."

" What do you think she'll say about it? "

" Well," she said thoughtfully, " I think she'll probably be a little upset at first. You know Mother. She likes things orderly—like her garden. She doesn't like changes. But, once she gets used to the idea—then I think she'll be very happy about it. Besides," she added, " there won't be much she can do about it! "

Then he asked her the question he had put off asking her. " When do you think you'll be going back? " he said.

" To-morrow . . ."

" To-morrow? "

" Yes, I must go back to-morrow. I'll—I'll fix your breakfast, see you off to work—and then I'll go. It's just that I can't leave Billy for too long."

" Yes, of course," he said.

" You understand, don't you? "

"Yes." Then he said, "You don't think—that you might bring Billy back?"

"Is it too soon, darling?" she asked earnestly. "Have we really had enough time to get to know each other again? Honestly, I don't know. At times, to-day, thinking about it, I thought yes. Then I thought—let's wait. But *I* can come back! I could come back next week-end. That is, if you want me too . . ."

"You know I want you to," he said slowly.

"Oh, I'm glad you do! Let's have week-ends together, two or three more, anyway. Just think—there's Christmas coming, then New Year's. Let's have two or three week-ends—clandestine, all by ourselves! Then, if we're really sure, then—then we can bring Billy here, and really begin."

He reached for her hand across the table. "I love you, Helen," he said.

"And I love you." She jumped up, brushing at her eyes with the back of her hand. "Well," she said, "let's do the dishes!" She began to clear the table. "This is what we need," she said. "This is what we never had any of, before. A little baby is—well, they take a little looking-after. We need every minute we can possibly have to get to know each other. It's been such a long time . . ."

He stood up and put his arms around her. "You know," he whispered, "I've been thinking all day—about last night. How wonderful it was. It was like it was way back at the beginning—before everything got mixed up. Isn't it strange? How everything got mixed up? But now—it's going to be all right now, isn't it?"

"There was a monster in both of us," she said.

The telephone rang. Helen started to reach for it; then, instinctively she withdrew her hand. "Let's let it ring," she said.

"All right . . ."

The telephone continued to ring. Then Jimmy said, "I'd better see who it is——" He picked up the receiver. "Hello?"

"Jimmy? This is Claire. Were you asleep or something?"

"No," he paused. "Where are you?"

"I'm here—about eight blocks away. At the Senator Hotel."

" What are you doing here? "

" Can I meet you? " she said. " Just for a minute? I've got to see you."

" What's happened? "

" Can I come up? " she asked.

" No, no——" he said quickly.

" Then meet me somewhere. Where can you meet me? "

Jimmy was silent.

" Where? " she asked. " Please, Jimmy, I've got to talk to you. It's terribly important."

" I'm trying to think——"

" Look," she said, " I'll start walking up the street and you start walking down. I'll follow the edge of the park, over to Capitol—I'll meet you half-way."

" Is something wrong? "

" I'll explain. Start walking down Capitol. I'll start walking up." There was a click as she hung up.

He replaced the telephone, then turned to Helen, who stood looking at him across the candle-lighted kitchen. " That was Claire Gates," he said.

" Oh," Helen said. " Is she—here? "

" Yes."

" She wants to see you? "

" Yes," he said.

Helen looked at him for a moment. " Then you'd better go," she said.

" Helen, I——"

She smiled. " You've got to go," she said. " I understand."

" Do you? "

" Yes." She went to the closet and took his raincoat from the hanger. " It's a miserable night," she said. " That poor girl——"

" Why do you say that? "

" Because—I like her, really," Helen said. " Now hurry."

" Are you sure you understand? Why I have to see her? "

" Of course I do, darling. Just——"

" What? "

" Just hurry back! " she said, smiling. " And remember——"

" Remember what? "

" Nothing. Now hurry."

At the door he stopped and turned. " I'll be right back," he said.

He went out the door and down the steps to the street. The rain was coming down with a slow, steady drizzle, and there was still a sharp, cold wind that rattled the fronds of the ornamental palm trees in front of the apartment house. The sidewalk was deserted and quiet; a few cars splashed by on the street. As he walked down Capitol Avenue towards the park, Christmas trees glittered from several lighted windows as he passed. Then, ahead of him, emerging through a puddle of lamplight, he saw Claire walking towards him. She looked small and cold, her shoulders hunched close together. She was wearing a short mink jacket and white Angora mittens. He waved to her, and she hurried towards him.

" Oh, Jimmy," she said breathlessly when they met. " I'm so glad you could meet me. I had to see you." Her hair was loose and damp and her face was streaked with rain.

" What's happened? "

" I've left Blazer," she said. " I'm going home."

At first he didn't understand. " Home? " he said. " Where?"

" To Mars Hill. I've left him, Jimmy. I'm going to get a divorce. I'm going home."

" Oh," he said.

" Yes. Oh, Jimmy," she said, " I'm kind of frightened. But it's what I must do! Jimmy—kiss me! "

Without thinking, he bent and kissed her forehead. " Claire," he began, " I want to tell you something——"

She went on. " I moved out this morning," she said. " While Blazer was at the office. I had to. I packed everything in Scarlet O'Hara——"

" Scarlet O'Hara? " he said. " But I thought——"

" Scarlet the *Second*! " she said. " Scarlet's twin. Oh, what a week-end I've been through—you'll never know! Last night I drove all the way to San Gregorio—to the beach. I thought if I could only just *sit* there on the sand! Just sit there! Listening to the waves coming in, trying to find some kind of peace! I walked for hours—or it seemed like hours. Finally in desperation I had to talk to someone. So I called Daddy at Mars Hill. When I heard his voice on the telephone, all I could do was cry! Let's walk this way——" she said.

They started down the street. " But to-day was better," she said. " Now that I've done it—moved out—I feel so much better. Because I know it's all going to work out. Daddy said, ' Come home.' So I'm going home. Over the mountains—our mountains, Jimmy . . ." She turned to him. " You're coming with me! "

" No, Claire."

" Then you're following me—as soon as you can. You must, Jimmy. I need to be sure of that."

" Listen to me, Claire——" he began.

" Jimmy—I've got wonderful news for you. And you mustn't be angry the way you were last time. But I went to see Helen. I got her to promise—don't interrupt, darling—I got her to promise that she would go to Reno right away. She promised me, Jimmy! She's going to get a divorce very quickly. She gave me her word! "

He stared at her bright face, incredulous. " Claire! I——"

But she wouldn't let him speak. " I know, I know what you're going to say," she said. " You're going to talk about your job —how you have to stay here, in this dreadful state, and work. But you don't. You don't at all. Oh, Jimmy, think of Christmas time in New York. Christmas at Mars Hill! Remember the dances, all the parties? Remember how Connecticut comes to *life* at Christmas time? There are going to be hundreds—literally hundreds of parties! The Cotillion! Would you like to take me to the Cotillion? Won't it be wonderful? Jimmy—you must come back now, before Christmas! "

" I'm not going back," he said.

" What do you mean? Of course you're going back! You always said you would. Blazer's staying here—he's the kind that should—but not you! Please come back now, Jimmy——"

" I'm sorry, Claire."

" Listen, Jimmy," she said, " I talked to Daddy. He's setting things up for me. Mars Hill will be mine some day. Just think —Mars Hill all to ourselves. And do you know what Daddy's doing? He's setting things up so I'll have a bigger income. I'll have thirty thousand, Jimmy. Just think—that, plus what you have—we'll be able to have an apartment on Park Avenue, Mars Hill, a house in France. How much will you have, Jimmy? "

" How much what? "

" How much money—income? That was one of the great troubles with Blazer and me—he had no money. Do you see what I mean? It's comforting to have all that money, don't you think? That's why I can leave Blazer so—so easily. I have that cushion. It makes the hurt so much more bearable. Tell me one thing, though—am I being a bitch to take Scarlet O'Hara away from him? I don't want to be a bitch, but Scarlet O'Hara *is* mine—and I need some way to get home——"

Jimmy laughed softly. " I think you should keep Scarlet O'Hara," he said. " You've earned her."

" Oh, you're laughing at me! " She looked up at him. They stopped walking. " I'm so out of breath—so excited——" she said. " Tell me, how much will you have? "

" None," he said, smiling down at her.

She looked at him, puzzled. " None? " she repeated.

" Next to none—compared with thirty thousand."

" But what about——"

" My father's estate? "

" Yes."

" It didn't quite work out that way—I'm afraid I'm pretty poor now. Compared with thirty thousand."

" Oh," she said.

" Now, why don't you go back to Blazer? " he said affectionately.

" Oh, no, no! No, he wants to stay in California——" she said absently. Then she said, " Well, it doesn't make any difference, does it? Whether you're poor or not? I still love you."

" Do you? "

" Of course I do. I didn't mean to make it sound like it was the money, honestly I didn't. I just meant—well, I just thought that with what you had and what I had—but it doesn't make a particle of difference to me! " She gave him a brief, worried look, then looked away. " Does it? " she asked.

" Now I have to tell you another thing," he said. " And I don't want you to be hurt, Claire, because—because I don't. I want to tell you that I'm not in love with you."

" I see," she said.

" Helen's come back, Claire. She's in the apartment right

now. I'm very happy, Claire, and I want you to be happy, too, because you and I would always have been wrong for each other. We never would have been happy together—and we should both be happy to have found that out in time."

She was silent. Then she said, "Let's walk back this way—just a little bit. Then I'll say good-bye." They turned and started up the street again.

They walked in silence, then Claire said slowly, "It had to be you and Helen, didn't it? It always was, wasn't it? Even when you and I——"

"Yes," he said, "it always was."

"You affect me—" she said—"you affect me in the strangest way. I should say, 'I've been a fool,' shouldn't I? But I don't feel that way. You said I should be happy. So I will be happy. I'll be happy that it's going to work out for you . . ."

"Thank you."

"I fell in love with you. I shouldn't have. But I did. That day I went to see Helen the first time—it happened before then, I hoped that if I tried to help you two get back together again, perhaps it would help me, too, with Blazer. But it was no good. And I forced you."

"What do you mean?"

"It was all my fault. I wasn't innocent. I wanted it to happen—that night in the apartment. I wanted it to happen before that. That night on the mountain—that was when I decided I would make it happen. So don't blame yourself. It was my fault."

He was silent. "Claire," he said finally, "it was my fault, too."

"It doesn't matter. But I can't go on living with Blazer, anyway. Oh, look——" She stopped suddenly and pointed into the low shrubbery along the sidewalk. "What's that? Oh, it's a camellia. Look at it—in the middle of winter. Crazy California! Crazy California flowers. Jimmy—pick it for me."

He reached into the bush and snapped off the flower.

"*La Dame aux camélias!*" She laughed, taking it and putting it in the buttonhole of her fur coat. "What a crazy place. Everything happens backwards out here." She began chattering gaily and artificially. She put her hand through his arm and they began walking again. "Blazer!" she said. "Dear

Blazer! He wants to stay here. But you know I could never bear to stay. That's really why I left him. I couldn't bear the thought of living here another minute. You must stay here, though. Your place is here now, with Helen——"

She began to cry, and as she walked, she pulled softly on his arm and cried strange little sobs that made no noise. "Walk me a little farther——" she said.

"I'm sorry, Claire . . ."

"Hush," she said, "don't say that. You must stay here. I can retreat——"

"Retreat?"

"Yes, go home. Retreat to the warm womb of love. I can retreat to money. I'm going to be very rich. Daddy's setting things up—oh, but I told you all of that . . ." Then, just as suddenly as it had begun, the crying stopped. "I'll tell you one true thing," she said.

"What is it?"

"Even if—even if Helen hadn't come back. Even if you had told me you loved me, Jimmy. If you had said you loved me, wanted me to stay—if you had told me you wanted me to stay out here and marry you, I'd still go back. I wouldn't stay here—even for you."

"I'm glad you told me that," he said.

"You and I are different after all," she said.

They were. She had tried to fight a battle, but somehow she had lost it. And now she was trying to turn the defeat into a victory. She was ready now, ready to submit to whatever it was that came next, ready to stop fighting for anything. And yet, in a curious way, this submission was becoming her maturity. She was ready to go back to Mars Hill, to Junius Denison, to the Junior League, to the Smith Club, ready for all the things she had always shunned. She was ready to be rich, to follow the pattern of the rich. Perhaps she would take an apartment on Park Avenue, a *pied-à-terre*. Her Bohemian period was over, and her marriage, which had been an extension of her Bohemian period, really, was over. She was ready for New England again, for men in black ties and dinner jackets, smoked trout for breakfast, French toast, tea parties. She would never again eat spaghetti from a can.

What was it that pulled her back? he wondered. Was it

really because she had loved him, and now saw the hopelessness of that? Or because Blazer had decided to stay in California? Suddenly, he felt that he had known all along that this would happen, that her departure had been predestined, and predestined to take place this way. That some subtle difference between the East and West had shaped the courses that their lives had taken. And that, somehow, to Claire, the circling view of Manhattan from the Eastbound plane, or the view from the George Washington Bridge, with the towers of New York rising like the spires of fairyland, signified a world that she had never wholly left. She had never left the cotillions, the Colony, the shops on Madison Avenue, the thing she called the warm womb of love. She was not running away with a broken heart; she was returning to a life she had always loved more than any person.

He stopped. " We're almost back to the apartment," he said.

" Oh. Well, I'll leave you here." She looked up at him and smiled. " Don't worry about me," she said. " I'll survive. I'll get over you. I'm beginning to already! I've got my whole life ahead of me."

" You're such a funny girl . . ."

" We're both funny. But different. We'll be happy, I know it. Remember that song we played on the phonograph that night? ' Scarlet Ribbons——' That's what you gave to me, my dear. Scarlet ribbons . . . for my hair." She paused. " God bless you," she said.

It was a curious moment, haunting and pendulous. They stood there, holding hands on the sidewalk. They were saying farewell to nothing. The rain had streaked her mascara; he could not tell whether there were tears. Her make-up—she always wore too much—looked raffish and haphazard.

" Good-bye, Claire," he said.

" Merry Christmas, Jimmy."

" And a Happy New Year," he said softly. " Drive carefully."

" Of course," she said.

She released his hand quickly. Then she reached up and touched the camellia blossom on her coat. " Oh, I must get back," she said. " My flower is dying! "

She turned away and started back along the sidewalk. He stood there and watched her. The white Angora mittens disappeared in the pockets of the fur jacket. He thought that she might turn and wave good-bye, but she did not turn. She walked, without turning, to the corner. She waited, without turning, for the light to turn to green. Without turning, she crossed the street, and continued on, along the sidewalk out of the lamplight. Just before she vanished into the shade of the trees and the darkness, he thought that she must turn. But though he waited until she disappeared, she did not turn.

The rain was letting up. In the sky, a searchlight arced from Mather Field. Then there was a distant roar of an engine. The planes were flying again. To-morrow would be clear. Soon it would be April and summer again.

Slowly, he turned and walked towards the house. At the foot of the rough-hewn redwood steps, he began to run.

All Futura Books are available at your bookshop or newsagent, or can be ordered from the following address: Futura Books, Cash Sales Department, P.O. Box 11, Falmouth, Cornwall TR10 9EN.

Please send cheque or postal order (no currency), and allow 60p for postage and packing for the first book plus 25p for the second book and 15p for each additional book ordered up to a maximum charge of £1.90 in U.K.

B.F.P.O. customers please allow 60p for the first book, 25p for the second book plus 15p per copy for the next 7 books, thereafter 9p per book.

Overseas customers including Eire please allow £1.25 for postage and packing for the first book, 75p for the second book and 28p for each subsequent title ordered.